NABLUS GIRL

DEAN DILLEY

SAVINGTON PRESS

Published by Savington Press

Washington

Published by Savington Press.

ISBN 9798355722340 (pbk)

Cover design by Peter Selgin | peterselgincoverdesign.com

Typesetting by Stewart A. Williams | stewartwilliamsdesign.com

For M.

Chapter 1.

THREE blasts in the middle distance, sequenced with orchestral precision. A prolonged tremor followed and lingered in his stomach, like E-flat slowly played by double basses. And finally, as he looked up in anticipation, a breath of ancient dust sighed from a crack in the ceiling and settled on the keyboard of Amir's vintage laptop.

Below the screen, a scratched pink label read,

"A gift to our friends in the Holy Land, from Miss Lapham's seventh grade class, Edina, Minnesota."

Edina and its intentions were a mystery to Amir, but dozens of discarded laptops, along with other assorted yard-sale merchandise, somehow found their way to the West Bank each year with a pleasant but confused Lutheran clergyman. Amir wondered at this incongruous message from rich American Christians, who had contributed so much to holy war in the Middle East.

At 4:25 on a suffocating afternoon in Nablus, the New York Stock Exchange was about to open six thousand miles away. Amir tasted fresh oxygen when he opened his FREE*Trade Active Trader webpage, the only daily ritual that kept him breathing. For most of the day, he had watched the Asian and European equity markets, the futures market in New York, and an endless stream of Wall Street finance porn with its breathless speculations about the earnings reports that soon would be released. The volatility numbers were high—just where Amir wanted them for today's option trade. He was plotting a bearish bet on bank stocks, but he would watch the opening moves before placing his trade.

Three more blasts, louder this time. And again, the dust.

They were a little late getting started, he thought. For weeks, everyone in Nablus was aware that, this afternoon, soldiers from the Israeli Defense Forces would dynamite the Fawzy family home. This happened in Nablus infrequently these days. It was more common in Ramallah. There always was plenty of advance notice, including placards surrounding the site, which warned neighbors to keep a safe distance. But spectators were expected. After all, the whole idea was to make an example of the victims. It was all part of the operatic experience of Israel's military occupation of Nablus and the other Palestinian land squeezed hard against Jordan's western boundary. In the other direction, Israeli settlements multiplied like mushrooms, methodically dispossessing Nabulsi landowners whose ancestors had coaxed olives from the rocky terrain.

For his part, Amir never lost sleep over the political conflict for which Palestine was infamous. In his analysis, Palestine had lost; game over; move on. Still, he generally could muster a little outrage at the medieval practice of demolishing a family home, and displacing the occupants, as collective punishment for crimes by one of the family members. But Amir felt no outrage today.

The Fawzy house had just been obliterated because Ezz Fawzy, a ubiquitous classmate of Amir's from preschool to university, was arrested by the Israelis after a knife fight in one of the nearby settlements. No one knew, or at least was willing to reveal, what caused the incident. Although everyone survived, there were nasty wounds and hysterical television interviews with panicked settlers demanding more security from "Arab Terrorists" and "Palestinian Militants." Amir and everyone else in Nablus knew that Ezz was a serial troublemaker, and whatever happened in that knife fight, he undoubtedly started it. As early as the second grade, Ezz was universally labelled with a vulgar local slang term that meant loud, arrogant, and lazy. By age fifteen, he had a pockmarked face with the texture of ground glass, and Ezz used his slightly disfigured features to exaggerate the menace that he naturally projected.

For years, Ezz had bullied Amir and every other kid in school, practiced petty thievery in all the shops, relentlessly molested the local teenage girls, and generally distinguished himself as a committed reprobate. His family—especially Ezz's loud and argumentative mother—defended him fiercely but knew as well as the rest of Nablus that he was born to be a criminal.

Amir was not sorry that the Israelis locked up Ezz, and not too sorry that the Fawzy house soon would be a vacant lot. Still, local tradition required the community to turn out to witness the latest outrage by the army occupying Nablus, and Amir was expected to be there, if only to join in a mass expression of schadenfreude. But first, he needed to place that option trade.

The early trading in New York was flat—not what Amir expected. There were three bank stocks on his watchlist, and all would be reporting quarterly earnings later that day. Rumors swirled, especially about Citibank, which supposedly suffered heavy and unexpected losses in its mortgage lending business. But the stock price movements were directionless in the first ten minutes of trading, and Amir lost his nerve. Amir could barely keep his FREE*Trade account value above the $2,500 minimum required to trade stock options. In the last three months, he had received two email warnings when a couple of bad trades sent him briefly below the minimum. And there were some still-undiscovered irregularities in Amir's account application, like his casual click on the "yes" box about U.S. citizenship. But today, the market signals were too good to ignore. Amir inhaled deeply, and used his entire account balance to buy Citibank put options, a highly aggressive bet that the stock price would fall hard and fast.

His father shouted to him, something indistinct but urgent. Amir closed his laptop and left the house with his father and sister to join the ritual assembly to witness the Fawzy misery. It was a short walk, the silence broken by his father's familiar reminders that Amir had no job, and worse, no moral convictions that would arouse him to fight against the occupation of Palestine.

"It's true that Ezz is a hoodlum," his father admitted, "but at least he carried the battle to the bloody settlers. What do *you* do to defend the honor of this family, besides gambling on the stock market?"

Predictably, Amir's sister, Sara, piled on. "Amir's the Wolf of Wall Street, Baba. There are no arbitrage opportunities in fighting for his country."

Amir shrugged.

A small crowd had gathered under some market umbrellas outside the remains of the Fawzy house on Al Jazi Street. After the carefully engineered explosions, the property resembled an archeological dig, with toppled concrete columns and smashed pediments evoking the ruins of some defeated place. Most families brought paper plates of food wrapped in aluminum and placed their offerings on a plastic table where Mrs. Fawzy was seated with her sisters, some small children, and a hideously large photograph of Ezz, draped in black, suggestive of martyrdom. When cameras were pointed in her direction, Mrs. Fawzy stood and shouted dramatically, appealing to mothers everywhere to condemn the arrest of her child, Ezz the innocent. Nearby, Mr. Fawzy was leading a chorus of local men in repeating the loud and vulgar punchlines of bawdy jokes, while pointing rudely shaped objects at a soldier operating the bulldozer, who was methodically reducing the ruins of the house to a surface that resembled a clay tennis court. The rest of the demolition crew worked with businesslike efficiency to erase the Fawzy property from history, while Israeli troops provided a protective cordon.

Mr. Fawzy's strategy—initially lost on the soldiers—was to convey a sentiment of defiant ridicule, denying them the satisfaction of seeing wailing, newly homeless Palestinians, displaced yet again by heavily armed occupiers. Oddly, there was a party atmosphere with convulsive laughter from the onlookers whenever some concrete fragment catapulted in the direction of the troops, or the bulldozer was pinioned by a defiant strand of rebar.

At first, the soldiers didn't get the joke and seemed convinced there would be trouble. Inside a security perimeter of steel traffic barricades, armored vehicles sat idling under dense diesel clouds, providing cover for a nervous squad of troops, each carrying an absurdly large weapon.

The raucous crowd grew larger as the workday ended. Ezz's

delinquent friends turned up to celebrate his heroism and proclaim his bravery against the settlers. Soon, teenagers outnumbered the soldiers, deployed in gender-specific clusters, heavily armed with mobile telephones on which they were deeply concentrated. *Probably sexting*, Amir thought. Amir's sister joined one of the clusters and soon disappeared among the packs of rabid-looking adolescent girls, certainly more cruel and threatening than any of the soldiers at this party.

For a time, the bulldozer was immobilized by a concrete remnant of the Fawzy garden wall. Confronting the bulldozer, four elderly Nabulsi men attending the Fawzy event took an interest in the engineering challenge and approached the security perimeter to have a closer look. The nearest soldier looked anxious, elevated his weapon to a ready position, and radioed his commander for instructions. But it would be hard to describe this aging jazz ensemble as a threat, and they were left undisturbed to study the mechanical science of the situation. They fell into animated debate about the possible solutions, using their hands, and eventually their torsos, to simulate heavy equipment maneuvers that might free the trapped beast. One of the simulations, accompanied by hearty laughter, bore a striking similarity to dog sex, which the bulldozer operator considered a rude insult directed at him.

The soldiers eventually became aware that *they* were the entertainment at the Fawzy party, and the neighbors' objective was to shower them with shame. It was having an effect. The soldiers, all conscripts, understood that they were part of an army of occupation. Conscripts or not, they were still soldiers. None of them saw the honor in the dynamite detail, and the ebullient Fawzy block party was beginning to sting.

With the hesitation that accompanied all unpleasant social conventions, Amir and his father approached Mr. Fawzy. Amir's father offered the usual litany of repetitive Arabic greeting phrases, followed by obligatory sympathies and offers to help—none sincere. Amir contributed his best attempt at a sympathetic facial expression but said nothing. Mr. Fawzy nodded to both of them with his own expression confirming that the feeling of insincerity was entirely mutual.

Amir wanted to get back to his trading desk, but his father

insisted that manners required a decent interval between arrival and departure. This provided more opportunities for his father to mention his disappointment in Amir. It had been some months since Amir finished his university degree, and he had made no progress in the direction of a career, a family, or his father's favorite shorthand for everything, a "life of purpose." Amir thought his father's own life scarcely deserved prizes for purpose. He left Nablus in 1973 to work in Kuwait as a bookkeeper for a minor sheikh in a failed family trading business, finally fleeing in 1992 when Iraq invaded. The sheikh decamped to an improved party scene in Beirut and stiffed Amir's father for half a year of salary. Back in Nablus, his family found him a wife, an overworked nurse with a plain, expressionless face. Neither husband nor wife was especially motivated, but the community could not abide childless residents of their age. Amir's mother dutifully produced two children, Amir and Sara, then went back to work to support her new family, but mostly to combat the crushing tedium of life in Nablus.

Amir's father never worked again. His mother never did anything but work.

The FREE*Trade app on Amir's mobile was slow to open, and there was nothing but bad news for Amir when the quotes finally appeared. Citibank's stock price had barely moved since the opening bell, and Amir's put options were sagging against the bet of a down day. He could unwind the position and cut his losses, but that would mean another threatening email about his minimum account value.

What went wrong? Amir wondered. He quickly scanned the financial news, which reported nothing but an unremarkable trading day.

"Merde!" he mouthed, annoying his father, but lighting up Sara, who had just returned from her clutch of mean girls.

"Declines leading advances?" she asked maliciously.

"I have to go," Amir announced. "I think we've done our duty here, and I prefer not to be shot by one of these nervous kids in the uniforms . . . or stabbed by one of Ezz's friends."

"We will see you at home," his father said. "I want to sample the food."

"Me too," Sara said, knowing that her mother wouldn't return until early morning, so dinner at home would be . . . improvised.

As he left toward home in the fading light, Amir was surprised to find that he was wading against the current of an ever-growing crowd joining the Fawzy dynamite watch party. In a surreal scene, given the circumstances, there were now hundreds of people crowding the perimeter of the demolition site, with pop-up food stalls, improvised firepits, diesel generators, and pirated power cables feeding newly strung bistro lights. Amir could make out at least two competing DJs, from which a confused din of Danish rave collided with mid-century Egyptian love songs. With the rhythmic pulse of the music, the ground heaved for the third time that day.

A good time to leave, thought Amir.

Whatever the Fawzy family might have expected from this event, it was a smashing success in the intended humiliation of the demolition team and their armed military escorts. It was true that almost no one liked or cared to remember Ezz Fawzy. But the guests at this assembly felt the spontaneous collective thrill of signaling defiance to their occupiers by dancing amid the ruins. Amir shook his head in disbelief and pushed out of the crowd, just as the bulldozer skulked into the darkness, chained to a flatbed truck, and followed by its military convoy, sheepish and ignored by the undulating crowd now screaming Scandinavian lyrics.

Back at his laptop, Amir watched his quote flash red. He had intentionally picked an option close to the expiration date, betting on a low time premium, and a much better return if the stock price dropped, as surely it must. Trading across all the equities was sluggish, even among the highfliers that attracted sucker retail traders playing with their retirement accounts. There was a short time left before the market closed, but if Citibank's stock held its value, the option price would plummet toward zero, and Amir would lose everything.

Amir panicked and frantically entered the trade instructions to unwind his position. It would mean a $1,100 loss on the day, and probably, another suspension of his option trading privileges. But he had to cut his losses. His phone vibrated, and he imagined an incoming call from the FBI to confront him about his falsified brokerage account application. It was his mother. When he answered, she could tell he was rattled. Their relationship had never been loving, and she hardly hid her disinterest in Amir's sad life. She spoke with him in transactional prose, oddly trusting him more than her husband to deal with the monotony of bank deposits, rent payments, plumbing repairs, and grocery purchases. When he was upset about something, she noticed, but only because it might disrupt the fragile architecture of their domestic lives, which then would be an irritant for her.

"What is it?" his mother asked. She knew about his day-trading but also knew he never had enough money to worry too much about losing it all. She was dismissive, and strongly of the opinion that trading stocks was roughly like selling drugs, and only slightly less dangerous. Amir knew his mother's views of the subject and saw no value in discussing it. He ignored her question, asked if she needed something, made a list of her assignments to him, and ended the call with a frosty, "I have to go." He regretted it for a moment, remembering that his mother at least treated him as a responsible adult, without the relentless expressions of disappointment that dripped from conversations with his father. Possibly it was because she couldn't be bothered, but still.

She started to say something, but hesitated and then hung up.

While he was distracted by his mother's call, and just before he could click, "place order," on the FREE*Trade page, the market started to move. It started with a sharp drop in energy stocks, followed by legacy industrials, then tech, and the indices. Amir scanned the wire services. There was a photo of the Saudi Energy Minister with a caption about stalled OPEC talks and friction with the Russians. It wasn't the news he expected, but Amir was happy to take anything that would knock a few points off the market today. But as the general downward slope of the market materialized, Citibank's stock price held steady and unaccountably started to trend up. The wrong direction for Amir's bet.

Sunset was hours ago, and Amir realized there were no lights on in the house except the pulsing quotes on his laptop. The noise from the street subsided to an occasional crying infant and a distant televised football match. There was less urgency to place the trade now since his position was essentially wiped out. The market would close in fifty-five minutes. He might as well ride it to the bottom.

Amir remembered the classroom trading simulations from his "Capital Markets 425" class during his last year at university. There was the arousing feeling of penetrating an elite circle, of knowing the obscure and secretive language of the trading floor. It was like a selective global club whose members recognized each other merely by their knowing expressions and opaque vernacular. During four long years of boredom and indignity, the endurance contest for which Nablus University was famous, Capital Markets 425 opened his mind, for the first time, to the possibility of escape.

To Amir, the student experience at his university seemed intentionally designed to reinforce pointlessness and a sense of collective failure. Intellectual inquiry, debate, and novelty were discouraged, as were any expressions that varied from the simplistic formulations that appeared in decades-old texts and lesson plans. With only a handful of exceptions, the faculty members at Nablus University were men of advanced middle age with embellished and improbable credentials, and a fierce determination to be feared by their students, respect being too much to expect. Most were trained in Egypt, where they acquired special skill in haughtiness. Comically, they functioned like some ancient family of faded royalty, full of invented titles, pretentious courtesies, and petty cruelties for the students who failed to observe their silly rules of court. Each was to be referred to as "Doctor," though even the fabrications that littered their self-published CVs seldom stretched credulity as far as claiming an actual PhD. The university curriculum was rigidly grounded in math, chemistry, accounting, classical Arabic literature, and political science—all perfectly legitimate fields of intellectual inquiry except that they were reduced by the faculty to emotionless lectures, uninterrupted by students, unchanged by the passage of time, and distilled into final examinations that scored memorization as the best evidence of human intelligence.

Amir's university years were a shroud of boredom and waste.

Chapter 2.

BUT there were exceptions.

During Amir's final year at university, an adjunct faculty member appeared unexpectedly as the teacher of Capital Markets 425. The course had never existed previously, and it was offered as a last-minute addition during registration. There were no announcements, and it almost seemed the university was trying to keep it quiet. Only twelve students enrolled. The teacher was out of place, and dark rumors circulated immediately that he was CIA, a label attached commonly to Americans in Arabia when their presence did not seem motivated by making money. The rumors flew most furiously, and with the most fantastical conspiratorial elements, among his faculty colleagues.

It was clear to Amir that Charles Aynsley Bridges broke all the faculty rules of self-importance. When a student emailed him about course prerequisites, and referred to him as "Dr. Charles," the always punctual reply began with, "Hi. Call me Charlie." The tenured faculty set to work immediately to undermine Charlie.

Charlie joined the faculty for a semester as part of a university exchange program sponsored by the U.S. Agency for International Development, an American government foreign aid office universally known by its initials, AID. It was never clear what, if anything, the university exchanged for Charlie's presence, but one of Amir's classmates found a notice on the AID website with a picture of Charlie and four other Americans who had volunteered to teach in the Occupied Territories of Palestine. Amir learned that Charlie was a forty-five-year-old Princeton graduate, formerly a star trader at Morgan Stanley in New York, where he ran sophisticated hedging strategies for insurance company portfolios. Then he joined the world's most prestigious investment bank, Burr Acheson, and became wealthy. It seemed impossible, and indeed suspicious to everyone at the university, but Charlie took a six-month sabbatical from his Wall Street career to teach an introductory course about securities markets to undergraduates in Nablus.

Charlie admitted to his class that he had no experience as a teacher. Amir and his classmates had no experience with a teacher who actually taught. He distributed a real syllabus by email a week before the first class, with an astonishing collection of links to market research tools, trading simulation platforms, and even video interviews with prominent traders, investment bankers, hedge fund managers, and two Nobel Laureate economists. Charlie promised, and delivered, four live video guest lectures from traders he knew at Burr Acheson, Goldman Sachs, Morgan Stanley, and Deutsche Bank. Each spoke with messianic passion about the transcendent powers of the securities markets. At Amir's resource-starved university, his basement classroom for Capital Markets 425 mysteriously was outfitted with specialized equipment to simulate the trading floor, including a battered but functioning Bloomberg terminal with an English/Arabic keyboard. The strong suspicion was that Charlie funded these exotic teaching tools himself.

It would be fair to say that Amir and all the students were deeply unsettled by the level of classroom participation and engagement that Charlie expected, having never experienced it before. A few challenged him, describing his approach as quite unlike the university's traditions. But Amir was mesmerized. This was the life-defining moment that had eluded him in every other endeavor in encircled Nablus, and he saw clearly now—and for the first time—his exit route.

Charlie arranged the classroom like a trading floor and sat among Amir and the other students. He had a natural flair for theater, inventing elaborate narratives about fictitious businesses on the verge of an initial public offering and describing actual companies that had experienced legendary trading histories—good and bad for investors. An oversized video monitor above the classroom door was Charlie's special prop for building and maintaining suspense, with countdown clocks displaying the opening and closing of markets across the world, a crawl at the bottom of the screen with ticker symbols, and a split screen with market news commentators from London, Hong Kong, and New York. Charlie assigned each student an invented client with an institutional portfolio of cash and securities and then launched the class into a frenzy of simulated trades, providing energetic commentary in the obscure language of Wall Street. At the end of each day, the class website posted the trading results for each student, as well as Charlie's. The flurry of student text messages that followed these posts dripped with acidic commentary about the winners and losers. It was fast, fiercely competitive, and exhausting—like a high-intensity, semester-long spin class, in which the riders raced for rankings displayed on a ubiquitous flat screen.

When Charlie spoke in class, the market was personified with vivid human characteristics, always feminine. "She" teased us with pulsing moves, daring us to guess her secrets; hiding and selectively revealing her desires that only a special touch could satisfy; giving and taking restlessly, unapologetic for her impetuous moods; prolonging her gentle caresses to amplify the climax of unwinding a trade; and flirting in after-hours trading to lure us back to her bed tomorrow. Sometimes after these remarks there was silence in the classroom and dewy perspiration on the foreheads of the students. It never felt crude or suggestive. It was poetic and reminded Amir of a sonnet about doomed lovers.

Charlie was not handsome exactly, more like beautiful. He was tallish, with a striking jaw that might have been carved by Donatello. His skin was fair; his nose sunburned. Always. He moved gracefully, and he had that kind of athleticism that seemed effortless, like the apocryphal triathlon competitor who paused before biking, and again before running, to calmly smoke a cigarette. During class, he was never without a No. 2 pencil braced above an ear, which he used to good effect during animated class debates—pointing the sharp end to celebrate and punctuate an incisive student remark, and the eraser end to register his disappointment.

He dressed in a paradoxical style that conveyed simultaneously his familiarity and comfort with elite traditions, and his determination not to be seen by anyone as pretentious or privileged. When his suit jacket was draped over the back of a chair in the classroom, a subtle label was visible: "Anderson & Sheppard, London." The royal warrant appeared below, an unnecessary afterthought since the exquisite suits bespoke for themselves. But in defiant contrast, Charlie's shirts were ancient, mass-market Brooks Brothers button downs with frayed collars and the occasional elbow emerging from a worn sleeve. The capstone of his uniform was one of a large collection of vintage Hermes ties, indifferently knotted, in the flamboyant blues and pinks popularized during the era of Concorde flights and leveraged buyouts.

Without question, Charlie violated the rigid faculty dress code established by the university's professorial mafia, and it was well noted. Before his arrival, faculty members could be seen only in a dark fecal-brown suit, sized to exaggerate the girth of its occupant. A stained tie of unrecognizable color was affixed to a shirt produced from unnatural fibers, either yellow, or perhaps white at some moment in its distant past. The ensemble was made more memorable by the fragrance of mothballs. The contrast with Charlie's look was perceived by the rest of the faculty as another intentional slight; a challenge to authority and traditions; and still more evidence of the American government's subversive intentions in deploying adjunct faculty in Palestine.

Only four women enrolled in Charlie's class. After the first week, each one of them, or all of them together, happily would have slept with Charlie. Though they had only the dimmest understanding of what that meant, they were certain they were ready to find out. The attraction was not just Charlie's exotic charms and rule-breaking confidence. He was deeply respectful of the female students, pointedly interrupting the men during their ill-informed monologues to call on Meryem, or Manal, or Omniyah, or Rana, inviting them to make the opposite case, which Charlie invariably rewarded with a wave of the sharp end of his pencil. Charlie shared with the class extraordinary statistical studies, sometimes dubious in their authority, to show that female securities traders were significantly more profitable for their firms and clients. He called this a "known fact," attributable to clearer thinking, a natural resistance to reckless gambling, and a deeper appreciation of risk. No one had ever spoken to these women like this.

Amir felt a disorienting affection for Charlie. He found himself lingering after class on the pretext of asking Charlie some technical question about an assignment or raising a point of philosophy in the capital asset pricing model. His feelings for Charlie disturbed him briefly as unnatural or suspect, but he noticed that everyone displayed similar feelings. Charlie himself encouraged the growing sensation among his students that they were members of a posh club that knew secrets of the universe that would never be revealed to others.

Several times during the semester, a student shrieked or wept uncontrollably during a simulation in class when a trade went wrong. Charlie had a special ability to maintain his composure, though preserving the frantic simulation atmosphere was important to him. He never relaxed the trading floor pace. There was the sense that precious seconds were being lost forever, and the prosperity of humanity hung in the balance. But when a student became momentarily unhinged by a bad trade, a missed signal, or market meltdown, Charlie could interrupt his invented high drama by quietly murmuring something to the student like, "Short your index position, and hedge by buying the January 340 calls." He spoke with precision, elegance, and confidence. The unmistakable message was that the forces of the universe could be known, and every individual could be the master of her fate. In Charlie's class, the markets were the proxy for the deepest truths of human existence. It was unthinkable that anyone in his class would feel powerless or humbled by their circumstances.

"There is a winning trade for every situation," Charlie repeated.

The students were Charlie's devoted acolytes. If he had proposed hacking the Bank of England to empty its currency stabilization fund, his students would fight like starved cats to be team leader.

It was Charlie who first suggested to Amir that he should open a FREE*Trade account.

Back in his upstairs room, Amir heard his father and sister returning. As they entered the room below, their voices dropped to a conspiratorial hush, signaling the abrupt suspension of yet another round of their usual conversation entitled, "What to do about Amir." Fueled by their father's anxiety about Amir's hopeless lack of direction, Sara enjoyed tossing lighted matches into the handwringing. She suggested darkly that the girls who knew Amir considered him a little effeminate, and maybe he had a drug problem, and perhaps he needed psychiatric help. But tonight, his sister's attacks were not Amir's highest priority. Something was happening in the markets, and with less than twenty minutes before the closing bell in New York, Amir watched his trade miraculously edge toward recovery. The sell-off in Citibank stock accelerated rapidly, with a dramatic and favorable impact on Amir's options. In the final nine minutes of the trading day, Amir sold his entire option position, and exited with a loss for the day of $71.

It seemed that Amir lost consciousness briefly, as if his parachute opened late but just in time, and the shock interrupted his breathing. He realized he was cold, despite the evening heat that crawled up from the street below. But he was just wet with perspiration and momentarily chilled. The markets closed, and Citibank's stock continued its fall in after-hours trading. Amir felt vindicated in his research and prescience about problems with the stock, but five clicks on the Bloomberg site led him to the real story. New York's largest hedge fund released its quarterly report an hour earlier and revealed a dramatic reduction in its bank stock holdings. Amir never saw that coming. He felt betrayed, like the real story was intentionally hidden from him, and his careful research just led him into some ruse orchestrated by market manipulators.

But then Amir remembered Charlie's loving portrait of the markets. "She walks in beauty," he would say of the securities markets, "and the tortured love she commands comes as much from your desire to know the secrets she will *not* share, as from her occasional tender caresses." He said these things with genuine poetic passion, sometimes with apologies to Byron or Charlie's other influencers. The women in the class swooned. But the takeaway was clear. Real romance, and specifically our romance with the markets, is derived from mystery. If we knew her secrets, desire would evaporate, and the relationship would just be crass, transactional, and momentary, like prostitution. Amir remembered that Charlie made the uncertainty of markets feel exciting, even erotic. His infectious confidence inspired Amir to think that, maybe, despite all the contrary signals, Amir had possibilities.

With only a few weeks remaining in Capital Markets 425, Charlie did something that, once again, shocked his faculty colleagues, and even his students. At the end of an especially intense Tuesday class in which his students simulated NYSE trading on September 15, 2007—the day Lehman Brothers announced its bankruptcy—Charlie invited the class to be his guests for dinner at Chef Baghdadi, an unassuming pizza restaurant near the university. It would be "his treat." Even Charlie knew that this invitation violated unwritten but never-questioned rules that prohibited fraternization between faculty and students. These rules were designed to reinforce the pedestalization of faculty and to avoid settings in which they might reveal their mediocrity. Charlie offered the invitation casually, for the following Tuesday evening, as an alternative venue for the scheduled class that day. He called it an "off-site," an unfamiliar term at Nablus University.

Within an hour, student social media accounts lit up with breathless speculation about whether this would be the last straw for the shadowy American adjunct faculty member. The inevitable trolls appeared, darkly intimating that this was more evidence of his CIA connections. He would disarm his students with pizza to recruit them into his world of espionage. Almost certainly, sex, drugs, and alcohol would be involved. But as the smartphone war raged, the tide quickly turned in Charlie's favor, first with swelling student support for his fresh teaching methods that treated students like adults. The surge brought a withering attack on the rest of the faculty, and the university, for its institutional disregard for students, for a failure to deliver real-world teaching, and for perpetuating a bankrupt system in which a university degree was valueless. By the time the electronic insurrection was discovered by faculty, there were memes and provocative video highlights from the Arab Spring, and it appeared that a student rally might be mobilized, possibly a strike. Someone said they knew someone who knew how to contact an Al Jazeera film crew. Within minutes, the university authorities went nuclear and posted their own statement threatening expulsion, *and arrest*, of any student advocating or inciting the "disruption or disharmony of our academic community."

Charlie received a call from the dean, "Dr." Al-Houty, who suggested a meeting that evening in Charlie's basement classroom, which by now had a cult-like reputation at the university. Dr. Al-Houty was not an imposing man. He followed the rigid dress code of his colleagues, faithfully armored with the *de rigueur* cheap brown suit scented with naphthalene. He was memorably short, and spoke in a nervous, halting prose, interrupted with long and awkward pauses, during which he seemed to be hoping for some rescue from his reflexive discomfort in the presence of others. The poor man often spoke inaudibly, as if trying out his words to assess the reaction, before he fully committed. Deep creases and dark shadows in Dr. Al-Houty's face exaggerated his haggard features. The worried lines in his forehead looked like a map of the Nile Delta. The apparent prestige of his title was a running joke among the faculty, who knew that the dean's salary was lower than most faculty members because he had no teaching responsibilities and because he reported to a board that second-guessed every decision. His title came with no authority. Still, the faculty expected Dr. Al-Houty to defend their prerogatives and wage their petty wars, and he did what he was told.

It was past 9:30 pm when Charlie opened his classroom door to the small, timid man who had come to lay down the law. Dr. Al-Houty greeted Charlie formally as "Dr. Bridges," but his anxiously prepared speech trailed off as he paused to look in wonder at the array of strange hardware on the trading floor, connected to wild bundles of cables suspended from the ceiling. Oversized monitors provided most of the light in the dim space, with red or green illumination from their nervous ticker crawlers.

"Dr. Bridges," he began again, shaking slightly, "I was astonished to learn that you intend to meet with your students in an unsanctioned private event outside the university. Surely you know this is not permitted. I realize you are not formally trained as an academic, and you are a guest among our faculty. We are grateful that you volunteered to be here, but this is a serious . . .."

"Dr. Al-Houty, my friend," Charlie interrupted with a wounded look. "May I tell you how much this teaching experience means to me? I have never seen such outstanding students and faculty. This is an exceptional university. You should be sending faculty to teach Americans. We have a lot to learn from you."

Dr. Al-Houty, like his Egyptian-trained peers, was accustomed to a confrontational style of communication, in which every human encounter necessarily included some contrived grievance or personal slight that would be negotiated into an equally contrived resolution in the course of the conversation. He was unprepared for Charlie's conciliatory approach and worried that it was a trap.

"But . . . yes. Well, thank you, but this is not why I wanted to speak to you. There is a problem."

Dr. Al-Houty realized he was standing while Charlie was seated, but they were almost face-to-face. Charlie's shirtsleeves were rolled, pencil behind his left ear, elegant tie even more intimidating in the reflected glow of the Bloomberg terminal. A deferential manner signaled the opposite of guile.

Charlie resumed his disarmament campaign. "Look, I'm teaching something that most people consider deadly dull, and, of course, *unlike you*, Doctor, I have no qualifications as a teacher. But I'm so proud of my students. They have mastered the material, and now, I am learning from them."

This last remark confirmed Dr. Al-Houty's view that Charlie was a menace and a threat to the order of the university.

"I heard there was some traffic on social media about my restaurant invitation," Charlie continued. "Really, it was a simple thing. I just wanted to celebrate my students in an informal setting. I learned this from my own college professors, years ago. It was very effective in building trust. I was surprised it provoked a reaction here."

"You must withdraw the invitation," Dr. Al-Houty said. "Faculty and students cannot be together in social settings. It is wrong. Faculty must be respected—even feared—or we will have no order here. Maybe this is not an American point of view, but I have to answer to powerful people in this community. Remember that you are here only for a few months. But this is my university and my career. There can be no compromise on this point."

Then the very little man played his high card. "And people will question your motives. They will ask if you are seeking . . . intimate relationships with your students. I have already heard that some of your classroom lectures include . . ." He paused, as if afraid to say the next word out loud. "Sexual references."

"I am sure you don't want to be the subject of this kind of speculation," the little man added.

Neither man spoke for a while. From the pained look on Charlie's face, Dr. Al-Houty felt sure he had crushed this insubordination.

The video terminals in the classroom seemed monstrously large, and their crawls cast shadowy images that Dr. Al-Houty suspected of being evil and predatory. Adjacent to glowing, incomprehensible charts and volatility indices, small boxes on the screens silently displayed garish television transmissions of animated interviews conducted by defiantly blonde women in tight dresses. Dr. Al-Houty wondered if his dark insinuation about Charlie had some truth to it. *After all, why was he here, really?* A rich American volunteering to be in this remote place, in the company of impressionable young women (and young men!), shielded from the scrutiny of his family and peers. Who would believe that his intentions are honorable? And what exactly was he teaching his students? Stock markets were gambling enterprises, famously the playgrounds of the unscrupulous, who used their money and influence to seduce and corrupt. As he thought about it, Dr. Al-Houty felt himself growing taller, ennobled by righteousness.

Charlie removed the pencil from his ear, pointing the eraser end at his visitor and speaking quietly. "I will call off the restaurant invitation. And you will have my resignation in the morning."

He was insulted, but Charlie was serene and professional. "My students are sufficiently near the end of term. I can schedule a final exam, so they will receive the course credits they earned."

"But let me ask you something," Charlie said. "You must see that everyone here in Nablus is trapped. There is no future here, and no one is coming to help. But I saw something in my students. Besides awareness of their hopeless situation, they are at least thinking about what an escape might look like."

Charlie stood and put his hand reverently on the Bloomberg terminal. "They should believe they have choices, or at least possibilities. I watched the students interact with the faculty here. There is this heavy-handed rhetoric of authority and submission. Why is that the message to these kids? If you're not going to march with them to assault the barricades, you should at least give them something to hope for."

"You don't belong here, Dr. Bridges." For emphasis, Dr. Al-Houty added, "*Your* people make this mistake a lot."

He left Charlie's classroom, still shaking slightly, but relieved that he could inform his colleagues that this troublemaker soon would be gone. The students would get over it, and with the threats of disciplinary action, social media would quickly revert to anodyne photographs of food. Later that night, Dr. Al-Houty thought it seemed a little too easy to get rid of Charlie. *Maybe Charlie actually was up to something with one of the women in the class,* he thought. In Arabia, no explanation could possibly be satisfactory without an element of conspiracy.

That evening, Charlie posted a notice on his classroom webpage, apologizing that a scheduling problem required him to cancel his restaurant invitation. The students knew what happened and also knew enough to remain silent. Nablus had been cowed years ago. The reward for protest, righteous or not, was always the same.

This was when Charlie changed Amir's life.

Days passed, and Charlie's students returned sullenly for his Tuesday class. Surprisingly, Charlie was ebullient. A thick envelope for each student had been placed in front of their terminals, with a label that read, "Capital Markets 425—Final Exam." The envelopes apparently had been repurposed from some of Charlie's old office supplies. In exquisite Helvetica typeface, the envelopes displayed a venerable Wall Street address.

There was mild panic among the students, unaware that this would be their last class with Charlie. When he spoke, there was unfamiliar calm in his voice, and it was clear that this would not be a normal trading day in the classroom. Charlie apologized to the class again for canceling his social invitation, but quickly added that "unexpected personal circumstances" required him to return to his banking job, and he would not be teaching the last four weeks of class. The women despaired audibly, especially Omniyah, who weeks earlier had abandoned all female pretense of restraint and reserve in Charlie's presence. Amir too was crushed, enraged at the leaden-headed university administrators who, without doubt, engineered Charlie's early departure.

Removing the pencil from behind his ear, Charlie reverted to his poetic allusions. "But we have miles to go before I leave you. In our short time together, I watched each of you develop your own appreciation for the beauty and subtlety of the market. Now you know how to charm her, and occasionally bend her to your will, but you also respect and fear her inscrutable will. Like me, your love for her looks on tempests but is never shaken. This is what makes you real traders."

Charlie offered a conspiratorial smile. "Our classroom simulations have been fun, but now it's time to move beyond the foreplay and have a serious relationship. Time to trade for your own accounts."

Amir had imagined this before. There was the usual problem of money, but also the seeming impossibility of establishing a brokerage account, especially for stateless persons like Amir and his classmates. Soon after enrolling in Capital Markets 425, Amir made a playful visit to the Morgan Stanley webpage, and began the application process for an individual brokerage account. The obstacles were the financial equivalent of confronting a West Bank border crossing checkpoint. Amir abandoned the experiment after confronting empty boxes for SSN/EIN, U.S. address, backup withholding certificate, and the ominous declaration, "I am a United States person." The minimum account value was the least of his problems.

But Charlie had thought about all that. He told his class that their final exam would consist of opening an online brokerage account and executing an actual trade. Using his AID credentials, Charlie had arranged for a widely used day-trading platform, FREE*Trade, to open brokerage accounts for each of his students, "for educational purposes," provided that he acted in a supervisory role. Each of the "Final Exam" envelopes contained a completed FREE*Trade account application, prepopulated with the information Charlie had negotiated. The customary minimum account value was waived for the duration of the course. With unexpended AID funds for "teaching materials," Charlie had deposited $500 in each of the student accounts. A signature would be sufficient to open the account, and a single trade would assure an "A" in his class, Charlie announced.

No one spoke for a while, as the students imagined the long list of laws that this almost certainly violated.

"Let me explain my goal," Charlie said, not quite anticipating their silent reaction. "You learned the traders' skills, and then—surprisingly quickly—you advanced beyond the skills to develop instincts. I watched you in the simulations—plotting your moves, assessing the risks, measuring the upside, and pulling the triggers. This is fine art, but like art, there is a difference between holding the catalogue and holding the brush. The market is not theoretical; she is the source of endless possibilities. You don't have to think small or live inside the fences that others built for you here. FREE*Trade can be your new passport."

There were many unanswered questions. His devoted students avoided the questions they knew he could not answer, though Omniyah raised her hand and asked hopefully if Charlie really would have a "supervisory role"?

He smiled, pointed the sharp end of his pencil at her, and said, "Omniyah, I watched you fearlessly selling naked put options, one of the riskiest trades of all. You don't need my help."

When he said the word, "naked," Omniyah whispered in Arabic, "*Anytime* for you, Dr. Bridges."

Charlie told his class that some tech people from the AID Mission in Amman would be removing the classroom equipment in a couple of weeks, but in the meantime, the class was welcome to use the terminals as much as they liked. He added dryly that not all his faculty colleagues endorsed his teaching methods, so it might be best if the students said as little as possible about the final exam. Charlie then bowed slightly and said, "Thank you, all," and left the classroom for the last time.

In the days that followed, Amir heard rumors (attributed to the dean, Dr. Al-Houty) that Charlie had left the university that same night in a black Chevy Suburban with no luggage, headed for the Allenby Bridge, and from there to the airport in Amman. Amir heard a different version from Mr. Abdel Raouf, a legendary Nablus taxi driver who had a rapacious sense for being nearby when someone needed a clandestine run to a border checkpoint. Abdel Raouf told Amir that he drove Charlie to Allenby Bridge in his battered 1989 Mercedes, and after a ninety-minute drive in which neither spoke, Charlie paid in U.S. dollars with a generous tip.

Charlie's students each sent sad and grateful messages to his university email address, all of which bounced back with an error message. Amir, and some of the other members of the class, made faithful pilgrimages to their Capital Markets 425 classroom, fondling the Bloomberg terminal, or simply lingering in Charlie's residual glow. One day, as Charlie had promised, contractors arrived in an unmarked truck, and emptied the classroom without speaking to anyone. Dr. Al-Houty, now a hero among his faculty colleagues, arrived a short time later and locked the door. Capital Markets 425 disappeared forever from the university course catalogue.

To secure the "A" that Charlie had promised, each of the students placed a small trade order, virtually all of them purchasing a few shares of something familiar from the old industrials. They all preferred to buy a sexy tech stock, but $500 might buy only one or two shares. After a few days, the students sold their modest positions, converted the accounts to cash, and mostly forgot about their brief visits to Wall Street.

Amir bought shares of a chip manufacturer and watched it move wildly, up and down. It was often the most actively traded stock on the NYSE and was perpetually the subject of takeover rumors. The FREE*Trade app on Amir's phone buzzed breathless price movement alerts and news updates late into the evening. The ride was intoxicating, undiminished by the fact that the paper gains and losses never exceeded the price of a new pair of running shoes. After a few days, Amir's circadian rhythm adjusted to New York's time zone. Charlie's presence seemed almost undiminished, and just as he had suggested, it felt as if the walls had opened around Nablus, and Amir was commuting daily to Wall Street with the Goldman Sachs guys.

Charlie's dodgy arrangements to open brokerage accounts for his students could not possibly last, thought Amir. Indeed, on the last Friday of the university term, Amir received a message via the trading app, instructing him to respond urgently to questions about his account. But instead of the account closure notice that he expected, Amir received a "renewal notice," asking him to update his records. The account profile continued to reflect the uninteresting Washington, D.C. street address Charlie had provided, along with Amir's email address, and other unremarkable account preferences. The last entry was more perilous, inviting him to confirm, "I am a United States citizen." Amir looked uncomfortably in the direction of his father's Koran on the bookshelf, hesitated briefly while he contemplated life without a trading platform, and then checked, "Yes." An email arrived immediately, with the subject line, "Welcome, Amir. Keep trading!"

During the term break before Amir's final university semester, he earned a little money working in his uncle's shop on Jaffa Street, repairing shattered mobile telephone screens. But Amir needed $2,500 to satisfy the FREE*Trade minimum balance requirement for anything he considered serious trading. Amir could think of only one quasi-lawful way to generate that kind of money in a couple of weeks. He approached Abdel Raouf and offered to drive his taxi during the late-night shift. They would split the fares, Amir proposed. Eventually, there would be twelve harrowing checkpoint trips in predawn darkness, three of which were aborted after the passengers panicked without explanation and fled into the desert. Amir's share of the fares was enough to seed his account and feed his addiction.

A few thrilling months of day trading had passed since then. Amir was still cliff-walking every day with an account balance that barely exceeded the minimum. With his near-miss on the Citibank trade, Amir's net worth was essentially unchanged since his brief arrangement with Abdel Raouf. He watched the after-hours trading for a few minutes and then caught some of the whispered phrases from downstairs, where his father and sister continued their anxious colloquy about Amir's wasted life. This onslaught from Sara began a few years ago as classic sibling hostility. But she quickly began to enjoy her own performance, both perfecting her theatrics and vastly improving her ability to generate anxiety in her father.

Despite her mocking cruelties, Amir loved Sara. She was not a pretty girl, with her pumpkin-shaped face and thick ankles, but Sara was viciously intelligent. Her dark eyes narrowed whenever anyone spoke in her presence, as she prepared to dismantle any mangled facts, flawed syllogisms, discredited cliches, mispronunciations, and malapropisms. From a young age, her peers kept a wary distance, and her teachers only grudgingly gave her the grades she deserved, irritated by her patronizing remarks and barely disguised contempt. Amir loved to watch her take down the preening, self-appointed socialites in high school.

The three years that separated Amir and Sara seemed to dissolve after early childhood, when their combat evolved from brawling with kitchen weapons to exchanges of sharp-edged vocabulary. Sara was better armed than Amir. Lately, after a few rounds in their one-sided verbal battles, Amir simply withdrew to the warm embrace of FREE*Trade. But on this night, after the infuriating Citibank trade and the surreal Fawzy block party, Amir decided to throw himself into the family drama. With a prelude of exaggerated throat clearing, Amir went downstairs to join his father and Sara in the kitchen. Before Sara could deliver another biting commentary on Amir's circumstances, he made an unrehearsed announcement.

"I have decided to leave Nablus," he said.

Chapter 3.

AMIR'S only other awakening at university was Aisha.

In his final semester, the subversive euphoria of Capital Markets 425 had been excised by force from the collective memory of the university and academic life returned to soporific memorization. Amir made no pretense of caring since he had found his One True Religion in FREE*Trade. During classes, and after trading hours, he devoted himself to constructing an elaborate fantasy, increasingly rich in detail, in which Amir is recruited by Burr Acheson to join its options trading desk on Wall Street. Relying rather too heavily on the style and manner displayed by Charlie, Amir did his best to refashion himself as worldly and cosmopolitan, an aloof risk taker, intimate with the special Wall Street codes that unlocked enlightenment. He abandoned the ubiquitous European football club jerseys that everyone at university wore, embracing instead some preppy-looking knock-off polo shirts sold from the back of a donkey cart near the Al-Shifa Hammam. His family and friends didn't recognize the character he was trying to be, but it was clear that Amir wanted to be elsewhere.

To perfect his transformation, Amir enrolled in the university's only course on American literature, despite warnings about the famously lazy professor, Dr. Fathy Shambli. In fact, this was the university's only course on American anything, and Amir thought he should absorb whatever he could on the subject. The reading list, unchanged since the course was first offered two decades earlier, actually was copied from a freshman seminar offered at the University of Utah. Dr. Fathy studied there briefly before returning to Cairo to complete his degree at Ain Shams, where he became a faithful member of the Muslim Brotherhood before it was outlawed and forced underground by the government. The list of authors was unsurprising—Melville, Poe, Twain, Faulkner, Fitzgerald, Steinbeck, Baldwin, Vonnegut. There would be no new scholarship.

Dr. Fathy's lectures, which he read in Arabic at an excruciatingly slow pace from a large green notebook, tended to dwell on themes of social inequity, racism, atheism, and the moral failures of capitalism—all of which he described as the features that defined American exceptionalism. His understanding of the literature was shallow, and his thematic analyses were an amalgam of preconceived hostility to the United States, mixed with lazy literary criticism cribbed from Google searches. It was widely rumored that Dr. Fathy's resentments toward Americans emerged during his student days in Utah, after an embarrassing sexual encounter with a Mormon girl who was much better informed than he about bedroom procedures. Her laughter on that occasion was merely cheerful, but it was said, left a deep wound in Dr. Fathy.

In spite of the professor's superficial understanding of the subject, Amir immersed himself in the literature and believed he found different and richer themes, which he invariably anchored in remembered remarks from Charlie. The characters seemed to embody the opposite of the failures and bourgeois corruption that Dr. Fathy described in class.

Most of the students dropped the class after the first week, confident that Dr. Fathy's lectures would not improve with time. Only seven students remained, and the class relocated from a near-empty lecture hall to a dimly lit seminar room that faced a cloistered concrete courtyard with dying olive trees. At first, Dr. Fathy clung doggedly to his rigid lecture format for the class, but after some tentative rebellion, he acquiesced in the spontaneous classroom debates that sprang from the handful of remaining students. Like

Amir, most were in their final year at university, impatient with rote teaching, unworried about completing their degrees, and uncharacteristically interested in the course material. Reading in English, and debating mostly in Arabic, there were spectacular car crashes of cultural misunderstanding in the classroom discussions. But generally, some literary gravity pulled the students into exciting places where, despite its shortcomings, America meant wild ambitions and endless possibilities. Occasionally, Dr. Fathy rebuked his students for overlooking the injustice, structural prejudice, and godlessness that he saw as the thematic architecture of America and its literature. But he conceded that, during his brief studies in Utah, even he found the vastness and variety in America intoxicating—more than once mentioning wistfully his surprise encounter with a Ramadan tent near Provo, where he said he was welcomed warmly by dozens of Utah Muslims dressed in denim and flannel farm clothes.

Amir had not noticed the striking young woman before the classroom relocation, but when the students were seated at a seminar table, she had a magnetic presence, even before speaking. Amir knew her, though the two had spent their lives in Nablus and at university mostly in parallel universes, with only rare intersections. Aisha Dajani came from the Nablus branch of a prominent Palestinian family, most of whom had long since decamped to Amman or London. Amir's father spoke of the Dajanis in reverential tones, always dropping his voice by two octaves, as if honoring some ancient allegiance to their obscure Hashemite royalty connections.

The family lived in a cluster of quite elegant flats on Derya Street, near the archeological excavations of Hadrian's theater. As a young teenager, Amir and his family had visited the Dajani home once, along with everyone else in Nablus, to offer condolences on the death of Aisha's grandfather, Dr. Wafai, who was certainly the most photographed man in Nablus. A highly respected cardiologist trained in France, Dr. Wafai looked and dressed like a Geneva banker, despite having spent his entire professional life in a dusty Nablus medical office where he had delivered the ultimate bad news to hundreds of his friends and neighbors who were habitual smokers. Lean and tall, with trim black hair, he always appeared to wear a half-smile that reinforced his air of confidence and added a touch of elegance amid the mostly shabby surroundings. The local newspapers liked to print his photograph, usually with the pretext of an accompanying quote about some municipal tempest. In fact, everyone simply loved seeing Dr. Wafai's picture because it made Nabulsis feel beautiful, accomplished, and important. When he died (of heart disease), the whole community turned out, mostly to mourn the absence of anyone to take his place as the city's visual trademark. Everyone felt slightly diminished, suddenly forced to think of themselves in less photogenic images.

From his visit to the Dajani home on the day of Dr. Wafai's funeral, Amir recalled the uncommon sight of a piano in the living room. The keyboard was closed, and the instrument was silent. Its great polished black mass served as an aircraft carrier of family photographs, mostly in sepia and framed in tarnish. It was a universal truth among middle class families—whether in Nablus, Frankfurt, Omaha, or Mumbai—that the displayed images of earlier generations must tell a compelling story of the family's creation myth, preferably evidencing close consanguinity with recognizable royalty. While the images themselves often fall short of that standard of proof, gaps can be filled with well-practiced narration. Amir overheard some of Dr. Wafai's older surviving friends explaining that King Hussein, as a boy, was depicted in some of the photographs because the Dajanis were his "favorite school chums." Dr. Wafai himself appeared in a combat uniform in one photograph, alongside the king's brother, during the ill-fated Six Day War. Based on the piano photography, the Dajanis were indeed local aristocracy.

Amir vividly recalled seeing Aisha that day, along with eleven other granddaughters for whom Dr. Wafai was responsible. X chromosomes evidently ruled in the bedrooms of this distinguished family. The girls all had unmistakable attributes of the departed doctor—elegant, tall, lean, and slightly removed from their surroundings. But Aisha stood out even from that cohort. She said little but registered her presence, and even her opinions, unmistakably with her eyes. That day, Amir thought Aisha seemed impatient; respectful perhaps of the occasion and the ceremony it required, but not especially tolerant of the repetitious condolences or the rumpled visitors.

After Herodotus wrote in the fifth century BCE about the Syrians called "Palestinians" who lived between Phoenicia and Gaza, important pages of his text were lost to mistranslation, careless pagination, and starved mice cohabiting with his manuscripts in medieval monasteries. Tragically, history has no surviving record of Herodotus's detailed description of Nablus women, whom he studied closely and found more worthy of his attentions even than the brides of Nasamone who, by tradition, had sex with all the wedding guests. In the missing pages of his manuscripts, he observed that, during his travels in Palestine, a prosperous community of merchants lived in a village on the road to Gaza, which they called Nablus. In Nablus, the men devoted themselves to farming, but the women operated sophisticated international trading networks from Libya to Persia. In Herodotus's time, visitors sometimes fled in terror after encountering Nablus women, who were depicted by contemporary epic poets as taller than any man, so beautiful as to paralyze the men in their presence, and accessorized with a luminous aureole that projected a mysterious flame.

In Amir's time, these legendary qualities of Nablus women survived, more or less intact. Even the local women who did not quite resemble the paradigm managed to affect the imperious presence that Aisha displayed as naturally as breathing. Similarly, the Nabulsi men accepted with equanimity their lesser stature and status, taking consolation in their good fortune to be part of the genetic fruit of such lovely and extraordinary creatures.

In the years that followed Amir's memorable first encounter with Aisha, he saw her—at a distance—a few times a year, sometimes at school, at weddings, and once on the periphery of a tame street clash commemorating an anniversary of the 2002 Intifada. They never spoke. An impossible social gulf separated them, he believed, and each encounter reinforced that assumption. Mutual friends occasionally spoke about her in Amir's presence. He was interested, but in the same way that he might be attentive to gossipy news about European celebrities. Their news was more glamourous than his, but they were far away, never to be known. Like a distant celebrity, there was a rich tableau of rumors, legend, anecdotes, and hearsay about Aisha, and these gradually coalesced into a vivid biography that Amir quietly curated in his imagination.

When he discovered Aisha in his American literature class,

Amir was elated. In his dreamlike narrative, Aisha appeared like a Pre-Raphaelite enchantress, only semi-dressed, head turned meaningfully toward him, while emerging silently from the mist accompanied by a fawn. But two seats from him, her features were more sharply drawn, less serene than the imagery he had composed in his mind, and more prepared for battle. Her hair was sometimes covered, though indifferently, and the luminous dark strands that fell recklessly over her face signaled supreme self-possession.

Amir realized he had never heard her speak.

One memorable day, Dr. Fathy's lecture about Melville fell into a turgid monologue about minor characters aboard a whaling ship, supposedly fated to be victims of a cruel nineteenth-century American class system that converted their labor (and sometimes their lives) into profit for distant capitalists. From the professor's green notebook, the white whale was transformed into the evil invisible hand. Amir and the rest of the class doubted that this was the author's intention, but debate was not invited. With one exception, no one saw the point in challenging the silly man.

To everyone's surprise, Aisha spoke up, not interrupting exactly, but leaving Dr. Fathy startled and open-mouthed, unaccustomed as he was to being challenged—and by a woman.

"Excuse me, Doctor, but I don't agree with this interpretation," Aisha began, pronouncing "Doc-tor" at a contemptuous pace. "If I am not mistaken, early American whaling ships were famous for operating like a modern private equity investment firm. The expeditions were so risky that investors pooled their capital and appointed a captain to organize the ship and crew. The captain and every crew member received a percentage— they called it a 'lay'—of the proceeds from the whale fat they successfully brought back. Melville wrote about this when he described the *Pequod* crew and their percentage of the ship's income."

Dr. Fathy frantically leafed through his text to find the passage she described.

Amir noticed something about Aisha's expression. When she came to the point, or landed the punch of her argument, a steep arch appeared in her right (always the right) eyebrow—as if to say, "And I defy you to challenge me." The effect was paralyzing.

Aisha went on, "This hardly seems like the exploitation that you are describing, 'Doc-tor' Fathy. It seems to me that the ship's crew were, in fact, privileged investors, sharing in the risks and rewards. And by the way, the whaling ship model is not so different from the compensation formula that most investment firms use today to make giant fortunes."

Right eyebrow arched, she twisted the knife. "The whole story seems very American to me—all kinds of strange characters are thrown together in a high-risk adventure that they freely chose to join. And it will succeed or fail, spectacularly either way. I don't see the ruthless class struggle you described. And if we compare it to our own lives here in Palestine, we have to ask which is more cruel, no risk or no opportunity?"

The air in the classroom was still with stunned silence.

Of course, Dr. Fathy knew about Aisha's family, and despite his best effort to remain in charge, he felt the same involuntary reverence in her presence as everyone else. He had hoped to avoid direct communication with her, but he never expected her to press him— in front of his classroom—to defend the lame propositions that he had plagiarized from web searches to prepare his treasured green notebook of lecture notes.

The women in the class smiled with newfound admiration of Aisha, not entirely eclipsing their natural competitive resentment of her, but still delighting in seeing their pompous professor humbled and shriveled. The men, with the exception of Amir, were not sure what just happened, or whether they entirely liked it. Amir recalled the private equity compensation formula from one of Charlie's classes and found it amazing that Aisha knew its obscure origins. His imaginary biography of Aisha was in need of wholesale rewrite.

After a pause that eventually became painful for everyone, Dr. Fathy finally responded, glaring at Aisha. "I am glad, Ms. Dajani, that you are reading our texts so closely. But take care that you do not read things that are not there. This is a book about a whale."

Aisha looked fierce and started to speak again, but the professor launched a preemptive strike by ending the class early. He said dismissively, "I think we have fully covered Melville, and we can begin our discussion of Twain in the next class. Make sure you read the text. You are excused." He closed his green notebook with a theatrical slam and exited without looking up, wounded and indignant.

As the classroom emptied, Amir approached Aisha for the first time. "Where did you learn about private equity?"

Aisha stopped, a little surprised to be approached by Amir. "My grandfather loved this book. He used to read passages to my sisters and me when we were children, and he had answers—or made-up answers—for every question. I remember asking him about Queequeg's '90th lay,' and this was his explanation. It didn't make much sense at the time, but the story stayed with me."

Impatient, she pushed some wisps of hair from her face. "Honestly, I was only trying to be a little provocative, and put the professor in his place. Maybe he's right about his evil American imperialist capitalism theory. I don't really care. We are wasting our time in this class. He knows nothing about these books. I doubt if he actually read 585 pages of Melville."

"You don't remember me, do you?" Amir asked. "I first saw you at your grandfather's house, but everyone in Nablus was there, so I doubt I made much of an impression."

Aisha laughed. "Amir, this town is so small, everyone is competing for the same air. Of course, I know who you are. But I don't remember seeing you at my grandfather's house. I was what, maybe eleven? And why would you remember me?"

Amir, flustered, was slow to respond. He missed his moment. Aisha looked at the broken clock above the classroom door, which had been stuck at 6:45 for years, and she reverted to a hurried pace. "I need to cram for an exam. See you." Hair in the face again, a rushed smile, and then she was gone.

Aisha repeated her Melville performance a few more times before the semester ended. Each time, she was more confident and increasingly malicious in exposing Dr. Fathy as a comically shallow practitioner of lit crit. Worse than his ignorance of the books, his English pronunciation was so poor that even Amir, normally deferential to his insecure superiors, spoke up to correct the most calamitous errors.

"Sir," Amir said one day, hoping to soften the indignity of what came next, "I believe the obsession of Gatsby is 'Day-Z,' not 'Dee-Chee.'"

Dr. Fathy furrowed his brow but did not change his pronunciation. Aisha seized the moment and delivered a lengthy, intentionally pointless monologue on Fitzgerald's depiction of the dysfunctional Buchanan family, which gave her the opportunity to refer several times, with glorious emphasis, to "Dee-Chee."

That was mild compared to the savage attacks that followed. Near the end of term, Aisha experimented with a new form of torture, opening with a flanking maneuver, delivered in a coquette's voice, to ask an apparently genuine question inviting Dr. Fathy's wisdom. On one occasion, during a discussion of Baldwin, she actually posed this "question."

"Professor, I was so moved by Baldwin's description of the first encounter between Rufus and Leona. But at first, I didn't understand the meaning."

She paused and affected a helpless, searching look. "It was so brutal, but now I see that *he* was the victim. In that moment, alone with a southern white woman, Rufus faced the whole evil American capitalist, racist, imperialist enterprise that had crushed him and his people. Their first moments together were frightening and violent, but it was really Rufus *raping himself* to express the pain and helplessness of his subjugation. I see it as a kind of self-mortification, which eventually drove him to suicide."

"Don't you agree?" she asked sweetly.

Dr. Fathy's suspicions were disarmed momentarily by the superficial attractions of her argument, not to mention the seductive force of her lilt and those careless strands of hair. He began too quickly, without thinking, like a doomed bug crawling into a spider web.

"You are becoming a perceptive reader, Ms. Dajani. Definitely, the whole undercurrent of the book is America's problem with race, and the brutality it uses to enforce its class system. You raised an interesting question regarding the self-rape, as you call it, and I think this deserves . . ."

By this point, Aisha's sweet smile had turned to smug satisfaction, and several of the students were openly laughing at their professor's embrace of a satirical absurdity. Once again, the green notebook slammed shut, and an abrupt departure followed.

These episodes enhanced but complicated Amir's careful

cataloguing of Aisha's story, now obsessive in rich detail. He noticed—or imagined he noticed—new details about her features
when she spoke. She narrowed her eyes as a prelude to a sinister
remark. Her nostrils flared when another woman spoke, as if Aisha's
intellectual dominance of the room was briefly challenged; but her
most defining feature was the elegant, sculpted silhouette in her default expression of serene and sublime boredom.

Before leaving university, Amir had only one other close encounter with Aisha. There was a commencement party hosted by
the semi-wealthy parents of the class valedictorian, a sad and silent
young woman who cowered behind thick eyeglasses but excelled at
the memorization rewarded by the lazy faculty. The party was depressing, shrouded with tedious, self-congratulatory speeches by the
valedictorian's family members, including particularly offensive remarks by her father about *his* success in business (which everyone
knew was some kind of shady loan sharking).

Near a dying olive tree in a garish urn in the yard, Amir stood
away from the scrum of students and family, drinking tepid tea. He
looked west, beyond the barren terrain of Palestine and the tasteless
architecture of encroaching settlements, imagining New York in the
distance. To his surprise, Aisha approached him and sat close by,
on the edge of a garden art object that seemed to be missing some
essential pieces. She was dressed stylishly in a clingy silk dress, subtly patterned on a pale blue background with more than the usual
number of buttons open at the neck. Her hair was uncovered. With
her torso turned to achieve a precarious balance on the unlikely
seat, Amir could see a bright red bra strap. He imagined, or hoped,
it was intended to be seen.

In the soft amber of late afternoon sunlight, which backlit the
contours beneath her dress, Amir was stricken by her presence.

"Do you think it was worth it?" she asked with her default
facial expression.

"You mean, four years at university?" Amir thought about it and
then spoke without conviction. "Sure. I mean the alternatives were
all worse. I learned a few things; met some people; grew up a little.
But I know what you mean. It should have been so much more. What
about you?"

For what seemed like the first time ever, Aisha looked directly at Amir. The familiar veneer of invincible poise was briefly replaced by melancholy. He thought she might cry.

Recovering, Aisha finally said, "It reinforced my determination to get the hell out of here."

"I have an escape plan," Amir offered. "When I save enough money, I'm going to Wall Street to be a trader for Burr Acheson. That's my definition of freedom. There's nothing for us here."

Aisha laughed, gently; not dismissively. "That's ambitious. Did you find that inspiration in Dr. Fathy's class? Which character are you? Nick Carraway? And how exactly do you plan to get out of here?"

"Working on that," Amir said, not very convincingly.

Aisha twisted again, plainly uncomfortable seated on the art object; and again, presented Amir with a momentary flash of red against the flawless skin below her neck.

"Well, let me know when you get there," Aisha proposed skeptically. "I have my own plan. It's a bit less dramatic, but you know . . . one step at a time. I have a scholarship for a graduate program at Cairo University, starting in a few months. It's a two-year program in political science. Not much money, but I can live with my cousin's family in Zamalek. I heard Cairo is its own kind of hell, but maybe I can turn this into something." Her defiant poise returned, and Aisha added with finality, "In any case, I'm getting out of Nablus. That's a win, even if it's not Wall Street."

She added, with sarcasm drawn from Dr. Fathy's catchphrases, "And unlike you, Amir, I won't have to live in a bourgeois imperialist state like America. In Cairo, I will be free to flourish under the heavy hand of a misogynistic military regime in a failed economy."

Once again, Amir had to recalculate his narrative about Aisha. This sardonic side, intermittently sad and desperate, was a new feature. There was more vulnerability than he imagined, more humanity, and at least a narrow crack in the pedestal that had always kept her distant and unreachable.

The valedictorian's party was ending. Most of the students had relocated to the street. In the distance, there was raucous singing by a few loud boys, but the air was thick with the usual Nablus foreboding and sense of defeat—the sad celebration of another milestone of fake achievement, followed by nothing.

Aisha and Amir were silent for a moment, but without awkwardness, while they each considered the odds against their ambitions.

Aisha stood up abruptly. "I will miss you, Amir. I'm sorry we never really got to know each other." Before he could speak, she disappeared into a stuffy room with appalling window treatments, where the last guests were thanking the host.

She said it with finality and left quickly. Amir wondered if he would ever see Aisha again.

Chapter 4.

MONTHS after finishing university, Amir was no closer to Wall Street, except in his virtual daily commute to FREE*Trade. Now, standing in the kitchen with Sara and his father, Amir thought his escape might somehow be advanced if he announced it with conviction.

"You're leaving Nablus? Did you find a job?" his father asked, doubtfully.

Sara took a different tack. "Finally," she said. "Can I have Amir's room?"

Amir knew there would be nothing but derision if he said anything about his aspirations in New York, and privately, he knew that plan was a fantasy. He hastily invented a placeholder story instead.

"I'm applying for a graduate program in finance. There is a work-study curriculum offered by an American college in Bahrain, where I could intern at a bank while working on my degree."

Only some of this was true. Amir remembered seeing an advertisement on FREE*Trade for a small New England college named Brattley that offered an unaccredited business degree program, in collaboration with one of the government-owned banks. At the time, Amir assumed it was just another fraudulent online degree scheme with a fictitious college, and anyway, Bahrain was a joke. He knew that no one intentionally went to Bahrain except bored Saudis looking for a drink and a hooker. But for purposes of his impromptu kitchen announcement, Bahrain would have to do.

Sara challenged his shaky story. "What bank? They don't hire Palestinians in Bahrain—unless you plan to be a taxi driver."

Predictably, his father added, "Where will you get the money for this? You know I'm not going to finance another wasteful university degree for you."

Amir shrugged. "Don't worry. I'm saving money for this. I need a little time, but I plan to be out of here soon. Sara can live it up in my palatial room." He reached for a Coke in the refrigerator and feigning confidence in his invented escape plan, started back upstairs.

Sara had to have the last word. "Oh, right. 'Saving money.' Waiting for your big score in the stock market. Exchanging tips with Warren Buffet. Any day now."

Alone again upstairs with his laptop, Amir was painfully aware that there was no escape plan. His day trading was a mild opiate, just enough to discourage suicide. After a long flirtation with FREE*Trade's minimum balance requirements, Amir knew he was unlikely ever to have a seat on Burr Acheson's trading desk or appear on the cover of *Institutional Investor.*

And there was Amir's obsession with Aisha, a preoccupation that seemed disturbing, even to Amir. When he was not conjuring options straddles or hypnotized by the knockoff Bloomberg terminal on FREE*Trade's website, Amir was knitting a Baroque tapestry depicting his new life with Aisha. It was just a thought experiment, but it had all the rich detail of a Bertolucci film. There was some flimsiness in the storyline and a lot of cliché material, but Amir felt pretty good about his editing on the fly. Information gaps were easily filled with tidy Hollywood patches.

In the elevator version, Aisha's posh family and her naturally distant demeanor presented near-impossible odds for someone like Amir, lesser born and from the wrong neighborhood. But their brief chance encounters at university sparked deeper connections, especially a shared desperation with the literal and figurative walls around them, and longing for the open road. In his persistent daydream, new obstacles to romance appear when Aisha leaves for Cairo, but determined, Amir finds his way to New York, and builds a phenomenally successful hedge fund. At afternoon tea at Cairo's Ramses Hilton, Amir surprises Aisha with a ring. They move to Greenwich and spend the rest of their lives wearing Armani and flying privately.

When the elevator doors opened, Amir was back in Nablus looking at an email message from FREE*Trade marked, "URGENT."

> To our FREE*Trade customers. FREE*Trade was advised by law enforcement authorities of a security breach targeting users of our trading platform. As a security precaution, FREE*Trade requires that all customers update the telephone number linked to their accounts. This will automatically reset the security firewall. FREE*Trade is cooperating with the authorities to investigate this breach.

Again, *Merde*, thought Amir.

Quite apart from the vertigo induced by his actual trades, there were two anxiety-generating problems with Amir's intimate relationship with FREE*Trade. One was his precarious cash balance. The other was his reliance on account identity information that was plainly false. A rudimentary security review would reveal that the telephone number attached to his account would be answered by a junior human resources manager at AID in Washington, who would be very surprised to learn that she was one of FREE*Trade's busiest day traders. Amir knew that the telephone number attached to his account came from some vestigial metadata in Charlie's syllabus for Capital Markets 425, and he was surprised when FREE*Trade continued to maintain his "educational purposes" account long after Charlie's departure. *Now*, he thought, *it's only a matter of time before I'm caught.*

The following day, a Saturday, markets were closed in New York, and Amir moved quickly to head off an expected calamity with FREE*Trade's security team. His uncle was in his shop early on Jaffa Street, patiently scratching a living from selling and repairing cheap mobile phones from off-brand Chinese suppliers. Uncle Jaber was resourceful. He had assembled a network of crooked middlemen in the settlements who provided bulk access to wireless plans that he could resell to pay-as-you-go customers, producing small but steady income for his tiny shop. When Amir opened the door, his uncle was positioned as usual on a tattered counter stool facing the rear, with strips of torn Naugahyde forming a kind of Polynesian dancer's skirt below his ample bottom. The shop was spare in its furnishings, with one singular exception. In a frame displayed above a pile of cannibalized cellphone parts, there was a faded magazine photograph of a Palestinian supermodel whose ancestors governed Nablus in the eighteenth century. She pouted for the camera, advertising something for Dior.

"Sabah al-khair, Uncle," offered Amir.

He mumbled a mechanical reply to Amir's morning greeting, without looking up. His hair and beard were always meticulously trimmed, and except for the girth in his hindquarters, he was an exemplar of good grooming. One ritualistic oddity was the subject of everyone's first observation. Every day—every single day, without exception—he wore a gleaming white shirt, starched and pressed with edges like the blade of a German chef's knife, and beige linen trousers, creased for a military inspection and cuffed with a slight break over exquisitely polished cordovan loafers. His appearance mattered to him, even if his business barely paid the rent.

Uncle Jaber had always been good to Amir, convinced that his brother's wife—Amir's mother—was a neglectful parent with no serious interest in her family. When Amir needed some quick cash, Uncle Jaber usually could be relied upon to provide odd jobs. Beyond the steady demand for restoring cracked mobile phone screens, Amir had intermittent employment with his uncle to collect bulk shipments of SIM cards and deliver duffel bags of cash to shadowy characters near the settlements, always after dark. On one occasion, Amir was assigned to a delivery that involved exchanging bird calls to confirm the identity of an unseen counterparty on the opposite side of a hulking settlement security barrier, and then hurling a canvas postal bag over the top. Uncle Jaber insisted on practicing the bird calls with Amir before the mission and seemed undisturbed when Amir pointed out that no such birds inhabited Palestine.

Amir broached today's mission carefully, not entirely sure of Uncle Jaber's ethical or legal boundaries but confident that he could suggest a solution. After some time-killing conversation in which Uncle Jaber could plainly tell that Amir was warming him up for something, Amir said, "I'm working on some job applications abroad. How can I get a U.S. telephone number that will ring on my mobile phone here?"

"What kind of job?" he asked.

"Well, I was thinking, maybe in banking," Amir proposed, "And I imagine it will be better if they see I have a U.S. address and phone number."

"I see. Tell me, does this have anything to do with your stock trading?" Uncle Jaber didn't miss much.

Amir was silent, but he hardly needed to reply.

As time passed in silence, his uncle made some playful turns on his stool. The Naugahyde twirled. He stopped finally, facing the rear of his shop, and asked calmly, "What state?"

"What state?" Amir repeated.

"There are fifty," his uncle observed. "Where do you want to pretend to live?"

By the time he left Uncle Jaber's shop, Amir was a resident of Boca Raton, Florida, with a SIM card that magically operated with a 561 area code. Amir knew better than to ask too many questions about this arrangement, but his uncle volunteered that some of his "business associates" had family in Boca Raton, and no one would question Amir's Florida residence. He added, in a joke that Amir did not get, "You will fit right in. There are millions of Florida residents who don't live there."

When he returned to his laptop, Amir felt newly naturalized. And like a good new citizen, he obediently set to work complying with the FREE*Trade security warning. A click on the security warning link led him to "Update Account Information," and moments after entering his new identity provided by Uncle Jaber, another automated FREE*Trade message arrived.

Thank you, Amir, for updating your FREE*Trade account information. Congratulations, you are now protected by the most secure trading network on Wall Street.

Relieved, and apparently safe for now from securities regulators, Amir could turn to his other passion, which was following Aisha—at a respectful distance—on her social media accounts. She was an indifferent user before moving to Cairo, but since then, Aisha posted regularly, with a few dozen followers in Egypt, the West Bank, and some unexpected places like Copenhagen. She was not quite an influencer or endowed with the coveted blue validation of her posts, but her photographs were tasteful, even artful, in their portrait of a happy student's life in the smelly stew of Cairo.

Aisha's departure from Nablus enhanced her alluring legend back home. It was said that her parents were furious. Her family continued to maintain a polite distance from most of the community, in keeping with their carefully curated social status. But one of Aisha's younger sisters, Noor, took a job as a teaching assistant at the university and suddenly was a ubiquitous presence in Nablus cafés or in the late afternoon promenade near the Hammam.

Noor was a statuesque, younger replica of Aisha, but playful and less judgmental than her older sister. She was one of the rare approachable women of the Dajani family. Noor was comfortable laughing, both at the tragicomedy of life in Nablus, but also at herself. She made friends easily and became close to Amir's sister. Amir was wary of this connection, suspicious that Sara would somehow undermine his path to Aisha. But Sara chose to focus on her own good fortune to be admitted into the Dajani orbit where—modeled on Noor's example as a gracious friend—she softened her edges and left her forever war on Amir out of the conversation.

As it turned out, Sara became a welcome new channel of information reporting about Aisha. She would share harmless gossip during dinner with Amir, while their father sat silently at the head of the table rereading old editions of Nagib Mafouz novels, from which desiccated mouse droppings sometimes fell as he turned the pages. Sara was aware of Amir's infatuation with Aisha, despite his care in expressing disinterest in the news from Cairo and total silence about his brief but memorable encounters with Aisha. But Sara was a keen observer, and it was not difficult to see that Amir's expression changed when Aisha's name surfaced or that he was absorbing the fine details of every anecdote to fill in the narrative gaps in her social media posts. But oddly, Sara restrained her reflexive impulse to ridicule Amir's impossible ambitions. She just smiled when he inquired obliquely about life inside the Dajani bubble.

A short time after Amir updated his FREE*Trade account details, his Boca Raton telephone number suddenly was very popular. There was a frenzy of unfamiliar incoming calls, identified on his mobile phone either as "No Caller ID," or with baffling origins like Batumi, Santa Monica, and Abidjan. Amir answered a few calls, worried that they might be important to verify his FREE*Trade credentials. Most were robocalls, alarming in their urgency and claims of official authority. The actual human callers were absurdly transparent scams. Amir stopped answering unfamiliar calls. He guessed that either Uncle Jaber's SIM card provider, or possibly "the most secure trading network on Wall Street" had sold his new telephone number on the open market within minutes after it was assigned to him. *Maybe,* Amir thought, *this is normal for Americans, and the flood of calls would reinforce the authenticity of his new identity.*

Downstairs, Amir could hear Sara on her telephone planning an outing with Noor. She spoke in the irritating clipped cadence of contemporary nineteen-year-old women, abbreviating everything to monosyllables or acronyms, as if they were being charged by the word, or were determined to confound the intelligence agencies listening in. Their conversation receded to the background of Amir's attention, until he heard Sara mention Aisha. Something indecipherable followed, a collision of Arabic, English, and girlsarcastispeak, with the impressive fluency in all three that could only come from years of screen time. Amir opened Aisha's feed, but there were no new posts; only a three-week-old selfie at sunset in Zamalek, anodyne except for an unusually comprehensive head covering with no hint of her signature splash of playful hair. Amir wondered if the conservative mood in Cairo was having an effect on Aisha's defiant style. He worried she might test the boundaries of the latest junta's benevolence or reprise in her graduate program the classroom savagery for which she was famous in Nablus. But the photo captured Aisha's familiar half-smile above a serene, elevated chin. She seemed unchanged by Cairo so far. Still achingly beautiful, and far from Amir's reach.

While conducting a telephone conversation with Noor, Sara left the house, pausing for a perfunctory kiss for her father. Amir was determined to avoid a conversation with his father, who inevitably would insist on probing the details of his Bahrain announcement. But Amir was intent on following Noor and Sara at a discreet distance, eventually orchestrating an accidental encounter in which he could casually inquire about Aisha. He came downstairs in a rush designed to convey urgency and to preempt conversation.

"Just a moment," Amir's father said with formality. "I want to know more about this graduate program you described. I have an opinion about Bahrain, and it's not favorable."

"Baba, it's just an idea. Nothing is finalized yet. I thought you wanted me to find a career. You don't seem very supportive."

His father went on the offensive. "I'm supportive of realistic goals. You should get a job here in Nablus. You may not think the opportunities are glamorous, but it's time to be honest with yourself about what is possible." He wasn't shouting, but it was as close as he ever came to that volume. "And stop your foolish dreaming about the Dajani girl. There are plenty of girls from families that are closer to our. . ." He didn't finish the sentence and didn't have to.

Amir didn't realize his father was paying attention to any of his dreams, especially the Aisha dream. No doubt that virus was spread by Sara. She had diabolical skill in manipulating their father's anxieties about caste. Amir decided to ignore the Aisha reference. His father was on shaky ground in advising Amir to stay in Nablus since his own career path memorably involved fleeing to Kuwait, where Palestinians are as welcome as lepers.

Amir regretted his words even before he said them. "Who are you to tell me about what's possible? Am I supposed to follow your example of success in work and marriage?"

His father stood up, red-faced, dropping his book and losing his place amid the 1,313 tedious pages in the trilogy he was reading, ironically the chronicle of another failed family trapped in Arab territory occupied by foreigners. And then he came to the point.

"Don't you see that this is exactly what they want?" He was referring to the settlers closing in on Nablus.

"They can wait, and what they are waiting for is for us to die or leave. I will die, and you will leave. Then they win, and Palestine is finished."

Unlike his father, and most of Nablus, Amir did not spend time brooding about the occupation or the Israelis. He didn't really think they were bad people. To Amir, they seemed just like everyone else between Tripoli and Damascus, skirmishing endlessly over desolate terrain, debating imaginary lines that were drawn a century ago by eccentric Europeans after too many glasses of port. Amir refused to spend his life being a victim. One state, two states, no state—it didn't matter. *Time to move on*, he had decided.

Amir chose not to reargue this topic with his father. "Baba, I can't stay here. I need something different, or at least I need to try."

Awkward silence followed. Deescalating, Amir changed the subject. "How is Mama? I haven't seen her in a few days."

Amir's father looked defeated, and much older than his age. There was dark swelling under his eyes.

"She loves her job . . . or she hates her home. I didn't give her much of a life, it's true, but why can't she at least pretend to have some interest in this family?" He picked up his book, found his place, and retreated back into the dust and mouse droppings of his novel about old Cairo.

On his way out, Amir offered to make dinner later. There was no reaction from his father.

Noor and Sara were making wide, flirtatious reconnaissance sweeps with the rest of the afternoon crowd at the bazaar, mobile phones at their ears to signal the importance of their mission, despite there being no one on the line. Amir intercepted them there, acted surprised, and offered to buy ice cream. Sara wasn't fooled, but she let her brother's little performance unfold, eager to see how he would introduce Aisha into the conversation without appearing suspiciously interested.

Noor saw it coming too, but possessed of all the gentle kindness that Sara lacked, she rescued Amir by asking casually, "Have you heard from Aisha?"

Amir was visibly relieved. "Not since she left for Cairo. I saw a couple of her posts." He tried to appear only faintly interested.

The pedestrian traffic was dense, and it was difficult for Amir to see Noor's face as the three of them walked with dripping cones. An ambulance was lodged in the Saturday traffic, its siren locked in a brain-crushing single key. He thought he saw Noor's eyebrow lift as she made an emphatic point that was rendered senseless by the background noise. Frustrated, Amir absorbed nothing of Noor's report on Aisha in Cairo. They turned off the main street, tossing their cone remnants in a trash bin, and Noor became audible again.

Amir's phone murmured. A call from El Paso. He ignored it.

"The really strange thing," Noor said, momentarily audible in mid-paragraph, "is that she never said anything about Cairo until she announced she was going. No consultation with my parents, nothing about the scholarship or the accommodations, and who knew she was interested in political science? My father just looked at her blankly and said, 'You're acting crazy, Aisha. No one wants to live in Cairo.'"

Noor stopped, leaned into a conspiratorial huddle with Sara and Amir, and whispered, "It has to be some kind of love affair. There is no other explanation. But Aisha confides in me about everything—except this Cairo thing."

Sara said some polite, predictable things in Aisha's defense—references to her "good judgment," she "'must know what she's doing,'" her well-known independent nature, and all the rest. But Amir was rattled by the love affair theory. *It made sense,* he thought. Her departure was abrupt, and not accompanied by the usual street chatter that would be expected for any successful escapee from Nablus, especially a member of the local gentry who also happened to be a beautiful young woman with no known love interest. *But wait,* thought Amir, *that should generate even more gossip.* Was he missing it, or was the scandal so profound that no one will speak of it, as a gesture of respect for the honor of the Dajani family?

Trying, but failing, to appear uninterested, Amir asked Noor if Aisha would be coming home for the Eid holiday in a few weeks.

"That's another thing," Noor said, exasperated. "Our family is always together for the Eid. I overheard my parents complaining that Aisha was noncommittal this year, offering vague excuses about exams, and the hassle of traveling in and out of Palestine. My father is furious with her."

Another call on Amir's phone, from Billings, Montana. *Enough!* he thought. Amir pressed "Block Caller."

"Noor and I are meeting some friends now. See you later, Amir," Sara suggested firmly, with an edge in her voice. Amir could tell that Sara was getting impatient with his lingering presence. He knew she was possessive about the Noor relationship—still in its formative stages—and Sara made it clear that Amir's infatuation with Aisha was silly and bordered on social climbing.

While Amir was fashioning an angle to stay in this conversation, his phone awakened again. A call from Palm Beach, Florida, the screen announced. Now that Amir was a Florida resident, he felt obliged to at least take this call. Skeptically, he answered.

"Omar!" the caller said. "How are you? It's Lance Bruckel at Burr Acheson Private Bank in Palm Beach. We're offering some incredible refinance options right now. I can offer you a ten-year interest-only jumbo on your primary residence for thirty basis points over Treasuries. Obviously, we don't make money on that spread. But we want a banking relationship with you! So we only ask that you move at least a million in your securities portfolio to the Burr Acheson wealth management desk. Give us a chance to show you we can outperform the market!"

Lance said all of that without taking a breath, in approximately the time required to say, "You have the wrong number." Sara and Noor had walked away and disappeared down Yaffa Street.

Lance continued before Amir said anything.

"You're probably wondering where this market is going. The volatility stats have gone nuclear in the last two months, and real yields are negative. Just like the rest of us, I know you're looking for some decent risk adjusted returns. I'm confident we can get you some Alpha."

Amir recalled Charlie's explanation of "Alpha." He said that active stock traders almost never beat the returns of a passively managed fund that simply bet on the whole market. But once every few years, a mystic appeared who could briefly outperform a blind market bet. It never lasted. But it had cachet, so Wall Street gave it a virile-sounding name, and everyone began "seeking Alpha."

Still apparently not breathing, Lance pushed on. "Can I send you some numbers to model your refi options? I see you live in Boca, so you're probably sitting on some nice appreciation on your house. We can help you pull some cash out to roll into your securities portfolio—though technically, we would have to call it 'home improvements' or something like that. But don't worry about that. We can make the numbers work for you."

This was the closest Amir had been to a live Burr Acheson encounter since he took Charlie's class. His mind raced. *What is this guy talking about, and why did he call me, and can I convert this cold call into a Burr Acheson job interview, even though I have no house in Boca, no mortgage to refinance, and no securities portfolio to transfer?*

Amir remembered his American literature class at university, and the first words he wrote on his final exam. Dr. Fathy's essay question, which he borrowed from an online book club chat room, asked, "What is a recurring literary narrative in all of the reading assignments?"

"Endless Possibilities," Amir began, as if suggesting a self-help book title. Dr. Fathy marked his answer, "Unclear," adding, "It seems you did not attend my lectures." Amir received a C on the exam.

Think fast. Seize the moment, Amir told himself. *This opportunity will not come twice. Alhamdulillah, thank God, for Capital Markets 425.* Amir could speak competently—or at least convincingly —about Treasuries, spreads, risk-adjusted returns, and even basis points.

To suppress the street noise, Amir stepped into the doorway of a filthy shoe repair shop, where an ancient man with gray stubble stared at him blankly. Amir paused for effect, and then adopted his best imitation of Charlie's trading floor voice.

"Lance . . . glad you called. If you can give me a spread of thirty basis points, I'm very interested. The thing is, the timing is not ideal. I'm abroad at the moment, working on some deals." Charlie always said, "abroad," never "overseas," and definitely not "in Nablus." "But in a month or two, I'm planning to put a tenant in the Boca property, and your refi would be perfect to manage my cash flow and monetize some of the unrealized appreciation."

Amir was doing his best to smell like a big fat fish to Lance. He was betting that Lance's cold-call targets rarely said things like, "monetize."

"Listen, Omar, we would love to work with you on these details.

Normally, we need to secure the note with your primary residence, not rental property. But hey, if the loan-to-value ratio looks good, as I'm sure it does, we can make it happen. And I can't lock in these rates forever, but if you can move some of your securities portfolio to us in the meantime, you have my word I will persuade the underwriters to give you the same spread."

Amir held his phone high above his head to capture ambient noise, and then said—as if to a roomful of hedge fund partners and lawyers— "Look, guys, I'm not closing on this deal unless you subordinate the tranche from Deutsche Bank. And I need to know by Tuesday night when I leave for Dubai!"

The shoe repair man looked around his shop for the other unexpected visitors to whom Amir apparently was speaking.

"Omar, are you still there? Omar?" Amir felt the urgency in Lance's voice.

"Yeah, Lance. Listen, I'm in the middle of something here," Amir said, returning the phone to his ear. "Can you put me in touch with your wealth management people, so I can follow up on your portfolio idea?"

Lance was talking fast again. "Absolutely. I'll speak to my guys in New York today . . . or wait, better yet, I have a Wharton buddy in wealth management at the Burr Acheson office in Dubai. If you're going to be there this week, I'll have him call you to arrange a meeting."

Merde, thought Amir, realizing that his careless Dubai reference would be hard to walk back. Recovering, Amir said, "OK, Lance, but my schedule is really tight. If you can make an introduction to your friend in Dubai, and text me his name and number, I'll call him."

Lance's tone became even more inappropriately familiar, as if he and Amir had played together on the lacrosse team at Andover.

"Excellent, Omar. I'll do it right now. My guy in Dubai is Pete Hampton. He will take good care of you. Our back office is going to need some paperwork from you. It's a hassle, but we need to check the boxes for our lawyers. I'll text a new account application to you. Send it back when you can. Looking forward to working with you . . . *Bro.*"

The call ended. Clearly irritated, the man in the shoe repair shop flicked his blackened fingers at Amir, as if dismissing an insect from his kunafeh. Back in the street, the Saturday chaos was settling into late afternoon. Amir walked in no particular direction, seized with a panic attack as Lance's text message appeared. "Pete Hampton. Burr Acheson, Dubai. Mobile +971 55 727 6262." Another text followed, accompanied by a new account application.

Lying to Lance probably was not the best strategy, thought Amir. On the other hand, Amir now had a name and number, and a chance to pitch himself. On the next call, maybe he could put off the refinancing discussion, without necessarily admitting that the house in Florida was nonexistent. And transferring a million dollars from his "portfolio" to Burr Acheson? Amir knew it would be harder to make that disappear, since it was the whole point of Lance's cold call. Amir decided he would mostly level with this fellow, Pete Hampton. He would tell him the refinance was a misunderstanding; he's happy with his current portfolio manager; but by the way, are there any job openings at Burr Acheson?

As he rehearsed the lines, his pitch felt hopeless, even preposterous. He considered abandoning the whole thing, ignoring any calls from Lance or Pete, and focusing on more conventional avenues to find a job on Wall Street. Except, as he well knew, you can't get to Wall Street from Nablus.

Then there was Noor's disturbing news about Aisha and her suspected "love interest" in Cairo. Amir didn't see that coming, but he realized he should have. *It made perfect sense,* he thought. And the guy doesn't have to be Egyptian—maybe he is a Brit, or worse, an American. Amir imagined someone like Charlie Bridges, maybe a diplomat at the U.S. Embassy or an investment banker. Someone as tall as Aisha, suitably elegant and polished to meet her impossible standards, fluent in all the right languages, and always greeted by name in the British Airways First Class lounge. *How did they find each other?* he wondered.

His father was out by the time Amir returned to his darkened house. *It seemed more shabby than usual,* Amir thought. All the lights were off, and the weak shadows of dusk produced a strange phosphorescent glow in the patina of dust on every surface. Alone with the laptop in his room, Amir probed every web reference to the Burr

Acheson office in Dubai, and also catalogued the career histories of Lance Bruckel and Pete Hampton. On social media, they left a rich photographic trail during college and business school, flush-faced and smiling with bosomy blonde companions at the Yale Club Christmas party, and sailing in Narragansett Bay while their future first wives sunbathed on the foredeck in racy bikinis. That path turned colder after they went to work, replaced by professional head-shots and white broadcloth shirts. Amir imagined a stern memo from their employers reminding them that careless social media images were not consistent with the bank's brand, or the behaviors expected of captains of the securities industry.

Amir memorized the promotional lines that decorated the Burr Acheson webpage. From these elaborate narrative portraits, it seemed that he wanted to become a "financial advisor," in "private wealth management," helping clients "align their portfolios with their personal values."

They have a lovely vernacular, he thought. Fulfilling, honorable, even noble. Nothing crass about making money. And the website images of beautiful people, giving and receiving wisdom, all depict-ed serene, well-groomed members of a world in which afternoons were spent mixing cocktails on a private dock, or calmly affixing a carabiner to a rock face in the Dolomites. *A long way from Nablus,* Amir thought.

He didn't hear his father return and retire silently to bed. Sara came in around midnight, banged around the kitchen for a few min-utes, and disappeared into her small bedroom, guided by the light in her phone while it delivered a low murmur of voices in a multipar-ty conversation. It was about 3:30 am when Amir heard his mother arrive, as usual, after her ICU shift ended at the hospital. She wore blue scrubs, battered clogs, and glasses balanced on top of her dark hair. Her professional uniform had not changed for years.

It was the sad ritual of his family that they maneuvered silently around each other like this. They were like small planets in orbits that never intersected. Occasionally, the gravity of one influenced the path of another; but it was not resonance as much as conscious avoidance. Amir couldn't remember a time when it was different. His mother was a ghost.

From downstairs, Amir heard the sound of ice and glass. Amir's mother was casual about her alcohol. Other women in Nablus drank, but furtively, stimulated by feelings of guilt, or the electricity of small Islamic infractions. Often in Nablus, alcohol was blamed on visitors, usually relatives from Amman or Beirut, who brought gifts in bags marked "Duty Free." It was considered a stylish present, though a subtly insulting reminder that the giver had escaped to the wider world, and the receiver had not. Those gifts never appeared in Amir's house. But when his mother returned from the hospital each night, apparently exhausted by trying but failing to save every patient, it was her custom to sit silently in the dark kitchen with a glass of Johnnie Walker. She was neither secretive nor ashamed, and no one in the family ever spoke of it.

Amir wasn't sleeping tonight, vexed by Aisha's duplicity and Burr Acheson's flirtation. He made enough noise on the stairs to announce his approach and then joined his mother at the kitchen table. Neither spoke for a while. The ice in her glass made a cracking sound, a cue for one of them to speak.

"Why are you awake?" she asked.

"When you were my age," he began, "did it seem that everything you wanted was out of reach?"

"It still seems that way," she answered without expression.

Amir knew only a little about his mother's early life. Neither of his parents spoke about it, and there were no family photo albums or chatty relatives to reveal those secrets. He did know that she left Nablus as a teenager when her father took a job in Tehran, working as an engineer for British Petroleum. There were rumors of wild days and nights among the expatriate community in the late 1970s, during Iran's approximation of Weimar, before the ayatollah abruptly closed the cabaret. Amir heard that his mother's family fled, forced to leave his grandfather behind. After a harrowing journey, the bedraggled survivors were adopted as charity cases by cousins in Nablus. His grandfather disappeared into Tehran's lusty spree of counterrevolutionary purges and executions. Amir's early childhood memories had large blank spaces for his mother's history, except that she often read and spoke to him in Persian, a poetic, lyrical language that disguises the apocalyptic, self-flagellating mentality of the new Iran.

It would be easy and cliché to think that his mother's cold and distant connection to her children resulted from the presumed horrors of her escape from Iran and the murder of her father. And indeed, when the topic of his dead grandfather surfaced, the remaining color in his mother's face drained suddenly. But Amir imagined there was something even deeper that haunted her.

She poured another two fingers of whiskey. "There are rumors at the hospital that you and Sara are getting friendly with the Dajani girls. You can imagine the stupid and hateful things people say about that. It's none of my business, but are you sure this is a good idea? That family doesn't exactly welcome . . ." She stopped to consider the right word.

"Nonmembers," she said finally.

Amir was incredulous that the most tentative, superficial, or even nonexistent social intercourse in Nablus invariably emerged as a lurid screenplay before the actual participants knew they had been selected for the cast. If this was a topic among the hospital nursing staff, what version had Aisha heard in Cairo? Was Aisha's mother having a similar conversation with her about "nonmembers"?

Amir thought it would lighten the mood if he reverted to Persian with his mother. "Well, I can't speak for Sara. But if you are referring to Aisha Dajani, I assume you know she is in Cairo. And I am here. So, I wouldn't describe that as 'getting friendly.'" In Persian, this sounded less defensive, but also slightly Shakespearean. Something like fated love doomed to result in tragedy.

He recovered by adding, in the harsher inflexion of Arabic, "And you are right that this is none of your business. Are things really so slow at the ICU that the nurses have time to debate class-based barriers to bourgeois mobility?"

His mother stiffened, slightly embarrassed. "You would be surprised at the gossip that goes on during a tracheal intubation, and the doctors are even worse than the nurses. Nothing goes on in Nablus that isn't critiqued by a thousand amateur judges of morality and fashion."

After an awkward silence, Amir's mother spoke up suddenly, eager to anchor her advice in something more solid than gossip. "I just remembered something about Aisha Dajani. I first saw her at the hospital a couple of years ago. She was a teenager, but very poised and confident, like all the women in her family. She was with her mother, who was preparing for some kind of procedure, and the surgeon was a visiting doctor from Tehran. The surgeon was struggling to communicate in Arabic, so I offered to translate. Aisha's mother was very curt and swatted me away like I was a bedpan attendant. Aisha looked embarrassed but said nothing."

His mother paused before adding, "The Dajanis are blueblood Hashemites. The time will come when they insult you too."

More dark mystery, Amir thought, strongly suspecting that his mother had recounted this episode with a few facts missing. But he was not about to acknowledge his longshot romantic aspirations in a conversation with his mother, so he shoved this topic into a cupboard by asking, "Have you ever been to Dubai?"

She looked startled. She said she had not but still volunteered plenty of opinions, including the usual local resentment of Gulf Arabs as new-money hillbillies, barely a generation out of their Bedouin tents, undeserving of the wealth showered upon them by an accident of geology. "Why do you ask?" his mother probed, suspiciously.

"I'm looking for a job. It's pretty uncertain, but I have a contact in Dubai." *That was mostly true,* he thought.

Amir's mother looked doubtful, and then a little upset. "Your father told me you mentioned something about Bahrain. Where are you finding all these contacts in the Gulf?"

They danced around Amir's dubious facts for a while, ending with a strangely desperate warning from his mother.

"I know you're unhappy. But I don't have to tell you that I rely on you to keep this household minimally functioning. Sara is still a teenager, and your father checked out years ago. If you leave, things will change here, and not for the better."

Amir didn't speak.

"Just think about it." She stood and then went to bed.

Upstairs, Amir wondered if his mother's concern was based on some other, unspoken concern. They both knew he wasn't contributing much to the "household."

He turned off the lights and took a last look at Aisha's feed. Nothing new.

What am I looking for? Amir asked himself. *Her secret lover obviously is not going to reveal himself on social media, but maybe there will be clues—a change in hair or makeup, the luminous face of a newly enraptured woman, perhaps a softening of her familiar indifference.* Nothing. It was the same days-old photo that revealed a familiar Aisha in a perfectly ordinary Cairo moment. Amir closed his eyes, worried and frustrated, as his phone purred with news of missed calls from Almaty, Tbilisi, and Abilene.

Chapter 5.

ON Sunday mornings, the international banking houses in Dubai open for business like everyone else in Arabia. But with the trading markets closed in Tokyo, New York, and London, the office atmosphere is sleepy, and the wealth management teams are expected to use these slow days to pitch clients to "rebalance their portfolios," a picturesque name for churning investments to generate fees. The pink sheets that guided these pitches half a century ago had been replaced by overnight emails from New York or London with elaborate talking points and trading strategies to shove at clients. The objective was to persuade them to exit the same positions and strategies that the firm had put them in just a few weeks earlier "in order to adapt to the new landscape."

Pete Hampton was good at these pitches. He avoided burnout during his first three years on Wall Street by neglecting his tedious analyst assignments and insinuating himself into client dinners. There, he deployed his considerable charisma, with legendary results for the bank. He quickly become the essential cohost when foreign clients were present. Pete grew up on military bases in Europe and the Far East, absorbing dialects, idioms, mannerisms, prejudices, and the unspoken fears and loathings that were the essence of every population. After fifteen minutes over dinner at Le Bernardin, a client from Norway, Chile, Singapore, or Brunei would be leaning across the table to share an inside joke with Pete, usually at the expense of some ethnic group back home, and in a language unfamiliar to anyone else at the table. It was said that Pete closed a dozen deals this way during his first two years at Burr Acheson. In short order, his junior analyst work was redistributed to Pete's irritated young colleagues on the twenty-seventh floor. Ahead of his peers, he was given a bespoke promotion to a position that required him essentially to attend dinners.

When the firm opened its office in the Dubai Financial Centre, the new head of the office refused to relocate unless Pete was assigned to him. Pete seized the opportunity to move abroad, where he proceeded to perfect the fine art of delivering clients over dinner.

On this particular Sunday morning, Pete was mildly annoyed by an email from Lance Bruckel at Burr Acheson's office in Palm Beach. Lance wanted him to call a prospective client who was passing through Dubai. Sure, they were friends at Wharton and joined the firm together, but while Pete's career took off in New York, Lance went sideways into selling down-market products like mortgage refinancing. Within Burr Acheson, everyone was admonished to cross-sell and pursue leads provided by other offices, but Pete felt mortgage lending was beneath him and should be left to—sniffing with contempt—regional banks. Still, the refi pitch required the client to move cash or securities to the bank, and if the deal closed, Pete could end up managing the portfolio and collecting a few bips. He finished his third coffee and replied to Lance's email. "On it."

Amir awoke before sunrise to the sound of Mrs. Darwish, a cruel and obese woman who ran an unlicensed pharmacy across the street, the local source of opioids smuggled mostly to desperate housewives in the Israeli settlements. Berating her delivery drivers for their unwashed appearance, her shrill aria held an impressive prolonged middle C, ideal for fracturing a wine glass. It had been a night of interrupted sleep anyway. Mrs. Darwish was just one more reason to quit trying. Amir's grinding teeth accompanied endless rehearsals for his call with Pete, and every take led him deeper into humiliation. He briefly considered telling the truth, but in the dim reasoning of half sleep, that seemed infinitely less appealing than doubling down on his original fraud. Now awake, he considered the implications of submitting a mortgage refinance application for a nonexistent house in Boca Raton, followed by a credit history check that would reveal his nonexistence. A police investigation seemed likely.

And yet, he thought, *this was undoubtedly his one chance to open a door at Burr Acheson.* Quoting a hockey player and pointing his pencil eraser at indecisive students, Charlie used to say, "You miss one hundred percent of the shots you don't take."

As the sun rose, Amir scribbled talking points for the call, punctuated with some of the inane phrases he heard from Lance ("Totally, risk on! I'm all in."). He would let Pete talk, encourage him to make his portfolio management pitch, and then casually mention his own trading experience, without referring to his difficulty in maintaining a trivial minimum account balance. Amir would say he is definitely interested in refinancing, but politely suggest deferring the application until the market stabilized, or maybe until his next deal closed, or perhaps just until never. But for now, Amir would mention the value he could add at Burr Acheson. *They must be looking for fresh approaches,* he reassured himself.

When the call from Dubai appeared on Amir's phone, all his anxious preparation congealed, like a neglected nosebleed, into the stubborn fact that he was not remotely a client prospect for Burr Acheson.

Pete introduced himself, mentioning the referral from Lance. But to Amir's surprise, he wanted to talk about Amir, mentioning for example, his accent, which Pete guessed was Palestinian. Pete fondly described a Palestinian girl he dated in college who, years later, called him to flirt at odd hours from a 970 landline in the West Bank. He was charming, even as he drilled relentlessly into Amir's fiction. In the time required to peel a tangerine, and with less effort, Pete persuaded Amir to reveal that he was unemployed and living with his parents in Nablus, where his "portfolio" consisted of a FREE*Trade account that would seem ridiculous to any of Pete's summer interns.

The line went quiet as Pete completed his disabling cross examination and calculated the value of his time just invested in this prank. But graceful to the last, Pete dryly observed that perhaps there had been a "misunderstanding," and began to apologize— with a gentle edge of sarcasm—for wasting Amir's time.

Amir felt the moment slip away, like the hesitation that dooms a first kiss. He spoke rapidly, worried that his voice rattled with desperation, but he was determined to keep Pete on the line. Amir described options strategies that had been perilous but successful, his expectations for an imminent cyclical rotation in the U.S. markets, a downside hedge that he was working on that involved utility stock index funds, and a tip he heard about currency arbitrage in Russia. Each random topic seemed to frame a question, suggesting an invitation for Pete to comment, but Amir kept moving to head off the inevitable train wreck at the end of this hopeless call.

Pete attempted an interruption. "Look, thanks for taking my call, but I don't think there is anything . . .."

And then, by accident, Amir scored. "Pete, by the way, do you know Charles Bridges? He taught my Capital Markets course at university. He's back in New York, I believe. Or maybe London. Amazing guy. I learned so much from him. You must have heard of him?"

Pete instantly froze. Amir thought he had hung up, and nearly abandoned the call himself, when Pete finally spoke up. "You know Charlie Bridges? Really?"

Before Amir answered, Pete continued. "He's a legend. I met him once when he spoke at a training session for the first-year analysts. Every one of us was in a spiritual trance after thirty minutes. Bridges is a trading shaman, who speaks in beautiful poetry. And they say his esoteric hedging operation made more money for his firm in 2009 than all of M&A."

"Listen, Amir. I don't know what we can do for you, but you should speak to Hodding. He and Bridges are close. If you hold on, I'll see if he's here."

"Who's Hodding?" Amir asked. But Pete was gone.

When the line came to life again, a male voice with an Alabama accent got right to business. "How do you know Charlie?" the voice asked, without introductions or pleasantries.

Hodding Easterbrook ran the Burr Acheson office in Dubai. His odd career path took him to Washington in the last quarter of the twentieth century after raising campaign funds for a U.S. President from the deep south. Despite his Tuscaloosa style and Bull Connor vocabulary, Hodding leveraged his peripheral contribution to the President's election into a "government relations" job with Burr Acheson's Washington office. To the surprise of nearly everyone in the partners' dining room in New York, Hodding proved skilled at opening doors in Washington. He often described his work as "securing unfair advantages for those who could afford to pay." Hodding was very good at that.

Eventually, Hodding persuaded Burr Acheson to plant its wealth management flag in some new, target rich markets abroad like the Middle East. His friends at the State Department told him that the very new money crowd in the Emirates was eager to be taken seriously in Washington and would pay for the privilege. Like generations of strivers before him, Hodding rebranded himself. He became a self-described "Arabist" and persuaded the bank to give him a budget to launch a new wealth management operation in Dubai, where he proved to be fabulously adept at generating new clients with portfolios they were willing to commit to "discretionary management."

In his first call with Hodding, Amir sensed an unexpected kinship. He didn't yet know Hodding's backstory, but after describing his spiritual awakening in Charlie's Capital Markets 425, Amir felt the conversation return repeatedly to his dreams of escaping Nablus and finding purpose on Wall Street. Hodding sprinkled into the call occasional anecdotes about Charlie, but afterward, Amir wondered if this was a test of Amir's authenticity. At one point, Hodding asked if Charlie still kept a ballpoint pen balanced over his ear, aiming it like a weapon when he was making a point. Amir hesitated, and then said he remembered it as a pencil. Apparently satisfied, Hodding moved on.

He was seductive, Amir thought, in a style completely different from Pete's, but even more successful in drawing out fine details that Amir had neither intended to share, nor expected to be of interest. Amir found himself describing the tortured relationship with his sister Sara, his mother's all-consuming career in the ICU, his discovery of *Moby Dick* in an American literature class at university, and the Persian language skills that he absorbed in his childhood. Hodding lingered with special interest on this last point, and practiced on Amir with a few rudimentary phrases he said he picked up in Dubai.

With dreadful pronunciation, Hodding said in Persian, "My secretary is sexy."

Amir let that pass.

Remarkably to Amir, Hodding seemed uninterested in the comic twists that led to this telephone call. Pete must have mentioned it, but Hodding apparently was unbothered by the Boca Raton refinancing charade.

After twenty minutes on the telephone, Hodding said, "Amir, I want you to come to Dubai and meet some people. It's not Wall Street, but we're doing exciting things here, and there may be a place for you. Anyway, I owe Charlie some favors, and I know he would want me to help one of his students if I can."

"I'm going to ask my office manager to call you to make the arrangements. She's very German. A Nazi really. But she makes things happen. My advice is, do what she says, or else."

"See you in Dubai!" Hodding concluded, making the emirate sound like a strip mall in Birmingham: "Doó—Buy!"

Amir was speechless.

Another panic attack struck him as he considered the obstacles in actually traveling from Nablus to Dubai; the impossibility of obtaining a visa; the expense; a forbidding list of Israeli occupation rules designed to guarantee that Palestinians cannot travel. But by lunchtime, all the arrangements were made. In a curt, no-nonsense call from Ms. Greta Speer in Hodding's office, Amir received precise instructions and was told to expect a courier package with all the necessary documents. He would be in Dubai next Wednesday.

It would be a short flight from Nablus to Dubai if there was such a flight. Traveling from Chicago to Shanghai is easier, safer, and faster. Even if magic documents appeared in Fräulein Speer's package, Amir knew he would need some local help. On his way to Jaffa Street, he stopped for a haircut, for the first time insisting that the barber replicate a photo that Amir had downloaded on his phone. The barber was dismissive of the image of J. P. Morgan's CEO, declaring his haircut to be the work of an amateur. When he arrived later in Uncle Jaber's shop, Amir looked and felt older, more experienced, even distinguished—just the look he was going for.

His uncle patiently listened to his improbable escape plan, skeptical at first, but gradually absorbed by the adventure. Pulling a pencil from a teacup under the supermodel's photograph, Uncle Jaber produced a freehand map. He carefully numbered annotations marking the navigational traps that Amir would confront in getting out of the West Bank, across Allenby Bridge to Jordan, and on to the airport in Amman. It was only seventy kilometers, but there were at least three intermediate stops, his uncle said dramatically, where he would be speaking to someone at gunpoint. Uncle Jaber had never actually made the trip, but Amir knew he had paid smugglers to move Chinese electronics through the airport cargo terminal in Amman, so his plan had some credibility. As was common in Nablus, he held contradictory sentiments about Dubai, observing with contempt that the Emiratis were silly, spoiled children who "got lucky" with oil, but with God's grace had built the greatest city in Arabia, an architectural masterpiece "envied in London and New York."

As Amir was leaving with his treasure map, his uncle quietly offered a warning. "Your mother won't like this."

Amir decided to postpone that conversation for the present. He sat quietly through dinner that evening as his father and Sara bantered about nothing. The shallowness of their conversation sparked a mood shift in Amir, and he felt himself smiling involuntarily. All the anxieties that had weighed so painfully on him—the humiliating accidents and subterfuges exposed in his phone call with Hodding, and his dubious qualifications to actually work at a Wall Street firm—disappeared from his consciousness like forgotten stains in freshly laundered linen. Amir's achievement was what mattered. His impossible fantasy about Burr Acheson had been converted into something real. He would finally join the rest of the world, outside the solitary confinement of Nablus, and experience such ordinary rituals as flying across continents to business meetings, exchanging stock tips with his fashionably dressed colleagues, deciphering inscrutable commentary during analyst calls with CFOs in Hong Kong, Palo Alto, and Stuttgart, and debating the fine points of sushi presentation during lavish client dinners. Amir had studied, even memorized, all of these images on the websites of global investment firms, and he was struck by their uniformity, which transcended global boundaries, cultures and languages, and gender roles. Everything, it seemed, converged with existential harmony in the lovely tapestry of global capital. At last, Amir could see himself in those images.

He slept deeply that night, as if in the cool, cleansed atmosphere of what Amir imagined to be a just-delivered airliner, comforted by that perfect ambient symphony of rushing air, precision machinery and time travel. Not quite dreaming, exquisite high-definition videos unspooled scenes of his new life, and at length, Aisha appeared— as she had so often —emerging silently from a mist, or just mystery. A scrim of drapery separated him from her naked contours, and a gently backlit dawn produced subtle brushstroke effects in sfumato. There was a thrilling blur of the outlines of her perfectly sculpted hips, her regal chin, and the climactic vanishing point above her silken thighs. But this time, and for the first time, Aisha was beckoning.

That word haunted Amir, from its first appearance to him in Dr. Fathy's class notes on Melville, with an evocative reference to an apparition of the famous white monster luring the crew of the Pequod to its doom. He had to look up the word, and there was no sensible version in Arabic. *Was it inviting or threatening?* Amir wondered, but of course, in context, it was both.

Aroused but unsteady, Amir caught his breath as he reached to pull away the drapery blowing gently against Aisha's glowing form. His hand brushed against her breast. Aisha's eyes closed in slow motion above parting lips. Her nipples visibly hardened. And then . . . the mythic scene evaporated into the dusty darkness of his bedroom in Nablus. The call to prayer was underway, in a hoarse recorded broadcast from the cheap loudspeaker at the El-Kebir mosque.

Chapter 6.

DESPITE the fancy name, the Intensive Care Unit at Nablus Martyrs Hospital was really just another stained corridor, with fewer than the usual number of expired fluorescent lights. It was built, or rebuilt, or possibly just repainted, after the second Intifada, when it served as a battlefield triage unit for the steady stream of young gunshot victims of street warfare with the occupying army. Amir's mother remembered those days vividly. The standard issue rifles supplied to Israel under America's generous Foreign Military Financing program were legendary for their 5.56 mm projectiles designed to tumble upon soft tissue impact, which produced exit wounds the diameter of pita bread. There wasn't much the ICU could contribute to those patients, but the nursing team was efficient in tagging the bodies.

In more recent times, the ICU dealt with fewer geopolitical forms of trauma, though the occasional skirmish with settlers, usually on Fridays, provided the medical staff with regular training in the treatment of stab wounds. More common, especially during the graveyard shift when Amir's mother ("Chief Nurse Hala," as she was called in the ICU) was on duty, were victims of the prosaic nighttime horrors of communities everywhere—young wives with swollen lips and bruised eyes, blue-hued children who swallowed something just large enough to produce a tracheal obstruction, terrified teenage girls whose DIY abortions had gone horribly wrong, and narcotic abusers alternately screaming for an 80 mg tablet or curled into a shivering mess on the floor. In her blue scrubs, Chief Nurse Hala projected calm and confidence, even if the physician on duty was not entirely interested in, or qualified for, the particular emergency. If they were conscious, the patients were reassured by her professional air, though the hysterical relatives considered her cold and unsympathetic, and accused her of having "German manners."

After fourteen years in the ICU, Chief Nurse Hala had presided over medical emergencies for virtually every family in Nablus. In those moments, they placed a kind of hopeful trust in her, and if things turned out all right, she was remembered as a savior. If not, she was at least remembered as the steadiest hand in the room. With this well-earned reputation, the physicians were deferential to her, the other nurses were afraid of her, and her superiors on the hospital staff kept a wary distance. In this environment, she effectively ruled the ICU and was accountable to no one. Even the hospital administrator, a notorious abuser of every other woman on the staff, would avoid encounters with Chief Nurse Hala, with grudging acceptance of her unimpeachable status. It helped, of course, that he knew that she knew of his petty larcenies with hospital finances.

Among other things, her status meant that no one questioned Chief Nurse Hala about the hour or two when she would disappear behind the locked door of the "Records Storage" room. A small examination room had been repurposed years earlier as the repository of carelessly piled boxes of medical records, patiently awaiting an indexing that would never come. Amid the hopeless tangle of radiographs and lab work reports, there was a very old desktop computer atop a gurney with wheels that no longer turned, an uncomfortably tall stool, and nearby, a hideous overstuffed chair, upholstered to resemble the Hindenburg. Despite its shortcomings in design, the chair looked inviting for unsanctioned on-duty naps—or in the dirty imaginations of the junior nursing staff, frantic late-night couplings.

Chief Nurse Hala's visits to the Records Storage room began innocently with a bona fide search for records. One night, while assisting a visiting Iranian doctor who was treating a long-neglected intermetatarsal neuroma, the two made a failed search for the patient's earlier treatment records. With the patient sedated after presenting in a state of swollen agony, the two found themselves crawling on the floor of the storage room, sharing expletives about the unprofessional state of hospital management. One thing led to another, and long-suppressed spirits of hope and meaning were awakened that night in Hala, as the visiting doctor called her with a degree of familiarity that no one else in the hospital would presume. They never found the records, and the patient left with a Percocet prescription that eventually, after inventive combinations with raki, killed him. But the encounter that night was a resurrection for Hala.

Between the doctor's monthly rotations to Nablus from his distant hospital residency, Hala made nightly visits to the records storage room. Patiently nursing life into the aging computer, she maintained a steady electronic correspondence with the doctor, encrypted with an application popular in third world surveillance societies. Things she thought were lost long ago were found again. She began to dream in color, vividly reliving her teenage years, which—with exaggerated memory—were filled with party music, eager displays of new decolletage, and grand plans. The doctor was handsome enough, but the attraction came from the things he knew and shared with Hala. There were his exquisite gifts that she hid in a box of ancient floppy disks that would never be of interest to anyone but her, and between visits, his secret messages revealed glimpses of a life to be awakened. He taught her an exquisite cadence of sensations—anticipation, desperate longing, fear, reckless determination—all exploding into the monthly episodes that reinforced her conviction to risk everything to have what the doctor offered her.

He promised her the safe return of her beloved father who was, after all, alive in a Tehran prison.

Chapter 7.

AMIR was distracted from his normal Monday FREE*Trade ritual. He had neglected the financial news for days, instead absorbing more portraiture and vernacular of wealth management websites. He was preparing for his interview by studying endless images of financially secure, impeccably dressed models. Religious incantations floated in the spaces above them—never casting a shadow on the sleek designer blouse, the trainer-toned forearms, or the exquisite Swiss wristwatch—but firmly invoking the stern commandments of God, whose grace will reward dynamic asset allocation, scrupulous portfolio rebalancing, and attention to risk adjusted returns. Amir memorized the portraits and the prayers, convinced that they would unlock the gates to Wall Street, and from there, deliverance.

Around noon, a tiny white Toyota van, with tires the size of vinyl LPs, appeared at Amir's house. The driver clawed through cardboard containers in the rear, finally emerging with a bright yellow overnight courier envelope marked "Urgent." He pressed the doorbell. Inaudible. Broken long ago. He pounded twice on the door, dropped the precious package in an unsanitary-looking damp spot on the front step, and drove away playing a high-volume remix of Arabic hip-hop. From his bedroom window, Amir shook his head at the driver's uniform, a clownlike red and yellow riot, familiar in fast food takeaways in East London.

Inside the package, there were treasures unlike anything Amir had seen or imagined. Several plastic sleeves were clipped to a letter printed on the weighty, elegant stationery of Burr Acheson. A subtle watermark confirmed its authority, along with the flamboyant signature of Hodding Easterbrook. In the clearest prose, the letter confirmed Amir's invitation to attend an interview in Dubai on the appointed day. A meticulous itinerary was attached, no doubt the work of Fräulein Speer, with prearranged flight details, and specifics of his every movement in Dubai. One sleeve contained a series of travel documents and entry permits in multiple languages, with redundant red and blue stamps evidencing the bloated bureaucracies that persist in places once touched by the British Empire and its civil service. There were printed round trip tickets confirming his business class seats on Emirates Airline, with tiny maps helpfully pointing out the locations of Emirates' "premium" lounges at the airports in Amman and Dubai. Instructions guided him to the meeting point for his car service in Dubai, and another page explained the amenities he could expect upon arrival at the Grosvenor House Hotel, where the general manager, Dieter Günther, looked forward to attending to his every need. Another small envelope, sealed with red tape that left a kind of indelible skid mark when opened, contained one thousand U.S. dollars and a sternly worded Burr Acheson form declaring that all travel expenses must be "documented."

Finally, Amir came upon a twenty-two-page disclosure statement, prefaced with microscopic references to the U.S. Securities and Exchange Act of 1934, a long list of regulatory citations, consent decrees, interpretative findings, and admonitions about the criminal penalties that apply to false or incomplete statements. He would be expected to complete this form with surprising details about his life, including a multipage description of his prior positions in the investment industry, which he would—embarrassingly—leave entirely blank.

His go-to taxi driver, Abdel Raouf, responded immediately to Amir's text, and they met on the street near the university for a conspiratorial-looking conversation to plan the trip out of Nablus.

Abdel Raouf was proud of his reputation for discretion and eager to exaggerate his clandestine image. He interrupted Amir several times to say, in brusque Arabic, "I don't need to know that." The plan was hatched, including the "handover" to one of Abdel Raouf's associates who would meet Amir once inside Jordan for the drive from Allenby to the Amman Airport. A price was agreed upon. He was visibly disappointed when Amir told him that he had all the required travel documentation for the trip. Abdel Raouf's expression signaled a concern that his stature might be diminished by undertaking a trip that did not depend upon his unique skills for rule-breaking, risk-taking, and exposing supposed shortcomings in the Israeli security measures in the West Bank.

Amir skipped the opening bell in New York that afternoon. He packed and repacked a small overnight bag several times, eventually opting for a plastic garment bag to protect his one business suit, an insouciant choice he had seen validated on the Emirates website in a photograph of important-looking executives taking their seats in business class.

At dinner, his father listened impassively as Amir revealed his news. He edited out the details about Boca Raton, and without plainly lying, left the dubious impression that Burr Acheson had searched the world for someone with Amir's skills, and found him in Nablus. Amir could see the skeptical expression on his father's face, conveying confidence that there was much more to this story. But he didn't press for details. Instead, expressing a familiar sentiment that captured his lifetime of disappointments and resentments, his father said simply, "Well, if this is what you want."

"But you should speak to your mother," he added, deploying a universal marital hedge.

To his surprise, Sara did not heap ridicule on Amir's story. She seemed stunned by the possibility that he might actually be converting his Wall Street fantasy into something genuine. And Amir knew that, even in Sara's cynical world view, a job interview in Dubai had cachet that could not be dismissed. She left the table without speaking, evidently mortified that she might be left behind in the wasteland of her family and Nablus. By Amir of all people. As she had often reminded him, a great consolation in Sara's life always had been the confidence that, at least, she was not the loser that Amir was.

Hours later, Amir heard his mother's arrival, followed by the sound of ice cubes. He chose not to join her for one more joyless encounter, in which his sense of personal achievement would be twisted into some version of betrayal, cowardice, and irresponsibility. Amir was leaving all that wreckage behind.

In the company of Abel Raouf, the cannonball run from Nablus to the Jordanian border was mostly uneventful. Uncle Jaber's scrawled map and checkpoint tips were reassuring, but the promised gunpoint encounters were—with one exception—just routine embodiments of the banality of military occupation. The soldiers manning—and often womaning—the checkpoints were even more bored and resentful than the bulldozer escort team in Nablus that erased the Fawzy residence. With thick eyeglasses and Nietzsche paperbacks shoved into the midthigh trouser pockets of their ill-fitting military uniforms, Amir thought they looked like anxious undergraduates, sleepless after cramming for an exam on European intellectual history. Conscripted from comfortable student lives to be sentries in the desert, pointing a lethal weapon at children huddled in filthy and stifling taxis, the soldiers' expressions had hardened into a combination of loathing, absurdist theater, and routinized cruelty. Beyond good and evil, indeed. They were less menacing than Amir expected, and like him, they just wanted to be somewhere else.

There was one exception, at the last stop before the Jordanian authorities exercised their shaky jurisdiction, just before General Allenby's bridge was transubstantiated into King Hussein's bridge. Like one last pointless insult, a military outpost sporting a blue and white flag appeared on the way out of the West Bank, and forced Abdel Raouf's creaking Mercedes through a maze of concrete barriers that required drivers to navigate a tedious crawl. At the last turn, a steel barrier rotated up from the roadway like the mouth of a white whale, signaling wordlessly that drivers would either stop or be eaten by the monster. There was no security purpose to be served by this checkpoint. The weary travelers who presented themselves were *leaving*, and about to be searched again and interrogated by Jordanian troops. But when national boundaries are disputed, and fictitious in any case, it was important for the claimants to behave like owners, marking their territory with the military equivalent of cat spray.

At a bomb-safe distance from the whale's jaw, a concrete box with one-way glass sat silently in the desert sun. There was no sign of life. Eventually, a single soldier emerged, in full battle dress. His (her?) face was obscured by a balaclava, finger on the trigger of an automatic weapon pointed, more or less, at Abdel Raouf's nose. The soldier approached, stopping five meters from the car, and then shouted at them in Hebrew. This was another piece of essential choreography in the ballet of asserting disputed sovereignty, advancing the fiction of an official national language that was used by few of the natives. Both Abdel Raouf and Amir responded with blank stares, intentionally, but also genuinely, not comprehending what the soldier said. The second attempt was in English, with an American accent. "Get out of the car and show me your travel documents." He inserted an expletive that was understood in every language.

A great show of officialdom ensued, with papers examined under brusque questioning. Abdel Raouf explained that he was merely delivering a passenger and would not be crossing the border, after which he was ordered back to his taxi. Amir stood in the sun for a long time, while the soldier reviewed his documents, speaking to someone via a radio strapped to a chest pack. Impatient at being asked to repeat himself several times to the radio voice, the soldier pulled the balaclava beneath a smooth chin, now revealed to be that of a young man of approximately Amir's age. He questioned Amir about the usual details but lingered on his ultimate destination—Dubai.

Amir had been coached by Uncle Jaber and Abdel Raouf on checkpoint protocol. Be brief and solicitous. Cast your eyes downward in a submissive pose. Above all, don't argue; remember that he has a gun. After disappearing for a while into the concrete box, the soldier returned, walking with purpose toward Amir, evidently troubled by something in his documents.

"Your exit authorization was processed in twenty-four hours. That doesn't happen. Did you bribe someone?"

Amir explained politely that he was going to a job interview at an American bank in Dubai, that the paperwork was submitted on his behalf by the bank, and that he was sure it was all properly done.

"What bank?" the soldier asked.

Amir hesitated, wondering if there was some kind of blacklist, or if this was a trick question that might lead to messy revelations about his Boca Raton credentials.

"What bank?" the soldier repeated.

"Burr Acheson," Amir said quietly.

"How the hell did you get an interview at Burr Acheson?" He didn't wait for an answer before speaking again, now in a strangely collegial tone. "I had a summer internship there when I was at NYU. That place is hyper-competitive, and they didn't give me a job offer when I finished college. In those days, they were giving all the analyst jobs to women to try to clean up their frat house reputation. So my U.S. visa expired, and I ended up back here—in this . . ." He didn't finish the sentence, but motioned with his hand at the bleak landscape, as if the missing descriptive term was self-evident.

The solider looked at Amir with a mixture of resentment and admiration. Amir thought it best to say nothing. He knew that the bundle of travel documents in the soldier's hand included a letter from Hodding Easterbrook on Burr Acheson letterhead, confirming the date and time of Amir's job interview. That was more authoritative than anything Amir could say, so he cast his eyes downward in his best imitation of Jim Crow deportment and waited for the soldier's next move. In Amir's peripheral vision, he saw Abdel Raouf smoking a cigarette, looking at his shoes, and listening carefully to every word.

The soldier's mood changed abruptly. Removing both hands from his weapon, he carefully folded Amir's travel documents and returned them to him reverentially, as if the bundle of paper was the diploma presented at a commencement ceremony. He seemed to reach as if to shake Amir's hand but then didn't. The soldier smiled at him and said, "Good luck, man," before pulling up his balaclava and disappearing into the concrete box.

Back in the taxi, en route to the Jordanian crossing, Abdel Raouf grinned proudly at Amir.

Inside Jordan at last, Abdel Raouf's "associate" met Amir in a taxi that looked weirdly like the one he just left. Amir wondered how it was possible that so many Mercedes sedans from the 1980s found their way from Stuttgart to the Middle East. And why, he wondered, were they all the color of a sun-blanched canary? The driver barely spoke but did his job. In an hour, he dropped Amir at Queen Alia Airport and then disappeared into a flock of other faded birds.

Onboard the Emirates flight to Dubai, Amir's seat in business class was comfortably appointed with maple, mirrored surfaces, and butter-colored leather. He was offered an array of amenities by female flight attendants dressed in costumes with absurd headgear, presumably designed to be evocative of Arabian Nights. Their uniforms reminded Amir of an old television sitcom he watched on a pirated satellite channel in which an American astronaut inexplicably shares his Florida home with a partially dressed concubine, who happens to be a genie. As the aircraft wheels left the tarmac, Amir tapped a pictogram in his armrest, and the seat reclined to cradle his body in a gentle boat pose. The dust of Nablus felt far away.

Chapter 8.

WAITING in the immigration line at Dubai's airport, there was a strong sensation of a childhood visit to the pediatrician and the odor of antiseptic, suppressing the existence, or at least awareness, of anything unclean. In the UAE, everything that required human hands was done with imported labor, except the handful of positions necessary to maintain internal security. To preserve a thin thread of social structure, the native Emirati population mostly withdrew from the visible scene in the 2000s—like a Wahhabi rapture—cloistered in splendid walled compounds, or in extended stays at Geneva or London hotels. Left behind was a vast expatriate population, toiling either under a brutal sun or in refrigerated cubicles, segregated spaces where they are invisible and inoffensive to the tiny community of Emiratis. There were Nepalese construction workers, Indonesian nannies, Sudanese accountants, American lawyers, and everything in between. But to the Emiratis, they were all the same—just hirelings with temporary work visas, eager to do the dirty jobs.

Fräulein Speer had booked Amir at the Grosvenor House Hotel, a glass icon astride the Dubai Marina, a neighborhood that was manufactured to resemble a clean version of Miami. From his hotel room, Amir watched the early evening sun set and dribble into the cerulean water of the Arabian Gulf, as motor yachts left their moorings for an evening of conspicuous consumption. Slovenian models posed playfully with the mooring lines, in crepe de chine dresses that uncovered more than covered their made-for-television breasts and thighs. The daylight faded, and a handful of lights snapped on in the forest of anonymous residential towers that spiked up from the desert around Grosvenor House. With few exceptions, the buildings were entirely dark. As Amir would learn, property ownership in Dubai was seldom intended for occupancy.

On his printed itinerary, the evening of his arrival in Dubai was described as "Check-In and Free Time," followed helpfully by swank restaurant suggestions and the mobile number of Allesandro, the Grosvenor House Concierge, who "takes special care of Burr Acheson's guests." Amir elected not to test Allesandro's skills that evening and instead chose a cubist leather chair in the hotel lobby, where he ordered grapefruit juice and settled in to watch the show.

The Grosvenor House in Dubai was named for a venerable property on Park Lane in London, where the earliest new money in the Arabian Gulf traded Bedouin tents for hotel lobbies in the 1970s. Every August, the London version was fully booked by Gulf families visiting to enjoy the mild weather, Bond Street shopping, afternoon promenades of black abayas above designer sneakers at the Serpentine in Hyde Park, and the generous cash allowances of their tribal patronage systems. The lore of these London visits half a century earlier, embellished and passed down to successive generations, gave Dubai's Grosvenor House a mythic quality, rich with images of luxury and good-natured rule breaking on the edge of the Arabian Peninsula's tolerance. The lobby parade of arriving, lingering, and departing guests was a fantastical scene—equal parts Federico Fellini and George Lucas. Nothing in Palestine's parochial prejudices and uninformed advice about Dubai had prepared Amir for his experience in this hotel lobby.

Dubai's early evening flight arrivals from every odd time zone brought a surge of exotic visitors to the Grosvenor House. They were greeted inside by a blinding, polished marble expanse, leading to the reception desk in the distance. Flanked on both sides by spectators in lobby bar club chairs, and accompanied by ambient music from the Buddha Bar hiding discreetly behind a rope line, there was the unmistakable feel of a runway show. Most of the arrivals rose to the occasion when they saw the spectators, quickly erecting their postures, making micro adjustments to their garments to reveal luxury brand signatures or hints of fine black lingerie, and stepping with exaggerated purpose like the models at a Milan couture show. There were the Russian oligarchs, with thick, cruel faces and expensively barbered stubble. On their arms were much taller, leaner, and younger Valkyries, sex dolls trafficked from the slums of Bucharest and Sofia. Close behind them came bankers from Zürich, handsome women and men in immaculately pressed navy suits, wearing identical expressions of serene confidence, smugly in possession of the secrets and mortgages of everyone who mattered. And then, with more clatter, a Gulf sheikh arrived, followed by his family and entourage. Defiantly not in step with the music and splendid in the glorious whiteness of his thobe, he walked at a sheikhly pace, slow and measured, as if a priceless antique Koran were balanced on his head. Some other guests, also in thobes, appeared from nowhere, and the sheikh paused for the deeply meaningful ballet of nose kissing, in which his tribal stature was affirmed for all present. Women in abayas and sunglasses followed at a discreet distance, carrying immense designer handbags. Behind them, a half dozen Indonesian maids, heads scarved, lightly superintended a clutch of bratty children. A trio of young women, models arriving for a fashion shoot, laughed and spoke too loudly in Italian, but quickly collected themselves for the runway show, lips pursed provocatively and hips in motion under spray-on leather jeans, trailing flashes of red under Louboutin slingbacks.

All around Amir, the lobby bar patrons absorbed the show, nodding in recognition at some of the arrivals, and occasionally elevating eyebrows in judgment of fashion missteps or decorum breaches. It seemed to Amir to be a kind of exclusive club, in which few of the members knew the others, but all knew *of* the others. Like all truly exclusive clubs, there evidently were rigid unwritten rules, which could only be revealed by breaking them. Suddenly discouraged and intimidated, Amir wondered if he was sufficiently prepared for this interview. His careful study of the images on bank websites had not profiled *these* characters. He wondered who he would encounter at Burr Acheson.

An image of Aisha flashed into his head. She seemed naturally to belong in this cosmopolitan place. He imagined her commanding the hotel runway, provoking awed silence among the lobby bar spectators, casting withering looks at the globotrash delaying her check-in. Amir checked her feed. Nothing new from Aisha. *Probably with her secret Cairo lover,* Amir thought, dejected. He slept poorly.

His interview the next day was set to begin early. Burr Acheson's working hours were dictated by the rhythms of global capital markets, and Dubai's time zone at GMT+4 meant that the office could trade live for some slice of each day in every major market from Tokyo to New York. But that required a long day in Dubai for the traders. Amir was expected at 7:30 am.

Stepping out of the hotel to meet his driver, Amir was knocked senseless by a ferocious flash of silent light and heat. It was the color of flaming phosphorous, white and blinding. He imagined the first microsecond of the Hiroshima blast, but this was just a September morning in Dubai. His eyes adjusted slowly, dialing up the f-stops in his pupils. In the nick of time, just before he was incinerated by the morning sun, his driver opened the car door, and Amir felt gently sucked into the refrigerated interior of an understated white sedan. The Bangladeshi driver was silent during the thirty-minute drive along Sheikh Zayed Road, a futuristic high-speed motorway flanked by office towers distinguished only by their remarkable sameness. At last, they arrived at the Dubai Financial Centre, a cluster of glass boxes surrounding a central building that looked like a giant Scandinavian end table, and Amir found his way to Burr Acheson's seventh floor offices.

Behind the efficient-looking woman commanding the reception desk was a glass wall that revealed an open office arrangement, an entire floor in which clusters of smartly dressed young people—mostly men—sat or stood facing their computer monitors, Bloomberg terminals, and flat panels of broadcast financial news, all speaking into one or sometimes two telephones. The shape of the clusters was familiar. Charlie had produced a much smaller replica for Capital Markets 425. Amir smiled at the reveal. *A real trading floor,*

Amir reflected, moving fortunes at the speed of light, building and toppling empires on every continent, unshackled from the impasses and crooked political deals that crush the spirit of Nabulsis and people everywhere who don't have the will or the imagination to confront the white whale.

I am ready, Amir thought.

After a silent electronic signal from the receptionist, Greta Speer appeared. Amir thought she looked tightly wound, both in manner and grooming. Her hair was secured above her neck with invisible hardware, and sharp lines defined her nose and jaw in an expression that said clearly that disorder will not be tolerated. She walked and stood with Wehrmacht precision, holding a black leather portfolio hard against her breast, from which she eventually produced a single sheet of paper with Amir's interview schedule.

"I hope your travel arrangements were satisfactory," she announced with an inflection that admitted no possibility that they might be otherwise.

"Mr. Easterbrook is looking forward to meeting you later today. Until then, we have arranged for you to meet some of his colleagues, who will tell you about our firm. Shall we get started?"

It was rhetorical. Amir was in her custody, and he murmured his submission as she turned to lead him through a door beside the glass wall. To his surprise, there was no roar or frenzy of trading energy, and no discernable expletives from the dozens of telephone calls in progress, despite the obvious urgency pressed upon the room by a hundred video screens delivering signals from twelve time zones. The prevailing sound was a gentle Venturi rush of cleansed air from discreet overhead slots, providing both the reassurance of atmospheric purity and the background music of measured efficiency. *It was,* Amir thought, *like the deck of a well-captained sailing ship, on which the crewmembers performed their difficult and dangerous mission in synchronized harmony.* The sensation was even more thrilling than Amir had expected.

The interviews began with individual meetings in a frosted glass conference room, looking out onto a fake forest of non-native tree species. Amir met with three analysts/account managers, each impressively credentialled. One woman was recruited by Burr Acheson from Stanford's engineering school. She smiled uncomfortably, as she sprinkled little quiz questions into the conversation. "Do you think the inverted yield curve is a trigger, or just a data point?" she asked, as if gossiping about a mutual friend who might be getting too intimate with the wrong person. "Have you noticed a relationship between commodity price volatility and the emerging consensus toward easy money at the European Central Bank?" she casually proposed, while nervously dangling a matte black pump from the toes of her right foot.

Another analyst about his age drilled into Amir's university studies, less interested in Capital Markets 425 but apparently fascinated by Dr. Fathy's American literature class. Did Amir think that the themes captured by Twain or Faulkner were "sufficiently universal to resonate in Nablus, or were they too parochial— too unique to the American experience?" the analyst asked. "What was the students' reaction to Baldwin?" he wondered. He referred to his upbringing in Nebraska, and implied that Nablus might be similar in its natural resistance to boundary-pushing authors and their enablers in university English departments. Amir demurred on that point but conceded that the classroom discussions sometimes—Aisha's sadistic ridicule of Dr. Fathy flashed into his head—took literary criticism well beyond the authors' plausible realm of contemplation.

Amir felt he was fielding the interview probes with respectable competence, having prepared reasonably well for the finance questions by scanning the online archive of articles in *The Economist.* The unexpected questions about literature seemed designed mostly to test his fluency in English, and again, Amir thought he scored well enough.

The third interviewer was Pete Hampton, the dubious voice on the telephone during Amir's transparently fraudulent story about coming to Dubai. He didn't seem (presently) bothered about that episode. While Pete looked a little too often at his watch during the interview, he was good natured about the unlikely circumstances. Pete did most of the talking, as if he had been instructed by his superiors to persuade Amir to join the team, or perhaps because he was always selling and didn't have a ready alternative approach for human encounters. *He was a character straight from the Burr Acheson website,* Amir thought. Very white in complexion and bearing, pumice-scrubbed and trim, in a European suit framing an open collared blue shirt, subtly personalized with a tiny burgundy monogram at his left ribcage. Pete spoke about the office team, their talent and dedication, his excitement at penetrating a relatively new regional business opportunity, and the thrill of working for a "visionary" like Hodding Easterbrook.

He's really selling, Amir thought.

Amir asked some anodyne questions about the business, all openings for him to display his command of the vernacular of securities markets. Pete appeared to recognize the routine, and he brushed it aside like the tiresome self-promotion that it was.

"Let me tell you about Dubai," he interrupted, as if suddenly losing patience with the interview ritual. "I've never seen anything like it. The clients come to *us.* They pitch *us.* I won't say they are very sophisticated about investing; they're not. And you have to explain some pretty basic things to them, like diversification, asset allocation, risk hedging, all the basics. For Christ's sake, when they first walk into the office, the only thing they think they want to do is buy trophy hotels in Los Angeles and Miami Beach, like they learned about investing from playing Monopoly. But usually they come around, and let us build high quality portfolios for them, with great fee generation for us."

"There is a messy side," he continued, lowering his voice. "We don't know where some of this money comes from. A lot of these guys obviously come to us for a makeover. They come in with these blemished, wrinkled assets from some dodgy commission deal in Kazakhstan, or from flipping a dacha on the Black Sea, and it's like they hope to leave our day spa with a new look—a portfolio that's papered, portable, and rebranded as a Burr Acheson client portfolio.

"Our compliance people in New York are all over us. We have to turn away a lot of the money that walks in. And then there are all the characters subject to U.S. government sanctions, the 'politically exposed persons' category, and the firm's own 'no fly' list. Realistically, the engine of the Dubai economy is converting mysterious cash into local real estate and flipping that into a securities portfolio that looks respectable to regulators in Zürich, London, or New York. But if there was an actual country club here, you could probably reconstruct the members' roster from the U.S. Treasury Department's sanctions list."

"And the Iranians are the worst," Pete rattled on. "They have these bag men flying into Dubai for the weekend, looking for places to park cash for the ayatollahs and generals. Those guys take a cut of everything their government buys, and then they try to convert it to hard currency as fast as possible. We have to stay a million miles from that money, but the spiderweb of shell companies and Emirati intermediaries is unbelievable. I remember one time—" Abruptly, Pete stopped talking.

Amir nodded with a serious expression, as if to dispel any suspicion that his own creation myth might expose the firm to problems. "Yes, I guess money laundering is a constant problem here."

Pete waved him off, looking uncomfortable, as if the L-word should never be spoken aloud. "It's manageable," he said, and then changed the subject to Amir. "Look, I don't know what Hodding has in mind for you. Your career path is a little unorthodox. You definitely said the magic words when you mentioned Charlie Bridges. But I have to level with you. If you joined us, you probably would start as a junior analyst, working under one of the wealth management teams. It's not very glamorous. You won't be trading or building portfolios, and there wouldn't be much client contact."

As Pete was managing Amir's expectations in a downward direction, Fräulein Speer opened the conference room door. "Mr. Easterbrook would like to see you both."

They followed her to a corner office, with a view of Burj Khalifa poking through humid cloud cover in the distance, its top thirty floors residing comfortably out of view in the upper atmosphere. Hodding's office was a riot of peculiar interior design, an assemblage of Victorian clutter that looked like a Raj encampment preserved in glass. There was a campaign desk (reproduction), with several brass nautical instruments (also reproductions) strewn about. A grotesque wing chair in red leather sat hulking in the corner, with its back to the windows. On the worn faux Persian carpet, old unread books were stacked in small towers that served as tables for guests and their coffee. The only thing missing was a grand fireplace with brass andirons and a well-worn bumper.

Hodding was on the telephone when they arrived. He motioned to Amir to sit in a University of Alabama captain's chair near the desk, part of Hodding's homage to the Confederacy. Pete was swallowed by the wing chair. Amir recognized the voice from his one telephone call with Hodding; a slow, exaggerated Southern cadence, syllables stretched for emphasis, and littered with colorful references to boxcars, shotguns, hound dogs, and Jesus. He was handsome, with rakish eyes shaped like mischief, and a full mustache drawn from 1940s Hollywood. Unlike the others Amir had seen so far at Burr Acheson, he was dressed haphazardly, in driving shoes, golf trousers, and a blazer with some kind of prep school crest peeling off the breast pocket—a crucifix above crossed quills.

When he finished his call, Hodding shook Amir's hand firmly and asked, "How the hell are you?"

Amir began to introduce himself, but Hodding pressed ahead. "Look, I called Charlie Bridges in London, and he told me he remembers you from that class he taught in . . . um . . .."

"Nablus?" Amir suggested.

"Right. He said you have a natural instinct for the trading business. That's hard to find, you know." He eased into a rhythmic rocking recline in his desk chair, looking reflectively into the distance. "It's easy for me to recruit quants. Christ, I have quants crawling out of my boots. They're fine for reading signals and spotting arbitrage opportunities. But they climax over a tiny spread, just because they found it and no one else did. That crap barely pays the rent here. I'm running a *client* business. I want people who know the markets, but also know how to talk to clients and *sell!*"

Hodding leaned forward, fondling a sextant on his desk, and gestured toward Pete, polished loafers peeking out from the wing chair. "And then I've got a couple of people like Pete here. No one sells better than Pete, though I might have to give him a C+ on his market insights." Pete looked at Amir with a smirk, not disputing that grade.

"Still, he can convince a Pakistani nawab to trust us with the ancient family fortune. Or in fifteen minutes, Pete can charm a Kuwaiti princess out of her abaya *and* her knickers, until she's standing there in nothing but her Manolos, begging him to ram some Alpha into her portfolio."

Amir contemplated the imagery. He felt he should say something, perhaps seize the opening and talk about *his* selling skills. He began tentatively, but Hodding ignored him and kept going.

"You know what I like about Dubai?" he asked rhetorically. "It has absolute clarity," he answered, as if finally solving the puzzle of string theory. "Everyone is here for one purpose. Making money. There is no pretense about being a cultural center; no bullshit about building a knowledge economy; and no 'National Vision to be a leader in building sustainable human human capital.' " He pronounced "sustainable" with twice its usual number of syllables, conveying contempt for New Age mission statements. "It's just money," he said with finality. "Plain, simple, and sometimes honest."

Hodding continued his monologue, rich with portraiture. Amir sensed he had given this book talk a few times before, refining it along the way to employ phrases and ideas that sounded like deep thinking and bold insights, even if not.

During a pause between paragraphs, Pete stood up to excuse himself for an earnings call. Hodding also stood, signaling that the meeting had been a success and was now over. Amir had said nothing.

"Thanks for coming in. You're joining us for dinner tonight, right? Greta will send a car for you. See you tonight." And then, Fräulein Speer was at the door with her black leather portfolio, still tight against her bosom, her eyes forming a wordless command that Amir was to follow her.

"He likes you," she said unaccountably as they returned to the reception area. "It's his style to make judgments based on a first impression. If he keeps talking after you sit down, that's a good sign."

"I thought he might want to ask me a few questions. He doesn't know me."

"Of course, he knows you," she said with the smallest hint of a smile. "He received an entire file on you. I saw it." Fräulein Speer handed Amir a page with information about the dinner arrangements, and his departing flight the following day. "The car will be at your hotel at eight thirty." He was dismissed.

In the Middle East, everyone assumes they are under surveillance, more or less at all times. This is part of the cultural fondness for conspiracy. Amir always thought it was silly and presumptuous of his friends and family to imagine that anyone—especially the perpetually-suspected Americans with their ubiquitous signals intelligence capabilities, and rogue agencies—cared enough about their tedious lives to intercept their conversations and text messages. *But if Hodding has a "file" on me,* Amir thought, *someone must be collecting information.* He considered what might be revealed, for example, by his FREE*Trade account history, his university transcript, his social media accounts, or even his memorable encounters with the notorious girl in his chemistry class. *Not much,* he thought. He wished there was something more interesting about him.

For what seemed like the duration of his interview, Amir's phone had vibrated impatiently. In the freezing car returning Amir to his hotel, he finally looked at the screen. A few missed calls from Central Asia, one from South Bend, and one from his mother, followed by a terse text. It was very unlike her to text. In fact, Amir was sure she had never texted him before.

His mother wrote, *You were wrong to leave without speaking to me.* Then there was one from his sister. *You are in deep s*.*

Amir decided to deal with this when he returned. He didn't want to add fresh content to Hodding's "file" while he was still in Dubai. And anyway, he had no intention of accommodating his mother's insistence that he devote his life to keeping his dreary household from falling apart. *Not my problem,* Amir thought. Still, he wondered what really triggered this sharp reaction from her.

When he arrived at the restaurant a few hours later, a queue of SUVs—strangely, all white and highly polished—snaked ahead of him. The winking pairs of taillights reminded him of the provocative red flashes from the heels of women arriving in the Grosvenor House lobby. The guests emerging from their vehicles appeared to be the same cohort of characters Amir encountered at his hotel. Some had exchanged inappropriate daytime attire for inappropriate evening attire, but otherwise, they all seemed to be there. When the car doors opened, the women presented themselves, bronzed legs and footwear-first, in carefully practiced moves designed to feed salacious paparazzi appetites.

Hakkasan was the kind of restaurant where Dubai's upper-bracket expatriate community could assemble in safety to admire themselves. The cuisine was nominally Asian, but the fusions on the menu provided something for every taste. The interior was dark with blue accent lighting that presented all the guests in silhouette, their features and complexions reimagined into a uniform contemporary glow, recasting them as a specially bred ethnic community unburdened by squalid earthly ties. As Amir was led to his table, he received critical glances from blue faces speaking a dozen languages.

Hodding had arrived ahead of him. He was seated at the center of a banquette, with an elegant Italian tie that was clumsily knotted, and half glasses balanced on his nose to lend gravity to an inspection of the wine list. Amir was introduced to the other guests, some familiar from his office visit earlier in the day, and a couple of new, severe-looking faces who were introduced with complicated names and vague affiliations.

Hodding's wife greeted Amir too loudly with, "Hi, sweetie. Come and sit by me." Lindsay Easterbrook was a Southern woman, middle-aged and fading, even in Hakkasan's generous blue glow. Her fuselage, once sleek and engineered for the jet age, had weathered into something like Gaudí architecture. A shameless name-dropper, Lindsay was a Vanderbilt graduate, a résumé feature that she sprinkled liberally into the conversation. By the time Amir was seated, Lindsay was deep into a reminiscence about "her days" in the White House and some minor patronage position awarded to her in exchange for organizing dark money political campaigns. Amir wasn't following many of her obscure inside-politics references. She seemed lost and sad in a place where no one recognized her social status and past glories.

Seated on his opposite side was the Stanford woman, Emily, who interviewed Amir earlier that day. More relaxed now, her hair and nails restored, she suggested that he try the lychee martini—which sounded dreadful to Amir, and suspicious, since Emily was halfway through a bourbon served neat. Amir opted for watermelon juice, which prompted her to laugh.

"You impressed me today," Emily said. "We must have read the same *Economist* article about the inverted yield curve. But I think you absorbed more of the nuance than I did." She used her index finger to swirl the ice in her whiskey. "I have to ask," she said tentatively. "Why leave home for Dubai? I mean, sure, the job is a résumé-builder and the tax dodge is good, but honestly, it's the loneliest place you can imagine. Everyone here is on a two-year plan. Their exit date is circled on the calendar taped to the refrigerator, and that's the built-in expiration date for every commitment. Your apartment lease, rental car, gym membership—even your Thursday fuck buddy."

Amir was startled when she casually mentioned her Thursday commitment, like it was something that popped up on her mobile phone in a calendar reminder. Emily had a plain face and a fragrance of sadness, even dressed up for the Hakkasan crowd. Amir tried, but failed, to conjure an image of Emily, frisky in lingerie.

Amir worried that his interview might still be in progress, and he wasn't really sure how to turn this line of questioning in a winning direction. But since her question was more about her than him, Amir batted the shuttlecock back. "Well, I was going to ask why you left California to come here."

A reflective, slightly miserable, monologue followed, like something she would share with a therapist. Emily mentioned a couple of false starts in the tech industry, where the people were "not nice." There was a romance that ended badly and the need for a "reboot." Amir imagined a cat in her life.

Meanwhile, Hodding had inspected and rejected a bottle of wine after it was opened, sending the sommelier away, stoic but furious. Hodding leaned into the assembled table guests to draw the house lights to his performance and said darkly, "*These people* are infamous for relabeling wine. It was a pretty convincing effort, but I know the difference between a Saint Julien and Lebanese table wine." He laughed at his cleverness.

Lindsay beamed proudly, the Old South triumphing again over the less worthy. She interrupted Emily's therapy session, put her hand on Amir's arm, and resumed her own performance.

"So, you're from Palestine! You know, when *I* was in the *White House*, I had a good friend—also *from Vanderbilt!*—who was the chief mapmaker for the State Department's Israel-Palestine Peace Process negotiators. Can you imagine? For almost twenty years, she went to work every day, drawing and redrawing the same geography, just moving the boundary lines back and forth to display the latest proposals. All those drawings would make a pretty good coffee table book, don't you think?"

Like his meeting in Hodding's office, Amir could tell that his expected role in conversation with Lindsay was to absorb her words eagerly and say nothing.

Anyway, Amir thought, *she obviously had no idea how an actual Palestinian might react to the image of a mid-level bureaucrat in a shabby Washington office, adjudicating with her colored pencils the dislocation of ancient families.*

A waiter started to distribute menus, but Hodding waved him off, announcing, "Everyone OK if I order for the table?" It was not a question. He commanded the waiter to his attention, and proceeded to dictate, from memory, a long list of house staples with exciting labels—tiger prawns, duck with truffles, dim sum with caviar, dry aged Wagyu—each followed by a Hodding off-menu variation, certain to enrage the chef. "But skip the pomegranate," he would add. Or, referring to some "dragon" concoction, "There was too much soy ginger last time." "Anyone need gluten free?" he added, with obvious disdain, dismissing the waiter before anyone could respond.

The imperious woman seated across the table extended her hand to Amir during an unexpected pause in the performance. "Hello. I'm Katrina Vanderlipp."

The improbable-sounding name somehow fit her perfectly, Amir thought. Northern European, the complexion of a Finnish February, purity in her genealogy, unburdened by humility.

Noticing her introduction, Hodding inserted himself. "Amir, I thought you should meet Katrina. She is an old friend and my favorite competitor here in Dubai. Katrina runs the best bank no one ever heard of. Below the radar, you know. Sometimes, that's what the most special clients want."

Appetizers arrived, distracting Hodding and the rest of the table. Katrina tossed some softball questions to Amir about his interest in finance, and she listened intently as he delivered a version of his elevator pitch. She shared only a little about herself, mentioning that she studied finance in Zürich, and came to Dubai a few years before to launch a wealth management practice for Bank Von Raab, which she described as an old Liechtenstein private bank. A colleague from the bank, seated to her left, was hastily introduced. After nodding with nineteenth century formality to Amir, he said nothing.

"Hodding tells me you speak Persian," Katrina said.

An odd thing to mention, Amir thought.

He and Katrina exchanged some rudimentary phrases. Her vocabulary was simple; mostly bland references to wealth management products and investment clichés. She smiled, the way a tarantula might, and said in Persian, "Buy low, sell high."

Trying to be clever, Amir responded, also in Persian, "Past performance is no guarantee of future results."

Katrina's accent was good, and even in their brief exchange, she dropped some surprisingly authentic colloquialisms that would be familiar mostly among young professionals in Tehran. Emerging from her extreme blondness, Amir thought the lyrical cadences felt shocking and out of context.

Hodding took a phone call and excused himself from the table to stand in the distance, listening more than speaking, backlit in blue. Emily was well into an oversized glass of Chardonnay, and Lindsay was chattering to no one in particular about how "shabbily" *("shaa-aab-E-Lee!")* Hillary had been treated in Washington. Ignoring her, the other table guests ate and murmured gentle praise for the food. Amir noticed Hodding signaling to Katrina, who wordlessly left the table and joined him in the blueness. They conspired mysteriously for a while, as Hodding returned intermittently to his phone call. Then they both looked at Amir, and Hodding beckoned.

It felt awkward, but Amir joined them. The remaining guests pretended not to notice.

Hodding put his hand on Amir's shoulder. "Look, Amir. Things went well for you today, but to be honest, it's going to take time for me to run this through the traps in New York. You should hedge your bets. That's why I invited Katrina tonight. I know she's looking for analysts, and I wanted her to meet you. Can you delay your departure tomorrow and stop by Katrina's office? She runs a first-rate operation. You really should see it. What do you say?"

Katrina looked at Amir expressionless, with a face of cold rolled steel.

Amir was crestfallen. Burr Acheson was his dream, and he had already pictured himself in a seat on their trading floor, smoothly delivering ingenious portfolio maneuvers to distant clients, and joining the ranks of international trading whales. "Well," Amir began.

"Perfect!" Hodding said. "I'll call Greta, and she can rebook your flight. This will work out great for everyone."

Back at the table, the evening rolled along in a pleasant wagyu afterglow. No one mentioned the *off-piste* gathering, as Hodding held forth with well-practiced exhibitions of his deep thinking. Amir tried to follow the impossible subject matter segues that flew off his tongue. But it was all just clickbait, assembled from random sources, and designed to keep all eyes on Hodding, while discouraging anyone from probing too deeply. It was dazzling but felt fake, Amir thought. *Was my Burr Acheson interview fake too?* he wondered.

The lobby at Grosvenor House was throbbing with energy when Amir returned after midnight, though the assembled guests looked slightly more dangerous than before, alternately caffeinated and intoxicated, with costumes *en deshabille*. Buddha Bar music pulsed like an elevated heartrate through the marble floor and even into the elevators, where it was more felt than heard. Amir's room was frigid, the thermostat evidently set by the housekeeper during evening turndown, at a temperature measured in Kelvin. The view from his window was blurred by condensation. A frozen orchid petal lay on his pillow, next to a specialty chocolate box sized for an engagement ring.

Amir tried to replay the unexpected plot twist at dinner, wondering if his handoff to Bank Von Raab was really a polite rejection by Burr Acheson. He ignored the accumulated alerts and messages on his phone and trolled the bank's ghostly presence on the web. Nothing but a few references on obscure European websites, with bland nomenclature about charters and licenses. A simple website listed a street address in Vaduz, with some perfunctory emblems of supposed validation that meant nothing to Amir. *Association des Banques et Banquiers? It sounded like a secretive luncheon club for bureaucrats and their mistresses*, Amir thought. There were none of the website visual flourishes that he had come to expect from wealth managers; no comforting images of the affluent and urbane, trusting their fortunes to exemplars of good grooming. And nothing about Katrina Vanderlipp, except some snapshots of a namesake in Muncie, Indiana, who obviously was very distantly separated from the Liechtenstein banker by many layers of consanguinity and taste.

Before he closed his eyes for the night in despair, Amir scanned his incoming messages. The ever-efficient Fräulein Speer had updated his itinerary and flight arrangements, adding a morning interview at Bank Von Raab's office. A few incoming messages later, FREE*Trade reminded him of its "enhanced" website security procedures (*"The most secure trading platform in history!"*).

Two text messages from his sister piqued his interest. "Hey, lover boy. Guess who's back home from Cairo this weekend?". And then, "BTW, Mama is still steaming mad at you."

Amir checked Aisha's feed and lingered over a new photo. Shot from behind her at a juice bar on Zamalek, Aisha's lush hair was uncovered and draped provocatively over a bare shoulder. She looked away from the camera lens, behind glamorous sunglasses. The 6th October Bridge was a faint sketch in the hazy distance, and beneath it, the banks of the Nile blurred into the dust, noise, traffic, and bedlam. As usual, there was no caption; only the allure of her very photogenic presence. *She didn't take this picture*, Amir reminded himself, *so it must be him.*

Amir slept fitfully, haunted by flickering film noir images of Aisha, locked in a violent, rhythmic embrace with her faceless lover. She looked back at Amir, laughing wickedly. He awoke in a sweat, feeling frightened, aroused, and cheated.

The visit to Bank Von Raab could not possibly have been more unlike Amir's experience at Burr Acheson. He arrived early at an anonymous glass tower in Dubai Media City and waited a long time for the security guard in the lobby to clear his entry through an unmarked door leading to a bank of elevators. Nothing in the lobby revealed information about the building's occupants, and indeed, when Amir presented himself on the twenty-third floor, he noticed that the name of the Bank appeared nowhere. The receptionist, a striking woman with the cheekbones and posture of a runway model, greeted him, first in Arabic and then in Californian English. While Amir waited for his appointment, she answered a few incoming telephone calls, always with the same greeting. "Vaduz 3333," she repeated, now with a German accent.

A pale young man appeared and introduced himself as Richard Swallow, Ms. Vanderlipp's assistant. It was Katrina's silent table mate at Hakkasan. Mr. Swallow spoke in careful sentences, all extraneous words excised, with the practiced manners of a London solicitor trainee. He led Amir into a frosted glass corridor flanked by offices marked only with four-digit numbers and no names. All the doors were closed, and the occupants invisible, apart from barely discernable shadows moving within their translucent cubes. Unlike Burr Acheson's offices, there was no trading floor, and no roar of restless energy emerging from a reactor core of money production. Mr. Swallow stopped at 4384, knocked imperceptibly, and then held the door for Amir to enter Katrina's office. She was genetically camouflaged, her complexion almost disappearing into the whiteness of the room. The monochrome was broken only by her blue eyes, more intimidating now that they were not competing with the ubiquitous decorative lighting of Hakkasan. Her office was a like a Bauhaus shrine, with form ruthlessly following function in the glass and steel furniture. The only decorative object was a large black and white photograph behind her desk, an image of a New York skyscraper, shot at a dizzy, oblique angle. There was no view from her office windows because exterior louvers were positioned to prevent visibility of anything on a horizontal plane.

Katrina made a perfunctory reference to the previous evening, and then went right to business. She described Bank Von Raab as a "typical" wealth management business. Their clients were comfortable with low-risk portfolio strategies, she said, often preferring negative yield bonds denominated in Euros or Swiss Francs.

"It might sound boring," she added, "but most of all, they value our . . . *discretion.* We give them safety for their portfolios and secure investment vehicles in reliable banking jurisdictions that will respect their privacy. We are *not* a hedge fund," Katrina said sternly, as if referring to racketeering.

She pressed Amir on his university training, not just Capital

Markets 425, but also the broad array of courses that interested him as a student. She lingered on American literature but expressed no interest in Amir's nominal major in economics. Katrina seemed pleased when Amir said, with some embarrassment, that this was his first trip outside of the West Bank.

"It's good to be anchored close to home," she proposed and then pressed a button on her telephone, which produced Mr. Swallow at the door a little too quickly.

"Richard will ask you to complete some paperwork now. I'm very grateful that you changed your travel plans to meet with us today. Let's see what happens," she said cryptically.

Mr. Swallow, expressionless, led Amir to a conference room where four neat piles of paper sat on a white conference table in front of a white leather chair. In the briefest of conversations, Amir understood that he would be completing certain "tests," and this was expected of all employees of Bank Von Raab. "All very routine," Mr. Swallow added as he left Amir alone in the ice-cold room.

They were indeed tests. Two of them consisted of comprehensive questions about finance and investment, subjects that Amir had read about but had hardly mastered. He soldiered through the questions but worried that his command of the subject matter was superficial at best. The third test was something like a personality profile, soliciting personal information about Amir, followed by a series of multiple-choice questions designed, it seemed to Amir, to provoke uncomfortable introspection about workplace interactions with subordinates, peers, and management. And then, the fourth and last pile of paper was, oddly, a test of his language skills in Persian. There had been no context for this last test, except—now that he thought about it—both Hodding and Katrina seemed unusually aroused by that topic, with more than a passing interest in an irrelevant novelty. Adapted from an Oxford Persian Language Proficiency Test, as the copyright notices indicated, Amir completed these questions with ease.

Somehow, Mr. Swallow seemed to be monitoring Amir's progress, because he stepped silently into the conference room just as Amir was returning the completed tests to their neat original piles.

"Right!" Mr. Swallow said, using that inimitable British term announcing that something of consequence had just been completed, and something of further consequence was about to begin. He gathered the piles into a file folder, and then led Amir briskly back to the reception area, through the same uninhabited glass tunnels. Mr. Swallow informed Amir that he would hear from Katrina in a few days, but he should certainly not hesitate to call in the meantime if any questions occurred to him. This last invitation seemed politely obligatory, rather than genuine.

Chapter 9.

THE return trip to Nablus was uneventful and considerably faster than Amir's outbound leg. Once on the ground in Jordan, provided his luggage contained no rockets or C4, no one was very interested in a traveler who wished to *return* to Palestine. As Amir crossed the barren frontier toward home, the border crossing and military checkpoints were like a version of the Berlin Wall in which the weapons and surveillance devices, not to mention the soldiers, were welded in place, facing only one direction.

On schedule, Abdul Raouf met Amir with his dusty taxi, back at the whale's mouth on the even more grim side of Allenby Bridge. Both were silent as they drove back to Nablus. The town looked more defeated than before, and the late afternoon atmosphere was thick with diesel residue, mixed with dirt and failure. Amir remembered turning to take a last look at the Grosvenor House lobby when he departed that morning, wondering if the Nablus reentry would be too much to bear. *Indeed, everything seemed smaller than before*, Amir thought, *and the clocks had all stopped long ago.*

Amir was angry at Hodding. The whole episode at Burr Acheson felt like a charade at his expense, followed by the rude, blue-stained handoff to Katrina Vanderlipp and her so-called bank, selling negative interest rates to their clients.

I'll die in Nablus, Amir thought miserably.

His father sat reading in his usual chair when Amir returned to the dark, forlorn house. At this time of day, his mother would be starting her evening shift in the ICU, and Amir planned to avoid the inevitable encounter with her as long as possible. Amir greeted his father formally and started upstairs.

"You may as well know that your little vacation was not popular here. Especially with your mother. True, you gave *me* fair warning. But I think you are being selfish and reckless about your responsibilities to this family." His father gave this speech without looking up from his book, an Arabic translation of *The Memoirs of Richard Nixon.* In the dim light of the room, Amir thought his father looked remarkably like pictures of Nixon in his final White House days— brooding, defeated, undone.

"You don't need to worry," Amir said to his father. "The interview was a disaster. Looks like you and Mama got what you wanted. We can all resume our slow death march here in Nablus."

His father let him have the last word, which infuriated Amir, who disappeared into his upstairs room. He considered calling Hodding, or possibly Pete, to see if he could salvage a job offer, or maybe find out why the tide had turned so quickly against him in Dubai. In a passing flash of optimism or desperate wishful thinking, Amir wondered if perhaps he had misread things, and he was still under consideration at Burr Acheson after all. He dismissed that idea. Killing time, Amir scanned his FREE*Trade account history, with its pathetic series of tiny trades—like the income statement of a lemonade stand.

"Account Balance: $2,612.47. YTD Return: -0.42%."

Embarrassing, he concluded. *Why bother?* In a box on the FREE*Trade screen, a svelte young woman in a turquoise swimsuit reclined by a sunny swimming pool, her face partially covered with a white Panama hat. The caption asked, "Are you ready for retirement?"

Amir heard Sara open the front door downstairs, followed by the usual storm of carelessly dropped possessions, one side of a loud, gossipy telephone conversation and desperate kitchen foraging. Her father ignored the damage to his repose, but when she saw him deep in his book, she suddenly was filled with questions. "Is he back? Did

Mama see him? Did he get the job? Where is he? Did he bring anything from Duty Free?"

"This doesn't concern you," he said, as if that mattered.

Amir didn't want to speak to Sara, except that she might have some intelligence about Aisha and her alleged return to Nablus for the weekend. It bothered Amir to depend on Sara for such information. She was, after all, only interested in the vicious sport of ridiculing his attraction to Aisha. He opened his door, and almost collided with Sara as she charged through the narrow corridor leading to the storage closet that had been repurposed as her bedroom.

She is wearing too much makeup, Amir thought. He wondered if Sara's attempt to cut the line in the rigid queue of local society would lead to tears, but then he wondered why he cared.

"Hey, Mr. Rockefeller, when are you moving to New York? I didn't see your driver outside. And where is your personal assistant? Picking up your dry cleaning?"

Amir had never been able to fight with Sara on her level, slashing at tender exposed flesh and sensibilities, cutting deeply sometimes. Was this something girls had evolved to do, skillfully and without regret? He remembered Aisha and her ruthless swordplay with the hapless Dr. Fathy. Were they all like this? Did they do this to their lovers and husbands?

Amir changed the subject and abandoned all pretense of aloof disinterest. "You texted me about Aisha. Is she back in Nablus?"

Sara managed a few sober sentences, for once, dropping the sarcasm. "Noor told me she is visiting for a few days. Supposedly, her mom is sick. But I think the family is worried about what she really is doing in Cairo, and they summoned her home to sort it out. There is some ugly speculation, even in the buttoned-up Dajani family."

"What *is* she doing in Cairo?" Amir asked, a little too eagerly.

"Why don't you ask her yourself?" Sara turned and closed the closet door behind her.

It was midafternoon in New York. To distract himself, Amir returned to FREE*Trade to catch the last couple of hours of the trading week. His eccentric news feed spit out some analyst rubbish about expected market volatility. Amir was feeling reckless and a little self-destructive. But then he reminded himself that the stakes

weren't too high with his child-size portfolio. He placed a relatively low risk trade option trade. And then he let the flickering price
movements work their magic, pulling him out of Nablus, like a psy-
chotropic drug that hits hard and fast.

Amir daydreamed vividly, alternately picturing Bosch-like apocalyptic scenes of half-eaten Wall Street traders and gauzy sepia stills
of Emily in Dubai, tattooed and licking the keys of her Bloomberg.
The value of his position moved explosively, mostly down, sometimes
at or near zero; but occasionally doubling without reason. A client
alert flashed on his screen, announcing that his account value had
fallen below the required minimum; a warning so familiar to Amir
that its shock value had passed long ago. He was breathing hard,
suddenly aware that he was unconsciously crushing a pencil point
into the cover of his well-worn copy of *Moby Dick*.

Amir unwound his option bet with four minutes left in the trading day, at a gain of $1,200. Stupid, dumb luck, he knew. It was his
best daily gain ever. He opened the camera on his phone and inspected his face. Sweaty, shadowed, hair matted, the face of an ax
murderer. Amir laughed at himself and went to bed.

The sound of ice and glass was louder than usual. A deliberate
noise this time, intended to be heard, not muffled. Amir was awake
when his mother returned just before 3:00 am. A lonely dog barked
in the distance. After an interval, he heard another sharp collision
with ice, fiercely intentional. Amir was being summoned.

In her scrubs, his mother looked intimidating. For Amir, it was a
uniform that announced special knowledge and power, both confident and unfazed by confronting life-and-death moments. Tonight,
she was angry. Amir joined her at the kitchen table, and they didn't
speak for a while.

"You look terrible," she said, finally. She spoke softly but not gently. Amir could tell she was suppressing rage.

She continued, exaggerating the harsh consonants of Arabic. "I
can't force you to stay with this family, and I can't make career decisions for you. But you don't know what you are doing . . . what you are
risking. You are safe here, but in places like the Gulf, you're taking
chances that you don't understand." As she lifted the glass to her lips,
her hand trembled.

Amir was baffled by her choice of words. He had assumed his mother just resisted change to the routines of their fragile family. But "taking chances"? What was she talking about? She cut him off as he started to speak.

"Don't ask me to spell it out for you. I can't. You need to listen to me and do as I say."

Amir inhaled deeply and braced himself for full throated combat. But he had never seen this side of her. She was terrified of something and determined to conceal it. Whatever it was, Amir was sure this had nothing to do with his contribution to the household. He chose a tactical retreat.

"I didn't get the job in Dubai. I'm not leaving Nablus." Amir delivered the news like an obituary.

The tension in the air remained, but she turned away for a moment, as if to hide tears or relief. He had never seen her cry. Amir studied the photograph on the security badge clipped to her scrubs. It was an old picture of her. She had full lips, some eye makeup and even the hint of a smile. Amir had no memory of that look, which was long gone—replaced by her signature face of resignation.

She turned her face back to him. "You need a job," she said, abruptly. "I approached the hospital administrator. He's a crooked bastard, and always too free with his hands when he's with the young nurses. But he knows I could report him for his fake purchase orders, so he will cooperate. There is a job in the accounting office that normally would be reserved for one of his lazy nephews. I can arrange an interview for you, and if it works out . . .." She let that possibility linger.

As Amir imagined himself in that job, his first thoughts were suicidal. "I don't think I'm qualified," Amir said, without looking up from an old scar in the table surface. "But I agree with you," he continued. "I'm wasting my time now. I'll find a job."

"At least think about the hospital interview," she persisted. "I admire your ambition but not your snobbery. I know you think it's beneath you. Just consider it." She offered this last plea in Persian, which softened the tone.

Amir thought it was odd that his mother asked him nothing about his Dubai trip. Whatever terrible mystery provoked her determination to keep him away from the Gulf, he would have expected some curiosity. It was, after all, a place of endless fascination for most Nabulsis, and despite the universal narrative that it was a tasteless theme park for new-money Emiratis, everyone wanted to go. The news would travel quickly that Amir had just returned, and he expected this to elevate his social standing, or at least generate gossip that momentarily would lift him out of obscurity. He wondered if Aisha had heard about it, and whether she would care. Surely the Burr Acheson story would get her attention, even if nothing came of the interview. She might see Amir in a different light, as a kindred spirit in chasing a dream that was far away from Nablus.

"I think I've lost your attention," his mother said, returning to Arabic. "It's late. Go to bed." She stood to get more ice and whiskey, with her back turned to Amir, and their meeting ended.

As Amir drifted into sleep, he felt deep sadness for his mother. She must have had dreams once. Clearly, she had secrets—whatever they were. But for as long as Amir could remember, she had withdrawn into a nocturnal existence, disengaged from her family, descending without a struggle into advanced middle age and the inevitable end. It felt like his future too.

Saturday morning, Amir woke feeling strangely bold about pursuing Aisha. She always was, and almost certainly still would be, out of reach. But his sense of defeat in Dubai brought freedom and an exciting sensation that, right now, this was the moment to make his move. He had nothing to lose. When he considered all the imagined risks of breaching the invisible barriers around the Dajani women, the stakes felt comically insignificant. What was the worst that could happen? And after all, the last time they spoke, it was Aisha who had approached *him*. Of course, there was the secret Cairo lover to contend with, and the painful fact that, apart from his Dubai adventure story, he really had nothing new to improve his pitch. He was still unemployed, without prospects, living with his parents, in a down-market neighborhood where the Dajanis sent their laundry.

Amir felt he needed a contrivance to meet Aisha while she was back in Nablus. He decided that Sara was not a reliable interlocutor. Despite her friendship with Noor, who might serve as a family gateway, there was high probability that Sara would scheme to sabotage any respectable communication on Amir's behalf, or that Aisha herself would wonder why the little sister was Amir's intermediary. The least bad option was also the most obvious. He sent Aisha a text.

Heard you were back. Meet for coffee?

She responded immediately. *Yes.*

It was not, "Yes!" But still. Amir was surprised and unprepared. The details were quickly settled. They would meet Sunday afternoon at a coffee shop near the university.

Amir abhorred rehearsed social encounters, but he found it impossible to approach this one without detailed preparation. What would he say about his failed Burr Acheson ambition, which likely would be the only thing she recalled from their previous encounter? A colorful description of the Dubai trip seemed like a good topic, perhaps with some playful imagery of the beautiful and damned at Hakkasan. After all, just leaving Nablus—even if briefly—is an accomplishment that distinguished him from almost everyone else. *And*, Amir reminded himself, *I haven't actually been rejected yet by Burr Acheson.* He could be truthful, and even a little mysteriously interesting, by just saying that the interview was rigorous and the outcome uncertain.

But while Amir was assembling this slide deck in his head, it occurred to him that what he really wanted was to hear Aisha speak. Obviously, she was aware of the gossip. Would she set the record straight or perhaps revel in the speculation? *The latter would be more her style*, Amir thought, *and anyway, why would she tell him?*

Mercifully, the time passed quickly, and all of Amir's anxious preparation ultimately dissolved into the simple goal of seeing her up close.

She arrived ahead of him at the brightly painted coffee shop, where Amir found her seated at a small outdoor table under a torn green and blue umbrella that read, "Jawwal Telecom: 3G is Coming!" The weather was cool, and Aisha wore a dark blazer over a white tee shirt. No visible undergarments this time. He recognized the sunglasses from the latest Cairo photo in her feed. She was reading some photocopied pages and balancing an orange highlighter between two ringed fingers like a flamboyant cigarette holder. Her long legs in blue jeans were crossed gracefully, calves parallel, evocative of a

Rodin bronze. Amir cast a shadow on her work as he approached the table, and Aisha lifted her sunglasses to the top her head, where they served to corral her spectacular, wild hair.

Skipping all customary greetings, Aisha threw down her papers and asked, "Did you know that the utilitarian philosopher, John Stuart Mill, wrote that pleasure is the only thing that has intrinsic value? And two hundred years later, Qadhafi published a book in Libya that he privately said was strongly influenced by the same Mr. Mill?" Her eyes flashed with mischief.

Amir smiled. "I couldn't agree more with Mill. As for Qadhafi, I think he was confusing Mill with Mao."

"I said the same thing in class on Thursday. The professor told me I missed the point." She added, "I lost my temper and eventually walked out of class."

"Aisha, when I think of you and your professors, it doesn't seem like a fair fight. Maybe you should try a different sport."

Amir ordered Turkish coffee for both of them, and they flirted like this for nearly an hour, until the sun started to sag behind the nearby university buildings. Amir probed delicately, but Aisha revealed essentially nothing about her life in Cairo. She was vague about her political science studies, dismissive of the professors, and fiercely critical of laziness among the students. She complained about her roommate and the women's dormitory. She summed up Cairo as "loud, self-important, and ridiculous," but then, returning her sunglasses to the bridge of her nose, and looking reflectively at the setting sun, she added, "At least, it's something different. Like I said before, maybe something will come of it." The sunglasses were sent back to restore some order in her hair.

She is mostly unchanged, Amir thought. Aisha was still the confident woman placed on earth to serve as a style guide for the wretched, somehow never slipping into haughtiness or the other bad manners of the entitled. But there was something else. In the space between her high cheekbones and penetrating eyes, there were new folds that suggested worry. *She was chasing something that was outside her comfort zone,* Amir imagined.

They were quiet for a while as some nearby students argued and then reconciled and apologized theatrically before separating and disappearing.

Dubai had not been mentioned when Aisha finally said, "I heard from a pretty reliable source that you had an interview at Burr Acheson." She looked directly at him, which was new.

After all his preparation, Amir still hesitated and then chose a half-truth. "I feel good about the interview, but it's really competitive. I haven't heard from them yet. I honestly don't know what to expect. The job is in New York," he lied.

She pushed him for more details about his interview, and he was glad to paint lush images of the Emirates flight attendants, the blue faces in Hakkasan, and the Grosvenor House lobby show. She laughed happily at his adjectives, and for once, Aisha was not the world-weary woman that intimidated Amir. Finally, he thought, *Chemistry.*

It didn't last. She turned abruptly, looked at her watch, and stood.

"I need to get back. My parents and I are battling about Cairo. They don't want me to go back to school. But they know I'm not going to stay in Nablus. It's silly. The outcome is a foregone conclusion, but you can't skip the ritual. And everyone has to hug and make up in the end. It's exhausting."

She blew him a little kiss as she walked away. "Thanks for the coffee. Good luck with Burr Acheson."

Aisha paused a few steps away, turned again, and said, "If you want to know what I think, New York is the perfect place for you. Get out of Nablus." And then she was gone.

Amir was euphoric. After months of navigating an imaginary world in which Aisha existed only as an exquisite apparition, he had just spent an hour alone with her, so close that he could study the delicious imperfections that made her, at last, real—a small cut on her left ring finger, half covered with a frayed bandage; a stain from the orange highlighter on her jeans; a clumsy tangle of hair and sunglasses; and best of all, that momentary lapse when Aisha looked directly at him, revealing something that felt like a connection. Amir decided there was no secret lover in Cairo. She was doing exactly what he was doing—working on an exit strategy, still tentative, but with purpose and conviction. Amir felt taller as he walked home, and he lifted his chin the way Charlie always did.

The early morning light brought a sting of reality. That stupid barking dog. Mrs. Darwish and her unwashed opioid runners. The relentless dust in the air. Amir was still in Nablus and going nowhere. He considered a call to Fräulein Speer, with an earnest-sounding charade about returning some unused expense money and a probe to find out if he had misread Hodding's disappointing signals. Possibly a polite call to Pete or even to sad Emily. As he played out the options, all of which were transparently pretextual, his phone vibrated, gently levitating in an eastward direction across the floor beside his bed. It was Hodding.

"How the hell are you? So glad you were able to join us in Doó-Buy."

Amir launched a litany of effusive thanks with accolades for the impressive talent that Hodding assembled in his office. And etc. Hodding cut him off.

"You know, my wife told me you reminded her of a good-looking guy she knew at the White House. I forgot his name, but I think he got indicted." Hodding laughed at his joke, and Amir laughed too, nervously.

"Listen, Amir. I told you that our firm has to deal with these impossible compliance people in New York. I would love to have you on my team here, but to be honest, it would take months to run your background check through that system. And even then, I think we both know there are some . . . *issues*."

They let that word linger for a moment, its meaning clear to both of them.

"I called Katrina and made a pitch for you. I can't promise anything, but I think you're going to get good news from her. And I really hope you accept. She can teach you a lot."

Panicked, Amir recalled Aisha's parting comment about New York. Burr Acheson was his only realistic gateway. He took another run at Hodding.

"Mr. Easterbrook, I don't want to impose on your kindness, but please reconsider this and give me a chance. I can resolve any questions in a background check, and you won't regret having me on your team. Of course, I was impressed with Ms. Vanderlipp, but to be honest, her bank seems a little . . ."

"Stiff and European?" Hodding suggested. "Sure, I guess it seems that way. Their style is different, but they have a strong reputation here. Katrina works below the radar, but her bank has a lock on a segment of the market that none of the rest of us can penetrate. Give it a chance. You'll see."

There was a muffled interruption while Hodding, distracted, spoke to someone about an incoming wire transfer. When his attention returned, he sounded rushed and dialed back the Alabama accent. "Anyway, it's the best I can do for you. Take the job, Amir." The call ended.

Not long after his call with Hodding, the sky over Nablus darkened, as the prevailing wind from the Sinai carried tiny particles of sand into the lower atmosphere, choking off light, air, and the last remnants of hope. It lasted for days, and local cranks referred to it in apocalyptic terms as a "black banner." The week crawled sideways like a version of administrative detention, as Amir waited to see if there would be another call from Dubai. He watched the markets in New York and London, mainly for distraction, but wasn't motivated to trade, feeling unlucky after his undeserved options trading windfall. Nothing new appeared on Aisha's feed, though Sara reported that she had indeed returned to Cairo, supposedly after a big row at home. Amir hid from his family, and they from him, an enduring routine now considered entirely normal among them.

He replayed the encounter with Aisha endlessly, finding new clues each time that suggested additions or amendments in his hagiography. The portrait that he was meticulously painting in his imagination grew ever more nuanced and detailed, still a form of idealized beauty—on some days, an odalisque with jewels at her neck and ostrich feathers tickling her loins; and on others, a highly polished marble Aphrodite from the second century. He still battled doubts about the secret lover's existence and found himself particularly tormented when he puzzled over an anomaly in Aisha's account of Cairo. During their coffee rendezvous, she referred in passing to a roommate in the women's dormitory, and then hastily changed the subject. Amir distinctly remembered Aisha's first mention of her Cairo plans, when she said she would live with her cousin in Zamalek. And Amir knew her parents would never allow Aisha to be in Cairo, unchaperoned by family, living in the iniquity of a *dormitory*. He couldn't reconcile those versions. She was hiding something,

Amir worried. Or it was nothing.

Five days after she blew him that kiss, Amir's frantic imagination left him paralyzed with speculation about what was really going on in Cairo. He sent her a text, which required hours of editing before he settled on the final version: "Good to see u on Saturday. Hope u will visit me in NYC."

There was no reply.

The sky started to clear after a few days, and Amir's anxiety devolved into debilitating boredom and wretched defeat. He started rereading favorites from his American literature class, with the subliminal intention of arousing memories of Aisha during a less complicated era, when he could worship her exquisite perfection at a safe distance. He began with Hemingway but tossed it aside after three chapters, feeling more depressed by the hard cadence of the spartan noun-verb-adverb sentences, stripped of flavor or flourish. He retreated to Baldwin. For Amir's present mood, it felt much more "in the moment"—dark and melancholy, with flashes of frustration, anger, and resentment—all in a place designed to stifle the ambitions of the protagonist, though he conceded it was a stretch to compare Nablus to Greenwich Village. Baldwin held his attention, deepening his depression for a couple of days. More than once, he was tempted to reach for Melville to remind him of his own doomed quest, but he wasn't yet ready to give up entirely on capturing Aisha's interest.

Just as his bookish retreat was beginning to feel melodramatic, the call finally came from Richard Swallow at Bank Von Raab. Even on the telephone, he sounded as if he was lurking somewhere nearby. After a very perfunctory introduction, he said, "Hold the line please for Ms. Vanderlipp."

Katrina's telephone voice was icy calm. "I spoke to my colleagues at the bank's headquarters in Vaduz. We are offering you a position here in Dubai."

"I should mention that you received a very strong endorsement from Hodding Easterbrook at Burr Acheson. This means a lot." She let this point ferment in the bottle.

Somewhere between Hemingway and Baldwin, Amir had decided he would accept Katrina's offer, if extended. It was not Burr Acheson, and it was a very uncertain bridge to New York. But the alternative was slow, agonizing martyrdom in Nablus, where Amir was certain he would become increasingly uninteresting to Aisha. He never had a job offer before, so he was unsure whether to accept immediately and gratefully (too eager, perhaps?), or say that he would consider it against his other offers (too dishonest, definitely). He chose not to test Katrina's patience or credulity, and simply said "yes, he looked forward to working with her, and he appreciated the opportunity." Katrina exited politely, and Mr. Swallow returned to the telephone line to recite the terms of the offer. Amir would start as a "Trainee-Analyst," commencing with a four-week training program, with a starting salary and "expat package" that seemed highly extravagant. Mr. Swallow apologized for the "modest" compensation terms, explaining that the bank was obliged to adhere to the market norms in Dubai but assured him that there were promotion opportunities, adding enthusiastically that the tax circumstances were "uniquely advantageous."

With the housekeeping matters settled, and a starting date agreed upon, Mr. Swallow concluded with his signature expression, "Right!"

Amir was aware that his moody hesitation about Bank Von Raab was foolish, even petulant, and he chose to adopt a new attitude. He would be the model bank employee, dedicated to the success of the enterprise and the wealth of its clients. And meanwhile, he would leverage this opportunity into a prestigious position on Wall Street and a spacious co-op that he and Aisha would share—eventually. With this new perspective, he kicked Baldwin under his bed, shaved and bathed, and emerged into the daylight as a banker.

Chapter 10.

AMIR'S immediate challenge was his family—more specifically, his mother—and her inexplicable admonitions that he should stay far from both Dubai and Aisha. There was no point in debating her since she clearly had no intention of providing a sensible explanation of her objections. Oddly, now that he was about to leave, he had a nagging dread that his sister and father might slip more deeply into listlessness, deprived even of the satisfaction of criticizing Amir's empty existence. He was especially worried about Sara, whose well-practiced sport of ridiculing Amir transparently disguised her deep insecurity as a daughter with an absent and indifferent mother, barely keeping her head above water amid unforgiving social currents. It would be best, Amir decided, for him to lie to everyone.

He would invent a story that was hard to disprove. It would need to reassure his mother by placing him far from her stated fears and simultaneously comfort his sister by giving her a credible escape narrative of her own. And if he was lucky, his invented story might eventually come true, and everyone would get over the lie.

"I'm moving to New York," Amir announced at a rare afternoon family assembly in the kitchen, as his mother was rushing to leave for the hospital in her scrubs, Sara was between social climbing engagements, and his father found a natural pause in the interminable reindexing of his library.

Silence and startled expressions. Amir continued, expecting skepticism, but determined to stick to his story, buttressing the fiction with a few genuine facts.

"I accepted an analyst position with a European bank. It's a good job with a very good salary. It starts with a training program . . . um, in New York. I will be leaving next week."

Silence.

"I was thinking," he continued, "that maybe, if things work out, Sara could apply for college in New York, and she could join me there. Not right away, of course, but once I get settled and she finds a good program. I might be able to help with the finances, and we could manage the costs by sharing an apartment." Amir paused, worried that perhaps he was spinning this a little too hastily.

Sara brightened as she considered the possibilities, and Amir thought he may have scored. His mother had the look of a cornered animal, threatened, but unsure of the right response. She finally said, "Well. This will change things." And then, simply, "I'll be late for work," as she closed the door behind her.

His father offered a strangely hopeful note, before returning to his bespoke card catalog. "You know, they have very fine libraries in New York."

Alone with Sara in the kitchen, Amir watched her glow with previously unseen energy. He worried about the prospect of someday dialing back this story, but he was very committed now, and there was nothing to do but embellish.

He suddenly remembered his encounter with the young soldier at Allenby Bridge. "You should think about applying to NYU. I read that they really like foreign students, and especially women. It's in the middle of Greenwich Village, where *everything* is happening." Images from Baldwin darkened that advertisement, but he stayed on message.

Sara teared up. "Why are you doing this for me, Amir? I've been nothing but a bitch to you for as long as I can remember. I'm ashamed."

"I haven't done anything yet. It's just an idea for you to think about. I need to get myself to New York first and get through this training program. A lot of things could go wrong. But nothing good is happening for either of us in Nablus. This is the first big break I ever had. I'll share it with you if I can."

She made a tentative, awkward move to embrace Amir, but that was a bridge too far for both of them. Sara composed herself. "Please don't fuck this up," she whispered, with determination, anticipation, and fear.

It was the first and last time Amir heard Sara use that word. He wasn't shocked as much as he was made painfully aware of how much she was betting on his fraudulent invention. And it now dawned on him that, in Nablus and beyond—certainly in the chaotic time-space geography of social media—his new life in New York would become common knowledge, and difficult to protect from exposure.

I'll worry about that later, Amir decided, though he resolved to simply stop posting on his feed, which he conveniently would explain (to anyone who asked) is essential for bankers to comply with client confidentiality rules.

He felt no incipient nostalgia about leaving Nablus behind, perhaps for good. Its past glories, if they ever really existed, had been carted off or wrecked long ago. All that remained was suppressed rage and quiet desperation, as the settlements relentlessly closed in, and even the narrative charade of eventual statehood, self-government and international recognition decayed from remotely possible to entirely laughable. There were no lifeboats, Amir knew, and the only survivors would be the realists—like Aisha and him—who got out by any means necessary.

In the remaining few days, Amir thought it prudent to say as little as possible about his departure, minimizing the number of people to whom he would need to blatantly lie. The eventual unwinding would be difficult enough. He did feel a need to say something to Uncle Jaber, if only to preserve a connection that someday might be necessary if everything fell apart. And Amir knew that, whether he spoke to him or not, his uncle would hear the rumors, decipher the truth, and keep it all to himself.

Back on Jaffa Street in the late afternoon, the scene in his uncle's shop was frozen in time, including the fiercely pressed white shirt and linen trousers. Amir decided to say simply that he was leaving Nablus to join a bank, with the destination unspecified. It was not Uncle Jaber's style to ask too many questions. If an obviously relevant fact was omitted, there was a reason, and it would violate his uncle's personal code of discretion to press the matter. And he would find out anyway, so why embarrass his guest? True to form, his uncle accepted Amir's announcement without comment, and in fact, he barely looked up over the half-glasses nearly falling off his nose. Amir wandered around the tiny shop in silence, pushing a few electronic components around their dusty graves on glass shelves.

For no clear reason, Amir added, "My mother is not happy about this." He regretted it as soon as he said it.

After a pause to reflect, Uncle Jaber removed his glasses, and looked sternly at Amir. "Let me tell you something about your mother. She has a secret that haunts her, and I tell you, it has been hanging over this family like recurrent cancer since she married my brother. I have my suspicions about it, but it's none of my business. I'm just going to tell you that, whatever it is, you need to watch yourself when you leave here. This thing, her secret, is not something silly or trivial—like an embarrassing love affair, or some petty larceny. It's bigger than that. It's something dangerous."

Startled, Amir turned to press the matter, but his uncle held up a forbidding hand. "Like I said, it's none of my business. Just remember what I told you."

That warning preoccupied Amir as he visited two more dusty shops, acquiring one dark suit, and a few safe, identical white shirts—all patterned on Amir's recollection of the male uniform he recalled from his day at Burr Acheson's office. His purchases were cheap, and cheaply made, but he hoped that their utter lack of distinction would be a safe look, at least until he could afford something else.

The evening before he left, Amir feigned deep concentration on his packing and other preparations, as a means of avoiding questions from his family, and their general curiosity about how a stateless person from Nablus gets through the literal and figurative gates that surround New York. They seemed mildly satisfied by his breezy deflections about how "the bank handled everything." There was no farewell party and no proud send-off speech from his father. As she left for the hospital, his mother lingered momentarily in the doorway of Amir's bedroom, and finally said, "I just hope you know what you're doing." She didn't wait for a reply.

Amir had plenty of doubts about whether he knew what he was doing. There also was the murky business of managing his fiction about New York and the ominous warning from his uncle. When he thought about all his lies, he had the disturbing sensation that he was covered in soot, as if he had sneezed in a chimney. In his imagination, the water ran black as he washed his hands, and it seemed that everything he touched left a trail of forensic contradictions about who and where he was.

There wasn't much to pack. His wardrobe would require a complete makeover, and his other possessions seemed pointless for Dubai. In addition to his newly acquired office uniform, he ultimately chose some jeans and a small collection of ragged paperbacks. Hesitating, he removed the weighty Melville from his bag, replaced and removed it again, and finally buried it under his well-worn sneakers inside the canvas duffel.

It was late evening, but he was too rattled to sleep. Amir's improvised countdown clock reminded him that there were thirty minutes remaining before the closing bell in New York. Somehow, FREE*Trade seemed like the perfect place to retreat for safety and reassurance—his private club, where he knew the rituals and rules, and was welcomed by his fellow members. Returning to his laptop and trading app, greeted by his generous friends from Minnesota, he felt a warm embrace after so many disorienting changes. After some hasty pencil calculations, Amir chose the simplest day trade of all, betting his entire account balance on call options, expiring that day, on the day's most volatile stock. Any upward tick would yield many multiples of his investment. It was the Wall Street equivalent of a roulette bet by a drunk, placing all his chips on number seventeen. He entered the trade order in a state of sublime calm and then sat back, eyes closed, imagining a steaming sauna, with the gentle sound of wind chimes in the distance. His saw himself looking out from one of Burr Acheson's website images. Exquisitely dressed men and women, led by Aisha with an admiring Amir nearby, teeing off on the back nine at Piping Rock. A polished Hinckley 42, gently heeling on a starboard tack, with Aisha at the helm, reaching for the jib sheet and catching sunlight on her breasts beneath a carelessly buttoned white shirt. And finally, the winning shot, of a smiling Aisha and Amir, arms linked, as they mounted the stairs of a sleek Gulfstream, trailed by the copilot with their luggage.

Gliding gently back to earth, in a state of beautiful tranquility, Amir opened his eyes just in time for the closing bell. There had been no uptick. His options expired worthless, and a familiar automated message immediately appeared on his screen, "Warning. Your account balance is below the required trading minimum."

Abdel Raouf was jolly when he collected Amir and his baggage for another desert road rally through the gauntlet of checkpoints to reach the Jordanian border. He already heard the news about Amir's job in New York, and to celebrate the occasion, he presented himself proudly in a necktie the color of American currency, shepherding his familiar taxi, freshly washed for the first time in a decade. In a flourish resembling what he imagined to be the custom among drivers assigned to Manhattan bankers, Abdel Raouf saluted as he opened the car door for Amir. In the back seat was a copy of the Wall Street Journal (some weeks old), and a small, wrapped package containing a pirated DVD of *Breakfast at Tiffany's* —the "quintessential New York film," he explained.

Overnight, there had been another stabbing in one of the nearby settlements, and to the south, some troublemakers in Gaza fired a few rockets that fell harmlessly over the Israeli border. The military would retaliate, as always, and that would include additional misery for anyone who happened to be traveling that day in the occupied West Bank. Amir worried they might close the border crossing, or just make random arrests, but Abdel Raouf was unperturbed, joking his way through the gunpoint interrogations. During the drive, he spoke without interruption, narrating a hilariously inaccurate introduction to New York City for new arrivals. In his version, some of its famous landmarks were actually fixtures of London.

When they reached the whale's mouth, Amir wondered if he might again encounter the NYU soldier who had his own failed dream about Burr Acheson. They waited a long time in a line of cars at the approach to Allenby crossing, inhaling dust, diesel, and contempt from the troops, predictably ruder and more battle-dressed than usual. Abdel Raouf passed the time by recounting iconic episodes of *Seinfeld*, the teleplays slightly amended to render the twisted humor somewhat comprehensible in Arabic. It seemed to Amir that his versions included laugh tracks in the wrong places, but who could say what was funny about that show? Finally, back at the steel-jawed whale mouth, travel documents were produced to a heavy-set creature in a balaclava, who disappeared into the concrete structure with one-way glass. After two more mangled trailers of *Seinfeld* episodes, a different figure emerged from the concrete, shouldering his rifle as he approached the taxi. Amir recognized the accent ordering them out of the car. The soldier inspected the letter from Bank Von Raab, stapled atop Amir's collection of essential travel documents, with their idiotic attestations and smudged purple stamps from redundant functionaries.

"What happened with Burr Acheson?" asked the familiar soldier with the NYU backstory. He sounded genuinely interested.

They commiserated like schoolmates about their shared experience with rejection and disappointment, even joking about how—in comparison—the European banks were in a second or third tier of investment sophistication. But in the end, it was uncomfortably obvious to both that one of them soon would be sitting at a Bloomberg terminal in a glass tower sipping Perrier, and the other would still be . . . well, not.

Suddenly impatient, the soldier sent Amir on his way. Presumably acting on his superiors' instructions to be gratuitously difficult whenever possible, he said curtly, "Tell your driver he is close to making this trip one too many times. If I see him here again, he's going to be picked up for . . . questioning."

Abdel Raouf smiled and saluted one last time to Amir, handing him off to the relay driver who would complete the trip to the airport. Before leaving, he called out to Amir, "I was in the pool! I was in the pool!" and then laughed uncontrollably. The soldier frowned, recalling the line from *Seinfeld* and assuming the joke was directed at him.

The Emirates flight to Dubai felt familiar, though it seemed noteworthy that he was seated in the economy cabin this time, evidently reflecting his new employer's more austere style. Still, Amir felt like a seasoned traveler on the third flight of his life, and dutifully filled out the application for Emirates' loyalty miles program.

A flight attendant in a genie costume, whose badge identified her home as Bucharest, offered a heavily accented, "Welcome back," as she collected the application from Amir. She returned to offer him champagne from a tray. Amir accepted a glass, contemplated the frantic bubbles, but handed it back untouched as the aircraft pushed back for takeoff. For a moment, he thought he recognized one of the other passengers seated nearby, perhaps from his previous trip. But on closer examination, Amir realized that what he recognized was a look, rather than an actual person. That same look occupied almost every seat on the plane. They were anonymous figures, scrubbed and sculpted, similarly attired, vaguely androgynous, with uniform expressions of emptiness—as if they were neither leaving home, nor going home.

Settling into Dubai, Amir discovered that there was a vast industry there that made arrangements for people like himself, the office worker class that parachuted in for an indeterminate, but definitely temporary, duration. A driver employed by this industry collected him at the airport and handed him an envelope filled with the accessories of his new life—security fobs, apartment keys, car keys, a temporary driving license, a temporary Dubai identification card, and a small stack of rental agreements, each interrupted at intervals with tiny yellow flags that read, "sign here." Reviewing the documents casually, Amir was reminded of Emily's sad reflection that everything in Dubai had an expiration date. Everything in his envelope ended in two years.

Deposited at a glass apartment tower, with the Orwellian name Harbour 7, Amir encountered a desk clerk in an ill-fitting shirt with epaulets. No words were spoken by the clerk, who checked Amir's name on a computer display and directed him silently to a bank of elevators. The interior air had the distinct fragrance of newly manufactured goods, and indeed, some of the elevator buttons were still covered with the same pink anti-corrosion coating that was applied when the panel left the factory floor in Wuhan just a few weeks earlier. Once inside his apartment, Amir imagined that artificial intelligence had designed the interior decorating. Every surface and

fixture was inoffensive, in harmonious shades of black, gray, and ma-
hogany, reeking of newness. Not novelty or freshness, but the unmistakable odor of recently removed packing materials. The windows
admitted only faded daylight, filtered through an exterior coating of
the fine particulate produced by desert sand, and interior conden-
sate reacting to the frigid temperature inside. Amir shivered with an
involuntary spasm. The thermostat was hidden, but once he found it,
the control buttons were locked. A small label read, "For your comfort, temperature settings are maintained by management."

Still nothing from Aisha. No response to his text and no new
photograph. *She must have heard about New York by now,* Amir thought.
Does she care? He considered sending another message. *Too desperate,* he decided. Telephone her? Out of the question. The thought
of a Cairo lover resurfaced and lingered in his imagination, as Amir
pictured her alluring presence, surrounded by desperate Egyptian
graduate students. He looked back at her earlier postings and stared
for a long time at the photograph of her bare shoulder. The back-
drop was out of focus with the Ramses Hilton rendered like a hasty
vertical brushstroke beside the Nile. Amir hadn't noticed it before,
but there was a newspaper, *Al Ahram,* on a table next to Aisha, underneath a tiny coffee cup with a vivid smear of lip gloss in a deep red
color. It was exciting, or frightening, like a bloodstain out of context.

Who took this picture? Amir wondered.

Richard Swallow greeted him the next morning at Bank Von
Raab and delivered Amir to the small translucent glass cube with
high gloss white furniture that would be Amir's office, discreetly marked like a storage locker, "4090." As ever, Mr. Swallow spoke
concisely, previewing Amir's month-long training schedule— "shed-
yule," as he called it—which would begin immediately. A thick binder on his desk contained a syllabus with dry materials on securities
regulations, compliance rules, and ethics guidelines. Beside the
binder and wrapped in plastic was a hardback version of the classic, *Private Wealth Portfolio Management,* by Günther Alberich. Mr.
Swallow pointed reverently at Alberich's masterpiece and spoke in a
deep tone that would be ideal for a eulogy.

"It goes without saying that you should come to know this work
as you would . . ." Evidently on the verge of making a reference to

the *Aeneid* or some other catechism of English public-school boys, he paused to consider cultural or religious landmines. Falling off the wind, he simply said, "It's a fine book. I suggest you read it carefully."

Amir wasn't excited about a month of training but took the matter in stride, hoping that there would be opportunities for trading, or perhaps training alongside one of the bank's traders. He gently inquired about a Bloomberg terminal for his tiny office. Mr. Swallow looked at him blankly and said he would "pass along the suggestion."

"Follow me, please."

Mr. Swallow led Amir to the room where he had taken the tests a few weeks earlier, where they found a young woman adjusting the settings of a video display on the wall. She was thirty-five-ish, an archetype of the passengers on Amir's flight the day before, but rather more polished. Mr. Swallow introduced her by her surname, an affectation of formality that he employed for all occasions.

Ms. Curzon interrupted him and said to Amir, "Please, call me Fiona," adding with a distinctly chilly tone, "Thank you, Richard." Mr. Swallow dismissed himself.

It was the first day of a seemingly endless collection of "modules" designed to indoctrinate newcomers into the "culture" of Bank Von Raab. Fiona was pleasant enough, despite the suggestion of English nobility in her name and accent. And if there was any natural colonial impulse in her regard for Amir, she disguised it well. When the training materials lapsed—as they often did—into blinding statements of the obvious, she would click ahead to a new topic, remarking acidly to the invisible author, "Yes, we get the idea." She entertained Amir's questions patiently, but a pattern quickly emerged in which he looked for openings to discuss investment strategies, and Fiona dodged skillfully back to the bank's "operating principles." The leaden term, "discretion," appeared so frequently in her slides that, whenever Fiona paused for a breath, Amir repeated the word with mock seriousness. She didn't smile at his irreverence.

It seemed to Amir that his "training" was more like an extended interview. Fiona faithfully followed the modules but quite often pressed Amir to comment or react. It was a rhythm not especially tied to the substance of the training topic, but seemingly designed to elicit self-reflection from Amir. Fiona made this feel natural, and Amir grew increasingly comfortable speaking candidly about his life, opinions, and ambitions. She was good at drawing him out. Meanwhile, Fiona revealed nothing about herself.

Their daily routine was unbroken for some weeks, and even the ubiquitous Mr. Swallow was scarcely visible. Amir sometimes encountered other variations on the Emirates Airline passenger theme in the bank's corridors, but there appeared to be no tradition of spontaneous gathering and no interior spaces other than the glass isolation chambers that were the extent of Amir's experience with the bank. He spent his evenings alone, shivering in his monochrome flat, dining on takeout meals delivered from a Hyderabadi restaurant that left menus on his car windshield. A potent residual aroma of lamb biryani lent dissonance to the arctic air. He worried that his meal choices would be discernable to Fiona, the way cigarette smokers' clothing betrays their habit to anyone nearby. But the cleaning crew that surreptitiously visited his flat each day while he was away waged mortal combat against airborne contaminants, leaving behind as evidence of their victory a persistent scent of chlorine.

One night, while Amir was flipping the pages of the Alberich tome and watching Al Jazeera, breaking news brought an endless live feed of sirens and flashing lights from Cairo, where a "terrorist" detonated an "explosive device" in the legendary Mogamma building in Tahrir Square. The Mogamma was a hulking government building infamous for its Soviet-style architecture and for the administrative bureaucracies within, torturing Egyptians—literally and figuratively—whether they were present involuntarily in the custody of state security officers or simply renewing their driver's license. Smoke poured out of a seventh-floor office window, as firemen in the square below smoked cigarettes and appeared to debate whether to save the building or let it burn. On air, breathless commentators and Egyptian officials confidently implicated the Muslim Brotherhood and the other usual suspects. With this pretext, a broader government crackdown seemed likely. Amir had no news from Aisha since their coffee shop rendezvous in Nablus, and no new social media posts. He worried that Aisha was not cautious in expressing her opinions, which was not an ideal personal security strategy in contemporary Cairo.

Was she safe? he wondered.

NABLUS GIRL

By the next morning, the news from Cairo had evolved. In the light of day, all that remained visible was a massive black scar above the targeted office of the Mogamma. On the streets below, the incident apparently was forgotten, and the familiar chaos of horns and near-miss pedestrian incidents was restored. Al Jazeera reported that no one was injured in the incident, which involved an argument between an office clerk and a married couple attempting to secure the necessary documents to finalize their divorce. Infuriated by monthslong delays, the couple apparently reunited, finding common purpose in setting fire to the clerk's office. According to the police, the couple and the clerk were arrested and held for interrogation in another Mogamma office.

"Another day in Cairo," Amir said to himself; but thinking of Aisha, he was relieved.

During Amir's empty evenings, while waiting with increasing desperation for signs of life from Aisha, he felt the inevitable challenges of keeping up with the New York fiction he left behind in Nablus. Sara, a permanent resident of social media, predictably had been indiscreet about alerting her friends to Amir's adventure. Within days, there was a low-level hum of NYC memes and other digital litter produced by Sara and her followers. To feed this appetite, Sara's message traffic to Amir began with the merely curious, but degenerated quickly to urgent and demanding. Amir worried that she was already filling out the NYU application and consulting crooked rental brokers in the West Village. Amir considered, but decided against, posting some stock images of New York with breezy comments, just to calm Sara and quell suspicion. *Too risky*, he thought, considering his ignorance of New York, and the scrutiny that certainly would follow. He chose instead a few safe text messages to Sara, emptied of substance, but reassuring.

Life is good in the Big Apple but working 24/7—more later, he wrote. And then, something more adventurous. *Learning to love the subway!*

While deflecting Sara, Amir's main preoccupation was Aisha's silence, fueling increasingly irrational suspicions. But adding to the dilemma of his natural reluctance to appear too eager, he knew she would be aware of his "move to New York," and had no idea how he would navigate one of Aisha's pointed questions about that. Lying to her felt wildly foolish. Among the attributes assumed in Amir's pedestalized version of her was a kind of omniscient awareness of truth, and as in her unforgettable university performances, a ruthless energy to reveal and expose fakery. This fear left Amir paralyzed, unwilling to awaken her, terrified about what she might already know, and certain of a looming confrontation from which there was no escape. And as always, there was the haunting question, "Does she even care?"

On a Thursday afternoon, at the end of his third week in training, Fiona startled him by inviting Amir to dinner at her flat. This coincided with the completion of her segment of his training, and she explained that he would be working directly with Katrina Vanderlipp on the final module, which would focus on "client development." The dinner invitation seemed spontaneous, and she delivered it with the same unremarkable inflection that characterized her training style. Amir politely accepted, the details were exchanged, and Fiona left him alone in the glass box.

In the bank's opaque organizational hierarchy, it wasn't clear where Fiona fit. He couldn't find her on the bank's website, which barely revealed the bank's existence. It was not apparent that Amir was her subordinate, and clearly no one was Amir's subordinate. Oddly, his training materials included precise instruction on the bank's policies regarding acceptable behaviors among employees, but nothing quite described Fiona's invitation. He chose to regard it as something entirely normal in the customs of Dubai's professional class and tried to dismiss his reservations as provincial and a vestige of his dusty Nabulsi conservatism. He arrived on time.

Her apartment, in yet another Dubai architectural calamity called Port Tower 11, was large and spare, but distinctive for its collection of large-scale canvases in the style of abstract expressionism. Amir's eye for fine art was untrained, but he could tell that Fiona, or her decorator, had assembled quality pieces with a thematic uniformity. Violent brushstrokes, dominated by red and black, achieved the artists' presumably intended effect of unsettling the room, which felt like a crime scene. One large piece in particular dominated the interior space, with its strong suggestion of a severed torso surrounded by faceless spectators. There was specialized, expensive-looking gallery lighting focused on the art. Noirish ambient light drifted in from the city outside her windows, interrupted by intense kitchen illumination that drew the brightest light to large sharp knives and vegetables in precisely symmetrical arrays. Dissonant jazz, sweaty and suggestive, drifted in from another room.

Fiona was gracious but formal in accepting Amir's gift—a glass vial with microscopic filaments of saffron—and led the way to her kitchen, wielding a tall glass of Sauvignon Blanc like a traffic baton. She poured a glass for Amir and put him to work dicing ginger and garlic. In her exemplary received pronunciation, marked by disappearing diphthongs, Fiona previewed for Amir a menu centered on sea bass. Her cropped hair was framed between a dazzling pair of aquamarine drop earrings, which exaggerated the frosty temperature of her all-white ensemble of jeans and an oversized V-neck sweater. Watching her naughtily massage the fish with extra virgin olive oil from a tall, bullet-shaped bottle, Amir wondered why such a woman would abandon Belgravia for the desolation of a desert kingdom, particularly Dubai, where inauthenticity was the defining virtue.

They exchanged refined small talk, about her art collection, the local cuisine, and the price of a barrel of crude oil. He hadn't noticed before, but Fiona had lovely full lips that remained slightly parted in an almost-smile when she was not speaking, as if reflecting the space between her thoughts and the words that would follow. And in a departure from her training sessions, she spoke with the highly visual prose of a Bloomsbury author. The preliminaries progressed to her dinner table, where the sea bass filets now lay in repose on a serving platter, scantily clad in capers and dill. Amir drank his wine and forgot his apprehension about Fiona's invitation. It occurred to him that this was exactly the kind of scene that he left Nablus to explore. It was not quite New York, but pretty similar to those coveted images of high-net-worth clients displayed in all their glory on the websites of private banks.

After the fish was dispatched, Fiona folded her legs into a relaxed curl, and kicked off her heels. She pushed the hair behind her ear, releasing a very subtle scent.

Maybe narcissus or rosewood, Amir thought.

There was a moment of silence, so Amir filled it, surprised to feel entirely at ease. He spoke much too freely—about his introduction to Charlie Bridges, his day trading, and his Wall Street ambitions, but was vague about the improbable series of accidents that brought him to Dubai. He volunteered vivid images of Nablus, his family members, and almost mentioned Aisha, but then hedged with a reference to friends from "the better families" of Nablus. Fiona nodded along the way, sympathetic eyes locked on Amir, lips parted, silently drawing out more details. He revealed more than he ever had to anyone about his tortured relationship with his mother; about his conflicted love and resentment of his sister Sara; and about his longing to leave all that behind and find purpose in an entirely new place. He waxed forward, using terrible clichés, unconsciously dwelling on Sara, even speculating that his deep feelings for her were a substitute for what was missing in his relationship with his mother. Amir admitted, ruefully, that he had lied to Sara about his job, inventing a New York presence and promising her a place at NYU. This prompted a raised eyebrow from Fiona.

Occasionally, Fiona would say something earnest-sounding and apparently genuine. "Your mother seems like a very strong woman."

Involuntarily, Amir responded to such flat prompts with volumes of information, complete with asides of self-analysis. In one such moment, he found himself telling Fiona that he couldn't recall being touched by his mother. Ever. A long silence followed. There seemed to be nothing he wouldn't share with Fiona, who projected invisible rays of encouragement, comfort, intimacy, and safety. She refilled his glass.

The temperature felt unnaturally warm for a Dubai interior. As he settled ever deeper into his excessively candid autobiography, Amir imagined that dinner might continue in bed. He was certain he saw a dewy glow in the space between her breasts, her loose sweater now draped to reveal more than office protocol prescribed. He sensed a deeper rhythm to her breathing. Something expectant, with the hesitation and anticipation that precedes an eager, reckless move. Coltrane's tenor sax pressed harder with its foreplay grind, his #5 reed stroking the air to produce a warm penetrating series of harmonic progressions. Any moment, Fiona would stretch one of her long legs into Amir's lap, tracing playful arcs with her polished toe. Her eyes would narrow in an expression of determination. She would take his hand firmly to lead him away from the table, stopping abruptly to kiss him urgently in front of one of her more nightmarish oil paintings—a massive canvas with deep slashing strokes of angry color, something like a giant ship smashed on rocks, surrounded by drowned victims. A spotlight above the painting would send dizzy, refracted patterns from her earrings onto the canvas, as their kiss fissioned into a double grapevine on the floor.

That didn't happen.

When it finally occurred to Amir that he had said far too much, he abruptly went silent. Fiona read his chagrin, quietly smiled with a look of satisfaction, and cleared the remains of dinner. Standing in the harsh light of the kitchen, she pretended to glance at her watch and then delivered the universal body language and polite but point-ed phrases that signal an end to the evening. He stammered clumsy thanks, and promptly found himself in the corridor outside her flat, where the air was cold again.

Amir sat in his car for a long time before starting the engine. He wondered what just happened, certain that he had breached mul-tiple standards of conduct and revealed personality disorders that disqualified him for any serious work—not to mention, internation-al banking work. And worse, as he reconstructed the unlikely invita-tion, the disorienting setting, and Fiona's captivating performance, he was convinced that this supposedly ordinary dinner party among business colleagues was really an interrogation, entirely designed and executed for that purpose, by a professional who very obviously was trained for it.

Was it recorded? Amir wondered with some terror, as he acceler-ated in darkness onto the E11 motorway, facing a crush of weekend traffic and taillights. In his confusion, the scene through his wind-shield looked like uncorrected astigmatism, as the relentless heat ris-ing from the pavement distorted the light into red swirls.

Chapter 11.

HIDDEN in plain sight in a mostly respectable Tehran neighborhood, there was a walled compound of single-story cinderblock
buildings painted the color of sand after an oil spill. In one of
the windowless buildings, there were twelve identical prison cells
with steel doors. There were no names on the doors. One cell was
numbered "361." Six guards worked in the building, but they were
not armed—at least not with guns. They sat at desks in a cramped
office, working at antique computer terminals. Their mission was
to maintain meticulous records of the prisoners assigned to cells
in this building, noting for example, the special dietary meals that
Number 361 received this week, a visit from his cardiologist, and
the contents of the letter he will send to his daughter tomorrow,
in which he reports the good news, once again, of his imminent
release. But Number 361 and the eleven other prisoners in this
building died some years ago.

Number 361 is, or was, Amir's grandfather.

The building in this Tehran community adjacent to Vali-e Asr
Avenue was referred to by its neighbors, and by foreign intelligence
agencies, as "Prison 59." It was operated by the Iranian Revolutionary
Guard, or as they preferred to call themselves, the "Army of the

Guardians of the Islamic Revolution." No one is sure if "Prison 59" is a real name.

Are there fifty-eight other prisons? some people wondered, very privately.

The appallingly ugly buildings were hastily constructed in 1979, when the inhabitants of Iran lurched explosively from a wretched excess of oil-fueled wealth and debauchery, to a mass clinical psychosis in which the apocalypse was a dream devoutly to be wished. Years later, the wreckage wrought by international isolation and institutionalized internal repression had produced fantastically sophisticated systems to alter or invent the truth, using tools far beyond the imaginations of the most determined Stalinists. At Prison 59, there were actual prisoners at some point in the past, but most were dead before the current guards were born. According to reliable rumors, the prisoners' visits generally were brief—sometimes overnight—which was all the time necessary to complete the due process formalities between accusations of counterrevolutionary collaboration with the Great Satan and public hanging. But the bloody fun in 1980s Iran eventually produced its own Thermidorian reaction. The cruelties at Prison 59 evolved into the current incarnation in which actual prisoners had been replaced by the painstaking creation of fictional narratives about dead prisoners, whose lives endured indefinitely to torture and manipulate their loving and desperate families.

The guards working just outside the cell of Number 361 included five young men in their twenties, supervised by another man who, auspiciously in Iran, was born on the day Ronald Reagan was elected president of the United States. The older man, a captain in the Iranian Revolutionary Guard, looked about twice his actual age, the result of a lifetime of tobacco abuse and the psychic trauma of his job. The younger men all had beards that were meticulously groomed in the current fashion—pretentiously suggestive of religious fervor—often receiving morning touchups at sidewalk barber stalls on the way to work.

On his pale cadaver skin, Captain Sadegh had a kind of permanent dark stubble, like pernicious weeds in sidewalk cracks, which could neither be shaved nor groomed because of the deep creases in his face. It was a look that his subordinates considered metaphorically perfect for a man in charge of keeping the dead alive.

The younger men were conscripted to the Revolutionary Guard, separately from local jails, where they were each serving "Level Six" sentences. They were convicted of more-or-less identical internet crimes that involved addictive online gaming that drifted into pornography, or what the prosecutors called "criminal propagation, distribution, and trading of vulgar or pornographic content in violation of Article 14 of the Cybercrime Law." In other words, they were normal kids. They narrowly escaped flogging sentences, possibly fatal, having received mercy from God in the form of three-year terms in lice-infested jails. But mercy upon mercy, the basij who were responsible for their religious reeducation found them to be uniquely blessed with internet skills and active imaginations that could be turned to the service of the Supreme Leader as sergeants third class under the charge of Captain Sadegh at Prison 59.

The ingenious mission of Prison 59 materialized quite by accident from the early days of the Revolution. The young, reckless, and soon-to-be-executed early soldiers of the Revolution discovered to their astonishment that the Americans in Washington with whom they were exchanging hyperbolic rhetoric were gullible beyond all imagination. In their desperation for civilized discourse and diplomatic breakthroughs, the Americans seemed willing to believe the most ridiculous fictions, exposing themselves to comic humiliations involving cakes, Bibles, and Nicaraguan rebels. But the Americans never lost their appetites for believing lies. Gradually, the Revolutionary Guard professionalized a sort of Bureau of Fiction—though no one called it that—which manufactured diplomatic bargaining chips out of elaborate untruths about ballistic missiles, unconventional naval warfare, spinning centrifuges, deuterium production rates, cyber combat forces, and all manner of spurious narratives.

Prison 59 was a spinoff of the Bureau of Fiction that recruited foreign agents, normally by threatening their family members still stuck in Iran. Those schemes penetrated deep into the Iranian diaspora in Los Angeles, producing a steady and tolerably useful intelligence harvest from the California spy satellite industry. But as the Great Game of Iranian nuclear brinksmanship began to eclipse all other battlefields, Prison 59 expanded its blackmail and recruiting operations to other venues.

The American desperation to penetrate the Iranian nuclear program led down innumerable blind alleys. After many disastrous attempts resulted in gruesome failures, they gave up the ambition of actually running agents inside Iran. Flipping the occasional diplomat or sanctions-busting oil trader from Tehran during their infrequent visits to Vienna or Geneva proved to be both improbable and irritating to the local authorities. But one angle produced results for the frustrated clandestine service officers in suburban Washington, and it emerged from the most obvious and universal principle. Follow the money. The Revolutionary Guard officers that oversaw Iran's nuclear and ballistic missile programs also ran impressive operations to convert illegal oil sales and endless other transactions into hard currency, normally through Emirati banks, with the help of some Malaysian fish exporter or other collaborator willing to supply fictitious invoices.

But best of all, the Revolutionary Guard skimmed a percentage of every Iranian government purchase. The proceeds fed the personal portfolios of its officers, with a fat slice, of course, for the ayatollahs. It was common knowledge in Tehran, but in the artistic hypocrisy of crooked governments, it also was punishable by hanging—though almost no one was stupid enough to be caught. Hiding all that personal money offshore became big business for the wealth management industry in the Emirates, and a good excuse for the occasional dirty weekend in Dubai for senior Revolutionary Guard officers to visit their bankers, mistresses, empty condominiums, and shell corporation partners. The Americans eventually converted these weekends into blackmail opportunities. A visitor from Tehran would be approached in the shadows and told he could keep his money only if he revealed names and locations of the secretive club of physicists who ran Tehran's Manhattan Project. The flood of resulting leaks about Iranian nuclear research forced Prison 59 to expand its operations, recruiting operatives to spy on the Americans who were spying on the Iranians.

Captain Sadegh loved "His Boys," as he called them, in Prison 59. At home, all he had were two mouthy teenage daughters and his fat, dictatorial wife—from Najaf, of all places, where he had to spend time with her freakish relatives. But the young criminals under his command were genial and obedient, not to mention fantastically imaginative in devising convincing narratives about long-dead prisoners. Some of their detailed webs of invented intrigue made him howl with laughter. Sadegh's dour senior officers imagined a steady flow of brutish threats were enough to keep the prisoners' distant relatives motivated to provide intelligence, an operating model as simple as the dead prisoner's fake text message: "Do what they want, and they won't kill me." But His Boys took this extortion racket to a new level, fabricating lush correspondence from Prison 59's long gone guests, promising safe return to their families abroad in exchange for just one more favor for the Islamic Republic. Sadegh wondered if His Boys developed this skill from their manic immersion in online gaming, and all their twisted Tolkien-in-Las Vegas story lines. He loved watching their caffeine-blasted minds work. Sadly, he had to tone down much of what they wrote, before sending it up for approval by "the Colonel." Still, he felt they had achieved impressive success in giving eternal life to a string of dead prisoners whose relatives desperately clung to poignant biographies, and in exchange, had penetrated more than a few American intelligence operations.

Prisoner 361 had been one of Captain Sadegh's early successes, an operation he led long before His Boys arrived and while 361 was even alive. He couldn't help admiring the old man who, despite decades of incarceration in miserable conditions, maintained the erect bearing of a Luftwaffe officer. He betrayed no one, and never succumbed to the pathetic begging by so many others. Prisoner 361 seemed to take his situation in stride, even remarking once to Sadegh that he "knew the risks when he came to Tehran." Working for British Petroleum was a capital crime once the ayatollahs arrived. From their leisurely interviews together, Captain Sadegh felt he learned enough to craft authentic-sounding letters from 361 to the old man's daughter in Nablus. He wasn't as creative as His Boys, but he could invent medical conditions that required special medications or surgical interventions, and fictitious sympathetic guards who could be persuaded to smuggle in letters from his daughter. One time, Sadegh even plunged deep in melodrama by creating an abandoned kitten that found its way into 361's cell and became his most faithful companion. The nonexistent creature was tolerated somehow by the guards and comforted the old man in his declining health by licking his chin and curling into his lap during long lonely afternoons in his wretched concrete cell.

This was a masterstroke of invention, Sadegh thought, producing tears of anguish on the other end of the correspondence trail in Nablus.

The meandering, frantic reply letters that arrived from the old man's daughter revealed one of those epic father-daughter relationships from literature. There was nothing she wouldn't do for 361, and she would suspend disbelief if there was the slimmest hope of bringing some small comfort to his life. She sent him vials of precious medications, stolen from the hospital in Nablus. She sent packages with warm sweaters, fleece-lined slippers, knitted gloves, even a tweed jacket that looked like it had been left behind at a Cambridge dinner to award mathematics prizes. He gratefully acknowledged these sentimental tokens, and asked for more, which produced a steady supply of gifts for Sadegh and His Boys. And at last, when Sadegh's pulp fiction correspondence introduced the possibility that 361 could be released if only she undertook some small, harmless missions for his captors, she was all in.

The Colonel, who communicated with Captain Sadegh only by shouting, made it clear that he was under pressure to recruit assets in Dubai who could neutralize the Americans' increasingly successful efforts to disrupt Tehran's money laundering. In a few rare but horrifying cases, American operatives were even successful in flipping Revolutionary Guard officers into talking about the money flows *and* the nuclear research program, before disappearing them into comfortable new lives and identities in the Arizona suburbs.

"This stops *now!*" the Colonel told Captain Sadegh, implying that his own tiny slice of the vast grift was at risk.

The Nablus Connection, as Sadegh named it, proved to be fruitful. The daughter of 361 had respectable cover through her job at the hospital, and it was not difficult to arrange communications with her through a monthly visit by an unassuming Iranian internist, Dr. Reza, whose visits were tolerated as part of Iran's chintzy foreign aid program to the beleaguered Palestinians. Dr. Reza brought "news" of 361, including hopeful signs of improved conditions at Prison 59. Sometimes he brought letters from her father. In their clandestine meetings, late at night in a deserted file storage room in the ICU, Dr. Reza and 361's daughter also exchanged target lists and progress reports. She was a natural at tradecraft, and once in the game, increasingly sophisticated in recruiting assets, running their cover, and producing actionable intelligence. In what seemed like no time to Captain Sadegh, she had deployed an operative to Dubai who was sleeping with the Deputy Chief of Mission at the U.S. Embassy in Abu Dhabi, a weasel-faced, underpaid, career foreign service officer who was happy to share embellished stories about American spy operations, while having her toes sucked.

There was a "cost of doing business," as the Colonel chose to characterize some early missteps with Prisoner 361 and the assets recruited by his eager, resourceful daughter. A petite young woman, who graduated near the top of her class at Amir's high school, had been carefully placed as a nanny with an Israeli family in a nearby settlement. The family included two data analysts with the Bank of Israel—husband and wife—who were helping the Americans track Iranian money laundering in the region. The nanny disappeared after a few weeks into the industrial scale "administrative detention" system the Israelis operated to take suspicious Palestinians off the streets, unburdened by legal niceties. Another recruit, a sweet local girl, who visited the hospital in Nablus after a particularly vicious beating from her abusive father, happily signed up to go to Beirut. Her mission was to get close to the American intelligence officers interrogating shady brokers who converted Iranian cash into Dubai condominiums. She ended up dead in a suite at the elegant Berytus Hotel, the bloody mess efficiently tidied up by helpful local authorities and explained as an accidental overdose of nonprescription antihistamines. This kind of thing happened so often in Beirut that the U.S. Embassy had established a standard gratuity rate for the hotel housekeeping staff to handle and keep quiet about "private accidents."

"You win some; you lose some," said the Colonel. In Persian, the phrase didn't quite capture the significance of disposable human beings. But they were receiving a steady flow of decent intelligence from the recruits who survived, and the mild-mannered Dr. Reza gave optimistic reports after his monthly visits to Nablus. The Nablus connection, Amir's mother, showed no signs of drying up.

And then, Prisoner 361, Amir's grandfather, died quietly in his cell one morning.

The Colonel panicked at first, but Captain Sadegh had seen this coming. Prisoner 361 had been flagging for a while, and medical attention at Prison 59 was not exactly a national priority.

"We are ready," Sadegh assured the Colonel, feeling clever, "to keep 361 alive indefinitely. He might outlast his daughter."

And indeed, with the help of His Boys, the intimate correspondence between 361 and his daughter continued, with deeper and more complex emotions filling ever more lengthy exchanges. Sometimes late at night, alone and reflecting upon his own unhappy family, Sadegh would reread and linger over the long letters that came regularly from Nablus. There was longing, deep loneliness, and a recurring theme of failure, almost as if *she* were the one imprisoned. He could picture her, graying prematurely, fallen breasts, thin lips pursed with resignation, quietly resentful about the opportunities she never had or took, reproaching her own bad decision to tolerate a wasted life. Sadegh looked in the mirror but turned away quickly.

But the magic of the Nablus Connection was that, in desperation, hope is a survival instinct, even if, like any cognitive bias, it is irrational. The dangled promise of 361's secret pardon and release from Prison 59 "any day now" had so excited the imagination of Chief Nurse Hala that she successfully recruited the agent who would provide Prison 59's greatest win over the Americans.

Chapter 12.

AMIR returned to Bank Von Raab when the work week resumed and went directly to Fiona's office. He wasn't sure if he would demand an apology or apologize himself. But he expected a confrontation either way, still feeling the sting of humiliation, worried about how much he had said and mystified by why it happened. Her office door was locked, and the translucent glass walls hinted at no signs of life inside. Amir knocked a second time, really just to express annoyance. Behind him, Mr. Swallow materialized, silently and like some science fiction figure that can rearrange its atoms anywhere in the universe.

"Miss Curzon returned to Vaduz," he reported. "But I have your schedule for the week."

Amir felt that, by now, he had graduated from any expectation of deference owed to Mr. Swallow. What *was* his job anyway? He suppressed the temptation to be dismissive.

"When will she return?" Amir asked, as if his interest was merely academic.

"She was here for your training. I don't expect we shall see her again."

Mr. Swallow looked at his watch. "Right!" he announced, coming to military attention. "Miss Vanderlipp would like you to join her for some client meetings this week. The background materials are on your desk, and here is a schedule of pre-meetings at which you will meet the portfolio management teams. Please study the materials and be prepared to meet tomorrow." Mr. Swallow handed a printed schedule to Amir, and then rearranged himself elsewhere.

Amir felt disoriented. Fiona had given every impression of being long settled in Dubai, and a fixture at the bank. The decorations in her flat, and elaborate details like the art and kitchen tools, seemed unmistakably to be stylistic extensions of her rarefied presence. There was none of the aseptic flavor that wafts from a transient's apartment or clues from the occupant, like searching vainly for the Himalayan sea salt or the micro plane zester. It's true that she was all business during their training sessions, which might have been identical in Singapore or Frankfurt. But she had *local* knowledge too, occasionally tossing around colloquial Arabic phrases, knowing references to the business styles of the Khaleeji Arabs, and a passing familiarity with Dubai nightspots. It seemed impossible that Fiona had just parachuted in for Amir's training.

The mystery was heightened by Amir's cyberstalking. Fiona had no digital footprint—no reference on Bank Von Raab's site, no detectable social media presence, not even a blurry background image in which a character of the same name is misidentified at an obscure London charity opening, flanked by handsomely tanned and cleaved benefactresses. She was a ghost.

Alone, in his cold glass space, Amir told himself that Fiona was just one more eccentricity of Bank Von Raab, and he should stop brooding and puzzling over her peculiar role. From the beginning, he had reservations about the bank, reinforced by the vivid contrast between Hodding Easterbrook's team of real live securities traders at their Bloomberg terminals, and Katrina Vanderlipp's haunted house of pale characters lurking about. But Amir reminded himself that Bank Von Raab was an intermediate stop for him. Imperfect or not, it was his ticket out of Nablus, and he was determined to convert this opportunity into a comfortable seat on Wall Street.

The binders that Mr. Swallow left with Amir were beautifully bound, with slide decks printed in rich colors on heavy vellum, as if intended for a place someday in the Laurentian Library. The

Europeans still did some things with a glorious intensity, producing beauty for its own sake. The contents carefully catalogued the essential features of important clients, with photographs and CVs of the principals, financial statements and projections from their opaque business ventures, bubble diagrams depicting interlocking webs of shareholders, investors, offshore trusts, lenders, and contingent beneficiaries, all captured with luminous portraits of their investment portfolios carefully constructed by Bank Von Raab.

As Amir studied the materials, he felt restored. His doubts about the bank lingered, but he was determined to leverage this position and moderate his impatience. *After all, this was a long way from day trading*, he told himself. Amir swam deep into the slide decks, eagerly building spreadsheets to summarize the highlights of key client portfolios, sorting the data by asset classes and risk-adjusted returns, creating his own formulae to compare objectives and outcomes. He would be ready when Katrina summoned him, and the clients would be impressed.

There was uniformity among the clients and their portfolios, Amir noticed. He guessed that a certain type of investor would be drawn naturally to a conservative, Northern European bank, as opposed to, say, Burr Acheson. In the slide decks in front of him, the typical client was a Dubai LLC, all special-purpose vehicles with banal names like Dhow Creek Trading, Consolidated Engineering, or Deepwater Gulf Investments—endless iterations of meaningless terms and labels, intentionally anonymous. In Dubai, almost every form of commerce was transacted through a backstop of some kind—a front company with an Emirati as the general partner. This preserved the ancient local protection racket, assuring that Emiratis took at least a small percentage of every transaction, even if the undisclosed foreign shareholders held essentially all the beneficial interest and voting stakes. It was comfortable for everyone and legal in Dubai, though it challenged the occasional local regulator who pretended to investigate money laundering whenever the Americans sent one of their counterterrorism officials to complain to the UAE Central Bank. That was all for show and never slowed the great engine of capital flows.

Beautifully crafted new spreadsheets took shape on Amir's computer, patterns emerged, and he felt confident and ready to go head-to-head with Bank Von Raab's portfolio managers. There wasn't much imagination in the investments—no option spreads, currency swaps, collateralized debt obligations, not even a convertible bond. They were all safe asset classes in Euro or Dollar denominations, with pathetically low coupon yields, sometimes negative. The portfolios were parked in classic tax havens like the Channel Islands, where brass plates appeared like stamp collections pasted on the moldy brick facades of quaint Georgian structures. Inside were the imaginary domiciles of thousands of trusts with names like "Peregrine Fund" and "Saqr Trading." Birds of prey were particularly popular as naming conventions among the bank's clients, Amir noticed. And although it was less obvious in the slides, there were layers of "management" fees imposed on the clients by every intermediary—banks in three continents, trade clearing houses, accounting firms, and comically-named law firms in Saint Peter Port and Saint Helier—guaranteed to produce a negative total return. Evidently, a return was not the investment objective, Amir concluded. Still, as Amir's spreadsheets confirmed, the investment portfolios all grew over time through a steady inflow of fresh deposits, and none was valued at less than eight figures.

His first appointment on Mr. Swallow's schedule was captioned, "Client Development Meeting, Team 4." Teams 1–3 were not mentioned. Amir arrived a few minutes early and found two analysts—both thin young men in dark suits, no ties—seated in a conference room, flanking a screen with the image of a familiar slide deck. They introduced themselves very formally and then went quiet when Katrina Vanderlipp arrived to preside over the meeting. By now, Amir was accustomed to her signature glow of whiteness, which seemed to unsettle the pixels on the conference room screen as she passed by to take her seat. She looked at Amir, asked if he had found the background materials clear, and without waiting for a reply, nodded to the analyst on her right. He stood and plunged into the slide deck.

The analyst spoke with precision, in clean English prose, with a faint trace of Continental Europe, possibly Scandinavia. There were no wasted words or flourishes. *His command of the material was impressive*, Amir thought. But the investment portfolios received only brief attention. The focus was on the clients—their backgrounds, personalities, family connections, and most of all, links to other investors. Amir had hoped to display his command of the portfolio details, and he came to the meeting armed with his spreadsheets, along with carefully devised questions about uncorrelated asset classes and diversification models. He was disappointed.

Katrina interrupted the presentations only to drill down into the elaborate graphic slides that depicted the clients' interlocking investor relationships—beautiful Pantone color wheels and spiderwebs, meticulously linking exotically named individuals and their special purpose investment vehicles, across continents.

The presentations moved quickly, as if both analysts carried a relay baton through the slides. Amir struggled to keep up. Each segment ended with a slide labelled, "Development Target," and a single name followed by a value with many zeros. Katrina and her analysts lingered over those slides, rehearsing elements of a sales pitch, in each case settling on a few talking points to offer Bank Von Raab as the ideal destination for the client's money. Katrina then delivered a curt, "Thank you," dismissing the two analysts. Amir started to follow them, but Katrina motioned for him to stay behind.

"Impressions?" Katrina asked Amir.

Amir remembered that Charlie Bridges had a wonderful talent for responding to his students' questions, while he clearly was still formulating an answer. He would begin with the confident expression, "Two things!" Then he provided a patiently cadenced description of the first thing, usually obvious, stalling while he hastily developed a second thing, more incisive, that really addressed the question. Amir tried it.

"Two things!" he said, without hesitation. "First, these clients are unconventional. I don't think they are looking for relationships with traditional money center banks in London or New York."

Katrina's face registered acknowledgement that Amir clearly grasped the obvious.

Amir pressed on. "Second, we need to differentiate our bank. Make it clear that we can provide something different. And . . ." He trailed off, having not successfully formulated anything intelligent.

There was an awkward silence, eventually broken by Katrina's merciful election to ignore his two things.

"I want you to join me for some client dinners this week. We will see the principals that were discussed today. I know it's early in your training. At this stage, I mostly want you to watch and listen. But client development is the most important thing we do here. And soon, I expect you will be building your own relationships."

Katrina stood, and then, so did Amir. "How are you settling in here in Dubai?" she asked, with a very faint trace of genuine interest. And as she so often did, Katrina did not pause for a reply. "Before she left, Fiona briefed me on your training results. You did well. She was impressed with your, um . . . diligence. We are glad you joined our team."

The reference to Fiona revived a sharp pain, like a deep splinter that resisted removal. Amir wondered what kind of "training results" were reported and winced at the realization that Katrina had heard all the personal and family dramas that he had so carelessly shared during the non-seduction in Fiona's flat. This time, he chose to be discreet, embracing the famous tradition of Bank Von Raab. He thanked Katrina for including him in the client pitches, to which he was "very much looking forward," imitating the odd, formal syntax favored by the analysts who had just left. The meeting ended, the pixels quivered again on the screen as Katrina passed, and Amir stood alone in front of his unused spreadsheets.

Back in his flat watching the sun disappear behind Dubai's brooding forest of empty towers, Amir had other work to do to. His fictional presence in New York required media maintenance, which he had neglected. Text messages from Sara expressed increasing irritation with his infrequent and indifferent replies. She reminded him of NYU's application deadline, asked if she should also apply to "safety" schools, pressed him for news about an apartment, and generally fretted about her hopeful but uncertain future. He also had a text from his mother. "Send us news, please." A later text read, "Your father wants to know about something called the Morgan Library." Amir had to look it up, before deciding not to respond.

Amir felt he could rely on Sara to feed the gossip appetite in Nablus and whatever level of interest his parents might have. He chose to send her a longish email expanding upon his invented life in New York. He wrote:

I can't wait for you to see this place. Everything moves three times as fast as Nablus. The work is hard, but if you work, people respect you and give you opportunities. And then, after work, it's like Ramadan. The streets are busy all night. I will be in the bank's training program for a few more months. The other trainees are from everywhere in the world, so no one thinks it's strange that I came from nowhere. There are lots of legal requirements that we have to follow as bank employees. The bank told us to stop posting on social media (Amir made up this rule, hoping it would explain why there were no photos of him posing in front of the New York Stock Exchange). I visited the NYU campus, and it's amazing. It's the perfect place for you. But I need to get through this training program before we start planning for your arrival. Can you defer your application until the next semester? Tell Mama and Baba that everything is good with me. Missing you. Amir.

Amir reread the email. It sounded like he was in middle school. But not fake. *It would work for now,* he thought. Sara would be satisfied enough, and she would spread the word that he was alive and well in New York. She would share the email with Noor, Noor would send it to her sister, and Aisha would be intrigued, impressed, or at least reminded of Amir's existence.

It was agonizing that Aisha never responded to Amir's text. There had been nothing to acknowledge their evening encounter in Nablus a few weeks earlier, and Amir wondered if he had imagined the whole episode. She continued to post photos from Cairo regularly. Amir scrutinized her posts for important clues, like searching for the missile launchers in spy satellite imagery. A few days before, there was a photo of a dozen university students gathered for some benign solidarity event for earthquake victims. In one post, Aisha posed in a campy shot in a coffee shop behind a stack of thick textbooks, eyes closed, affecting exaggerated boredom, with El Fishawy's familiar blue sign in the background. Amir lingered over another striking photo, filtered in sepia like a Steichen classic, with Aisha in profile, chin high, looking up at the Mokattam hills in the distance.

He noticed that there always was some kind of recognizable Cairo landmark in the photos, like a visual geotag, though the metadata was missing. It was maddening. There was never anyone *with* Aisha in the photos. But who was taking these pictures?

Chapter 13.

EXITING the cool, clean airplane upon arrival at Cairo's airport, Aisha felt like she had been rudely awakened from an enchanted dream, as if interrupted during a deep-tissue massage at a Balinese resort. Her eyes opened, and she was a Kafka character, crawling desperately through grimy narrow corridors in which the default means of human communication was shouting. A ubiquitous patina of dust covered every surface, including the clothing and faces of the locals, rendering everything and everyone the sad color of a retired dun horse. As passengers and porters roughly trundled luggage and suspicious oversized parcels through the airport, every stumble provoked a little nimbus dust cloud that hovered and then disintegrated near the floor. The too numerous airport police, in their once white uniforms fitted for much larger occupants, greeted arrivals with crude manners, aggressively suspicious of all declarations, and the unspoken but unmistakable solicitation of bribes. A sign, badly translated in multiple languages, hung near the customs declaration zone. It warned visitors, without irony, that narcotics smuggling would be punishable by a large fine, or death, *or both*. Lurking in corners were sullen teenage soldiers, dressed in black paramilitary uniforms and armed with automatic weapons, evoking the at-the-edge atmosphere of a meeting of mercenaries in a warlord's encampment.

In Aisha's well-heeled family, they knew how to project sophistication and worldliness, though most—including Aisha—had never left Nablus. Her inexperience with travel was not a handicap, especially in a place like Egypt. Aisha knew plenty of Egyptians in Nablus. Instinctively, she knew what to expect from them, how to respond to their little social manipulations, and the careful balance necessary to feed, but not quite satisfy, their fragile egos. She would have no difficulty managing Cairo taxi drivers ("The fare? As you wish!"), hotel desk clerks (who couldn't seem to find the reservation until some cash appeared), or even the pushy young female "expeditor" in black jeans and head scarf who had been sent to greet her at the airport.

Expeditor Woman spoke fast and relentlessly, clicking through the tedium of airport arrival tasks, but not offering to help with her luggage. Her hard consonants made Aisha's teeth hurt, and she thought the young woman stood and walked a little too closely to her. Aisha maintained her aloof equipoise, even as they squeezed into a dirty Hyundai driven by an aging gangster and hurtled into the horns and constant near-misses of vehicular Cairo. The narration from her handler continued, but it was a relief that the woman chose the shotgun seat, leaving Aisha alone with the stale odor and upholstery stains in the rear.

Aisha's arrangements in Cairo were unorthodox for a new graduate student with a modest scholarship at Cairo University. They included an extended stay on the seventeenth floor of the Semiramis Intercontinental Hotel, a landmark near Tahrir Square, in the center of Cairo. It was not convenient to the university, but her student status would require only infrequent classroom visits. More important was her anonymity and proximity to an undistinguished office building in the nearby Garden City neighborhood, where she would spend long days for the next month, deep in study. The hotel stay was not part of the story she shared with her family and friends in Nablus, but she would find ways to manage the truth to conform to their standards of propriety for a young woman alone in a metropolis.

Expeditor Woman was brusque with the hotel staff, cutting the line at the reception desk, and checking in Aisha while she stood nearby. Some money exchanged hands, though not too visibly, and soon Aisha was in her room, alone with a thick envelope of materials she was told to study. Her room lacked the coveted Corniche and Nile views, but instead faced the menacing nearby tower of the U.S. Embassy, with its unique architectural flourish of windows set at oblique angles, with masonry baffles designed to prevent direct impact from antitank projectiles. The embassy flag sagged in the windless evening haze, projecting a flaccid aspect that defined the American presence in Egypt since the Arab Spring. By leaning over her balcony, Aisha could see Tahrir Square to the northeast. The din of car horns could not be suppressed.

The Semiramis was too expensive for the locals. It catered primarily to business travelers from Europe and America. Though it was close to the U.S. Embassy, it was not on the "approved list" for the embassy's official visitors, either because it exceeded the stingy *per diem* of the American government or because of some unfortunate security incidents in the hotel lobby in the 1990s. This fit the needs of Aisha's handlers, who wanted Aisha to look like she belonged there, but not attract attention from the wrong people. Aisha bristled at the parting instructions from Expeditor Woman. She was to keep her hair covered in the hotel's public areas and on the streets of Cairo, rely on room service for meals, and generally limit her visibility.

Aisha washed her hair in the shower, wrapped her head Marilyn-style in a heavy white hotel towel, and then slid into a long bath. Even after the shower, the loofa and the bath water seemed to turn slightly ashen as she scrubbed the residue of Cairo from her neck and shoulders. But the steaming bath softened the sharp edges of her arrival, and Aisha smiled as she considered the small victory of her escape from Nablus. When this unexpected opportunity presented itself, she was suspicious at first. It was improbable, and of course, inappropriate by almost any standard. But its clandestine flavor had its own attractions, and Aisha—overconfident by nature—was certain she could turn it to her advantage.

And what are the alternatives? she asked herself. Keeping up appearances for her family in Nablus was not an aspiration, and it was long past time for her to meet people—particularly men—with style, experience, and ambition. With the exception of the Dajani family patriarch, the men she knew in Nablus—boys, really—were disappointments. Like other places in the world that are habitually trashed by war, natural disasters, bad governance, or self-inflicted civil calamities, the native population of Nablus had settled into a culture of victimization, in which ambition was replaced by blame. The men were the worst practitioners, Aisha knew, wallowing in generations of inherited anger and reinforced by a collective narrative of failure that was "not their fault." *It was revolting*, she thought.

Her skin glowed, as the hot water flushed the toxins and free radicals. Aisha looked with satisfaction at her long legs, playfully lifting one in a ballet maneuver, pointing her toes to the ceiling. She admired the fresh waxing performed a day ago by Mrs. Al Qasem, a skilled artisan in the Hollywood style, which was both *au courant* and Islamically correct. Her discreet services available to select Nabulsi women, through a side door in her home on Al-Juneed Street, also included access to smuggled French cosmetics, Italian underwear, contraception, and freely rendered advice about sex that was so authoritative and graphic that her visitors often departed in a condition of flushed and urgent desperation. There was even a little lending library with books about female sexuality written by "social scientists," carefully disguised with dust covers and fictitious titles like "Motherhood and Faith." Like Aisha, Mrs. Al Qasem was a practical woman, unsentimental about anatomical apparatus, and patiently focused on helping her clients have what they want and, most of all, *deserve.*

In the warm bath, Aisha patiently attended to her own machinery. With eyes closed, she reviewed a catalog of images of the men she had known, if only in her imagination. It was a flicker in her mind, a series of rapid left swipes, some accompanied by dismissive laughs, and others, merely sympathetic sighs. She lingered for a moment on the young Danish internist from a group of volunteer doctors who had appeared in Nablus for two weeks to administer HPV vaccines, but the memory was hazy and glamorized by the surrounding controversy among local parents. Then there was her very cute cousin, who sometimes visited during Eid from London, where his family had built a successful catering business. He was awkward, though willing. But their consanguinity added a layer of confusion to their fumbling encounters. She momentarily considered Amir, the sweet boy who stared at her during American literature class at university, but he was bookish and impossible to visualize, prone, naked, and poised for a performing role in one of Mrs. Al Qasem's narrated skin flicks. And of course, under the present circumstances, Amir was out of the question.

After some modest success with her exercises, Aisha let her breathing return to normal, opened her eyes and considered herself, more critically now. Were her breasts too small, she wondered, by London standards, and were her nipples too . . . confrontational? Her hair, she knew, was slightly wild, and resisted capture in the sophisticated styles she saw in films and influencer images. The profile of her nose, every woman's preoccupation, was either too little or too much, depending on the light and infinite other variables during inspection. Her bottom, celebrated by Mrs. Al Qasem as Aisha's most perfect physical attribute, sometimes seemed to Aisha to be too lean, perhaps lacking in the contours that her jeans were designed to exaggerate.

Stepping out of the bath, she inspected her tall profile in the oversized bathroom mirror, standing unnaturally erect and affecting skinny arm poses with lip pouts adapted from online photos of celebrities. There were imperfections she hadn't noticed before, lending sincerity to her pout. Aisha resolved to use her time in Cairo to perfect the toning in her calves and upper arms through diligent visits to the hotel fitness center. She would emerge from this adventure, her "best self," as the self-care authors prescribed.

After her salad niçoise was delivered by a rude room service waiter, she settled into an oversized hotel bathrobe and channel surfed between Al Jazeera and Sky News, laughing as the same news was reported in diametrically opposed versions. Aisha opened the envelope from Expeditor Woman, which contained a catalogue from Cairo University, course descriptions for a graduate political science program, and copies of a few dry academic papers. There were titles like, "Utilitarianism and Political Economy in the Post-Modern Maghreb." Oddly, the papers were heavily annotated with marginal notes, in syntactically hilarious English, and blue or orange highlighting, as if authenticated by actual student use. The university's images in the catalog, as Aisha would discover, were digitally enhanced to insert lush gardens, with colorful flowers and mature trees, which expired half a century ago in the poisoned Cairo air. But she understood that the catalogue contents were a preview for her adopted identity, providing the small details that she would employ to lend credibility to the charade of her graduate studies. Before bed, Aisha composed a text message for her sister, Noor. "The students here are SO serious!"

It was a short walk to Tawfik Diab Street. The morning air smelled of diesel and burning tires. In the lonely lobby of a weary office building, the single elevator, inoperable, was marked with a repurposed No Parking sign, and Aisha climbed the dusty stairs to a third-floor office marked simply "393." She waited a long time after twice pressing a small button beside the locked door, which eventually opened to a cramped corridor of shabby offices, with peeling paint the color of lingering cigarette smoke.

A middle-aged woman, trim in a gray tunic, her hair carefully covered with a drab roosari, introduced herself as Leila. She was unmistakably Iranian. "I will be your teacher," she said, not cheerily.

There were a few other women and men in the office, also Iranian. They passed by Aisha without speaking, eyes averted. Leila led Aisha to a cramped corner room, closed the door, and began the instruction with a sharp admonition.

"Let's be clear about your role. You are not a movie star. You are a contractor performing a job. There are rules, and they are strictly enforced. The most important rule is that you will do as I say."

Aisha found herself nodding involuntarily. Leila projected authority. Her choice of words had a doctrinaire edge, but Aisha was glad she was a no-nonsense woman. As the morning progressed, it was evident that she had conducted this kind of training many times before. She mentioned, clearly informed by experience, examples of the kinds of mistakes that had led others into "difficulty," as she put it.

"Here in Cairo," Leila said, "you are Aisha Dajani. We will work on building a footprint for you. Photographs, school records, social media posts . . . normal life. The family and friends you left behind in Palestine will see the ordinary things they expect, and you will feed those expectations. Once you relocate, you will have a new identity, but your Cairo presence will continue just as before."

A young man with a close-cropped beard joined them, not introducing himself to Aisha and speaking to Leila in a low murmur. He left with Aisha's mobile phone and returned a short time later with a similar model. Leila explained that Aisha's SIM card was transferred to the substitute phone, which was modified so that the location monitoring system would place her in Cairo indefinitely.

With these formalities out of the way, Leila and Aisha settled into a routine that would fill their days for two months. Much of their time together would be spent in the same dirty room in Garden City, interrupted by occasional field trips to Cairo University, where the pair easily infiltrated overcrowded lecture halls in which the professors neither saw nor cared who was in attendance. Leila usually selected political science courses, consistent with Aisha's public presence for consumption in Nablus, but for variety, they also visited lectures on statistics, pre-Islamic history, and one very strange class in tropical medicine. The professors, all male, bore an alarming resemblance to Professor Fathy Shambli back in Nablus—invariably shaped like large eggplants, dressed in brown suits, reciting lecture notes clearly stolen from European or American university websites, and ignoring questions from the assembled students. On a few occasions, Aisha felt aroused to launch one of her nuclear attacks on the fraud at the podium, but in Leila's company, those dialogues remained in her imagination.

During the long midday breaks, the two women lingered in coffee shops, where they preferred outdoor seating. Using a battered digital camera, Leila staged elaborate photo sessions, assembling a catalogue of images of Aisha, always alone with some kind of familiar feature of Cairo.

She was a remarkably accomplished photographer, Aisha thought, *always attentive to the complex attributes of light and shadow.*

Some shots involved many takes before Leila was satisfied. She had a particular talent for adjusting the depth of field to blur the background, just enough to dramatize some feature of Aisha's vivid presence, while preserving something identifiable in the landscape. While composing the frames, Leila would speak knowledgeably about portraiture techniques of Peter Lindbergh or Richard Avedon, and once instructed Aisha to imagine that she was the subject of a Sargent painting, head turned in aristocratic profile and fingers projected to accentuate verticality. They would review the images together, sometimes debating compositional choices, or deciding to wait for the light to change before reprising the scene.

They did not become friends exactly, but at times they laughed together about some comical translation error in the training materials, or about the behavior of Cairo men, who were often stricken in Aisha's presence. Each admired the professionalism of the other. As expected, the training focused on tradecraft, much of it tedious and repetitive. Often, the layers of security seemed obsessive, bureaucratic, or just silly. But Aisha warmed to the phrases of her new field—legends, swallows, dangles—the imagery was thrilling. Eventually, the training progressed from the theoretical to the highly practical, and Aisha was studying lever arch binders with holding company organization charts, wire transfer records of money movements between international banks, and detailed biographies of women and men with aliases. The "target profiles" were dominated by Americans, all men with some kind of diplomatic background or affiliations with transparently fictitious enterprises. There were case studies of past operations, successful and not. Leila liked to dwell on "lessons learned." While never mentioned explicitly, Aisha could infer that some of the operations had resulted in unintended casualties. She internalized this fact but regarded it coldly, as an example of the failures of less-qualified people. Aisha could see that Leila admired her apparent indifference to the risks.

Oddly, or perhaps not, Aisha noticed that Leila seldom mentioned politics. The presumed evils, or even the abstract geopolitical competitive forces, that placed this project in conflict with its targets, were never discussed. Plainly, this was a war, and one that had raged—mostly beneath the surface of louder wars—since 1979. There was considerable wreckage above the surface too, including defeated or damaged presidents, dramatic exploits of espionage, and assassinations that were never fully attributed. Once, Aisha carelessly observed that the duration of the conflict had the feel of some kind of petulant feud among boy-men on both sides whose fragile egos prevented a practical solution. It was familiar to anyone from Nablus. Leila glared at her for a moment.

"We don't require you to have any opinion about this project. In fact, it would be best if you had no opinion. One of the attributes for which you were chosen is that you have should have no particular reason to care, one way or the other, about the two sides in this . . ." She paused to select just the right word. "Business," she said finally. She didn't say it harshly, but the message was pointed. Aisha would keep her politics to herself.

It was a lonely time too. After evenings spent alone in her hotel room, restricted in her movements, and almost certainly shadowed whenever she emerged, Aisha was restless. One night, when CNN International's apocalyptic breaking news intro music became too much to bear, Aisha put on heels and a mid-length dress, clingy but not excessively so, and strolled into the Ambassador Club Bar at the Semiramis, taking a seat in a high-backed chair facing the Nile. The walls of the bar were decorated in dark green silk, with paintings of nineteenth-century Ottomans in fezzes. The exotic interior, a persistent white noise from some unseen HVAC machinery, and the dim wall sconce lighting, were perfectly designed for a place in which shadowy people could conduct their business unseen and unheard. A waiter with a face like a camel looked disapprovingly at Aisha but wilted when she flashed him a fierce look and commanded him to bring coffee. In the darkness outside, the Nile was black with ripples of reflected light from the Corniche. The automobile horns were relentless. There were a few other men and women in the bar, but by design, the oversized chairs obscured all details except human legs and footwear. She heard whispered conversations, in Arabic, French, and English, but only an occasional, disconnected word was comprehensible. This being Cairo, the word she recognized most often was "dollars."

She wasn't precisely breaking the rules. Her instructions were to refrain from leaving the hotel, except to attend to her training. But she was sure that lingering alone in the hotel bar at 11:00 pm in heels was not part of her approved orbit. This improved her mood and reinforced her natural defiance. Aisha held her coffee like it was a martini, feeling uncaged.

The vibration of her phone was a reminder that a problem was festering back in Nablus. For weeks, with Leila's detailed curation, Aisha fed her modest but attentive social network a steady current of predictable images of student life in Cairo. Apart from the quality of the photography, there was nothing to provoke much attention. But reports from Noor, first melodramatic, and then alarming, made it clear that her parents' opposition to Aisha's move to Cairo had metastasized into a mortal threat to the family's honor. She tried to de-escalate the darkening mood with upbeat calls to her mother. Her father would not answer her calls. But her mother's famously measured poise, an affect that normally subdued any tension in her presence, suddenly was replaced on the telephone with unfamiliar, stern monosyllables. She ended the last call a few days before with, "Come home. Now."

Even Noor's normally playful, teenage prose on social media descended into ominous warnings. "Things are getting bad," she said, more than once, in reference to spontaneous outbursts from their father. "Never seen Papa like this before!" she added.

"Papa said he is coming to Cairo to bring you home!" Noor wrote.

When she arrived in Garden City the next morning, Aisha knew this was a subject she had to raise with Leila. But instead of the always punctual start to their morning session over tepid tea, Aisha sat alone in the conference room listening to indistinct but emphatic shouting in a nearby office. When the combat finally subsided, Leila appeared, unruffled, and took her usual seat at the table opposite Aisha. Aisha was wide eyed, but neither spoke for a while. Leila pretended to search for that day's topic in the binders on the table.

"When the time comes," Leila said quietly, "they will have to get used to the fact that you are a beautiful young woman, and you cannot complete this project by working under a shroud behind closed doors. But not yet."

Her face darkened. "You are making this difficult, especially for me. Did you think no one would notice you sitting alone in a bar? Especially *that* bar . . . where the local intelligence services play their little games of intrigue like a fraternity house initiation. We heard about it as soon as you left your room . . . from three sources."

Aisha started to protest that her outing was harmless, but Leila silenced her with a Persian hand gesture that was unambiguous.

"I dealt with it this morning with the station chief," Leila reported, "but now I have to explain it in a report to the directorate in Tehran. I will defend you this time, but don't make me do this again, because I won't."

Contrition was not one of Aisha's natural sentiments, but she bit her lip and nodded.

"And don't wear heels again while you are in Cairo."

She faux-inspected the binders on the table. Aisha calculated that it would be best to address all the bad news at once. She brought up the texts from Noor, and the growing "problem" back in Nablus. Leila did not seem surprised. She was, after all, stage managing Aisha's social media presence, and—Aisha assumed—monitoring every cookie and trifle that transited through her mobile phone. They reviewed the texts together, and Leila pressed for more details about Aisha's father, his personality, and likely intentions.

More tea arrived. It was barely warm. Aisha noticed a small insect floating in her tiny glass.

The risk was real, Leila concluded. She stepped out to make a call. When she returned, Leila said, "I'm sending you home for a few days. You need to work this out. Do you think you can?"

Aisha said yes without hesitation. She was, after all, a Nabulsi woman. Men were creatures who could be managed. And there was the added chemical reaction universally experienced by fathers and their daughters. She would test his patience, even provoke his wrath. There would be tears and shouting, but in the end, he could not say no. The travel arrangements were made, a carefully crafted text to Aisha's mother was dispatched, and the two returned to their binders.

A few days later, at the outskirts of Nablus, Aisha felt momentary panic, like she was rewinding the tape on her new life. From the taxi window, the dreary scene was worse than ever. Even after Cairo's spirit-crushing chaos, and the surveillance bubble of Leila's unseen directorate, it was demoralizing to return to Palestine's hamster maze of checkpoints. Long shadows were cast by merciless construction cranes in settlements expanding on the horizon, gradually erasing the community that had survived since Herodotus. Aisha looked away, determined to make this a brief visit.

She rehearsed the ballet to be performed with her father. She would present herself to him, moist eyes cast downward, *sans* make-up, and deep in chastity. He would speak first, with suppressed anger, reminding her that the family's reputation was now at stake, not to mention her own standing and prospects in society. And then, since he was a Dajani and considered himself an educated, modern man, he would pretend to acknowledge her side of the story, expressing sympathy that community standards were sometimes unfair.

"But we have to live with these people," he would say. Aisha had heard that spurious argument before and wondered how it would sound if they happened to live in a community of cannibals. But she would not challenge him.

Still looking down, she would say in a trembling voice that he was right, of course, and she "could only imagine" the terrible burden he must carry in looking after the family's reputation. A pause, a faint whimper, and then, the precision-guided weapon. "My whole life, I only wanted you to be proud of me," Aisha would say. "First Grandfather, and then you, always reserved your highest praise for educated women. My graduate program in Cairo . . . this was for you." Then tears.

Her father would look stricken, uncertain about where to go next, and finally put his arms around her. "I *am* proud of you," he would say, now on the defensive. And then, in defeat, "I think we can make this work." Her mother would watch the whole performance in silence, knowing in advance how it would end.

The town was sleepy. Compared to Cairo, the street traffic was like a silent film, and the pedestrians were merely walking, rather than fleeing for their lives. When Aisha stepped out of the taxi in front of her house, her sleeve brushed against the side mirror, adding an ochre stain to her ensemble. *The dust was dirtier in Cairo,* she reflected, *but dustier here.* Noor greeted her in the hallway, and then, pressing an index finger to her lips, pulled her conspiratorially into the small room beside the kitchen.

"You came back in the nick of time," Noor whispered. "Papa was making flight reservations when you texted Mama. But *now* what are you going to do?"

Coolly, Aisha explained her plan, adding that she had every

intention of returning and completing the graduate program in Cairo. Getting out of Nablus was the best thing she ever did, Aisha told Noor, and "everybody knows it."

Aisha was in costume for her performance— hair tastefully covered, long sleeves, no earrings, understated shoes. After a family dinner eaten mostly in silence, the curtain went up in her father's dark study, witnessed by several ancestors staring out of black and white photographs on book-lined shelves. The libretto was followed, exactly as rehearsed. This crisis was averted, and harmony restored. During their embrace, Aisha could tell that her father knew he had been maneuvered, but he accepted it with dignity.

In a coded text message that night, Aisha informed Leila that she would be returning to Cairo soon, the delicate matter having been resolved. Carefully following Leila's instructions, Aisha spent the next three days conspicuously meeting everyone she knew in Nablus to be sure they knew all about her life as a student in Cairo. She even accepted a surprise invitation from Amir to meet for coffee and brought along one of the helpful props provided by Leila, a dry monograph on political science, aggressively annotated and highlighted in orange to convey authenticity to her graduate student cover story.

Chapter 14

PERSIAN restaurants were popular in Dubai, an odd social contra-
diction considering that Persia was the existential hobgoblin that
haunted Emiratis more than any other. Their restaurants were presumed to be dens of Shiite conspiracy and surveillance, but people
went anyway. A few were even stylish, including Darya House, where
Mr. Swallow had booked a corner table for Katrina, Amir, and the
executive team from Bank Von Raab's client, Al Sharq Trading. In
the dim light of the restaurant, Katrina's usual phosphorus glow was
softened, and she looked a little less like the Swedish ice sculpture
that Amir imagined whenever he was with her in her office. Amir
had studied the client binders carefully and felt well prepared to
dive into the specifics of the client's portfolio. But he would watch
Katrina carefully for signals, before volunteering an opinion about
anything. He understood generally that the dinner was intended to
persuade Al Sharq to enlarge its position, but it wasn't clear why
Amir was there, except to watch.

Typical among Emirati trading firms, the chairman was a distinguished older man from one of the better families, Bedouin and
only one generation out of a tent, but now elegant and serene, as if
holding court in the Dorchester lobby, as indeed he frequently was.

The chairman rarely spoke. His son, Khalid, sat at his right, more animated and arrogant, speaking in the flat American English tone that he picked up in college in Oregon. And as Katrina had told Amir to expect, their "office director" was the loudest voice at the table. Lebanese, late-thirties, with slick hair, two mobile phones, a pack of Marlboros, and a frantic manner that seemed fueled by Dexedrine and Turkish coffee. In the Gulf, the office directors handled all the dirty details, in exchange for which a reasonable level of embezzlement was tolerated. The arrangement created a business environment in which the fast-talking Beiruti constantly behaved as if his job was on the line, and this meant he would ostentatiously (and tediously) fight for every last trivial concession and basis point.

Katrina's presence was highly tactical. These men were unsettled in the presence of a powerful European woman, intimidated by her knowledge of finance, bewildered by her inscrutable calm, but intensely gracious, insisting that all food and beverage deliveries to the table must be offered first to her. Katrina manipulated this chemistry masterfully, directing her eyes at the chairman, and speaking almost as seldom as he. She let the office director prolong his monologue about the bank's management fees until the topic and his manner became irritating and embarrassing to his employers, at which point Khalid directed a withering look in his direction, followed by a firm, "Khalas"—finished, enough, and shut up.

Katrina never asked for more money but skillfully painted lovely pictures of new investment opportunities available only to Bank Von Raab's most select clients. She referred to them as like-minded families who were "building wealth for future generations." It was a universal language. The next generation of the Beverly Hillbillies—whether from Tulsa, Mumbai, or Dubai—will go to Stanford, summer in Ibiza, and shop at Art Basel. The word "discretion" made its appearance often, but not too often, and always was received with reverence and a moment of silence.

Turning to the chairman, and apologizing to the table for a private aside, Khalid spoke to his father in Arabic. Amir noted several references to their "investors," and a favorable report on the bank's understanding of their business. The chairman leaned back, apparently persuaded. He mumbled something to his son in Arabic, which

Amir recognized as, "Let's go ahead." The whale was subdued.

As the table was cleared and coffee served, a large sum of money was mentioned. It was agreed that Amir would follow up with the Beiruti on the details. With business thus concluded in a mutually satisfying climax, the evening settled into a tranquil calm of soft-spoken pleasantries, like post-coital nuzzling. "Yes, good for me too," they all seemed to be saying.

As they left the restaurant, with unctuous handshaking from the Persian owner, Katrina offered a ride to Amir. Her driver opened the car door for him before he could respond. They were quiet as the car gracefully joined the late evening constellation of taillights.

"That went well," Katrina finally said.

Eager to appear useful, Amir spoke up. "You probably picked this up in the Arabic conversation, but the chairman made a few references to his *investors*. Who is he talking about?"

"It's an extended family," she said, "but the numbers are too big for just that. And their trading business doesn't generate enough cash flow for this kind of investment. But they have steadily increased their portfolio in the past two years. I think there's more where that came from."

Katrina looked out at the traffic and the dark buildings in the night skyline. "This is a perfect client for you to develop, Amir. There was good chemistry at the table. I want you to spend time with them. Get to know their business. Find out more about their investors, if you can, and let's keep growing their portfolio."

The driver dropped Katrina first, inside a gated compound of stylish villas on land reclaimed from the soupy water of the Gulf. Before the car door opened to the humid night air, she smiled with mischief. "This is going to be fun," Katrina said. "I will send Richard to you tomorrow to explain your entertainment budget. Our colleagues in Vaduz understand how this works. You will have everything you need."

Back in the chlorinated atmosphere of his flat, Amir felt newly relevant. He considered upgrading his wardrobe. Or joining the body sculpting gym that sent him constant unsolicited text messages. *Maybe I will redecorate this flat,* he thought. That reminded him of Fiona and her art collection, a haunting memory of their last evening together. But his scars from that encounter were suddenly more bearable. Whatever personality profile or sordid private details she may have shared with her superiors at Bank Von Raab obviously had not crippled him or his future in wealth management. Katrina seemed happy to give Amir a chance.

Before calling it a night, and before slipping on a pair of eyeshades provided during his last Emirates flight, Amir made a hopeful visit to Aisha's feed. Nothing new. But like a return visit to a beloved museum, Amir always made fresh discoveries in the collection of images he had studied many times before. In the darkness of his bedroom, he lingered at a photograph in which she was speaking to the camera and gesturing with her right hand, as if directing the composition of the shot. As she so often was in Amir's memories, Aisha was in command. Master of her destiny. Unburdened by doubt. In the image, a shaft of light fell upon her lovely face, which made it seem as if she was chosen for a special purpose. In the far distant background haze, over her shoulder, he could just recognize the white cap of Chephren's pyramid, and its defiant remnants of unplundered limestone. A detail in the photo he had not noticed before. Once more, as he closed the page, Aisha remained out of reach.

Chapter 15.

THE clock was ticking back in Cairo. When Aisha returned after a long weekend, confident in the resolution of her family crisis, she threw herself into aggressive absorption of the remaining training. Leila noticed a sense of urgency, as if the return to Nablus had lit a fuse. At Aisha's suggestion, they started their days earlier and ended later. For security reasons, Leila refused Aisha's request to take some of the binders back to the Semiramis to study at night, but she had meticulous notes in the perfect penmanship of a Catholic schoolgirl that filled her evenings with deep concentration. In their daytime sessions, Aisha began to finish sentences that Leila started. She had mastered the vocabulary, at least, of espionage. It was clear that she would be ready, and if she survived, she would be a formidable weapon. Leila noted this in her reports, and when copies arrived on Captain Sadegh's desk at Prison 59, he smiled with pride. He and His Boys had breathed immortal life into Prisoner 361, thus persuading Chief Nurse Hala to recruit and deliver Aisha, now a fierce warrior for Persia against the Great Satan.

Some of the role-playing in the final weeks of Aisha's training was clumsy. Leila, not unlike Mrs. Al Qasem back in Nablus, was never squeamish about discussing the mechanics of sexual encounters as tradecraft tools. Neither was Aisha. But the men in Leila's office who were propped up to act as mannequins for a few harmless scene-setting examples were ridiculous in the extreme. One of them, the IT expert, looked so uncomfortable that Leila finally ordered him out of the room, after a vicious Persian diatribe in which she accused him of confusing bedwetting with a vulgar term for intercourse.

Final preparations progressed to relocate Aisha with a fresh identity, while carefully maintaining her virtual existence as a Cairo graduate student. At modest expense, Leila recruited an actual student to preserve the fiction of Aisha's course load, exam results, transcript, even running email correspondence with a professor over a disputed grade in a course called, "Cultural Imperialism." When Aisha landed in her new home as scheduled in ten days, her Jordanian passport would identify her as Yasmine, armed with the elaborate backstory of a Christian family of academics in Irbid. Aisha and Leila spent their final days together in Cairo assembling a portfolio of photographs that would dribble out at carefully timed intervals on her feed, adding fictitious future date tags to correspond to the prescheduled postings. The composition quality, and indeed artistry, had improved so much that Leila worried that the photos might provoke suspicion. Perhaps they were "too good" and, therefore, inauthentic. But pride in their work convinced her the risk was low, and the photos were preserved in a file transfer application that would post them automatically on carefully planned dates.

The two women worked several late nights on the photo archive of Aisha in Cairo, editing the best shots, culling duplicative themes, and filling gaps with a few new images in less orthodox settings— El'Arafa Cemetery, an Austrian book shop on Sherif Street, and the unspeakably filthy Birqash camel market. Back in the office with her photo editing software, Leila kept returning to a series of images taken during Aisha's very first week in Cairo. There was an eagerness in her expression, and the wear and tear of Cairo's air was not yet visible. The best of these were shot in the rooftop bar of the old Nile Hilton, a pale blue LEGO® block of midcentury modern architecture that evoked early Bond films. Restored and renamed by new owners, the hotel still inspired nostalgia for happier days before Nasser's socialism wrecked the economy for good. Using the lens settings she favored for moody portraits, Leila experimented with positioning Aisha in the dim shadows of early evening light, finally announcing, "This is it!" With the camera now pointed to the southeast, the city center seemingly subdued in slow motion behind her, Aisha slowly raised her chin and directed her gaze at the lens, her lush lips concentrating the last light of the day. The effect was equal parts inviting and forbidding, a conflicted pose that Aisha delivered naturally. Leila fired a shutter burst and knew she had the image she wanted. With a black and white filter, and an imaginary cigarette between her fingers, it was Aisha at her most captivating. In their final hours together designing Aisha's fictional social media presence for the coming year, the two women agreed that the Nile Hilton shot was so good that it should be brought to the head of the queue for an early post on her feed.

Before Aisha left Cairo for the last time, Leila said she was her best recruit. Ever. It was sincere. This was unlike Leila, who normally had little admiration for the swallows she trained. Or perhaps, knowing the odds were against them, she preferred to refrain from sentimental attachments. But Aisha was different. She had calculated the risks, and there was no going back to Nablus. She was fiercely determined to complete this mission inside the prescribed six-month timetable. She would collect her fee and her new passport, as agreed, and then disappear into London society with enough money and fake credentials to cancel her past and guarantee her future—one more beautiful interior decorator with an ambiguous history, sipping champagne in Berkeley Square, watching her portfolio grow. In Aisha's cold calculation, everyone would get what they wanted, and the Great Game between Tehran and Washington would grind on with different chess pieces.

On the flight from Cairo, Aisha remembered her first encounter with Chief Nurse Hala, and the twisted path that led to her exodus from Nablus. It was a tense time. During Aisha's last year at university, her mother had a cancer scare, and the inexperienced doctors were too quick to prescribe taxanes in reckless doses that produced terrifying side effects. Late one night, Aisha's mother burst into her bedroom in a panicked state, shaking and clutching brittle hair in her fist. They went together to the ICU, in a harrowing taxi ride with a clearly intoxicated driver. The stricken, once beautiful, woman in the back seat howled like a mortally wounded animal. When they arrived to abruptly break the silence of the hospital, Aisha was horrified to see her mother berate Chief Nurse Hala for incompetence, as if she was responsible for the diagnostic sloppiness of the resident oncologist.

The chief nurse was calm in the face of withering verbal abuse from Aisha's mother, and eventually, the hysteria subsided into quiet tears. But if her mother was ashamed of her performance, it was not evident to Aisha. Chief Nurse Hala was the model of cool professionalism as she assembled the patient's vitals, consulted the on-call resident by telephone from another dark corner of the hospital, and sedated Mrs. Dajani. After leaving her patient, now reclining quietly in an observation room attended by a junior nurse, the chief nurse sat with Aisha alone on a battered bench outside in the stale night air near an overflowing trash bin and a mound of cigarette butts.

"I apologize," Aisha said softly. "She's upset."

Chief Nurse Hala was silent for a moment but then surprised Aisha. "Your mother is a very special woman. I admire her. And she's right. This hospital, this wretched town, the so-called doctors . . . we can't possibly give her the care she needs. She should be in Geneva or London."

"Hah, we all should be in Geneva or London," Aisha responded sharply. "Wouldn't that be nice?"

During the next four weeks, Aisha and her mother made several return visits to the hospital, invariably at night, as her treatments lurched chaotically between extreme medication and criminal neglect. At times, it was all but certain that death was imminent. Her body weight plummeted, and that magnificent statuesque poise of a Dajani matriarch was reduced to an unsteady, bent ghost. Chief Nurse Hala became a reassuring presence for Aisha during long nights in the ICU, and entirely out of character, Aisha began to confide in her.

Of course, Aisha knew that Chief Nurse Hala was Amir's mother. But this was a fact of no particular consequence to either woman. There were few degrees of separation and almost no secrets among the inhabitants of Nablus. Spatial proximity was nothing of significance, compared to the rigid grid lines of social hierarchy that governed every Nabulsi's boundaries. Even as Aisha and Chief Nurse Hala became ever more intimate, with Aisha eagerly sharing her personal secrets and looking for help, the subject of Amir never came up.

In the end, Aisha's mother recovered. It was not cancer after all, but an undiscovered septicemia acquired during a careless blood test at the superbly named Nablus Martyrs Hospital. In the brutal race that followed, the undiagnosed infection competed with toxic treatment of the misdiagnosed ductal carcinoma to decide which would kill her first. It was the chief nurse who finally countermanded instructions from the distracted oncologist, suspended the ill-advised cancer therapies, and conducted the simple test that revealed the near-fatal infection. Although the patient was saved, and even restored to most of her former glory, she never returned to the ICU to thank Chief Nurse Hala. Among women of very different strata in Nablus, the social code did not contemplate such gestures, which were as unthinkable as they were manifestly right. But Aisha knew what happened, and it only cemented her faith in the chief nurse as a rare source of good judgment.

For months after her mother's medical misadventure, Aisha would return to the ICU for late evening chats with Chief Nurse Hala. She would bring coffee, occasionally kunafeh, and the two of them sat outside in privacy, where Aisha did most of the talking. The chief nurse was a private person, sharing almost nothing about her past.

She was a patient listener, and there was, thought Aisha, *something wise about her.* But she was cautious about dispensing advice, which frustrated Aisha, who found herself pleading sometimes.

"I'm miserable here. Tell me what I should do," Aisha begged.

The recurring theme was Aisha's slow but certain suffocation in Nablus. It was a common affliction, and most people managed it by blaming the familiar malefactors, engaging in trivial forms of disobedience, or self-medicating. Aisha refused those options but had fashioned no better alternatives. Chief Nurse Hala's "Geneva or London" remark resonated, not because Aisha knew much about either—she didn't—but in her imagination, they became proxies for the life she wanted to live. Relentless travel via social media rein-forced those choices, and the pretty pictures eliminated all doubts.

It was a long time before the chief nurse offered to help, and when she did, the suggestion was so subtle that Aisha nearly missed it. It was buried deeply in obligatory rhetoric about the necessity of securing the blessings of Aisha's family, and considering her parents' feelings on the subject, and remembering that Aisha was still young, and so on. *This was the curse of membership in the Dajani dynasty,* Aisha recalled thinking. The local population imagined some meticulous-ly managed peerage system, in which births, marriages, deaths, and every intermediate event followed inflexible rules dictated by an an-cient astrolabe. No one wanted to be accused of encouraging rebel-lion in the noble order.

Even Chief Nurse Hala, who projected unusual self-confidence in her challenging near-death encounters with Mrs. Dajani, would naturally wish to avoid presumptuous meddling in affairs above her station. And yet, one night, amid leaden disclaimers that would be familiar in a London courtroom, she very clearly said to Aisha, "If you are interested, I may know someone who can help."

What followed was a teasingly slow unfolding of details, obscure at first, but tantalizing. It began with an introduction to Chief Nurse Hala's "friend," Dr. Reza, during one of his monthly rotations in Nablus. Aisha towered over him. *He was unremarkable,* she thought, in every way except his quiet sincerity. She saw none of the manipula-tive Persian that existed in the deeply held bigotries of Arabs. In his white lab coat, he projected comforting reassurance, and he listened carefully as Aisha spoke about her frustrated dreams.

All he said at the end of their first meeting was, "Let me make some enquiries." And then he was gone for another month.

During that painful interval, Aisha pressed Chief Nurse Hala for updates. She was noncommittal, but sprinkled crumbs of infor-mation about Dr. Reza's broad network of professional associations, his extensive travel in nearby countries—even Europe—and, mys-teriously, his "influential friends." But the chief nurse relentlessly added reminders that Aisha must "take care" to consult with her family about her future, and not "get ahead of herself." Finally, Aisha pushed back, with a sharp announcement that *she* would be making decisions for herself, and her family would "deal with it."

By the time Dr. Reza finally said, "I may have something of interest to you," Aisha already was determined to say yes and had begun the mental reorientation of a new life somewhere, anywhere but Nablus. When he explained that Aisha would be spying for Iran, she considered it merely a detail.

And now, as the pilot announced their final approach into Dubai International Airport, Aisha was more certain than ever that she was making a shrewd investment.

Chapter 16.

In the weeks following Amir's first client dinner with Katrina, the process was repeated, more or less identically with many more clients. The personalities and venues differed only slightly, and with few exceptions, the evenings ended with the same nods of satisfaction that signaled a new commitment of portfolio investments to be lovingly tended by Bank Von Raab. It was early, but Amir felt he was perfecting a personal style that eventually would make him Katrina's indispensable wingman for these dinners. Already, he felt the two of them were exchanging invisible messages, teeing up the pregnant pauses that preceded the subtle pitch, or the reassuring gesture, or sometimes, the coveted reflexive pronoun reference to "sophisticated investors like *yourselves*." In this delicate chase, harpoons would never do. Katrina might be the essential European at the table, but Dubai was a high context culture, with corners and shadows that Western civilization had jettisoned centuries ago. Amir could look inside these men, share their deeply felt self-doubt and suspicion, read the music of their language, and select just the right word at the right moment to persuade them that *they* were the shrewd negotiators with the upper hand in this deal. Here in the Arabian Gulf, investment returns were just intangible Western calligraphy, meaningless in comparison to the satisfaction of outsmarting your counterparty, especially a blue-eyed European like Katrina.

In her way, albeit cool and lacking emotion, Katrina encouraged Amir to see these skills in himself. He was careful to be deferential, and so far, had made none of the early career missteps that worried him obsessively: saying too much, speaking before Katrina telepathically provided the opening, or tolerating too many or too lengthy digressions into Arabic that might leave Katrina outside, rather than above, the moment. He even warmed to the sales role he was playing, despite years of assuming that traders occupied (and deserved) the upper floors, possessed of knowledge that transcended mere banking.

Amir maintained a meticulous journal of the client encounters, with granular details about the personalities, their positions in the local tribal ladder of consanguinity, government connections, menu preferences, even wristwatch choices—all cross referenced with their estimated business operating income, portfolio investments, and investor relationships. That last category, those relationships, proved most elusive. His journal was littered with question marks, or wild guesses. But Amir knew the investors were there, somewhere in the shadows, if only because gravity and other natural laws placed practical limits on the wealth that could be generated by something called "Al-Tahnoon & Sons Trading Company." The clients were circumspect and seldom strayed beyond obscure references to "our partners." But Katrina pressed Amir to discover those secrets; to "find the new money." She leaned hard on this point, sometimes using words, volume, and gestures that were entirely out of character for her. Alone with Amir in the car after one particularly long client dinner, which ended without the prized nods affirming a new portfolio commitment, Katrina nearly screamed in uncharacteristic exasperation.

"That prick, Hassan!" she said, referring to the client's CEO. "He's hiding the real assets. Do what you have to do to find them. Whatever it takes." Her voice was scary, as if ordering a drone strike on an *al Qaeda* wedding.

Amir knew it would be difficult to deliver what Katrina was demanding. The Arabian Gulf was famously opaque. Information did not flow naturally, and concepts like transparency and full disclosure were as foreign as plunging necklines in public. Traditional data sources in the finance industry were practically useless, especially for these clients, who studiously avoided tapping Western capital markets where they would be required to report such deep secrets as their assets and liabilities. Worse, they would be required to disclose *accurate* information, which was regarded as an outrageous interference in the internal affairs of places like Dubai, Riyadh, and Manama. The blank spaces in Amir's journal would not be filled by data from a Bloomberg terminal. So, Amir set to work building relationships with the local network of Lebanese office directors.

He had a natural entrée. Behind closed doors in Dubai, the natives never mixed socially with the help, but the weird social order placed Nabulsis and Beirutis in approximately the same orbit, which they navigated in dimly lit flats high above the city, where dinner parties stretched into predawn hours, propelled by gossip, tobacco, and whiskey. In these tastefully decorated settings, the dinner guests shared a safe space in which to laugh at their employers, who were ridiculed for their Bedouin provincialism and their childlike fascination with expensive playthings. The narrative was equal parts resentment and envy, sentiments that were familiar to Amir and to any modern Nabulsi.

Also, the parties were amazing.

There were false starts. Katrina pushed Amir to connect with the young Emirati CEOs, who occupied the confusing space between their Wharton MBAs and their fathers, who remembered poverty. She imagined a shared vocabulary—Arabic, English, Excel, WhatsApp—in which Amir could penetrate the encoded secrets that obscured Dubai's family fortunes. Because she insisted, he tried, but Amir knew that was not the right channel. He sent gifts from landmark European shops, with flattering notes on Bank Von Raab's weighty engraved stationery, and patiently requested audiences that would never take place. He went through the motions and kept Katrina informed.

Meanwhile, Amir targeted the low-hanging fruit. Consulting his journal for candidates, he recalled one client dinner in which the office director stood out for his quiet presence, dispensing with the more common show of indispensability in front of his employers. Rashid and Amir had exchanged business cards at the table, after the Emirati owners communicated with finger flicks that Rashid would attend to the paperwork horrors that accompanied the agreed portfolio commitment. It was Amir's opening.

Rashid was about forty, lean and well turned out in a finely tailored suit that was cut short, in the contemporary fashion of Dubai office directors. He had studied accounting in Beirut, but his family came from the Beqaa, a Hezbollah stronghold, which in the inscrutable logarithmic tables of Lebanon meant that there was an invisible asterisk beside his name, widely understood to mean "suspicious circumstances." It followed him everywhere, like a genetic predisposition. At their first meeting, Amir thought he noticed a subtle tension between Rashid and his employers, an unusual attribute not normally observed among men in his position. By custom, there normally was an equilibrium of suppressed sentiments: dependency, greed, treachery, subservience, and contempt. But Rashid had dignity and intelligence. Though he nodded in acknowledgement when the sheikh gestured dismissively in his direction, it was not a deferential bow but an affirmation that the matter would be handled correctly and professionally. By Rashid.

When Amir called him, it was entirely routine. They met in a conference room in the offices of the sheikh's family business, on an upper floor of a black glass office tower that, according to a plaque in the lobby, was owned by the sheikh. While presenting his credentials in the ground floor reception area, Amir noticed that the tenant directory listed most of the floors as vacant. Amir brought a bundle of trust amendment documents for signature in a stylized Bank Von Raab folder that Mr. Swallow delivered to him that morning. The weighty folder gave the impression that its contents were epochal. Inside were many pages of turgid text in the prose of English solicitors, who were determined to preserve their irreplaceability by employing a language that no one else could decipher. "For the avoidance of doubt," began dozens of subordinate clauses, which proceeded to create ample doubt. Rashid had seen it all before. As he and Amir quickly paged through the documents, Rashid applied yellow stickers to the signature pages, on which he scrawled "Sign

Here," in Arabic, with a cheap ballpoint pen. Rashid left him alone in the conference room while he went to secure signatures from the sheikh.

The tea boy came and went a few times before Rashid returned with the signed documents. Amir accepted the now priceless folder with two hands, in Asian solemnity, and then he and Rashid reviewed the housekeeping details, switching from Arabic to English when necessary to confirm wire transfer nomenclature, SWIFT codes, FBO references, and the other clubby vernacular of international bankers. Rashid and Amir both smiled at the trust names, more obscure birds of prey. It was a shared moment of unspoken ridicule of the romantic imagery to which the Emiratis clung, a generation or two after they had replaced desert bird hunting with indoor skiing at a shopping mall. Their business concluded, they shook hands, and agreed to speak again when the bank wires were confirmed. In the outer office, Amir handed the receptionist a package elegantly wrapped in deep blue Florentine paper with instructions to deliver it to Rashid. Inside was a bottle of very old whiskey, which announced itself with a giveaway bubbling sound when the receptionist accepted it. There was no message, Amir said, smiling to the receptionist as the elevator door closed.

In the custom of the country, there was no explicit acknowledgement of the gift. But a few days later, as Amir hoped, he received a text message from Rashid inviting him to a Thursday night dinner party at his flat, along with a few friends.

Rashid's wife, Rula, greeted him at the door of their apartment. She was holding a wine glass, and still laughing at another guest's joke as the door opened. In a disarming move, she reached for Amir's elbow and pulled him into the foyer, where he was introduced insensibly to four other couples deep in animated conversation in Arabic and French, who waved and smiled through a soft glow of cigarette smoke. The women were just a little overdressed, in strict observance of a fashion code among their set that included a tsunami of thick, dark hair, fierce eyeliner, and a form-fitting sheath dress that proudly announced their surgical enhancements. For these occasions, the style theme recalled Lebanon's late-twentieth century civil war, during which every party might be the last, and everyone behaved accordingly.

Rashid said hello with an unexpected embrace, as Rula glided Amir among the guests. Two of the women turned out to be Palestinian, both from Ramallah. They appeared to be unattached, or perhaps attached to each other. Despite their unfamiliar family names, they expressed instant kinship. They pulled Amir into a gossipy, improbable story about some corrupt local Palestinian official in Hebron who accepted bribes from Israeli intelligence officers and hid a pregnant teenage mistress in Jerusalem. The Ramallah pair were dressed as if competing with each other to expose as much of their breasts as possible, without being arrested. Rashid passed behind Amir, silently placing a glass of whiskey in this hand. The other men, presumably husbands of women in the room, were huddled around a professorial-looking Syrian man, who could be overheard calmly dismissing rumors about the imminent collapse of the ruling party in Damascus. Amir tried to lean into that conversation, but Rula pulled him deeper into the small living room where two Beiruti women interrogated him about his presence in Dubai. One of them, in a pearl choker and a black dress with a distracting zipper tracing her thorax, was smoking a cigar, a robusto that she held between thumb and index finger like a fencing foil *en garde*. Her green eyes narrowed like a venomous snake when she placed the object between her lips, leaving a slash of pomegranate lip gloss on the tightly wound Cuban wrapper.

"I don't recognize the name of your bank," she said, before offering an exceptionally well-informed analysis of the expanding Middle East market share of European banks since the latest Euro crisis proved that a robust monetary policy could defend the currency.

The other woman challenged her premise, offering very precise data about recent exchange-rate volatility, and concluding, "It's not the exchange rates. It's just that European banks are willing to look the other way when their clients' money is a little dirty. That's why they are thriving in Dubai right now."

Amir started to say something about Bank Von Raab's long history and reputation for "discretion," but Rula pulled him away with a pretext about helping with dinner. Some small children suddenly appeared in pajamas, shepherded by a diminutive woman in a head scarf. All the guests joined in loud, ritual admiration of their preciousness, before they were sent off to bed. Rula herded the guests to take their seats at the table, and as Rashid refilled glasses, a frenzy of food platters flew in all directions with no interruption in the several independent conversations. Rula seated Amir to her right, and in her elegant hostess style, gracefully inserted him in conversations with openings like, "I'm sure Amir has an opinion on this. What do you think, Amir?" The obedient guests would turn to him, and for the most part, he rose to the occasion, offering competent commentary on topics like OPEC's declining ability to manage oil prices, Turkish military meddling in the Middle East and haunting echoes of the Ottoman presence, ubiquitous social media pop stars branded with single names like "Ahlam" and "Elissa," and family scandals smoldering among the lingering remnants of minor European nobility. Between these gentle insertions to keep Amir engaged at the table, Rula put her hand on Amir's arm and drew him into private conversation about his family, or his progress in finding a girlfriend in Dubai. She listened intently, nodding with motherly interest. Amir noticed that many threads of conversation would reach a volume crescendo and impasse, at which point Rashid, at lower volume, would intervene. Speaking calmly and with natural authority, he was a model of equanimity, acknowledging the merits of all the positions expressed, and diplomatically steering the table to a new topic.

No matter what subject was consuming the table, Amir felt the shared sentiment among the guests that their presence in Dubai was temporary, like a long layover at a giant anonymous airport hub. There were income opportunities to be exploited there, along with indignities to be endured, but there was no fondness for the place, or even recognition that it *was* an actual place. Like Amir, they were all on their way to someplace better, and this—along with the alcohol—made them fellow travelers on a great pilgrimage.

Business was discussed only indirectly, with a lot of speculation about which families were ascendant in the great and fluid local race for status, where proximity and loyalty to the ruler were the essential measures, along with money. There were sneering references to the new-money manners of their Emirati employers, and inside jokes about the empty residential towers that proliferated like pernicious weeds. The women at the table offered viciously dry satire about the visiting oligarchs from semi-failed states who passed through Dubai with cheap suitcases filled with cash, and even cheaper girls, intent on rinsing both into respectability. Amir mostly stayed on the sidelines of these discussions, conscious that he and everyone else at the table were engaged in some version of this human laundry cycle. But when he interjected with a colorful description of the visitors he witnessed in the Grosvenor House lobby, the guests exploded in knowing laughter, impressed with Amir's keen insight into the charades on parade.

By the time coffee was served, there was a soft Renoir glow in the faces around the table. Amir had been admitted to the Club, mobile numbers were exchanged, and with three-cheek kisses, they dispersed into the night. Amir watched the two Ramallah women make hasty wardrobe adjustments as they left, raising zippers, and securing buttons, in case they encountered some local sensibilities in the elevator. Lingering husbands threw back the last two fingers of whiskey in their glasses and followed their wives. At the door with Amir, Rula whispered her delight at *finally* having a single man in their circle, adding that there were several nice girls that she would introduce to him. Rashid winked at Amir, and silently mouthed, "nice."

The night air was thick and enervating, like the hot breath of an old camel. Despite that, and the tedious traffic that never eased, Amir felt renewed. For the first time since leaving Nablus, he was sure he could convert this bet into a win. It would be boring for a while, he acknowledged, with no immediate prospect for a seat on a trading floor thumping with the music of arbitrage and naughty Wall Street lyrics about spreads and straddles. Katrina didn't care about trading; she just wanted him to find new money. That was the easy part, but if that's what she wanted, Amir would deliver. And once he had a track record, he was sure Burr Acheson would give him another chance. He thought about his close encounter with the eccentric Hodding Easterbrook. There was good chemistry there, Amir had imagined, and it still stung that he was handed off to Katrina and her obscure bank in the ladies' room queue at Hakkasan. But once Amir produced a respectable order book, he was sure Hodding would take a fresh look at him, and that would be his ticket to New York.

In the meantime, there was work to be done. Back in his flat, Amir filled several pages of his journal with names and notes drawn from his evening with Rashid and his guests, recording small details from brief mentions of local Gulf investors, their family feuds and succession plans, strategic marriages intended to grow their portfolios, and shadowy foreign partners with pseudonyms like "Dr. Strangelove," and "Mr. Mustard." He added this information to spider graphs and Venn diagrams assembled from his weighty client briefing binders at the bank, looking for connections that he could convert into the kind of intelligence that Katrina was looking for.

The early leads were promising, and his hunch that Rashid could open doors was spot on. Amir became a regular at Rashid and Rula's salon, where he built a network of the expatriate office directors, accountants, and project managers that kept the Emirati family offices functioning. Like Rashid, they were talented and calculating, highly educated refugees from once beautiful places that were collapsing under occupation, corruption, repressive regimes, civil war, or all these things at once. Like Amir, they all had a plan to be somewhere else. To Amir's surprise, his position with Bank Von Raab gave him stature within this group, as if he had somehow skipped some rungs on his escape ladder. He picked up their vernacular quickly, and also perfected his own style, projecting a slightly detached restraint during the good-natured shouting that was typical during their dinners. He always left the impression that he knew more than he could say. This proved effective, and soon his new friends started referring to him as "our banker."

As always in Arabia, trust was slow in coming, but it felt close. Amir found ways to do small favors for his new friends. His absurdly generous expense budget from the bank meant that he could pick up the tabs for lunch, but most of the serious entertaining took place in private homes, where the guests could speak, and drink, more freely. Amir adapted. He became the dinner guest who reliably could be counted on to arrive with ample supplies of the very best whiskey and wine. His gifts for the hostesses evolved quickly from flowers to designer sunglasses, and eventually to earrings and wristwatches. Inappropriate or not, the gifts always were accepted. The recipients sometimes were a little too grateful, whispering urgent entreaties in Amir's ear during stolen moments, or placing a firm hand on his "upper thigh" beneath the dinner table. Other times, Amir was able to help his friends with a bridge loan from Bank Von Raab to cover an unexpected medical expense, a school tuition bill, or an extortion demand from a mistress. Amir made sure he always was available to help in a crisis, making urgent late-night calls in the Bank's name to vouch for apartment leases in Toronto or Vancouver for his friends' children at university, or to persuade reputable law firms to defend their relatives after DUI arrests in Los Angeles or Miami.

In one memorable incident, Rashid telephoned Amir frantically one weekend with news that his youngest daughter, a six-year-old with dark eyes of heartbreaking beauty, was hospitalized in need of an urgent kidney transplant. Amir spoke to Katrina, and with her help, including some mysterious friends whom she did not identify, the child moved to the head of the pediatric transplant queue at a prestigious hospital in Zürich. The life-saving surgery was completed a few days later. Rula sobbed uncontrollably when she called to thank Amir.

"Our banker" lived up to his name, and the club members were in Amir's debt. Like a real banker, he faithfully entered these personal debits and credits in his now-priceless journal, which Amir hoped someday would become the definitive map for Dubai's hidden treasure.

Amir kept Katrina informed of his progress, without entirely sharing the details of his networking methods. He worried that she might not approve of the behavior or dress codes at the dinners in which most of his business was transacted. She was impatient, and at first, skeptical that anything useful would come from, as she called it derisively, "drinking with the B suite crowd." But she would let him run his table for a while and give him a chance to produce results. She never questioned his expense reports when they were brought to her by the ever-disapproving Mr. Swallow, who was visibly vexed when she signed her approval without even the most cursory glance or pretense of due care.

In the meantime, Amir and Katrina continued a regular schedule of her more traditional client development dinners—dull, formulaic, but seemingly successful. Still, even as they respectably grew the client portfolios, Katrina made it clear to Amir that she felt, somehow, the big prize remained behind the curtain and, so far, out of reach. On this point, she was increasingly fixated.

Chapter 17.

LEAVING the jetway, Aisha thought it odd that the airport smelled like a hospital. It certainly was cleaner than Nablus Martyrs Hospital. She was met at Arrivals by a uniformed driver holding a sign with her new trade name, "Ms. Yasmine Khoury." She had debated with Leila about the selection of this name. The Khourys were another old clannish family in Nablus, and after several generations, there were the usual accumulated resentments and prejudices between them and the Dajanis. But Leila prevailed. She had done her research. The Khoury family was much larger, and their diaspora was older and more dispersed. It would be easier, Leila concluded, for Yasmine to circulate in Dubai without suspicion. Everyone knew someone named Khoury. It was unremarkable.

Despite a thick haze of humid air that obscured the tops of most buildings, the city skyline made a dazzling first impression on Yasmine. She had seen images and studied the landmarks during her training in Cairo, but now, amid the aggressive newness and jutting heights of the place, she felt small, provincial, and intimidated. These were unfamiliar sentiments for her. The dense traffic crawled in the midday sun. Her driver was silent during the long drive, through thick forests of blue glass structures, and then over a causeway to a gated hamlet of modernist villas nestled against the sea. A few pleasure craft were moored offshore, looking more like decorative home furnishings than actual water vessels. Other than cars that presumably were occupied, and the occasional helicopter that passed silently overhead, Yasmine and her driver had encountered no visible evidence of human life since leaving the airport. Welcome to Dubai.

The driver made a muffled cellphone call as the car slowed in approaching one of the villas, which was unnumbered and indistinguishable from all the others. A small woman in pink rubber sandals, head covered, emerged from a side door, and waited to collect Yasmine's luggage from the trunk. The driver, still silent and inscrutable behind mirrored aviators, opened the car door for Yasmine, and led her to the front door, which was opened by another small woman, who was barefoot. Yasmine removed her stylish heels, which were making her feet ache, and followed the woman into a living room with a long glass wall facing the water. The room was decorated ruthlessly, with every visible surface and object assaulted and rendered senseless by Baroque drapery, gilding, carving, and mad ornamental flourishes. Grandiose chandeliers hung lifelessly, like victims of a reign of decorating terror. Bad oversize paintings captured scenes of cliché desert adventure—muscular white horses with signature tails carried high, and falcons in blitzkrieg attack dives toward doomed prey. A cold marble floor under Yasmine's bare feet contributed a kaleidoscopic trainwreck of inlaid marble arabesques.

"It's awful, isn't it?" Her new business partner glided into the room in a breezy caftan, exactly as Leila had described her. "But trust me, this is what all our clients want."

Nadia was one of those women whose features, accent and manner were impossible to localize. Mid-forties, sophisticated, educated (maybe, or just practiced), an air of the exotic (or perhaps the pretense of mystery), and distinct flavors of both Asia and Europe, as if she were born in a taxi on the bridge across the Bosporus. Important men, and a few women, were pulled involuntarily into her orbit in every room she occupied, rendered helpless by her magnetic force. She slept with none of them, but each imagined that they had established a special intimacy. She ran a successful interior decorating business from her villa in Dubai. This placed her in the inner circles of prominent new arrivals eager to make their real estate purchases look authentic, or the revolving door of diplomats trying to stand out in Abu Dhabi, or even some of the high-caste Emiratis who were happy to pay someone to legitimize their kitschy design tastes. Nadia knew everyone in the UAE and their darkest secrets.

Her design fees were known to be surprisingly modest, and she even worked *pro bono* for some of the diplomats, whose stingy government salaries tended to constrain their grand ambitions. Nadia could afford to be generous because her principal client paid a handsome retainer to provide cover for extended stay visitors like Yasmine. The terms of that deal were simple. Nadia would put Yasmine in circulation, with a semi-genuine job title, and make sure she was invited to all the right parties.

"Let me introduce you to my new design director!" Nadia would say brightly. In return, Nadia would be protected with plausible deniability, scrupulously *not* informed of any actual operations or intelligence gathering. Nadia had her own two-year plan in Dubai, and she was careful to make sure that, when the time came, there would be a clean exit with a nice portfolio, and no suspicious baggage exposed to sniffing dogs. Though she didn't know it, and didn't want to know it, Nadia's generous and protective client was Prison 59.

The spacious villa was ideal for everyone's purposes. Through French doors off the outlandish living room, there was a businesslike workroom, with a long trestle table surrounded by tall cabinets of swatch books. Nadia's living quarters were in a separate wing, which Yasmine assumed (correctly) to be off limits to her. Yasmine had a spacious suite on the second floor, with a terrace overlooking the pool, and a small windowless office accessible through a false bookcase door. Nadia put a finger to her lips affecting high drama as she showed Yasmine the bookcase latching mechanism, which required a four-digit code on a keypad and a gentle pull on a brass knob, all obscured behind seven volumes of Proust and a Larousse Arabic-French dictionary.

"For your spare time," Nadia said with mock seriousness, stroking the spine of *Swann's Way.*

Nadia left her to unpack, and the two agreed to meet later for a "working lunch."

Assembled in her luggage, Yasmine had traveled with a few wardrobe essentials, most of which were carefully purchased with Leila in secretive Cairo boutiques. The daywear was chic and professional, suitable perhaps for a meeting in the office of the Norwegian ambassador. For working evenings, the selection was more glamorous, perfect for a memorable entrance, and ideally paired with Yasmine's long legs, tall frame, and waterfall of luminous dark hair. Strangely, considering her own austere costume, Leila had a good eye for the right look, never over the top, always impeccably tasteful, and navigating that fine line between inviting and forbidding. Once her schedule of activities in Dubai was refined, and her appearance on the Very Best Invitation Lists was established, Yasmine and Nadia would shop together locally for more finely targeted wardrobe and jewelry additions. There was nothing that couldn't be bought in Dubai.

Yasmine quickly set up her small clandestine office with the tools Leila had provided for secure, encoded communications. As agreed, she sent a test message to her in Cairo. "The brocade wallpaper arrived." While waiting for the reply, Yasmine remembered Leila's dreary Cairo office, and wondered—as she had so often—what or who Leila had left behind in Iran to accept this grim job, with no apparent escape plan or timetable. The pre-arranged reply quickly appeared on Yasmine's screen. "Send invoice."

Time passed leisurely in Nadia's company. There was a gentle schedule of genuine work, visiting vacant apartments and villas with a measuring tape, and meeting with clients to gracefully guide them toward designs that were less monstrous than their natural inclinations. It seemed entirely natural that Yasmine was present at Nadia's side, and together, the two women quickly developed a rhythm that reinforced the clients' certainty that they had selected the very best decorators. After patiently listening to a fat, sweaty man from Belarus propose a dining room with murals of medieval hunt scenes and *trompe l'oeil* stag heads, Nadia would turn to her design director, slide her glasses down her nose for emphasis, and say, "I like where Viktor is going with this. Yasmine, doesn't this remind you of the flat we designed in Monaco for . . . what was her name? *Vogue France* did a stunning spread in their September issue. Do you think we could persuade the artist to do Viktor's dining room?"

"He owes me a favor," Yasmine would say, looking directly at Viktor. "He's expensive, but I don't think anyone has done work like that since the seventeenth century. I could call him. If you wish."

Viktor, helpless, stammered, "Please. Yes, you must!"

When newly arrived diplomats came to Nadia's villa to pore over fabric samples, they were paralyzed by endless variations of the same thing. Yasmine would silently pass a swatch book to Nadia, with an expression that might accompany the discovery of the double helix. As the clients watched in suspense, Yasmine looked with exaggerated certainty at Nadia and tapped her index finger twice on a rich sample of silk the color of a vintage champagne (US$768 per yard, thirty yard minimum).

"I don't know if it's available," Nadia would say with a worried expression. "It's a small fourth-generation shop in Deauville. This project may be more than they can handle."

The diplomat's wife, a desperate looking English woman eager to accelerate her social climb out of the ruins of Manchester's mills, preempted her husband's hesitation and suggested, "Tell them they were chosen by the *British* Embassy." She said it as if reciting a New Testament commandment from Christ.

After these grubby episodes, Nadia and Yasmine would wash their hands carefully and flee to long, lingering lunches, sitting alone at a corner table in one of Dubai's luxury hotels. Pecking at lavish salads, they laughed at the pretensions of the decorating business and the silly people who were its engines. But then, down to business. Yasmine made cryptic notes in a small leather notebook as Nadia deconstructed the complex social networks that connected Dubai's expatriate community. Because turnover was so high, she explained, new arrivals faced relatively low barriers to entry. Indeed, fresh faces were coveted entries on an invitation list, but like nineteenth-century Europe, they needed to be "introduced." Yasmine's local debut would begin according to the locally accepted fashion of attending events as Nadia's guest. As a pair of attractive women, with no apparent male encumbrances, their entrances would be noticed by those who mattered and enhanced by predictable, mostly unspoken, questions that were certain to arouse high-definition interest in Yasmine. Where did she come from? What is that accent? Her earrings . . . are they from Asprey? Are they lesbians? Nadia would make introductions (again, her "new design director"), but would carefully preserve mystery about all questions, spoken or unspoken. Yasmine would follow Nadia's cues, avoiding long conversations and focusing on brief, impactful appearances that would be followed by a dozen text messages appearing on Nadia's phone. "Who *was* your lovely colleague? You *must* bring her to our party on Thursday!"

Nadia was fluent in the language of influence in the strange circles that made Dubai momentarily relevant, despite lacking any history, tradition, or meaningful geography beyond its fungible air-conditioned cuboids in the sky. Even as they approached their customary expiration dates, the expatriates seldom were able to pinpoint with any accuracy their present location on a map, or their proximity to, say, the perpetual combat zones in Syria and Yemen. But they could define with precision who was hosting the best parties. Nadia explained the ruthless hierarchy, knowing approximately what kind of people Yasmine needed to meet, but scrupulously distancing herself from the specifics. The embassies, she explained, had chintzy entertaining budgets, and the worst were the Americans and British. Everyone joked that the U.S. Embassy soon would be adopting a cash bar tradition, but the joke was no longer funny after one ambassador imposed a strict no-alcohol rule, supposedly to honor his Muslim hosts. Some doubted that explanation, since the ambassador—a Texas evangelical who, during his Senate confirmation hearing, advocated crucifixion of physicians that performed abortions—sported a U.S. flag lapel pin with tiny crosses instead of stars. Another problem was that the embassies were in Abu Dhabi, a dull drive of about two hours from Dubai. Nadia described Abu Dhabi as a dour and unforgiving place, whose skyline ranked high in competitions for world's ugliest architecture, competing for the local version of London's Carbuncle Award, easily beating fierce competitors in Pyongyang, Warsaw, and Las Vegas. She summarized Abu Dhabi's embassy party scene as, "Soviet, without the vodka."

"No one attends the embassy parties," Nadia stated dismissively, "including their own diplomats and spies."

But there were better options, she reassured Yasmine. Just as whores were more abundant on payday, the weapons contractors, private equity funds, and multinational law firms were ubiquitous in Dubai, all selling easy virtue for top dollar. Their entertainment budgets were like legs spread wide, obscured behind a thin curtain devised by accountants who recorded them as marketing expenses. Their parties were organized with the same precision targeting of guided missiles, expertly populated with visiting U.S. Congressional delegations, military attachés, career diplomats, purchasing agents for subsidized state airlines, and sovereign wealth fund officials, all conduits for the big checkbooks. Among them, of course, *in mufti*, were the station chiefs and desk officers representing foreign intelligence agencies, unconvincing under their official cover as water safety experts or advisors in trade development. This was the intimate circle, Nadia said, in which Yasmine would find what she was looking for, "whatever that is," she added with pretended innocence.

And it was not really necessary to take it slowly, Nadia pointed out. The schedule of promising social events was more or less constant, slowing only slightly—actually just moving to less visible venues—during Ramadan. She would acclimatize Yasmine at a few of the bankers' parties, announced in invitations celebrating forgettable anniversaries like, "Thirty Years in the Gulf for Banque Finanz (Lugano) S.A." Nadia would make the essential introductions, and after a few well-timed entrances in which Yasmine's presence would be rationed just enough to assure that everyone would ask about her, the carousel would be hard to stop. Eventually, Yasmine would have her pick of invitations.

Her debut was a safe, smallish event organized by a German bank that was struggling to play catch-up among its continental peers who had built a presence in the desert years earlier. The bank had a venerable name, and a history of financing appalling, but forgotten, colonial exploits in the nineteenth century. But marketing is not a natural instinct in Frankfurt. In Dubai, the bank's business generation efforts fumbled between callow flattery and unabashed bribery. Still, they had a nice budget, and their newly appointed "Regional Vice President for Private Banking," who was the third person to hold the job in eighteen months, after some "irregularities" by his predecessors, was motivated to make a splash.

When Nadia and Yasmine arrived, there were a few minor sheikhs in thobes sipping carrot juice but a strong showing by the European and American companies that were hawking expensive wares at a prominent international trade show in Dubai. This particular week, the dominant trade categories were in-flight entertainment systems, aircraft fleet insurance, and software to manage passenger loyalty programs. The venue was a glittering "rooftop garden" sealed in glass to protect the guests from the implacable climate and decorated with explosions of exotic flowers flown in that afternoon from Pakistan. Guests were greeted by aggressively blonde models in brutalist hairstyles, apparently selected by the caterer to appear thematically consistent with the bank's provenance. Mysterious canapes circulated, but as usual, only the Americans ate. Yasmine assumed that Nadia would be a familiar presence, but she was unprepared for the palpable adjustment in the party's heartbeat when they entered. Everyone recognized Nadia.

Well-dressed men waved to her from across the room, abruptly interrupting their elevator pitches about avionics and reservations systems. Less well-dressed men, Americans in their boxy suits and cheap haircuts, winked in Nadia's direction. Women gesturing with champagne flutes would sometimes shriek her name, like fans of a teenage pop idol. More often, women cast an envious look in her direction, with a slow vertical scan appraising her fashion choices, which would clog social media by midnight.

It was a stunning display of social magnetism, Yasmine thought, as she stuck close by Nadia's side in hives of eager supplicants.

The dialogue was gossipy, but at least from Nadia, not trashy. As always in Dubai cocktail conversation, there were new arrivals and departures to be catalogued. There was concentrated analysis of the promotions, lateral moves, firings, mergers, marriages, and other liaisons that were material factors in everyone's relentless calculation of their place in the social order. It was obvious to Yasmine that no one considered Nadia merely a decorator, even if that subject invariably entered the conversation ("You *absolutely must* find time to look at my living room. It needs an extreme makeover."). She was more like the definitive repository of social intelligence and interlocutor of connections, large and small, that everyone relied upon to navigate successfully to their Dubai sell-by date.

As planned, Nadia introduced Yasmine as her business colleague but with an intentional vagueness that was certain to invite interest. Her debut attire, selected after several false starts in consultation with Nadia, placed a visual emphasis on Yasmine's bottom, which tortured the other women in the room with envy and resentment. Yasmine would smile at her new acquaintances, affecting a pose of beautiful inscrutability. Deploying the phrases and accents carefully practiced with Leila, Yasmine revealed almost nothing about herself, except that she was someone to be known.

With the benefit of her training in Cairo, Yasmine was quick to notice a young woman near the sushi station, aiming her mobile phone to photograph the celebrities hovering around Nadia. Looping her arm in Nadia's, Yasmine gracefully pivoted to face the opposite direction. A photographic record of her presence in Dubai was to be discouraged, as Leila had made clear. Just as they turned, the Austrian ambassador appeared. He was at the party to promote the business interests of some Vienna-based manufacturers, and, of course, to justify his secret five percent commission on the deals they closed. An elegant man with dubious morals, His Excellency kissed Nadia's hand and whispered something in German to her. She laughed and placed her hand gently on the lapel of his jacket, which had the effect of both encouraging his advances and keeping him at a respectable distance.

"And who is your lovely friend?" the ambassador asked. And so on.

The evening progressed like this, as the pair of women paraded among the guests. Exactly twenty-three minutes after they arrived, Nadia thanked the host, and as the bank's executives begged them to stay for the upcoming anniversary toasts, she and Yasmine waved while the elevator doors closed the curtain on their performance. As their silent driver returned them to Nadia's gated villa, the women methodically inventoried the names and credentials of the guests, plotting feints and enfilades to advance Yasmine's campaign in Dubai. Back in her quarters, Yasmine made notes and diagrams in her journal, before sending a coded dispatch to Leila with a preliminary report on the battle landscape. She knew that Leila, ever alert to the mission, would respond with fresh instructions before tomorrow's breakfast.

As explained to her in Cairo, Yasmine's objective was simple. She was to penetrate the American intelligence operation, presumed to be in Dubai, that was disrupting Iran's lucrative money laundering business in Dubai, crucially threatening the lifestyles and patronage networks of Tehran's leadership. The Emirati trading families had been reliable intermediaries for decades, and they still were trusted. But somehow, senior Iranian officers with impeccable revolution-ary credentials were being flipped with frequency, after which they and the ayatollahs' offshore money evaporated without a trace. The working assumption was that an American working in plain sight in Dubai was running agents inside the Emirati family businesses. But that was just a theory, and there were no hard leads. Captain Sadegh, His Boys at Prison 59, and Leila's cell in Cairo were certain that *their* lives quite literally depended upon solving this mystery, "as a matter of urgency," as they all had been reminded. For Yasmine, the game was merely transactional, but she knew the stakes were high for someone. Bolstered by her successful first parachute drop behind Dubai's social lines, Yasmine also had her signature confi-dence. From the binders she had absorbed in Cairo, it seemed there were only a finite number of possibilities. And the Americans, noto-riously inept at operating in the shadows beyond their borders, had almost certainly left revealing breadcrumbs that would betray their presence.

I can find this target, Yasmine felt certain.

Enjoying her casting in the spy movie genre, Yasmine dressed for bed in one of Mrs. Al Qasem's naughty nothings. As she slid easily into a deep sleep, Nadia's inbox already was filling with compliments and inquiries about her new friend, together with fresh invitations for Nadia *and Yasmine* to attend more of Dubai's very best events.

Chapter 18.

IT was late November, and the night air was almost sufferable. The traffic moved at a good pace on the E11, and there was no reason Amir would have noticed the white sedan that he overtook as he headed home after a mercifully short client dinner with Katrina. In the darkness, he could not have seen the two women in the rear seat, who had kicked off their heels and, uncharacteristically, relaxed into unfeminine shapes, taking a break from the hard duty of red carpet posing. One of them was writing in a small notebook.

Though he didn't sense her nearby presence, Amir was thinking about Aisha. In the twisted sense of world geography that Dubai encourages, Cairo seemed remote, and not on anyone's regular calendar for business or pleasure travel. For his colleagues at the bank, and among his new Lebanese friends, a long weekend in the Maldives was far more likely. Lately absorbed in his work connecting the dots of money flows, days would pass when Amir did not imagine a canvas or short film in which Aisha appeared, resplendent and just out of reach. But then, without warning, he would lose his junior banker focus, and the haunting, aching images returned. There were amalgams of noirish photos on her feed, which were appearing with regularity, each more artistically nuanced than the last. And though her photography seldom revealed more than face, hair and hands, Amir's imagination perfected a kind of radiographic imaging, mentally melting layers of fabric to reveal, in soft focus, neck, shoulders, teasing straps and hooks, a breast in bloom. And eventually, as if just beneath the surface of the ocean, her hidden treasure.

Before ending each day, Amir studied her growing portfolio of social media posts, always images of her, with Cairo unmistakably in the composition. The identity of the photographer continued to nag, though he felt grudging admiration for the artist's talent. It seemed strange that so much effort went into capturing these moments; work product that was alien to the dominant social media style of hasty, thoughtless selfies, empty of narrative, and plainly doctored by software cosmetics. Amir always returned to one image of Aisha, where he lingered, as if seeing it for the first time. It was the lifted chin with Cairo's city center behind her right shoulder. He had studied this photograph so carefully that he felt he could draw it, eyes closed, from memory; something he tried to do from time to time but abandoned because the graceful line of her nose was impossible to render correctly. Looking at it again in the darkness of his bedroom, Amir noticed for the first time that Cairo's Mogamma building was clearly recognizable in the background of the photograph. The depth of field left some grain in the architecture, but the facade was as familiar as Mussolini, hands-on-hips, and just as brutal. But something felt off. The front of the building, which faced Tahrir Square, was unblemished. It was not a trick of faded light or shadows since the afternoon sunlight fell where it belonged in other spaces on the image.

Amir checked the date tag on the photo and then returned to the Al Jazeera archive with articles about the fire started by the angry Cairo couple trying to finalize their divorce. Aisha's photo was taken and posted two weeks after the fire, but there was no evidence of damage to the Mogamma building.

Amir decided to let it go. These were the kinds of anxiety-provoked questions for which there always was a simple explanation, and he would not let his obsession with Aisha, or this anomalous photograph, distract him from his unexpectedly successful career at Bank Von Raab.

Focus, he told himself.

He closed his eyes and willed himself toward sleep by picturing spreadsheets of Channel Islands client trust accounts. *Peregrine, Saker, Gyrfalcon . . .*

His phone murmured. A text from Sara. Amir's correspondence with his sister had been increasingly neglected as he moved farther into the deep end of Dubai's pool of murky mixtures of work and play, and her patience had turned into anger and desperation. His promise to bring his sister to New York was not followed by any actual progress, and Amir's excuses about the stresses of his training program sounded repetitive and unconvincing even to him. For a while, Sara's messages were hopeful with practical references to her earnest preparations. She enrolled in an online SAT preparation course, scheduled her exam for English as a foreign language, and conducted elaborate research about America's byzantine student visa process. But every message ended with a plaintive tone, which captured the growing misery and desperation of her wait. The latest message string was more alarming.

Haven't heard from you in a while.

Going insane here waiting.

Decided to leave university and take a job in the settlements.

If the NYU thing is real, you need to tell me.

Now!

Amir turned on the light and read it again. It was not surprising that Sara questioned his masquerade in New York. He wasn't exactly diligent or creative in preserving the fiction. In fact, he had justified his indifferent communications by imagining that the more he surfaced, the more likely it would be for a suspicious inconsistency to emerge. A botched reference to the time zone or weather; a verifiably wrong observation about some New York feature; or a detail about his invented job that easily could be checked with a web search. These were just excuses. But Sara was smart. In the beginning, she was willing to suppress her well-founded doubts about Amir's New York story because the prospect of her own escape from Nablus was a powerful dream in which she could reside, at least temporarily, without much empirical evidence.

Amir momentarily contemplated telling her the truth. But he

wasn't ready for the withering recriminations that would follow. From Sara, there would be painful words like "liar" and "betrayal." From his mother, he expected worse. He remembered Uncle Jaber's cryptic warning about his mother's dark secret. "Something dangerous," his uncle had said. There was something about Dubai that really set her off. He closed his eyes, shook his head, and resolved to continue lying about his whereabouts with even more conviction if necessary. Anyway, eventually he *would* be in New York, and then no one would dwell on his hazy references to this brief interlude in his life.

Sara's reference to a "job in the settlements" could be a ruse, he thought, *designed to arouse my attention. But maybe not.* There were few real jobs in Nablus, especially for young women. A few chose to work in the Israeli settlements, provoking accusations that they were "collaborators," or worse. But Amir knew, and Sara knew that Amir knew, that this subject was more explosive than that.

For Nabulsis, their neighbors in the settlements were objects of scorn and envy. Scorn, for the obvious reasons. Envy, because in the popular imagination, the Israelis had somehow manufactured an international brand that was at once sympathetic and formidable. But the highest form of envy was reserved for the broadly accepted certainty—at least in Nablus—that their female neighbors from Israel, on the other side of the concertina wire, had magical sexual powers which they practiced with greater skill than any other women on Earth. No one knew the source of this information, but no one doubted it. For Palestinian men, who trembled with confusion and fear about the mysteries of women generally, this fact about their Israeli neighbors was merely lurid. For the women of Nablus, with their creation myth of historic glory, it was maddening and intolerable to be considered second-rate in this field. This created an epic paradox in which Nabulsi women were simultaneously determined to learn their neighbors' secrets and terrified that one of their daughters might be exposed to these dark arts. When a young woman in Nablus resisted her family's objections and took a job in the settlements, everyone assumed she would return . . . transformed.

Amir had his own experience with this peculiar reputation of his neighbors. His brief but intense relationship with the girl from his freshman chemistry class at university was like a religious experience. The girl, Aaliyah, worked intermittently as an *au pair* for Israeli families in the settlements on the periphery of Nablus. Indeed, she did return to Nablus with very specialized knowledge and was happy for others—especially the other girls—to believe that she did. An enthusiastic teacher, she shared some of this knowledge with Amir. He smiled involuntarily when he recalled the exquisite instruction he received from Aaliyah. But his smile disappeared when he thought of his sister in the settlements.

Amir telephoned Sara. She answered immediately.

"I'm at the office," he lied, "and I only have a minute."

"You always say that." Her tone was combative.

Amir tried to put Sara on the defensive. "Why can't you be patient? Do you think this is easy?"

"You made me a promise, and then you disappeared. Have you done anything to follow through on this? I don't believe you anymore."

He changed the subject. "What is this about a job in the settlements? Are you crazy? Baba won't stand for that, and your reputation in Nablus will be . . ." With a vivid image of Aaliyah on her knees, shouting commands and aiming her athletic bottom skyward like a French 75, Amir wasn't sure how to finish the sentence.

"I'm wasting my time at that university. The professors are a joke. It's not going to help me get into NYU, so I might as well make some money. An employment agency called me. They're checking my references, but if I get the offer, I'm taking it." Sara added, "Unless you send me a plane ticket."

Amir tried again. "What about Baba? How are you going to explain working for the Israelis? Do you really want to be considered a traitor?"

"Baba stopped paying attention to me years ago. He won't even notice that I'm gone. And who the hell are you to lecture me about politics, Mr. Day Trade Intifada? What have *you* done to fight for your homeland?"

Amir never came out on top in arguments with his sister.

"Look, I'm just asking you to wait a little. I need time to settle into this job. I told you I would bring you to New York, and I will. Just, please—"

Sara cut him off. "How do I even know you're in New York? Maybe you're in Cairo chasing Aisha, and you made up the New York bank story. It sounded fishy from the beginning."

Amir froze. From a very young age, Amir had a persistent, irrational fear that Sara could read his mind. She seemed to know when he was hiding something, and on the rare occasions when he was, Sara never failed to find the flaw in his cover story. He chose a tactical retreat.

"Aisha has moved on to bigger things in Cairo." With an air of dejection that had the benefit of being genuine, he added, "She was never interested in me."

Sara said nothing, which was unusual for her.

Before she could fashion a new line of attack, Amir said, "I have to get back to work, or the bank is going to fire me. And then we can *both* forget about New York. Please trust me on this and give me some time. Don't do anything stupid."

He hung up, unsure about how much of her tantrum was theater and whether she really doubted his New York story. He fell asleep quickly, and into a dream that haunted him for days afterward. Amir was a small child, standing in opaque water on a beach beneath a stormy sky. The water was above his waist and moving higher with the incoming tide. His mother was standing nearby, looking out toward the open ocean. Frightened, Amir called to her and reached out his hand. She turned to look at him, with no expression, and then turned away. She seemed to be expecting something to emerge from the ocean. Stunned by her reaction and unable to speak, Amir disappeared under a tumbling wave, and slipped into darkness.

The dream made no sense. Amir had never been to a beach, with or without his mother. There is no beach in the West Bank, unless you count the Dead Sea, and the Israelis restricted Palestinian access even to that perfectly named freak of nature. But Amir couldn't stop thinking about the blank expression on his mother's face, which was both familiar and terrifying.

The next morning, he felt a renewed sense of urgency to produce a few quick wins at Bank Von Raab, and graduate to Burr Acheson in New York. On the way to his office, Amir encountered Mr. Swallow in the corridor, and with no clear plan in mind, asked him to arrange a meeting with Katrina as soon as possible.

"May I know the subject of the meeting?" he asked, predictably.

Amir affected an exaggerated Eton accent. "You may say that it is a delicate client matter." He closed the door to his office.

In the several weeks since the memorable first dinner at their flat, Rashid and Rula had established Amir as a regular in their high season of soirées. There were some other favorite, recurring guests, particularly the flamboyant pair of women from Ramallah whose costumes and manners never failed to animate the no-tomorrow flavor of these parties. With each event, Amir widened his circle of new friends among the shadow intelligentsia of local business. By now, he had become close to just about every senior manager for an Emirati family office or trading company in Dubai, cementing these relationships with little private favors that never would be forgotten, especially since he made a point of asking nothing in return. However, he recorded them all faithfully in his journal as part of his increasingly detailed map of Dubai.

It became clear to Amir that Rashid was the unofficial grand vizier of a secret society of expatriate office directors in Dubai, men (it happened that they all were men) who disguised their power and influence through deferential phrases and body language in the presence of their employers. These were the public operating rules, but when it was time to actually make a business decision, the Emirati patriarch would summon his office director for a private meeting and ask what he should do. Men like Rashid knew how to manage up, and in general, their advice was in the best interests of the business. But quaint Anglo-Saxon manners like confidentiality, avoiding conflicts of interest, and refraining from self-dealing were just irritating insects to be swatted away by these power brokers who assembled after office hours to trade information and opportunities at the expense of their employers. In practice, they functioned like a Chinese central committee, running Dubai like a managed economy. And in the tradition of Beijing, they also managed to enrich themselves off the books.

Amir's new friends were careful not to share too much with him. It was an unspoken understanding that, while he was a confidante, Amir occupied a different position as a banker, and it would be wrong to compromise him. One dinner discussion came close to revealing that two guests had collaborated to arrange for their respective employers to bid on the same hotel purchase, substantially inflating the purchase price, and triggering a premium agent's commission that kicked back to both of the office directors. Rashid gently sidelined that discussion just before the punchline, one of many times that he stepped in to maintain the delicate balance by which Amir became well informed but not a co-conspirator.

The "nice girls" that Rula had promised to introduce to Amir proved to be an unwelcome distraction. The first was a recently divorced, very distant cousin in the labyrinth of Rula's family from Sidon. She spoke in an angry tone of voice, even when describing her quite generous divorce settlement, which included a well-staffed villa in Dubai and an apartment in Zug, carefully chosen by her former husband's tax lawyers. Amir politely declined her dinner invitation, on the pretext of a full schedule of bank client dinners. She wasn't offended, and in her present frame of mind, appeared to prefer her own company anyway.

Another young woman was strategically seated next to Amir at one of Rula's smaller dinner parties. A striking Circassian woman whose family had fled Damascus during the interminable civil war, Lina spoke Arabic in that educated, refined way that many Syrians do. She wore a modest black dress and suede pumps, with no jewelry, which seemed like a pointed stylistic challenge to the other women at the table, with their incendiary fashion manifestos. Lina's understatement was noticed, particularly by the Ramallah twins, who responded during dinner by adjusting their postures uncomfortably to restrain the natural designs and impulses of their flimsy bodice garments and the sculptures beneath.

Amir felt some attraction to Lina. Despite misgivings about being distracted from his Dubai exit plan, he suggested they meet again. Rula was ecstatic, flooding Amir with ideas for date venues.

They met for dinner at a high-style Japanese restaurant near the marina, in a dining room that was so minimalist and dark that Amir had to rely on Lina's golden hair to provide the crucial evidence that she actually was present at the table. She was nervous, and Amir pitched softballs to try to unlock some rudimentary dinner conversation. Eventually, he was successful, though he opened the wrong door, and regretted it immediately. In a halting narration, Lina told the story of her family's flight from Syria when she was a teenager, a harrowing and violent experience that obviously left her scarred, emotionally and worse. She cried, and between sobs, made sounds that reminded Amir of a small animal taking its last breath in the teeth of a predator. It seemed like the right gesture, so he reached his hand across the table to touch Lina's forearm gently. She recoiled with fearsome and unnatural force, toppling a delicate ceramic sake bottle and the overflowing cup that had just been poured for her, which crashed on the tile floor.

After that, Amir did not encourage Rula's efforts to find him a female companion. *Why waste energy on that?* he asked himself. With the rich visual landscape he had painted to capture Aisha in his imagination, she was a powerful presence in his daily experience. His brief live encounters with her were extrapolated into a fantastically detailed hagiography in which Amir immersed himself. She was the intellectually combative classroom dominatrix, the flirting seductress calculating and delivering measured glimpses of that red bra, and the playful schoolgirl wrestling with sunglasses tangled in the deep ocean of her hair. From these snapshots, enriched by the gallery of social media photography that she had chosen to tell her own story, Amir invented fine details about her—historical, psychological, and anatomical—and studied them pathologically. It was like the PhD dissertation that he would happily continue forever, hoping never to complete it. When he was lonely, Amir transported himself to one of those familiar, perfect places that existed on the websites of wealth management firms. With the snowy Alps in the distance, beneath gently lighted winglets framed by the signature oval windows of a lustrous aircraft, Aisha was nestled in his arms. A creamy leather cabin seat carried them like a magic carpet, far above the wretched emptiness of Nablus, Cairo, and Dubai.

Before Mr. Swallow responded to confirm his appointment with Katrina, Amir received unexpected calls from two office directors, new friends introduced by Rashid. Each offered to place respectably sized company portfolio investments with Bank Von Raab and said "they would be pleased" if Amir would handle the transactions.

These were new clients with no prior relationship with the bank. They weren't even on the list of prospects. The timing was fortuitous. Before receiving these calls, Amir had only a vague concept of what he would say when he met Katrina. Now he had concrete evidence of progress with his plan to penetrate the opaque realm of Dubai family offices, and their money, through the maneuvers and manipulations of their unassuming staff.

In Katrina's office, with Mr. Swallow taking notes, Amir was triumphant. The bright white room energized him.

"I know you doubted this approach," he began. "It took time, but I think this proves that we can use this back door to grow the business. 'Slowly-slowly,' as they say here, but this is working."

Amir laid out the highlights of the new investments. These were not especially large, but he predicted confidently that more would follow. Amir leaned back in his chair and waited for the praise that he had earned.

Katrina looked at Mr. Swallow, whose lips were pursed in an expression of dubious reflection.

"Really, Amir, I expected more from you." She spoke quietly at first, but there was an edge in her voice that foreshadowed a building storm. Amir was unprepared for the withering critique that followed.

"Was it really not clear to you," she continued, "that the crucial goal is to understand where this money comes from? We are chasing our tails with these little one-off investments. These are just crumbs falling from a giant bakery, which is as hidden and elusive as ever." Her tone turned fierce. "You are *not* helping me. You don't know anything about these investors or this money. I gave you every chance to get in this game and show results. Now I have to reassess your role here."

Mr. Swallow was writing furiously in his notebook, recording faithfully the phrase, "reassess your role."

Blindsided, Amir quickly calculated the relative merits of a gracious exit, versus challenging Katrina's completely unfair appraisal of his progress. With less than total conviction, he chose to stand and fight, sensing correctly that she might not give him that chance if he left her office now. His voice was less than steady.

"I think, Katrina, that we have to be more patient. There is no cultural presumption of trust here. It's exactly the opposite. They will test the water—maybe for a long time—but if we stick with them, and show—"

She cut him off. "Are you serious? Are you really going to lecture me about Bedouin sociology?"

The room went silent, like the harsh quiet that follows a catastrophic car crash. Amir heard only the relentless rush of chilled air from vents above his head.

Katrina recovered her signature poise, which at this moment resembled the calm of a serial killer in a Hitchcock film. She spoke formally.

"Please work with Mr. Swallow to prepare the paperwork for these new investments. You can assure these clients that we value their business, and we will give them the same excellent service that all our clients receive. Meanwhile, I want to reconsider our. . ." There was a pause. "Strategy." She swiveled in her chair to face the computer screen behind her desk. Amir was excused.

In the corridor outside Katrina's office, Richard Swallow walked slightly ahead of Amir and then turned abruptly to face him.

"I will send you the trust agreements and ancillary documents. I trust you will add the necessary client particulars, and other mandatory conflict information." "Man-duh-tree," he pronounced. He paused, apparently considering whether to offer some additional advice. He started to speak, but then walked away.

Chapter 19.

EVERYONE heard the blast during Thursday evening prayers in Qom, almost ninety miles away. There were no news reports, but social media lit up with wild speculation, misinformation, and quickly, the Tehran version of truth. It was an industrial accident at a fertilizer plant located on the edge of Meyghan Salt Lake. Attentions quickly moved on to more pressing matters, including the latest episode of the wildly popular television melodrama, *Estranged*, which featured boundary-pushing images of the lead character, a fiery young woman who has fled her abusive husband. The public was consumed with analysis of a full-frontal head shot that revealed uncovered earlobes peeking from beneath her head scarf. Were the censors relaxing the rules, or was this a one-off wardrobe accident? Foreign journalists wondered if this signaled the beginning of the end of the ayatollahs.

Meyghan is remote. It never featured in any of the breathless intelligence reports in Langley, and it was not on any international list of suspected nuclear sites. But beneath the modest Mosaddegh-era processing plant for diammonium phosphate, an extremely dull agricultural product, the well-guarded stairway led to a cramped space where a dozen physicists spent their days designing delivery systems for a nuclear weapon. Essentially, their challenge was to fit an unwieldy, unstable apparatus the size of a taxi into a warhead the size of a urinal. They were repeatedly told they were the "tip of the spear," but joked that this particular spear needed to be the size of a mature juniper tree. The work was tedious, and the secrecy measures took a toll. The scientists lived, separated from their families, in an isolated compound near the dead lake, where the local cover story described them as "agricultural inspectors." In the nine years since the Meyghan operation was launched, two of the physicists committed suicide, four were arrested and confined indefinitely to military psychiatric hospitals, and the rest barely subsisted on cleverly disguised forms of substance abuse. One year before the explosion, the Revolutionary Guard determined that some form of mental health intervention was critical for the surviving physicists. As an experiment, two of the most trusted were authorized to travel with their families, and heavily armed chaperones, for a long weekend in Dubai. The experiment results were inconclusive, and the idea was abandoned in favor of less expensive solutions, like beer and prostitutes.

The perimeter was sealed after the explosion. Picking through the rubble after the explosion, and identifying the mangled bodies, the team that arrived by helicopter from Tehran was able to account for all the physicists but one.

The physical damage was not a significant program setback. There was no fissile material at Meyghan, and no crucial equipment for either enrichment or weapon-delivery systems. Satellite surveillance and the other enemy detection systems would record it as an unremarkable industrial accident. That was the good news. But back in Tehran, at the somber incident briefing for the most senior officers of the Revolutionary Guard, there were blank stares as the men in the room contemplated the loss of the entire scientific team responsible for designing the delivery of Iran's nuclear weapons. There were no alternates for this expertise at Natanz or Fordow, and Tehran's operatives recruited in Pasadena were useless, broadly suspected (correctly) of sharing intentionally flawed engineering at the direction of the U.S. military. The substance of Meyghan's considerable technical progress was entirely in the physicists' brains, now splattered against white boards strewn about a blast crater like a deck of cards after a saloon shoot-out. On what remained of their scorched and crimsoned surfaces, the boards were still decorated with handwritten calculations of nose radius, free stream velocity, and peak surface heat flux.

The missing physicist, Dr. Mousavi, and his family in Tehran, had vanished. The briefing team reported that the explosion killed the security detail that monitored all the physicists' movements, but Dr. Mousavi was one of the physicists who had travelled to Dubai for a weekend a year ago.

In the ensuing rage and recriminations at the top, including a memorable incident in which the Supreme Leader hurled a weighty glass desk accessory at the intelligence minister (his son-in-law), a few heads rolled before an urgent new mission directive arrived at Prison 59 and landed on the desk of Captain Sadegh.

"Find the missing scientist," the directive succinctly commanded.

Captain Sadegh stood in his colonel's office. He was not invited to be seated. Tea was not offered. There was an unpleasant odor of fear in the room, generated by the awareness that this particular mission could be fatal for the present company if the results were not swift and decisive. *There wasn't much to go on*, Captain Sadegh worried, noticing that there was only a single sheet of paper on the colonel's enormous desk. The security team that accompanied Dr. Mousavi to Dubai was dead. The written report that followed his trip was missing, including the recommendation to abandon further R&R experiments for the Meyghan team. The contents of the missing report survived only in the hazy memories of two government psychiatrists who were pleading for their lives for suggesting the Dubai weekend in the first place. In a blinding vision of the obvious, the colonel concluded that Dr. Mousavi had been flipped by foreign agents while visiting Dubai, and recruited for this sabotage operation.

On the grim walk back to his office, Captain Sadegh paused to look in the empty cell of Prisoner 361. Some books were still piled neatly on a metal table. At least he had an asset in Dubai, he reminded himself, though she was still wet and untested. His methodical plans for her would have to be scrapped. Now there wasn't time for her to patiently build a presence, networking on the periphery before advancing on a prime target. In the immediate aftermath of the

Meyghan explosion, there would be gloating among the Americans in Dubai who were responsible for the operation, and with luck, someone would slip up and make a smiling reference to "an unfortunate crop failure in the region" or some other sophomoric version of speaking in code. He had to move fast, while the incident was fresh.

Captain Sadegh assembled His Boys around a conference table and warned them that no one in Iran must know what actually happened at Meyghan. But, he said, it was up to Prison 59 to find out. One of the Boys distributed cans of a grotesque concoction of taurine, caffeine, and sugar, and soon there was a spontaneous combustion of wild imagination, unfinished shouted sentences, schemes that were hilarious and terrifying, and impenetrable references to story lines from gaming products with names like *Warriors of God, Vegas Assassin,* and *Alien Bloodlust Revenge.* What Captain Sadegh loved about these sessions was the complete indifference to consequences; not fearlessness or heroics, but a wonderful, liberating sensation that nothing really mattered because, worst case, the game ended and you started over. He didn't interrupt the random thought generator as it played out before him, and he tried not to let his presence suppress any natural imaginative instincts in the conference room, which in this moment tended toward sex slaves and slit throats. Magically, impossibly, he saw a few realistic options emerge.

Closing the door to his stuffy office, Captain Sadegh switched on the antique Korean air conditioner, a purely decorative feature that was loud but produced no conditioned air. He frowned and wrote new instructions for Leila in Cairo. From the assorted comic book plots tossed into the air by His Boys, he quite liked a simple scheme in which his pretty sparrow in Dubai lets it slip that she has a new Iranian client for whom she is decorating a flat. "A strange guy, very nervous," she would say. "Some kind of scientist with awful taste, who pays in cash, dollars." In the right company, this little tease might get the party started. If there was interest, the Americans would look for an introduction, or they might follow her. Yasmine would eventually arrange a meeting with her fictitious client, at which the American flip team would reveal itself. *It might work,* he thought.

Captain Sadegh contemplated his cluttered wall chart on which a cobweb of moldy string connected low resolution photos of a dozen characters with supposed links to the American intelligence presence in the UAE. He settled on two figures who he had nicknamed Spock and Kirk, pseudonyms suggested by His Boys. Spock was a pale, emaciated looking diplomat in the U.S. Embassy in Abu Dhabi, who was accredited as "climate change attaché." Kirk was a lawyer in the Dubai office of a Washington law firm. According to the firm's website, he specialized in "project finance," a fancy term for building factories with mortgages paid by future sales. Both had been on the periphery of Prison 59's radar for some time. There were unverified sightings of them, separately and on different occasions, visiting a hotel that was popular with the Revolutionary Guard's chief accountant during his Dubai laundry weekends. The accountant was clean, or at least he was back home in Tehran, and the money was accounted for. He said he didn't recognize the photos of Spock and Kirk, even after some coercive interviews, and reminders that his family was "under protection" by the Revolutionary Guard.

His Boys thought the pair were too boring to be good suspects, but Captain Sadegh's intuition told him their public profiles were dodgy. Good, but not great, colleges and graduate schools; gap years with volunteer organizations teaching in inner-city schools; early career government jobs in backwater agencies like the Bureau of Labor Statistics and the Office of Management and Budget; divorced wives back in suburban Washington who spent their days in maniacal fitness programs and boozy book clubs, and curious reputations for attending all the best invitation-only parties in Dubai, but never drinking. Mainly, Captain Sadegh didn't like the way they looked.

After Meyghan, things obviously had changed since Yasmine was given her original assignment in Dubai. Captain Sadegh wondered how much more they needed to tell Yasmine about her mission. Obviously, nothing specific about Meyghan, but enough for her to recognize clues that she was digging in pay dirt. She already understood the objective of interrupting American operations to turn Tehran's money laundering into opportunities to recruit Iranian officers, bribing or blackmailing them for information. And Yasmine already knew that Iranian scientists were the subjects of greatest interest to the Americans. All she needed to know was that her targets may have assisted in a recent exfiltration of a scientist after a sabotage operation, and they would be trying to repeat that success. Captain Sadegh sent Leila four pages of encrypted instructions, introducing Kirk and Spock, and embedding a few of his favorite phrases and visual elements from the manic session with His Boys.

The reply from Cairo arrived within minutes. Leila was terse. The mission was clear, she said, but in future, "kindly refrain from supposing that our asset requires such micromanagement. She is resourceful and does not require talking points or handholding."

Captain Sadegh smiled at the reply. *This was classic Leila,* he thought. The sparrows she trained always became her gifted children. She protected them fiercely, and even when their missions failed, Leila could be counted on to deflect the blame, sometimes to herself. *Leila could be a real bitch,* he thought. And yet, when Captain Sadegh recalled the summer week she spent at Prison 59 attending the colonel's amateurish counterespionage awareness program, he remembered a woman of uncommon style—confident, intelligent, impatient with the relentless posturing in Tehran, and seemingly unafraid of challenging the doctrinaire codes of behavior that shrouded everything in an unfashionable shade of black. She excited him. Especially now when she was berating him, Leila aroused his most prurient, un-Islamic thoughts of ecstatic bedroom tempests in which Leila gave orders while wearing nothing but over-the-knee boots and a shoulder holster with a Glock 9 mm.

Happily unconscious of Captain Sadegh's distant leering, Leila set to work recrafting Yasmine's instructions. *Less is more,* she thought, as she reduced the content to a single page of crisp bullets, stripped of foolish drama. Yasmine would deploy her exquisite natural instincts to disarm and expose Spock and Kirk. Still, she wondered about this mission, and the thin threads that led to these peculiar targets, neither of whom seemed to Leila to have the keys to anything. She suspected correctly a massively embarrassing intelligence failure back home, and the customary reaction of launching a desperate, hastily conceived counterattack with little chance of success. She had seen this before. Despite her reservations, Leila sent the message to Yasmine.

As Yasmine eventually would discover, Spock and Kirk were exactly who they pretended to be, though they both enjoyed and encouraged whispering about their purported ties to the "intelligence community." They believed this improved their social standing, and particularly, the quality of the invitations they received. Without some enhancements to their backstories, they both would struggle to get past the interns guarding the door to the annual Tax Haven Navigation Conference, much less the A-list events like Davos in Dubai or the Sovereign Wealth Fund Leadership Summit. But a little résumé fraud was well within local thresholds of tolerance for professional behavior, and thematically consistent with Dubai itself, in which the very best addresses had never existed until recently, when they were pulled from the shallow waters of the Arabian Gulf by massive dredging machines.

Chapter 20.

NADIA's villa was a palace, thought Yasmine, compact but splendid in its comforts. She never felt like this in Nablus, where the un-magnificent Mounts Ebal and Gerizim collaborated with the relentless occupation to create metaphorical and actual barriers, condemning the inhabitants to a sadistic version of death row. She thought about her family back home, lying to themselves about the privileges of their social status, and repeating absurd slogans about resistance and independence, all just excuses for living and dying in the pathetic status quo. Here, Yasmine felt free to reimagine herself, and she liked the results. Nadia had a light touch as her guide and companion, a stylistic role model who relied mainly on unspoken communications to encourage Yasmine to experiment. Their daily rituals were rich in comfort and variety, like a long, leisurely European tour that skirted the touristy capitals in favor of discreet private chateaus as the invited guests of the last surviving nobility.

Early one morning, before the beastly Arabian sun turned the atmosphere into heavy gelatin with all the qualities of napalm, Yasmine woke to find Nadia swimming graceful laps in the pool between their villa and the sea. The garden architecture skillfully screened the pool with elevations that simultaneously revealed the dramatic view and precluded unwanted attention. Yasmine admired her athletic strokes and then looked carefully to discover that Nadia was wearing only the bottom half of a minimalist black bathing suit. When she emerged from the water, Nadia pulled her hair back into a sleek mane and faced the sun like a Degas dancer, projecting her chest and absorbing the warmth on her breasts. Her silent dwarf of a housekeeper appeared with coffee and a fresh white towel, while Nadia reclined into a chaise. *This*, thought Yasmine, *was a picture to emulate*, imagining herself in one of Leila's artistic photographs, wet and bare-breasted, breathing heavily after her own morning swim.

She was embarrassed when Nadia looked up to see her watching from the bedroom, but Nadia just smiled and gestured in the direction of the pool, an invitation for Yasmine to take her turn in the water. Yasmine waved a polite decline, not quite ready for this level of exposure, and feeling quite intimidated by Nadia's presence, serene and commanding in her secret garden of earthly delights.

Only a few days passed before Yasmine herself summoned the courage to rise at dawn for fifty laps in the stillness of the morning. Sensitive to avoiding the appearance that she was imitating, Yasmine selected a different bathing costume, abandoning a suit entirely. The housekeeper was expressionless when she delivered coffee. Yasmine considered the miracle of this little performance, free of the judgment and indelible stains upon her character that it would provoke in her prior life. She had not thought about it before, but there in proud naked display on the chaise, with the morning sun eagerly licking drops of water from her belly and loins, Yasmine resolved that she would never reemerge as Aisha.

But when it was time to work, the women worked. It was not lost on either of them that their lifestyle, including their happy—sometimes quietly competitive—transgressions of all manner of local social norms was made possible by the ayatollahs back in Tehran. So they did their jobs. The decorating business was, in fact, demanding, even if Nadia had skillfully outsourced most of the tedium to an enterprising entrepreneur from Mumbai who seemed never to sleep. He was on call, day and night, to produce sample books, masterful color renderings, order histories, price quotations, and invoices. In fact, he attended to almost all the boring details of a client-service

business. And when the exquisite sconces, tapestries, floor cover-
ings, and accent tables finally arrived from their exotic origins, the
gentleman from Mumbai would appear with his industrious wife
and daughters to supervise their installation. This freed Nadia and
Yasmine to attend to their clients' needy egos and fragile confidence,
reassuring them that it was perfectly fine to pair Louis XVI with pale
lavender silk brocade.

Then there was Yasmine's other work. Inside her hidden cupboard behind the Proust volumes, she decrypted the message from
Leila, drawing tiny diagrams and arrows in her journal as a kind of
battlefield plan to reach Spock and Kirk. She was electrified by the
urgency implicit in the new instructions. Her glamorous but slightly
vague mission seemed suddenly transformed with more precise targeting. But it was also unsettling. By the explicit terms of Yasmine's
arrangement, there was a deadline for completing her mission, and
her exit package depended on success. Surrounded by upholstery
samples in Nadia's workroom, the two women set to work building
a schedule that would propel Yasmine safely into the orbits of her
new targets, arriving with just enough velocity to be noticed but not
too much for a rendezvous that necessarily must appear accidental.
Nadia did not recognize Spock and Kirk, but after a few discreet
calls and text messages with her vast circle of confidantes, she had
their dossiers at her exquisitely polished fingertips.

"Let's start with Kirk," she proposed. "He frequents the bankers'
events, where he trolls—or maybe pretends to troll—for new clients.
Those are easy invites. But he's also tight with the American military officers who run the weapons sales into the UAE. I know some
of them."

"The military guys are pretty simple in their tastes," Nadia warned,
"so you may want to tone down your mystery ingenue theme for them.
Think Methodist, not Milan Fashion Week."

Nadia described Kirk as polished, always draped in a tailored
suit, spread-collar shirt, antique enameled cufflinks, and custom
shoes made by a legendary cobbler with a shop at the Mandarin in
Hong Kong. A bit pretentious too. He used funny vintage phrases
that he picked up from his solicitor friends in London. A messy situation was a "dog's breakfast," and his carry-on bag was his "kit." He

kept his law firm in the dark about what he did in Dubai, and they didn't ask too many questions as long as the billings and collections outperformed the other foreign offices. The U.S. military guys liked him, Nadia said, because he understood their business, and he used the acronyms and code phrases that served as a kind of key card for admission to their little club.

Surrounded by heavy bolts of damask positioned like sandbags in a bunker, the women plotted a series of introductions for Yasmine, built around the seasonal social calendar, and the natural marketing rhythms of Dubai decorators, who were always welcomed as party guests. Nadia would join the initial entry points, to authenticate and introduce Yasmine to the hosts and influencers around whom Kirk hovered. And then Yasmine would fly solo.

The first encounter with Kirk was intentionally understated, designed merely to place Yasmine discreetly into his proximity. Nadia and Yasmine arrived late at a party hosted by a munitions contractor from Missouri. There were too few women, and their arrival made more of splash than either intended. Champagne appeared in their hands, but even Nadia's well-practiced air of social elevation was challenged amid the scrum of beefy Midwesterners and uniformed Emirati military officers, who were offsides in Nadia's imaginary playbook. As they had practiced, Yasmine was introduced but said little. The idea was to present her as quiet, not aloof. The Missouri men had nametags with the company's logo—a violent splash of color on bars, lurking like Obersturmführer insignia above names like Bob and Fred. Nadia kept the dialogue moving, providing openings for the men to pitch and preen.

Kirk was visible nearby, leaning into a hushed exchange with some military men in uniforms. He glanced up occasionally, keeping an attentive eye on new arrivals. Yasmine was struck by his presence. Perhaps it was the contrast with the brutish styles of the others present, who reminded her of the crude soldiers who pawed her in repetitive searches—ostensibly for weapons—when she passed through the checkpoints on the way out of the West Bank. Kirk looked polished and elegant, like a Habsburg descendant from a distant generation. He was holding a glass but not drinking. At one point, Kirk looked up and caught Yasmine's eyes on him. She looked away but

felt she had made a beginner's error, looking too interested, or signaling to Kirk that the encounter was not random. Nadia glared at
her when she caught the incident.

In the very brief interval between Yasmine's recognition of her
mistake and Nadia's glare, Kirk appeared with a bottle of Veuve
Clicquot, from which he refilled Yasmine's flute.

"You're not from Missouri, I think," Kirk said, with a pronunciation that deliberately sounded like "Misery." He was trying to be
funny. As he poured, Yasmine noticed his enameled cufflinks displaying the cross of Saint George, a mild breach of decorum in
Arabia where crosses of any variant evoke anti-Muslim crusades and
where British emblems are reminders of the worst of all scheming
foreign invaders, even more contemptible than the Americans.

Yasmine accepted the champagne, but before she could speak,
Nadia intervened with one of her clever distractions. She put her
long, lovely fingers on Kirk's forearm, flashing nails the color of the
crosses on his cufflinks.

"We've met before, I think. I'm Nadia. This is my colleague,
Yasmine. You're with Deutsche Bank, correct? We did some design
work recently for one of your colleagues."

The pincer movement diverted Kirk, who dissembled for a moment, flanked by Nadia and Yasmine, their upper torsos draped
loosely to invite inspection.

"Actually, I . . . How do you do?" He introduced himself and then
gently corrected Nadia, informing her that he was merely a lawyer,
but he did know most of the local bankers.

Nadia kept him off balance.

"Really?" she said with mock skepticism. "You look exactly like my
friend Wolfgang. Do you know him? He used to be at the bank."

Nadia was referring to a local German, who formerly ran the
Dubai branch of a household name German bank. He was notorious
for negotiating fat signing bonuses and then shopping himself to
other banks to collect more front-end pay packages. Wolfgang was
desperately in love with Nadia and fed her limitless expatriate gossip,
which she deployed to great effect.

Reluctantly, Kirk averted his eyes from Nadia's breasts and recovered. "I know Wolfgang. He's much better looking than I am, but

thank you for suggesting a resemblance."

Yasmine read the cues correctly and slid quietly off the pitch to let Nadia take possession of the ball. She introduced herself to one of the Missouri nametag men and listened politely to an earnest description of the peacekeeping value of cluster munitions. He was programmed to sell, not necessarily to consider the audience, and she let him complete his talking points. In no time, he was sharing a wallet photo of twins with braces on their teeth. Killing time with this unremarkable fellow, Yasmine was struck by the paradox of his profound harmlessness, and the conscientious energy with which he promoted a military product best known for maiming children. Looking over his shoulder, Yasmine could see Nadia deep in conversation with Kirk. He looked like he was trying to speak but was unable to find the on-ramp. Yasmine waited for a signal, and finally it came. Their faces turned in her direction, and both their flutes leaned subtly toward Yasmine, like flowers reaching for the sun.

Nadia was in the process of disarming Kirk. She could see that he was the kind of man who carefully rehearsed all his most spontaneous remarks, probably practicing with a mirror while shaving, making slight adjustments in pace and expression to convey just the right insouciance. It was a technique that often worked. People probably wondered if he was one of those lovely characters whose backstory was vague and never quite revealed, but included Geneva boarding schools, weekend homes near foxhunt packs in Upperville and the Cotswolds, and equal comfort quipping in French and English.

Nadia was, however, a discerning listener, familiar with the inventions of Dubai's parachute class, who dropped from the sky with freshly printed credentials, fleeing failed marriages, career stumbles, or police inquiries. In six minutes of interrogation, Nadia concluded that Kirk was not who Tehran thought he was. The Iranians bought into his fake personality, apparently not understanding that this was never the profile of an actual intelligence officer. But Nadia knew this was not her decision. Yasmine would have to follow her instructions and carry on with Kirk for a decent interval, ultimately reporting that he was not a useful source. *Actually*, thought Nadia, *this may work out for the best. It was a safe dry run for Yasmine She could learn from her mistakes without tipping off the other side.* Nadia steered the conversation with Kirk to the decorating business, and then to Yasmine's "natural gifts" in interior design. In midsentence, Nadia's flute beckoned, and Yasmine excused herself from Fred's lively commentary on fin-stabilized fragmentation patterns.

When Yasmine joined them, Kirk reverted to his practiced air. "Nadia tells me you are here to rescue Dubai from its style wasteland. At last!"

With Nadia nodding her permission, Yasmine joined the pitch.

"That would be an exaggeration. But I would like to try some fresh ideas. The monochrome look has been dominant for too long. I think people like surprises in their homes; unexpected colors and patterns that provide personality."

It was stock footage but fit the bill.

Nadia put her hand back on Kirk's arm. "He wants us to help him 'breathe new life' into his flat in the marina. We'll work together, but Yasmine, you should really take the lead on this. I know he will love your color palette."

A site visit was quickly arranged with Kirk. Nadia, looking at her watch, reminded Yasmine of their "next appointment." And then, their champagne gracefully deposited on the tray of a passing waiter, Nadia and Yasmine executed a runway step formation toward the elevator, followed by admiring eyes.

In the car, Nadia was silent and looking away at the blurred skyline. Yasmine could read the message but hesitated before speaking up.

"Thanks for saving me. I know this was not a good start." She hoped Nadia would soften the impact.

"You're right," Nadia agreed, not gently.

Nadia turned to Yasmine with a withering expression. "Fortunately, he's just a lawyer cruising dull banker receptions for clients and younger women. He's not what you're looking for. But if he was, he would have *made you* in your first eye contact. And your little operation would be over before it started."

"I'm just going to remind you," Nadia continued sharply, "that I have other interests to protect here. I provide the cover story for you and make introductions. I'm going to help you. But win or lose, this is *your* operation. Don't make a mistake and drag me down with you. I have my own exit plan."

Afterward, back at Nadia's villa, there were no "good nights." The two women wordlessly retired to their separate spaces. Leaving her skimpy cocktail dress in a sad puddle on the bathroom floor, Yasmine sulked in her underwear at the small desk behind Proust, where she labored over her journal. Like a Catholic confession delivered in cursive Arabic, she recorded the details of her mistakes that evening, alongside a contrasting column with observations of Nadia's methods. Yasmine was determined to get it right. Nadia was almost certainly right about Kirk, she admitted, but a few more encounters were necessary to justify that conclusion and make a sensible report to Leila. Meanwhile, Yasmine turned her attention to Spock, and a fresh chance to prove that she was up to the job.

Chapter 21.

SINCE his sparrow in Dubai now had new importance, Captain Sadegh felt the need to reinforce his Nablus connection and get a temperature check. It was time for Dr. Reza to pay another visit to Nablus Martyrs Hospital, where he would provide hopeful news of the impending—all but certain, awaiting one final signature, any day now—release of Prisoner 361.

In a strange coincidence, on the very day of Dr. Reza's arrival in Nablus, Chief Nurse Hala ran into Mrs. Dajani. Despite the intimate geography and shrinking perimeters of Nablus, it was a clannish, segregated place. Chance encounters across social strata were rare, except in the stilted confines of condolence gatherings, or in this case, near the hospital, where Mrs. Dajani had visited a friend. The two women, startled and momentarily speechless, came face-to-face on the sidewalk along Rafedyah Street as Chief Nurse Hala, in her scrubs, walked with her usual intensity to begin the evening shift at the ICU. At first, it seemed as if the slender, elegant lady in the turquoise skirt and stylish handbag would just nod and continue on her way, and that probably was her strong preference. But in a choice that neither anticipated, Mrs. Dajani stopped and managed an awkward smile.

"You are well, I hope?" the chief nurse offered.

They exchanged more perfunctory greetings in formal prose, with automated, insincere inquiries about health and prosperity. Then momentary silence.

"You have children, I think?" Mrs. Dajani asked abruptly, surprising both women that she was prolonging the sidewalk conversation.

"I do. Thank you for asking. My daughter is here, on leave from her university studies. My son recently left us for America." Chief Nurse Hala paused, uncertain about the sound of that. "To work in banking," she added, in a nod to their mutual bourgeois sensibilities.

"Well," Mrs. Dajani began, unnaturally intimate, "I am sure your son will come home soon. It's strange that so many of them these days decide to travel and postpone starting a family. It's an odd choice, don't you think?"

Chief Nurse Hala offered a nervous smile, panicked at the direction of this conversation.

Mrs. Dajani continued, "You remember my daughter, Aisha, from our hospital visits? She left to study in Cairo. A graduate program in political science. I know I should be proud of her ambition, but Cairo? A wretched place. It seems strange."

Was this the prelude to an accusation? the Chief Nurse wondered. Had the Dajani social network informants, presumed to be everywhere, discovered Aisha's prolonged visits to the hospital, and implicated Chief Nurse Hala in her impetuous plan to flee to Cairo? Or worse, did the Dajani family tap its sources in Cairo and discover holes in Aisha's cover?

"I remember her well," the chief nurse said cautiously. The roar from a passing truck laden with steel barrels forced an interruption in their dialogue. Then it was quiet, and Mrs. Dajani looked at her wristwatch.

"Well . . .," they both said, as the sidewalk encounter appeared to have run its course. And then, after stiff valedictions, they continued on their separate ways.

Chief Nurse Hala's heart rate remained elevated until she reached the staff entrance of the hospital, where she stopped amid the landscape of cigarette butts to breathe deeply after the unsettling encounter. In the years since her covert collaboration with Dr. Reza began, there had never been a hint of suspicion, at least not this kind of suspicion. She was happy for the nursing staff to suspect that she and Dr. Reza were fornicating with abandon on the Hindenburg chair in the records room, even though he had never once touched her. If anything, that richly imagined story provided cover for her. Even if it *had* been true, it was hardly an infraction likely to have consequences. Certainly, the grifting hospital administrator would not risk exposing his augmented compensation schemes—or indeed his own indecent liberties with the young nurse trainees—by making an issue of Chief Nurse Hala and the visiting Iranian doctor. But the odd incident with Mrs. Dajani provoked paranoia and made her wonder. Did Aisha say something to her mother? Should she report this incident to Dr. Reza to protect the operation? If something went wrong, would this jeopardize her father's return?

Involuntarily, during her anxiety-reducing deep breathing exercises, she had a flashing image of Amir. It was the first time she had thought about her son in days. His adventure in New York infuriated her. It was blatantly disobedient and threatened the shaky order of her household. Even Sara was withdrawing into impossible schemes about studying in America, clearly inspired by Amir. Worst of all, it distracted Chief Nurse Hala, at this most delicate moment, from the defining purpose of her life. But she felt helpless to change the situation with Amir. Anyway, she reminded herself, it was not a priority. *My children were just like their father,* she thought. They were all ungrateful strangers in her home, not like *real* family members.

She resolved to carry on and stop worrying. The stakes were too high, and the finish line was too close, to risk a course correction or an unpredictable reaction from Dr. Reza's handlers. The chance encounter with Mrs. Dajani was just what it seemed to be, she told herself. There is nothing remarkable about two lonely mothers exchanging small talk on the street about their adult children moving on with their lives. Chief Nurse Hala stood tall, recovered the steely facial expression that was her workplace trademark, and resumed command of the ICU for another long night.

Dr. Reza arrived just after midnight, on schedule, after completing his rounds in the outpatient clinic. Since his last visit to Nablus, he had added some uncharacteristic facial hair, sharply carved, and unsuited for his age and mild temperament. It was a mandate, he explained in response to Hala's skeptical look, from the "guidance patrols" in Tehran, the self-appointed guardians of Islamic purity, whose stilted educations assured that they would consistently confuse religious doctrine with back street fashion fads. And like those who feel surges of pleasure pulling the wings off trapped insects, they never tired of enforcing arbitrary rules.

The young nurses at their stations greeted the doctor formally, and then shot spicy side-eyed looks at each other. For show, Chief Nurse Hala invited Dr. Reza to accompany her through her own ICU rounds, during which he studied some of the critical care patient charts and commented thoughtfully on the treatment plans. In addition to his other role, he was a skilled physician—well-trained, experienced, and compassionate. During the long war with Iraq, when he was conscripted to serve with triage units near the front lines, Dr. Reza had attended to thousands of young Iranian soldiers whose limbs, and sometimes heads, remained behind on the battlefield. That crushing experience left him resolved to withdraw entirely into his profession, suppressing all political and moral judgments, and finding solace, purpose and clarity in patient care. When he was approached by Prison 59 to carry messages to Nablus under the cover of his medical duties, he asked no questions, and simply did as he was told. The lunacy of such people, with their endless wars and collateral damage, would not distract him. Because he lacked a sufficiently twisted imagination, Dr. Reza assumed that Prisoner 361 was very much alive, and soon would be reunited with his daughter in Nablus, just as he would repeatedly assure Chief Nurse Hala.

The ICU was quiet except for the familiar background melody of several heart monitors. Alone in the records room, Dr. Reza and the chief nurse shared tea in paper cups. She was eager for news, but respectful of his methodical style of communication. It was somehow reassuring and had the strange effect of validating the information that he brought to her. This time, he carried a new letter from her father, abbreviated but enthusiastic, and produced on the same shah-era typewriter that generated all previous correspondence from his prison cell. The letter paper was artfully discolored, with carefully executed typing errors, all painstakingly contrived by Captain Sadegh's Boys to lend authenticity to the blatantly fraudulent object.

My dearest pet, it won't be long now. The doctors tell me my condition is improved, and it is safe for me to travel at last. I know it is real this time. Most of the others have been released already, and today I received a box of new clothes. They say I owe this all to you. I don't know what they asked you to do, but it will be worth it when we are together again. Soon. I hope you will recognize me, though I fear you will not. With love, Baba.

She read the letter a few times, never doubting that these were her father's words.

"What are the travel arrangements?" she asked, not for the first time. "After all this time, I can't imagine he has any documentation. And if the checkpoint soldiers suspect he came from Iran, we will lose him into another dungeon, maybe forever."

"They know how to do this," he said calmly, using the words he rehearsed before this trip. "For your father's protection, we won't know the details until he is here. You have to trust the process. You did what they asked. They will keep their promise."

He paused and looked at the door. There was whispering and suppressed laughter from a few of the nurses in the corridor. The chief nurse pressed her finger to her lips, and they both smiled playfully, visualizing the gymnastics they were presumed to be enjoying. For fun and mischief, she pushed a bundle of old radiographs off the table, sending them crashing to the floor. The noise dispersed the gathering outside the file room door.

"They told me your latest project is the most important yet," Dr. Reza continued. "Everyone was impressed that you were able to recruit the Dajani girl, and they think she is a good asset in Dubai. But they want to know if you think her cover is secure here in Nablus."

She never heard this question before and immediately thought of the strange conversation with Aisha's mother. Folding and refolding her father's latest letter like a postal clerk on the verge of a nervous breakdown, she feared that the wrong answer would derail his return.

"Very secure," she said, without hesitation.

Chief Nurse Hala watched him carefully for a reaction. He seemed to accept her answer with a simple nod, but she worried that

Dr. Reza suspected her of not revealing something.

"There's another thing about your recruit," he said, as if something delicate would follow. "So far, the reports from Cairo and Dubai are encouraging, but in Tehran, they still think of her as unreliable until proven otherwise. I don't know why, but *our friends* are nervous about this mission. Or maybe the stakes are higher. They want an insurance policy. In case she loses her nerve. Something that will persuade her to carry on to the finish line."

Again, thought Hala, a strange and unfamiliar turn in the conversation. *What is this? They trained her. They watch her every day. Has something happened to provoke this concern? And he never called them "our friends" before.*

Dr. Reza added hastily, "Of course, they would only use it if absolutely necessary."

There was an uncomfortable silence, modulated faintly and suspensefully by the distant music of heart rate monitors.

"Can you suggest anything?" he persisted.

It was her personal legend in the ICU to deal with crises, often multiple crises, with decisive action, delivered quickly, and without drama. The doctors, in particular, admired her for this. For this unique crisis, she calculated that it was crucial for Dr. Reza to return to Tehran to report that she was serene and entirely confident in Aisha for this mission. But if insurance was important, Chief Nurse Hala could provide that as well.

"She is close to her mother," the chief nurse said in a measured, sociopathic voice. She paused and then added, "Her mother had serious health problems not long ago. They might recur. It could be arranged."

Dr. Reza looked at her gravely, feeling compromised himself. In his too long association with Prison 59, he had contrived elaborate imaginary boundaries to persuade himself that he remained faithful, at least, to his professional integrity as a physician. This seemed intellectually possible if he was just carrying messages. He wished that Hala had not added those last four words. They would haunt him until he could fashion some new mental contrivance to pretend that he was not complicit in an appalling scheme.

"As I said, only if absolutely necessary," he concluded like a lawyer at a deposition, making a verbal record that this was merely an inchoate concept, not an actual plan in which he might be involved.

Chapter 22.

IN his chilly glass cell at the bank, Amir was still processing the startling encounter with Katrina when Rashid called. Amir had dinner with Rashid and Rula just a week earlier where, memorably, the Ramallah twins were absent, and the evening passed in depressing sobriety. Presumably, Rashid was calling to take credit for referring his friends with the new client business that had so totally disappointed Katrina, much to Amir's surprise. But Rashid didn't mention that.

"I have something new that might interest you. Can you meet me for dinner on Friday?"

Amir wasn't sure he would still have a job on Friday, but he agreed. Rashid texted him the address of a Persian restaurant that was unfamiliar to Amir. *Probably new*, Amir guessed. Making the rounds with Katrina and her client list, Amir thought he had sampled all of them. He could recite the menus, as well as the oily, solicitous parting remarks from the owners.

Katrina's performance reminded him that there was a lot he didn't know about Bank Von Raab. It had always been a secretive workplace. After several months in Dubai, he scarcely knew any of his colleagues. Unlike the animated trading floor and Alabama manners he had seen at Burr Acheson, human interaction almost seemed discouraged at his bank. Apart from Katrina, Fiona the ghost, and the inscrutable Mr. Swallow, Amir really knew no one. The occasional corridor encounter with other bank staff tended to be stiff and uncomfortable, accompanied at most by a suspicious nod or murmur. At first, Amir attributed this to Northern European formality, an impression shaped by the firmly believed and mostly uninformed prejudices in Nablus. But there were other anomalies. Unlike all the other banks in Dubai, with their lavish spending on advertising and entertainment, Bank Von Raab was practically invisible in the local business community. There seemed to be no marketing outside of the intimate client dinners that Katrina organized, and the origins of those relationships had never been shared with Amir. Bank Von Raab's website, which Amir had probed deeply after his unsettling evening with Fiona, was a pictorial masterpiece of beautiful affluence, seductive in its unsubtle suggestion that the clients of *this* bank inhabited a planet that had evolved far beyond work, want, weather, and even unfortunate facial features. But there was absolutely no information. Even the headquarters address on Pflugstrasse appeared on satellite images of Vaduz as a strange opaque rectangle, like a document redaction.

Finally completing the tedium of Mr. Swallow's new client paperwork, Amir left the office early, feeling resentful. On his way out, he caught a brief glimpse of two unfamiliar visitors entering Katrina's office. They stood out because they were not dressed like Emirates Airline passengers. Both men were tall, wearing boxy gray suits and dated club ties, and they had odd military-style haircuts. *Whoever they were, there would be no place for them on the bank's website*, Amir thought. Mr. Swallow closed Katrina's door after they entered, and spotting Amir, he averted his eyes and vanished in his usual sci fi fashion.

The atmosphere in Amir's flat was even more antiseptic than usual, and he wondered whether he would survive the toxic cleaning products that his unseen housekeeping visitors deployed. As usual, Amir spent his evening stalking Aisha, studying her latest photography, and trading sharp-edged text messages with his sister. Sara's pointed impatience had settled into a persistent whine, reminding Amir of his promises, and conveying an irritating combination of exasperation and disappointment. She continued to threaten to take a job in the settlements, using hyperbolic phrases transparently chosen to provoke Amir into accelerating her rescue. "Is prostitution really so bad?" she texted once. But to his great relief, he did not detect real suspicion about his presence in New York. Of course, it helped that she considered Amir to be a person of such modest intellect and limited imagination that an invention on this grand scale was inconceivable.

There were no new posts from Aisha. The most recent photograph, a week old, was not the best. She was seated alone, reading a heavy textbook, in some kind of library or academic building. There were blurred images of other students in the background, but the faces, including Aisha's, were mostly obscured in shadows. The scene was brooding, melancholy. As always, the photographic technique exhibited skillful use of light and patient attention to softening the portrait by manipulating the shutter speed. It was grainy, modified to look like it was taken with an old 35mm camera. These were not snapshots. He scrolled through the images, lovingly lingering on the most evocative. By now, the assembled archive totaled about twenty-five photographs of Aisha in Cairo, around which Amir had imagined a series of short stories, poems, and even the substance of a novel, unwritten but imprinted in fine detail in his memory. In his solitude filled by the richly detailed editing of this now voluminous work, Amir felt happily prolific, creating abundant narrative content illustrated by her social media posts.

But there also was a disturbing writer's block that frustrated all his creative energies, resulting in abandoned chapters and much discarded verse. In his literary architecture of recurring reconciliation and conflict resolution, Amir successfully inserted himself alongside Aisha among the beautiful narratives and characters. But despite his efforts, he could not produce any of the last-act dialogue that he felt so intensely and desperately wished to capture. In frustration and defeat, he could not craft the words that Aisha would say to him in these moments of high drama. They could pull themselves out of crises, or emerge triumphant from the schemes of double-dealing relatives, but he could not make her speak to him. He would turn to her for the inevitable words to accompany the cinematic finale.

She would present her exquisite face to him, lips arranging themselves for an explosive climax. The theater audience involuntarily would do the same—wanting, needing, expecting. And then nothing. Silence from Aisha. It was maddening.

There was the other plot puzzle that he could not reconcile— the Mogamma building in the background behind Aisha, unscarred by its legendary arson incident. To explain the inconsistency, Amir spent hours deconstructing metadata in her photograph, and trolling through news media images from Cairo that were taken before and after the incident. The mystery just deepened. Almost weekly, he watched Al Jazeera journalists broadcasting from their usual perch in Tahrir Square, usually reporting on the latest roundup of political dissidents. And there it was, plainly visible over the reporter's shoulder, like a smear of mascara below the eye of a woman abandoned in the rain by an unfaithful boyfriend. Like the Sphinx and everything else in Cairo, the damage to the Mogamma would never be repaired, and its origins either would be forgotten or wildly embellished by the predatory tour guides who attached themselves to lost tourists. But the scar was absent from Aisha's photograph.

Amir looked for forensic anomalies in Aisha's other photographs. He tried aggressively enlarging images to find dates on newspapers to compare with her posts, but the distorted pixels were never decipherable. He made an elaborate chart to track her photographic diary with Cairo's weather, looking for clothing choices that would be contradicted by the climate. But temperatures never varied much, and even in the hottest months, women in Cairo had not yet adopted the European and American summer street fashion of parading in their underwear. His weather analysis was inconclusive. Despite Amir's obsessive investigations, the Mogamma photograph just lingered as a curiosity. It never really occurred to him that Aisha wasn't in Cairo or that her photographs were entirely a charade.

When Friday arrived, he was glad at least that no shoes had dropped at the bank. People hurtled past him like subatomic particles, just glimpses that were already somewhere else before they were detected. Mr. Swallow continued to teletransport himself through time and space, silently materializing in unexpected places. Katrina was nowhere to be seen. Amir had passed the time by catching up on the latest favors he had promised to his office manager friends—liberating some exotic prescription medications from the bureaucratic clutches of a regulator in Brussels, arranging the details of a medical tourism trip to Istanbul where a human organ was purchased from a questionable source, and negotiating a tuition rebate from a California college that expelled Rashid's niece after a cheating incident. It amazed him that such things were possible simply with his polite intervention in the name of a European bank, lending a supposed imprimatur of respectability in all manner of shady deals. But his friends were grateful, and his favor bank deposits swelled. Amir was showered with gifts and courtesies, telephone numbers of women that he *simply must meet,* and outlandish whispered invitations at dinner parties that sometimes appeared to have the endorsement of everyone present. Once, Rula's younger sister visiting from Lebanon, an impetuous married women in her forties, pulled Amir aside after dinner and asked if he could help her free a reluctant zipper on her clingy dress, which was caught on an undergarment. The other women in the room followed this staged fabric crisis with their eyes, evidencing their collaboration in the episode. When Amir made polite excuses, the determined sister backed him into the empty kitchen and guided his hand firmly to a zipper that was high along her thigh, where Amir discovered there was no obstruction because there was no undergarment.

The Persian restaurant that Rashid selected was so new that the dominant aroma greeting the arriving dinner patrons was latex paint. Named for a tenth century poet, the restaurant Ferdowsi clearly had ambitions to attract the literati of Dubai. The interior spaces were extravagantly decorated with modernist interpretations of Persian mythology. Menus poked from within slim volumes of classic verse, bound in navy blue Morocco and placed like reading assignments next to the dinner napkins. The owner circulated among the tables wearing a velvet smoking jacket and bow tie, looking more louche than professorial. In a conservative floorplan, only men were seated in the visible portion of the dining room, though Amir saw the backs of a few abayas moving discreetly toward the "family" section of the restaurant. In a newish spin on Gulf gender segregation, there also were a half-dozen private dining rooms in which waiters attended to guests of both sexes, where the honor system allowed assemblies who were members of the same family. Local clerics with television talk shows were enraged by this trendy seating concept, convinced that it was an open invitation to debauchery during dinner. The "brothelization of dining," they called it.

Amir followed a waiter to one of the private rooms, where he found Rashid and two familiar Beiruti friends huddled in conversation. They stood formally when Amir arrived, a clear signal that this was not primarily a social occasion. Amir wondered if he might be asked for some really big favor. All four of them, including Amir, were dressed in the Emirates Airline passenger uniform. The Beirutis had accessorized with Marlboros and mobile phones, neatly placed on the table to their right. They looked like the cast of a dystopian film about genetic engineering.

While waiters came and went, there was easy conversation about nothing. They had all been together many times, socially and to arrange offshore investments with Bank Von Raab on behalf of the Emirati family offices whose affairs they managed. Amir also had discreetly helped each of them with a variety of private matters. Some of those were small things, but all three of these men had, at some point, confided in Amir to solve a personal problem that was very consequential—usually a career-jeopardizing incident of financial misfeasance or a deeply private family crisis with sordid ingredients like teenage pregnancy, mistress extortion, or a drug rehab clinic. Amir quietly applied himself to the resolution of all these things, never asking anything in return, and never breaching their trust in him. Their dark secrets were safe with Amir, and for this, he had acquired a unique stature. Amir was the friend of last resort.

Boat-sized platters of grilled meats sailed in and out of the small dining room, steered by rushed waiters under the command of the owner in his smoking jacket. In the familiar style of Persian restaurants, abundance was more important than flavor, the lamb having been transubstantiated nearly into charcoal. The absurd excesses of food eventually were cleared away, tea was served, and there was a moment of silence pregnant with anticipation. Rashid spoke with his usual authority and chose his words carefully.

"We are in your debt, Amir. It's time for us to show our thanks."

The others nodded gravely, and Rashid continued, "I'm sure you will not be surprised that the investments we have made together are not what they pretend to be. No one—not even our dim-witted Emirati employers—pays fat placement fees to an obscure Liechtenstein bank for the privilege of earning negative rates in a Channel Islands trust account named after a bird. Not unless there are . . ." Rashid hesitated, sipped his tea, and then found the right words. "Other objectives."

They all looked at Amir to see if he reacted. In fact, Amir always had assumed that, for their own reasons, the Emirati family offices were parking their money offshore in a slightly more modern version of burying chests of doubloons in the desert, simply to protect it from scheming family members, and profligate crown princes. In their world, where institutions were fragile and central banks were just private lenders to hereditary rulers, privacy and safety were more important than the rate of return. Amir felt slightly offended. He was, after all, an Arab. Why should he be surprised that the public version was not the whole story?

Amir looked blankly at Rashid, truly not expecting what he was about to say.

"All this money is Iranian," Rashid said, getting right to the point.

He went on to describe the invisible machinery by which the sermonizing leadership in Tehran, comprehensively sanctioned and embargoed in America and Europe, routinized the conversion of their graft proceeds into respectable offshore accounts. Rashid called it "elegant in its simplicity." The Iranian Revolutionary Guard Corps processed every large government purchase, from bulldozers to measles vaccines, not because the Corps was technically qualified—it was not—but in order to police the secret Bump and Split Rule. Whatever the real price was, the invoice was bumped up by fifteen percent. In exchange for keeping quiet, the bulldozer maker or vaccine manufacturer pocketed half of the bump and kicked back the remainder to Iran's "purchasing agents" in Dubai. Since the glorious revolution in 1979 when they learned this little grift from the European manufacturers of aircraft parts, the turbaned class in Tehran had accumulated private wealth that placed them statistically, if not sartorially, in an elite club with members like the Prince of Wales.

There was one problem. Hiding the Revolutionary Guard split was expensive, Rashid explained, and depended on the cleansing magic of Dubai. The venerable Emirati family offices that employed Rashid and his chums from Beirut quietly provided cover for the Iranians, depositing their splits in the accounts of perfectly ordinary local partnerships before moving it abroad. But the Iranians wanted their money in the rinse and repeat cycle. And they were willing to tolerate some shrinkage. For twenty percent, the Emirati family offices lent their names and bona fides to the creation of offshore trust accounts in secretive tax havens. With the help of a handful of banks, like Bank Von Raab, the toxic splits were resurrected as aristocratic old money—as unimpeachable as the two-hundred-year-old slave trade earnings that still supported modern British gentry—and fully controlled by a few dozen ayatollahs and their faithful generals.

Amir did not immediately register his alarm. He knew his friends liked this quality. He displayed the same steady face when they came to him with their personal family crises, almost always the predictable result of some appallingly bad judgment. He gave them every assurance that they could be open with Amir, and if he was judging them, it would never show.

But for Amir, it was like being told at a young age that he was fated to murder his father and marry his mother. Interesting information, but best not to know. Too late. It was now clear that Amir's Dubai exit plan depended on a business model that not only was illegal and fatal for a Wall Street future, but also likely to result in Amir's rendition to a black site in Romania. For the moment, he kept his calm. Rashid wasn't volunteering information to be transparent. A proposition was coming.

"For your protection, we didn't share this information with you," Rashid said with no apparent irony. "But then something happened. Our Iranian client asked to see me alone a few days ago. I had seen him before, visiting the office at strange hours, but he always met privately with the sheikh and his son. This time, he was brief and blunt. He said the Emiratis charge too much, and he knows they rely on people like me to actually get the deals done. He proposed to cut out the middlemen and give *us* ten percent to move their splits offshore."

Amir finally spoke. "Who is 'us'?"

Rashid looked at his friends. "Well, the dollar volume is large. To avoid suspicion, we will need to have a few local account holders. That's us. And . . . we will need *you*. An insider at the bank who can navigate the regulators and compliance officers. These deals will need to look routine, just like the ones your bank has been closing for years. We know you can make that happen."

"And we're offering you two percent," Rashid added hastily, in that inimitable Beirut style, as if placing the pen in his hand and rushing to help Amir trace his signature on the commitment.

Amir chose not to comment on his share. By not mentioning it, he felt somehow less implicated in the conspiracy.

"Don't you think the Emiratis will notice when their income drops?" Amir asked.

Rashid had thought of everything, it seemed. He explained that, just as before, the Revolutionary Guard money man would continue to meet his Emirati agents and arrange delivery of the splits for movement offshore. All the paperwork would look the same, and since Rashid and his friends handled the accounting and kept the books, they would faithfully record twenty percent commissions just as before. The Iranians would get their offshore deposits placed by Bank Von Raab, but the commissions would go to Rashid and his friends, at their cut rate.

"This plan is good for a year; maybe eighteen months," Rashid said. "By then, we plan to be . . . relocated." His Dubai "sell-by" date.

One of Rashid's friends passed a spreadsheet to Amir. It was a one-year projection of splits and the associated commission revenue. Rashid helpfully pointed to one number at the bottom. Amir's cut, politely labeled in the spreadsheet as "bank service fee," was slightly more than four million dollars.

It was quiet in the private dining room, except for the occasional sound of colliding plates and flatware outside the closed door. Some Marlboros were ignited in unison. A long time passed while Amir considered his options. He felt there was an obligatory speech to deliver, expressing shock at discovering the poisonous nature of their past transactions and declaring his objection to any further participation in illegal schemes. As for "his cut," he would have to dismiss the idea out of hand, using words like "unthinkable," even "shocking."

But where would that speech lead? he wondered. He was already half out the door at the bank after his last meeting with Katrina. His painstaking efforts to build a network with Rashid's little club would end in nothing. If he declined Rashid's proposal, it was hard to imagine a plan B in which things just reverted to business as usual. Vividly, Amir saw himself back in Nablus, sweating in his dust-covered room, struggling to reopen his long-blocked FREE*Trade account. And while he was in Nablus, he imagined Aisha in a beach cabana at Cap d'Antibes, nuzzling with an elegant Swiss banker, who undoubtedly had said yes to schemes very much like the one that Amir had just heard.

In Arabia, where yes means no at last half the time, Amir chose a third way.

"I'm really grateful that you came to me with this opportunity. I don't feel . . . worthy." He used an Arabic word that conveyed a subtle sentiment——something like, "Honored, but not deserving."

Rashid, who was apprehensive before, looked touched, like a father watching his young son exhibit a first flash of mature good judgment.

"But I need to be sure I can deliver. The stakes are high, especially for you. You have families to protect; responsibilities bigger than mine. Give me some time to test the systems at the bank."

Amir looked at their faces, which brightened. He had hit the right note. Rashid looked pleased with Amir's little speech.

"Akeed—definitely," Rashid said. "But we don't have much time. The Iranians want to move now. They told me the first twenty-five-million-dollar tranche will be ready in a week."

The suspense had lifted, and there were smiles all around. Even the cloud of tobacco molecules celebrated, swirling in excited eddies near the air conditioning vents above their table. Amir's title, "our banker," was repeated with new reverence and meaning, as if they were riding into battle together, rifles raised, proclaiming "Damascus!"

Their dinner adjourned happily. The restaurant owner mysteriously seemed to know when it was time to reappear. In his clown attire, he begged forgiveness for all the shortcomings of the meal and received in return the obligatory remonstrations and protests that, in fact, the guests had never experienced such excellence in dining. He led the foursome from their private enclave to the exit, past the patrons seated at less distinguished tables, producing a nice little spectacle.

In this high context culture, Amir meaningfully was pushed by his friends to the head of the parade. As he passed the other tables, people whispered, "I wonder who *he* is?"

Stepping into the thick night air as valets delivered their cars, it was one for all, all for one. "We'll speak soon," Rashid said to Amir.

Amir turned to acknowledge Rashid's parting words and was distracted by a glimpse of two women in black abayas entering the restaurant. He couldn't see their faces but was startled by the impression that a halo of amber light surrounded one of them. *Probably just a trick of the strange interior decorating,* Amir thought, as the door closed behind them.

Chapter 23.

AFTER Yasmine's fumbled first encounter with Kirk, Nadia's rebuke stung. But by the next morning, they were both back to business. Spock required a different approach, Nadia concluded, after offering a bulleted list of his eccentricities.

"No one knows what he does at the embassy, but he works long hours. They say his closet has five identical black suits, and five white shirts, which he wears without a tie. He likes restaurants, the larger the better, so he can be seen. He makes a great show of his encyclopedic knowledge of wines but doesn't drink. He never picks up the check. Oh, and Spock has a thing about his hair, which he wears in an early Beatles style. He gets his haircuts from a fancy stylist in one of the Marina hotels."

"I don't like him," Yasmine said, looking at a photo of him that she found on social media. Spock, pale and suspicious, had turned his head to the camera, away from some faceless companions at a table littered with remains of a mezeh menu.

"But I think he will like you," Nadia countered. "My friends tell me that he likes to be seen with tall women."

Yasmine looked again at the photograph, and indeed, Spock was beside some towering female figures, bowing as if to share a private joke.

Nadia exchanged a few text messages with her network and then said, "It's settled. There is a dinner on Friday to celebrate the opening of a new Persian restaurant. Spock will be there, and you will be the guest of a friend of mine from Bratislava, a girl I knew at university. She's tall, like you. A little plain looking, but an amazing storyteller. Usually dirty stories."

In the preparations for her dinner with Spock, Nadia told Yasmine to expect a private dining room at Ferdowsi. Yasmine's right eyebrow drifted up in feigned surprise. In a Persian restaurant, where Shiite disapproval collides with the naughty aroma of za'atar, mixing genders behind closed doors was . . . unorthodox. Nadia and Yasmine laughed and then moved on to select a chic frock for Yasmine for the evening, to be revealed ceremoniously at the table, after peeling off the abaya and head scarf that would anonymize her restaurant entrance. They debated shoes for a long time, finally settling on high altitude heels that would play to Spock's fetish for height.

Yasmine never made the same mistake twice. Spock would notice her before she noticed him. Once inside Ferdowsi, she and her companion, Michaela from Bratislava, let their head cover slide gracefully down to their shoulders, a maneuver of intentional accident that had been perfected years ago by adventurous Bahraini women in London restaurants. After a brief stop in the ladies' room, where their shapeless abayas were submerged into oversized handbags, the pair emerged as brightly colored butterflies with long, well-tanned legs and strappy heels. Leading the way into the private dining room, Michaela linked arms with Yasmine and made introductions.

Their host for the evening was an Egyptian "grain broker," a little more polished and cosmopolitan than his schoolmates from Heliopolis, but *still an Egyptian*, thought Yasmine. The dossier on Shafik Magdy, carefully fact-checked by Leila, described a new-money confidante of the head of America's foreign aid office in Cairo, a bloated bureaucracy responsible for distributing some of the annual bribes that persuaded Egypt to suspend open warfare with Israel decades ago. Shafik took a healthy cut for himself and protected his position by sprinkling cash liberally among the government ministers who arranged bid rigging and phony price supports. America's tax dollars at work. In the process, he threw lovely parties in smart restaurant venues from Muscat to Istanbul, taking special care to include even midlevel functionaries like Spock, a strategic investment in their future career paths. On this occasion, Spock was among a handful of embassy employees present, men and women with inoffensive titles and obscure responsibilities. With their invitations arranged by Nadia, Michaela and Yasmine understood that they were expected to be clever, decorative, and memorable facilitators of Shafik's generosity.

Michaela was exactly as advertised by Nadia. She commanded the room with breathless conversation, sometimes exaggerating her Eastern European accent to flavor the atmosphere with the scent of faded nobility. She fluttered between the huddled guests, making impossible connections that seemed to place everyone present within two degrees of separation. She introduced Yasmine in a conspiratorial whisper as her carefully guarded secret, a creative sensation who was on the verge of reinventing Dubai's dreadful decorating scene, which Michaela referred to as "Disney's Desert Kingdom." Yasmine responded with obligatory modesty and then dropped some design vernacular to establish her *bona fides* in a famously opaque trade. The other guests nodded as she spoke, pretending to appreciate the insight of a "collision type color palette," and her personal mission to resurrect black as a primary interior color. Shafik—bombastic and name-dropping—promised introductions to Yasmine that would yield lavish commissions from his well-placed friends. The circulation continued under Michaela's stage direction until finally, feeling peripheral, Spock approached and introduced himself.

With his Ringo hair, and deeply carved facial features, Spock looked like a wax museum replica of rock and rollers from the last century. When he extended his hand in formal greeting, it felt cold and flaccid. He held Yasmine's hand a little too long for her comfort. She acknowledged his introduction with only a nod, as he explained that he was "a diplomat with a niche portfolio," evidently hoping that she would ask him to elaborate. Rationing Yasmine's precious presence, Michaela swept her quickly away from Spock to a trio of women dressed in dour costumes, who were revealed to be

Yale-trained lawyers attending a conference on international arbitration. In no time, Michaela somehow established that she previously had met two of them at a human rights rally in Budapest and was distantly related to the third via an ancestor with the same name in Vienna.

The little room buzzed and oscillated like this while fresh fruit juices in jumbo burgundy glasses were passed by harried waiters. The silly man in a bow tie drifted in and out for occasional consultations with Shafik, who suddenly clapped his beefy hands, and commanded everyone to take their seats for dinner. Yasmine noticed that place cards had been arranged, and rearranged, during the pre-meal conversation, and she took her appointed seat across the table from Spock. Michaela sat on his right, where she could monitor and manage his attentions. Shafik tapped his water glass with the dessert spoon, and then stood to thank the assembled guests for their presence, extending a special welcome to "His Excellency," referring to Spock with an intentionally incorrect honorific, and the other "dignitaries" from the diplomatic corps, a pointed reminder that he was investing in future relationships that would be mutually beneficial.

Thus tapped by Shafik's annunciation, Spock launched some practiced conversation with his table companions, as a prodigious supply chain of food heaved into action. Yasmine measured every word from him, while affecting disinterest and maintaining separate conversations with men on her left and right who claimed to be experts in logistics. When Yasmine turned to her left to give her attention to the man discussing dry bulk carrier demurrage, she knew that the loose surplice of her little dress would invite Spock's attention. She had practiced this with Nadia, perfecting an upper body posture that was natural and graceful, but certain to share the intended view.

As predicted in Leila's dossier, Spock summoned a waiter and inquired about wine. The waiter looked paralyzed by the forbidden alcohol request, but Shafik intervened with some subtle hand signals, and the restaurant owner himself appeared with a precious-looking red leather book, placing it in Spock's hands like a giant communion wafer. He made a good show of inspecting the contents, consulting the owner, for all the guests to hear, on various options. When the bottle arrived with great ceremony, Spock tasted the wine and then made a dismissive hand gesture evidently meaning that it was tolerable and should be poured for those guests who wished to join him in the experience. A few accepted. Spock's glass sat untouched for the remainder of the evening.

Leila's intelligence about him was good, Yasmine thought, *or perhaps the wine was undrinkable.*

Michaela kept the ball rolling, gently providing openings for Spock to impress the table. He spoke about his climate change portfolio and clearly knew the subject. He had a truly tedious command of facts about the science of the upper atmosphere. Yasmine also noticed that Spock periodically would turn and direct his comments to her, as if Yasmine was chairing his dissertation committee.

Once, he said with intentional mystery, "Of course, with some countries, the climate subject can be a stalking horse for *other* things on the diplomatic agenda." Another time, he leaned in as if confiding in Yasmine, and whispered, "The back-channel negotiations are pretty interesting. Sometimes, we even talk about climate." He winked and smiled at Yasmine. After a few of these, she returned the smile, looking intrigued but not quite interested enough to invite him to say more. Spock persisted, and Michaela kept him talking, now and then placing her hand on his arm to flirt and assure him that his expertise was fascinating.

The others at the table more or less dissolved into white noise, as Michaela and Yasmine tag-teamed Spock. Yasmine—inscrutable, desirable, unsettling —was the target of his attentions, and Michaela—playful, eager, encouraging—kept him in play.

It was a promising start, Yasmine thought. While he hadn't yet slipped down any slopes that would compromise his presumed secrets, she was persuaded that his climate change portfolio was a cover. His conversation was sprinkled with more tradecraft terms than he could reasonably absorb from spy novels, and she had instinctive suspicions about his style. But she also worried that her impressions might be colored by wishful thinking. In the previous few days, the communications from Leila about Kirk and Spock were increasingly urgent. This was unlike Leila. Yasmine could tell she was under pressure from Tehran. No one had mentioned it recently, but Yasmine was reminded that her exit package had a deadline.

Dessert and coffee arrived, and then dispatched quickly. Led by the Yale women, the table guests commenced the ritual expressions of gratitude to Shafik, which signaled a collective sentiment that it was time to say good night. When Shafik stood, everyone did the same, and an awkward huddle formed around him so that contact details could be exchanged and hands shaken. Spock used this opportunity to maneuver to the opposite side of the table, out of range of Michaela, where he extended his cold hand again to Yasmine.

"I was very interested in your comments on the decorating business. You clearly have a good eye for design, and I could use your help." Predictably, he added, "How can I reach you?"

"You're nice to say that, but really, I'm pretty new at this," Yasmine responded with the required false modesty. "But somehow, my client commitments are keeping me busy. I'm not sure I could help you anytime soon."

Spock stood uncomfortably close to her as the host and other guests dispersed. Eventually, when it became inelegant for her to continue to deflect his attentions, Yasmine shared her mobile number, and Michaela arrived to sweep her away. Back to black in the disguises retrieved from their handbags, the two of them strode briskly through the crowded restaurant and disappeared into the night.

Chapter 24.

AMIR'S determination to go to Wall Street had already included a few ethical compromises. He told himself that these were small departures from God's commandments, unlikely to even catch His attention in a world that tested new extremes of depravity every day. Surely his harmless lies—to his family, to FREE*Trade, to Burr Acheson, even to Aisha—were nothing in comparison to the outrages that appeared in the daily news. What Rashid was proposing was a different level of dishonesty, with existential risks for Amir's grand plan, and perhaps even for his survival. Aside from the moral questions, which might be rationalized under a Dubai code of conduct, he would be building a long list of formidable enemies. There was, of course, the bank that would be exposed to ruinous media and legal attacks if his rogue trading was discovered. There were the Emirati families who surely would arrange for his disappearance when they realized that he was the conduit for diverting their crooked revenue stream. The Americans, with their ham-handed but relentless campaign to demonize everything Iranian, would hunt down Amir, and call him a terrorist. And finally, there were the Iranians themselves, at the top of their government, suddenly exposed to public awareness of their decades-long corruption. For

Amir, and for all Arabs, there was no prospect more unspeakably terrifying than facing the wrath of Persians provoked.

Would it even work? he wondered. Sure, he could probably navigate the know-your-customer charade with the sleepy compliance office in Vaduz. Except perhaps for the dollar volume, these new deals would look indistinguishable from the investments that he and Katrina had been chasing and closing since he arrived at the bank. Amir also was confident that Rashid and his friends could massage the books and keep their employers in the dark, probably for a long time.

The ultimate exit plan, he thought. *It could work.*

He and his partners would be long gone before this was discovered, and the victims would have to think carefully about whether they themselves wanted this scheme to break into the open. Finally, and inevitably, the money was a factor. Amir's upside obviously did not change the risks, but definitely, four million dollars sat heavily on the scale that weighed his internal calculations of the wisdom of Rashid's proposal. It wouldn't go too far in New York, but it would open some doors, perhaps to a respectable address with a doorman, membership in a good club, the summer rental in the Hamptons, and tuition for Sara at NYU. Most of all, Amir was certain it would change the way Aisha thought of him, which at the moment was not at all. He scrolled through her photographs again, subconsciously pasting them (and himself) into scenes on the recently updated Burr Acheson wealth management website, which ran like a loop in his head, filled with chestnut horses, orange handbags, and blond children.

Stop hallucinating, he told himself. *Prison. That was where this would end if Amir signed on to Rashid's deal.*

Amir stared at the ceiling of his flat, where a blank white slate appeared, erasing his scribbled, foolish notes about joining this bunco scheme. He could see clearly now. Amir would go to Katrina and give her a detailed account of Rashid's proposal, making it clear that he, Amir, would never involve the bank in such transactions. He would recommend that Bank Von Raab report the information to the Financial Market Authority in Liechtenstein and suspend further offshore investment dealings with Rashid and his friends. Katrina would agree, of course. She would commend Amir for protecting the bank and rejecting the lucrative side deal that Rashid offered. With the cleansing power of doing the right thing, this would restore Katrina's confidence in him, and surely revive Amir's career, though he would miss Rula's dinner parties and the kitchen encounters with her randy guests. He went to sleep feeling purified, as if by especially aggressive ablutions before prayer.

Amir called Richard Swallow before office hours, requesting an urgent meeting with Katrina. Impatient with Richard's telephone kabuki, and his insistence on knowing the subject of the meeting, Amir hung up and called Katrina directly. She accepted the call and coldly told him to be in her office at 10:00.

He wore a freshly pressed Emirates passenger uniform to the meeting and arrived early. Mr. Swallow, identically dressed, intercepted him and asked Amir to wait in a conference room until summoned. He waited a long time, gradually losing some of his nerve. The certainty and serenity that swept over him the night before now felt riddled with doubts. Mr. Swallow, a ghostly presence when he eventually reappeared without warning, led Amir to Katrina's office and closed the door, producing a disturbing sound like the hush of compressed air when a space capsule is unsealed. She looked imperious, offering no pretense of warmth or curiosity about the purpose of Amir's urgent presence. Neither spoke until the dead air became uncomfortable, and then they both spoke at once.

"Thank you for seeing me," collided awkwardly with, "What is so urgent?"

Annoyed, Katrina opened her palm in Amir's direction, giving him the floor.

"There has been a surprising development," he began, suspensefully.

Amir had rehearsed this lengthy narrative, including some previously unshared information about the favors he performed for his Beiruti friends, which seemed necessary to explain why he had been trusted with this unorthodox proposal. Katrina listened impassively, visibly startled only once—by his recounting of an incident in which Amir wired funds using a Bank Von Raab account to secure an abortion in Amsterdam for the teenage daughter of one of Rula's brothers.

When he approached the finish line, Amir concluded with a sentence he had carefully refined until it had what he thought was just the right combination of professional rectitude, sound business judgment, and solemnity without sanctimony.

"Obviously," he said with practiced gravity, "we have to distance the bank from these transactions."

Amir thought it was interesting that Katrina never took notes. There was no leather diary on her desk, and no paper or writing instrument of any kind was visible in her office. *Did she have perfect recall?* he wondered. He didn't consider the possibility that, in her position, some records should never be created.

Unexpectedly, Katrina drilled down into the mechanics of Rashid's proposal. The icy edge that greeted Amir when he arrived was replaced with something more like academic interest, and quickly evolved into eagerness.

"How exactly would the funds transfers be handled?" she wanted to know. "Who would be the nominal account holders in the bank's records? At what stage would the Lebanese partners divert their split? Have you met the Iranian partners? How much money are we talking about?"

Surprised and hesitant, Amir described how a hypothetical transaction might work, noting that Rashid had been meticulous in considering the small details, even to the point of insulating the bank from exposure when the plan ultimately unraveled. Katrina pressed him again on the likely value of the investments, and Amir repeated the staggering figures that Rashid had previewed.

The noisy silence of machine-processed air returned to the space capsule. Hoping to return to his script, Amir inhaled deeply and prepared to deliver his prescription for reporting to the bank regulators. Katrina cut him off, now smiling and contemplative, twice repeating the phrase, "Bump and Split." From her lips, moistened by a curious exertion of her tongue, it sounded like vulgar French shorthand for a fiery afternoon ending in damaged clothing.

"Let it play," she said.

Amir heard her but it was the last thing he expected. He was prepared for a furious accusation that he was somehow complicit in exposing the bank to legal ruin or that he should have detected signs of this dirty money earlier, or even that the whole story was invented to divert attention from his mediocre achievements in client development. He had not anticipated this reaction. Maybe she wanted him to play along until all the culprits and details were exposed, or until they could be caught *in flagrante*, with cops and bank regulators hiding in the next room, springing out with their guns when the incriminating documents changed hands.

"I don't know what you mean," he said, genuinely confused.

"I mean that these are important clients of the bank, and you may be jumping to conclusions. Of course, you can't accept the sweetener they offered to you, and the bank needs to keep its distance from any misleading recordkeeping. But that's not *our* business. As I see it, your friends are just bringing us more of the same transactions that we have always handled for them. If there are different middlemen or intermediaries, or placement commissions that they share among themselves, those are *private* matters that don't involve the bank." Katrina finished with a surprising little toss of her hand, as if to dismiss Amir's concerns as overwrought.

"Katrina, Rashid told me this is Iranian money. It's toxic for the bank."

"We don't know that," Katrina said with a breezy air. "The international sanctions rules are complicated. We're not being asked to transact business with the Iranian government. This seems to be private money that happens to reside in a UAE company, just like other offshore investments that we have handled a hundred times in Dubai. You're not a lawyer. Don't try to blow this up before we even know the facts."

"And by the way," Katrina added. "This is a huge win for you. I know I leaned on you hard to grow this business. I criticized your slow pace. But you pulled it off, and this will be good for you at the bank."

For a brief moment, Amir reconsidered his appraisal of Rashid's deal. Had he criminalized the concept too hastily? Could the bank, as Katrina suggested, compartmentalize its role, and maintain a polite, and legal, distance from the source of the money? Maybe they should leave this for the lawyers to sort out.

Katrina sensed an opening and pressed ahead. "I'm going to assign a team to work with you on this; to make sure you have all the resources you need. And I will stay personally involved. But this is *your* deal, and I will make sure you take the pole position. You should call Rashid today and tell him this is a 'go.' And make sure you meet with his Iranian partner. Let's find out who we're dealing with. Congratulations, Amir." She gave him a smile that seemed to say, "Now calm down, and go close this deal."

Katrina's eagerness helped to clarify Amir's thinking. Shaking off his momentary doubts, Amir remembered that he already considered the options and the risks. He would stand on principle, because it was right, and because the other choices were disastrous.

"You can't be serious about this." He spoke more loudly than he intended. "You are talking about joining a criminal enterprise. It isn't ambiguous. And if I take the next step, as you propose, there is no turning back. We are all implicated. I'm not doing this."

Amir stood and started to leave. Katrina, too calm for this moment, kept her eyes lowered, studying the empty desk in front of her. He could have simply walked out, but for reasons he could not explain, Amir waited for a reaction instead. It felt like a painfully long time.

Finally, she spoke, still looking down. "You're being cautious. I respect that. But let's agree that these things are not always black or white. There are experts that the bank *pays* to resolve questions like this. It's not up to you or me."

Then she looked directly at him, striking Amir with a blue blast from her hypnotic ray gun. "Let's not make a decision now. Sleep on it. And I will too. Let's meet again tomorrow morning, and then we will decide. Together."

Obediently, helplessly, Amir just nodded and left Katrina's office.

Amir returned to his cubicle and felt himself shivering, from the temperature or from the lingering tension of Katrina's office. He had a missed call from Rashid, a painful reminder that a decision was urgent. Retreating to the binders on his desk, Amir pretended to analyze the legitimate business opportunities that might be generated from his network but wondered what else Rashid had not told him. The day passed slowly while Amir distracted himself watching the rhythms of foreign stock markets opening, pulsing, and closing. The Nikkei bled into the Hang Seng. Rumors about Chinese real estate debt caused wild swings in Shanghai, and oil price spikes rippled through the markets in Mumbai and Riyadh. London opened directionless, and finally, at the opening bell in New York, financial stocks plummeted on inflation worries. They would all go the opposite direction tomorrow, Amir predicted, and the traders on Wall Street would celebrate both days. Movement either way means money. After the meeting with Katrina, his destination felt more out of reach than ever.

Amir wished desperately for someone he could trust. Someone to advise him. Charlie Bridges would know what to do, he thought, but Capital Markets 425 was a long time ago. And poor Charlie was railroaded out of Nablus by the university faculty thugs and their gangland protection racket. Even if Amir could find him, Charlie probably would not welcome any reminders of that episode in his otherwise impeccable career. There was Sara. Despite their tortured sibling relationship, she knew Amir better than anyone, and she always seemed to know the answer. But he wasn't ready to start unwinding his New York narrative, and Sara would be merciless when she discovered he had misled her. And last, there was Aisha, the permanent presence that glowed in his peripheral vision —watching, knowing, waiting. He remembered her at university, critiquing Faulkner with such confidence, penetrating the prose and pretention, always seeing the heart of the matter. She would know what to do.

He slept deeply but uncomfortably, locked in a senseless dream loop, repeating the same conversation with his Uncle Jaber in his shop on Jaffa Street. Amir waved his mobile phone, complaining that it didn't work.

"You can't call that number," his uncle said.

"But that's the only number I need to call," objected Amir. The phone rang, and the screen announced "unknown caller." Then the dialogue would repeat. The caller was never revealed.

When he returned to the office the next morning, later than usual, something seemed different at the bank. The disturbing quiet remained, but even the impression that others might be present had vanished. In the long, lonely corridor that led to his frosted-glass door impersonalized with etched numbers, there were no shadowed glimpses of movement, no subdued telephone ringtones, no nervous keyboard strokes. The corridor lighting, automated by detected movement, oscillated as he passed, from off to on, and then to off again, like the spotlight following him from a gulag guard tower. Amir stared at his terminal, expecting a message from Katrina or a meeting invitation, but there was only the bank's usual screen greeting, warning against cyber intrusions, and threatening careless users with referral to law enforcement authorities. He was ready for this meeting, resolved and steeled to stand on principle, refusing to expose himself and the bank to the obvious risks. If necessary, Amir was prepared to resign from Bank Von Raab, a conclusion he reached under the narcotic spell of wishful thinking, in which he imagined that Hodding Easterbrook would rescue him. It was one of the gaps in Amir's self-awareness that he often assumed, incorrectly, that he occupied a seat at the table in the consciousness of others.

He chose to believe that the delay in this meeting was intentionally staged by Katrina, elevating the drama, and forcing Amir to weigh the consequences of his refusal to cooperate. *I won't play this game,* he told himself and drafted a letter to Katrina.

Dear Ms. Vanderlipp,
With the deepest regret, I hereby resign my position at Bank Von Raab.
I will not participate in transactions that are plainly corrupt and illegal, notwithstanding your instructions that I do so.
Sincerely,

Amir reconsidered the "notwithstanding" clause, which pulled the pin on a hand grenade. He liked the legalistic formality of it, but he knew the presence of these words on paper would provoke deployment of expensive heavy machinery in the form of lawyers, internal investigations, and recorded interviews with solicitors and their supernumeraries. The blast radius would be large, and he would be within it. He used the backspace key to delete everything after "regret." A moment later, he deleted the whole document.

"Merde," mumbled Amir, angrily standing up and preparing to storm into Katrina's office. Amir threw open his office door, just as Mr. Swallow was about to knock, the dorsal side of his hand paused in midair.

"I believe you are wanted in the conference room." Any pretense of cordiality was long gone.

Amir followed silently to the familiar room, where Mr. Swallow left him at the door. Inside, Katrina stood stiffly, facing him from the head of a white marble table the size and shape of a whaleboat. Seated to her right was Fiona Curzon. Her nails flashed crimson, like blood stains on the gunwale.

"Of course, you remember Fiona," remarked Katrina dryly, still standing.

Amir's memory of his last encounter with Fiona was unclouded by time. The sting was still pronounced, and he could not suppress an accelerated replay of images from that night, the trailer of a psychological horror film. The sea bass in a provocative pose, the abstracted drowning victims slipping beneath the surface of painted canvas, Coltrane's grinding film score, the hint of rosewood when Fiona playfully touched her hair, the moist glow below her neck, her long legs tweezering depth and detail from Amir's confessional, and the abrupt silence as he stood alone in the corridor outside her flat. He recalled the feeling of having been undressed on television before a live audience, followed by a commercial for a laundry product.

Katrina continued, "I shared the details of our discussion with Fiona, and she decided to join us overnight from Vaduz. Obviously, it is important that we handle this correctly."

Fiona said nothing but looked up at Amir. A piercing look. Her ruthless, haunting beauty was exactly as Amir remembered, even in a black blazer layered above a crisp cotton shirt with an office-appropriate neckline. Just as before, he knew he would give her whatever she wanted. His protests, if mustered at all, would be just for show. Amir sat down, disarmed.

"We agreed to sleep on it," Katrina said diplomatically, as if to acknowledge that Amir's resistance was something as to which reasonable people might disagree. "What are you thinking this morning?"

Without conviction, and unsettled by Fiona's presence, Amir delivered his little prepared speech. "In all good conscience," he could not be a part of these transactions. He made no concessions to the possibility of another point of view and expressed "disappointment" that the bank would even entertain the idea. Then, in a heavily edited and cautious version of the draft letter he had just deleted in his office, Amir finished with, "If the bank has a different view, I will be forced . . . reluctantly. . . to resign."

If they were surprised, neither of the frost-covered women revealed it.

In an expression borrowed from the imitable Mr. Swallow, Katrina, still standing, simply said, "Right." Evidently unsurprised, Katrina turned to leave. "I will leave you to work this out with Fiona." Then she was gone.

Fiona chose not to insult him with, "It's good to see you again." Instead, she got to the point. "I suppose I don't need to mention that this . . . *opportunity* . . . was the result of your hard work in developing important client relationships. You did exactly what you set out to do, and what the bank hoped you would do. You were *chosen* for this, both by us and by them."

Not understanding, Amir quibbled with Fiona's word choices. "What *I* set out to do? You can't be serious. When I raised this with Katrina, she told me to 'let it play.' I thought she had gone rogue. This isn't some harmless corner-cutting with the bank's Know Your Customer obligations. You are talking about conspiring to engage in money laundering with government officials of a sanctioned foreign state."

"And you did the right thing in objecting," Fiona said with a patronizing, parental tone. "Now I need to explain something to you about Bank Von Raab. The bank has a special relationship with certain clients who rely on Katrina and her team to lead them to precisely these kinds of transactions. These clients have the legal authority to protect the bank. They are not traditional bank customers."

Amir wondered if Fiona was dramatizing the punchline with a suspenseful pause, or if she wasn't sure he could be trusted with the information. They watched each other in silence.

It was her move.

"Obviously, you know there is a lot of dirty money moving through Dubai. A lot of it comes in cash and is converted into empty apartments and villas. Those are bought and sold in a game of musical chairs, and after a couple of years, the proceeds look clean. That's the Dubai shadow banking sector."

"The front door is mostly closed to that money. Brand name banks left that market years ago when 'terrorist finance' was everyone's worst nightmare. The Americans used the dollar as a weapon to vaporize any bank that didn't cooperate. Sometimes the targets were actual terrorists, but eventually it was the full list of the Americans' political enemies—Russia, China, North Korea, Cuba, Venezuela, and, of course, Iran."

Fiona proceeded to tell a story—fantastical to Amir—that was equal parts Ian Fleming and Gustave Flaubert. Five years earlier, Bank Von Raab was struggling to emerge from its Old Europe origins by building a new presence in Dubai. Unfortunately, the bank's newly appointed regional director for the Middle East had never traveled further south than Basel. She was quite unprepared for the creative banking practices of the Arabian Gulf. The locals quickly appraised her as a bourgeois virgin from the provinces, eager for experimentation, and soon she was in bed, figuratively at least, with the fast money operators that made Dubai's desert carnival irresistible. That was Katrina Vanderlipp.

In a short time, she built a lucrative client list of no-questions-asked depositors. Katrina was the resourceful intermediary for investments in tax haven trust accounts, bearer bonds, limited liability companies, and other elegant black boxes designed to be untraceable. She introduced her clients to offshore jurisdictions that were, if not entirely respectable, at least friendly to the transnational frequent fliers and Politically Exposed Persons whose wealth was mysterious in its origins. For her success, Katrina was promoted and rewarded by the bank. The board in Vaduz, whose meetings and members easily could be confused with a Gilbert and Sullivan performance, was ecstatic. With Katrina's marvelous inventions of previously unknown transaction fees, the new Dubai operations reversed the steady decline in the bank's fortunes, after barely surviving what the bank's chairman, Baron Maximillian "Spatz" Angerholzer, always referred to as a string of bad luck. Others felt that "luck" had nothing to do with the 1923 *and* 1945 defaults in the bank's generous loan facilities with the Reichsbank in Berlin, or the reversals that followed a disastrous bet on British currency in 1967, or the massive and ultimately worthless position in Icelandic mortgage-backed securities in 2008.

Bank Von Raab's investment strategies were nothing if not consistent. Baron Spatz felt Katrina had arrived with providential timeliness and let it be known that the accountants and lawyers should not distract her.

With dramatic flair, Fiona described a visit from some unexpected guests, who disturbed Baron Spatz's aperitif one evening at the family Schloß. They included the chairman of Liechtenstein's central bank (the baron's cousin), a nervous-looking chief of the Police Grand-Ducale, and two Americans with ambiguous government credentials. In a memorable meeting, the Americans reviewed the high points of a document labeled, "INDICTMENT," which began with the words, "The grand jury charges that . . ." It required very little explanation to reveal that this document virtually guaranteed prison time for Baron Spatz, Katrina, and the entire Audit Committee of the Board, not to mention the ignominious dissolution of Bank Von Raab. The baron put aside his tiny coupe of Lillet and poured himself a generous goblet of whiskey.

Living up to their reputation for being transactional in all things, the Americans had a deal in mind. The baron could preside over the liquidation of his bank and try to fight extradition to the maximum-security facility in Florence, Colorado. Or he and Katrina could continue exactly as before, serving quietly as bankers of choice for clients of dubious provenance, provided the bank cooperated with its new American friends. Cooperation meant that the bank would pursue a very particular category of clients and share the details of the client's affairs. The Americans explained that they were interested in some specific individuals from Iran.

Baron Spatz was gracious to his American guests, despite their dreadful manners and frightful neckwear. Surprising no one, he accepted the proposal without hesitation, and invited everyone to stay for a very fine dinner.

Skeptical, Amir interrupted Fiona's story. "What's in this for the Americans?"

"Suppose they want some sensitive information—just hypothetically—about the Iranian nuclear weapons program. The bank tells them where to find the hidden retirement accounts of some well-placed officials, who then receive a proposal that is not so different

from the one Baron Spatz received. The Americans say, 'We can expose you and seize your money, or you can help us get to Scientist X.'
I think you can guess the rest."

"And who exactly do *you* work for?" Amir asked.

Fiona answered softly while admiring her nails. "I'm not a bank
employee."

Amir didn't necessarily believe Fiona's story, but he was relieved
to have at least a plausible explanation for his disturbing previous
encounter with her. Maybe she was never "training" him, he considered, but was evaluating him as an asset in her little game of flipping
Iranians. The story also was consistent with some of the other unex-
plained oddities about the bank, like the apparent absence of any
normal banking activity. But then Amir had a chilling realization.
In the improbable chain of events that brought him to Dubai, he
wondered exactly when Fiona and her friends might have chosen
him. Was the introduction to Katrina in the blue light of Hakkasan
a chance encounter, or step five or six in his recruitment as an
unwitting accomplice?

Amir was fitting together the pieces. He pictured the debates in
Vaduz about how much to tell him and what carrots or sticks would
be necessary to persuade him to play along. He expected some creative incentives from Fiona, possibly a comfortable landing in New
York if he agreed. She knew about his dreamy ambition because he
had shared that and a lot more with her during their memorable
evening together. No doubt, Fiona assured her colleagues in Vaduz,
and their American friends, that he would say yes in the end.

But Amir surprised her. "I don't know what you and Katrina are
up to, but I'm out. I already told Katrina that I wanted no part in this.
In her version, the bank just wanted to make some easy money. At
least her story was plausible. Now you want me to believe that you're
a spy, and I'm . . . what? The one who takes the fall when your crooked scheme unravels?"

Suppressing impatience, she tried one last time. "We can make
this attractive for you. During that lovely evening we spent together
in my flat, you told me exactly what you want in life. I can make that
happen. For now, we need you here to close a few very important
transactions. After that, you will have a seat on the trading desk of

your choice in New York, a passport from a real country, and some nice perks that aren't normally offered on Wall Street."

Amir was still disoriented to be in the same room again with Fiona. *She had no reason to invent this story,* he thought, but he had every reason not to trust her.

"If I were you, I wouldn't refer to our evening together. It doesn't inspire trust."

Fiona looked at her tank watch, a recent gift to herself to celebrate the Meyghan operation. "Fine," she said, clearly not intending to continue the pretense of being reasonable. "We tried the carrots, now let's move on to the other things. Of course, you know that if we can't make this work, staying in Dubai is not an option for you. When we notify the Ministry of Interior that you no longer are employed by the bank, you will have only a few days to leave. You may be willing to spend the rest of your life in occupied Palestine, though personally, I can't think of anything worse. That's your choice. But consider your family."

Fiona let the last word linger before continuing. Amir looked up.

"I remember what you told me about your sister, Sara. About how important she is to you. As I recall your words, you told me she fills some of the 'empty spaces' left by your difficult relationship with your mother. That was really . . . poignant."

Enraged, Amir flattened his palms on the cold conference table as a showy prelude to demanding that Fiona leave his family out of this discussion. But Fiona calmly continued. "Did she tell you she found a new job? Working for an Israeli family in the settlements. Surprising, right? You told me she's always been militant about such things, fighting against the occupation and all that. Well, I suppose people change and grow up. Except this is a special job. In fact, I arranged this job for Sara, including that cold call she received from a recruiter. That family works for us."

"Listen to me carefully, Amir. *This* is our insurance policy. Your sister won't be returning to Nablus until you finish your work here in Dubai. And if you walk out on me, or try to tip her off, Sara will disappear into Israel's famous legal limbo of detention for suspected terrorists. I can arrange for that to continue. Indefinitely and uncomfortably."

Fiona's serene facial expression and posh accent provided a special touch of spiritual *noblesse* to her threat, as if it was her divine right to maneuver Sara's fate for the greater good.

Amir felt he had no violent impulses. That had always been a point of pride for him. In that respect, at least, he was different from too many of his peers, like his miscreant non-friend now in jail, Ezz Fawzy, who seemed to feel that his shaky manhood needed the occasional theatrical display of bluster, threats, fists or worse. But in this moment, Amir could not resist imagining a high-definition scene in which a bludgeoned Fiona was splayed on the conference table in the style of a de Kooning canvas—at once beautiful, petulant, and grotesque, as the artist might say.

It's true that he was not a deep thinker. Fiona and Sara judged him correctly in that respect. Retreating from a passing lust for gore, Amir hastily calculated his options. He could dismiss Fiona's wild tableau as impossible fiction, except that her narrative elements lined up, providing a coherence to the seemingly random turns in Amir's recent history. There was, for example, too much coincidence in her awareness of Sara's strange job offer. In fact, as he considered it, all the odd accidents that had plucked him from obscurity in Nablus now lined up like obedient dominoes. He wondered who else was in on the scheme, but then wondered who *wasn't?* Maybe this started long before Hakkasan. Even the unsolicited call from Lance, the fast-talking mortgage broker in Palm Beach, now seemed entirely orchestrated. And from there, it was a nearly straight line back to Nablus and Charlie Bridges himself, waving his pencil in Capital Markets 425. In a state of wild paranoia, a long police line-up of suspects appeared before Amir, all sneering at his naïve trust in a world in which things just happened.

His father used to say, "God works in mysterious ways." *This has nothing to do with God*, thought Amir.

"I'm not going to wait for you to think about it," Fiona added. "This is not a negotiation. You need to call your Lebanese friend now and get to work. We both know you will do it. The sooner the better. For you, and for everyone."

She was right. Of course, he would do it. He almost laughed at the comic obviousness of his circumstances. Rarely in his life had he felt such clarity. The fog had lifted all at once. Monet became Magritte. And really, Fiona was the perfect messenger, with her extreme Britishness. From an early age, every Arab knew that, for centuries, the accursed English lurked and schemed behind every unhappy twist of fate. Even in advanced decline, they bent much of the world to their will.

Amir finally just nodded, and with that, the mood in the room instantly shifted to the business of structuring a mostly routine banking transaction with some very unusual new clients. Fiona produced a list of five names, distinctly Persian. It was a wish list of high value targets in Tehran, each known to be major players in the Bump and Split enterprise. Any one of them was well placed to reveal the intimacies of Iran's nuclear program. Amir would use his new business arrangement with the unsuspecting Rashid to become the trusted wealth manager for at least one of these targets, who would secure his financial future with numbered accounts denominated in the Great Satan's currency. Fiona and her friends would handle it from there.

There was one last thing. Fiona said the stars were aligned for very fast results, and if Amir seized this moment, he could be on Wall Street before Easter Monday. Just a few weeks ago, an "operation," as she called it, penetrated deep into Iran's most sensitive weapons program. "Some of their eggs were scrambled," she observed in her driest voice.

"We expect some panic-driven investors to appear very soon, desperately hoping to monetize their splits before the intelligence services in Tehran lock all the exits."

Amir nodded again. He considered insisting on some assurances—about Sara's safe return, about himself, possibly even about the perks that Fiona had mentioned. But he said nothing, choosing not to concede his fragile high ground, from which it was faintly possible to see that he was acting at gunpoint, not as a willing collaborator. And as a practical matter, any promises from her were hardly enforceable.

"I'll leave you to it then," Fiona concluded. She stood. The conference room door opened, as if by some silent command. Mr. Swallow was there, and the two of them disappeared into the dim corridor.

Amir returned to his office and telephoned Rashid.

Chapter 25.

RASHID clearly was relieved when Amir called. And he said so. Amir knew Rashid would be worried about the delay in responding to his proposal. With his South Lebanon world view, Rashid would expect Amir to create calculated suspense, with the intention of haggling over the size of his cut. Ironically, as Amir plotted his next moves, he worried that Rashid might be suspicious if he *didn't* demand a higher share. But in the end, Amir chose to stay on the high road, which had earned him the trust of his Beiruti confidantes. He accepted the terms as offered. They spoke in innocuous code on the telephone, ostensibly arranging for one of Rula's sisters to have an eyelid procedure in Mumbai where the exchange rate was favorable, and the cosmetic surgeons were "good enough."

Now things would move quickly, Rashid promised. And indeed, they did.

In a surprise that fit nicely with Fiona's purpose, Rashid revealed that the Iranian client insisted on meeting Amir to satisfy himself, Rashid said, that there really was a Bank Von Raab insider on the team. Of course, he would insist on that, Amir reflected. To preserve the impression of business as usual, they would meet in Rashid's office during business hours, and even include an audience with

Rashid's employer, the courtly Emirati sheikh who would be reassured that his future commission revenues were as secure and reliable as the arrival of the crescent moon.

The gentleman from Iran was Mehdi Golestani, the fourth name on Fiona's target list.

When Mr. Golestani arrived for the meeting, he was dressed in the pretentious uniform of the Islamic Republic's elites, the flavorless western suit paired with the supposedly anti-western mandarin collar shirt, *sans* tie. As everyone knew, at least since 1979, neckties were oppressive symbols of the despised Christian cross. The visitor was seated in the conference room when the sheikh arrived. The Shia and Sunni gentlemen exchanged formal greetings and embraces, each suppressing extremes of mutual contempt and suspicion provoked by their presence on the same planet. The sheikh smiled broadly, both to convey the superficial honor his guest expected, but also because he believed that the terms of his financial arrangement were absurdly one-sided in his favor, evidence of the infinitely superior trading skills of the Khaleeji Arabs. Of course, the sheikh was the only one in the room who was not in on the joke. With the ceremonies concluded, the sheikh left the conference room, a pointed signal that transaction details were clerical work far beneath his station. Whereupon Mr. Golestani commenced his due diligence.

Mr. Golestani was a short man, whose hair and beard were closely cropped in the severe style dictated by the Department for the Monitoring of Public Spaces. He did not smile, nod, or employ any of the other natural tools of human communication that complemented language, evidently wishing to avoid revealing anything about himself. There was a violent scar on his right cheek, which looked like the result of some industrial accident, or more likely, a battlefield injury. For anyone in his presence, it was difficult to resist staring at the scar. He exploited that distraction.

What Mr. Golestani did not reveal was that, in the small need-to-know circle of Iran's Bump and Split operations, he was the most trusted bag man of all. The Supreme Leader himself, and the six members of the Guardian Council that he appointed, all relied on Golestani to collect and manage the vast sums that were skimmed for them from the state's purchases of everything from copy machines to ammunition. He was the very private laundry for the A-list, personally circulating between Tehran and Dubai to oversee the modern alchemy by which the proceeds of gangster thievery were converted into genteel portfolios—anonymous, far away, and above suspicion. His clients were so lofty that Mr. Golestani's special services were not available even to the president, who had his own busy laundry staff. And while Golestani was well compensated, it was clearly understood that his investments never would be commingled with those of his very special patrons. He was meticulous in his affairs and trusted no one. It was his idea to end-run the Emirati sheikhs and their extortionate commissions. But first he had to make certain that Rashid, and especially his channels inside Bank Von Raab, were reliable.

Amir was well prepared by Rashid. He expected questions about his relatively brief tenure with Bank Von Raab, his lack of traditional financial training, and shrewd lines of inquiry intended simply to trip him up. Amir also knew that Persians had low regard for Palestinians, whom they consider parasitic poor relations of the Arab extended family. Mr. Golestani would not be shy about conveying that prejudice.

"You're not exactly the kind of person I would expect a European bank to employ," he said bluntly. It sounded even more insulting in his coarse version of Arabic, as if his tongue was sliding over sandpaper.

"You're right about that," Amir agreed, trying not to look at the facial scar. "But my European colleagues would be the first to admit that there are things about the local culture that they don't understand. And my track record speaks for itself." That final phrase had been suggested by Rashid, who nodded with satisfaction when he said it.

"Maybe, but now we are speaking about much larger transactions. How do you intend to protect this from the bank's regulators and the internal compliance officers?"

Amir was ready for this. He spoke confidently about the blind spots in the bank's compliance systems and displayed deep knowledge of the asset classification nomenclature that he himself had tested. These transactions, he assured Mr. Golestani, would appear in the bank's accounting entries as routine and unremarkable investments by longstanding bank clients with impeccable credentials.

"They will not be questioned," Amir said flatly.

Rashid was silent during this exchange, carefully watching their Iranian guest for any signs of suspicion or doubt. He was difficult to read, but Amir had been persuasive by using some of the same techniques that brought him into Rashid's circle. He was measured and discreet, never selling too hard.

The interrogation continued and drilled into the minutiae of back-office banking. Finally, the scar-faced visitor sat silently staring into Amir's eyes, as if watching for a nervous blink, or a suspicious dilation that might reveal evidence of a future betrayal. Amir kept his composure. Abruptly, Golestani spoke in Persian, in a slow and quiet cadence, almost *sotto voce*. Amir understood him but was careful not to react. He did not want to explain why he knew the language or invite inquiries about what his mother was doing in the shah's Tehran during her teenage years.

"I'm sorry. I only know a few Persian phrases," Amir lied.

Golestani translated for him. "I said, 'The stakes are high. We need to get this right.'"

Amir knew that what Golestani actually said was, "If this goes badly, we are all dead men." There was an expletive in there too, for emphasis.

With Golestani apparently satisfied with the interview, they turned their attention to the mechanics of the investments. Amir circulated closing checklists and took command of the transactional documentation, lawyers' opinion letters, government stamps, and other formalities that western civilization invented to subvert the intentional ambiguity that is preferred east of the Bosporus. The plan was hatched, and the details agreed upon. Mr. Golestani departed, unsmiling but clearly ready to proceed. The first tranche would move in a week and two more within the month.

Rashid was pleased and effusive in complimenting Amir on his performance. In a celebratory mood, he offered to organize one of his famous soirees in honor of Amir. He mentioned that the Ramallah twins had just returned from a shopping weekend in Milan and would surely appear for dinner, "*un*dressed in the absolute latest style." And Rula's sister with the memorable zipper malfunction might be persuaded to drop by. But Amir said he was superstitious and preferred to close the deal before counting their money.

"Always our steady banker," Rashid said proudly.

Over a sad ramen dinner in his lonely flat, Amir drew arrows and circles on quadrille paper. Several crumpled discards were arrayed like a dot plot on the floor around an empty urn, once home to a tropical plant that had expired from hypothermia. He was trying to map an escape plan that would reconcile his dizzying accumulation of lies, subterfuges, and frauds. He questioned whether Fiona would honor her promise to place him on a trading desk in New York, but as long as they had Sara on the wrong side of the wire in the settlements, Amir had to play along. One of his drawings, quickly discarded, imagined a cloak and dagger scheme, enlisting the ever-resourceful Uncle Jaber to engineer Sara's escape. But the risks were not manageable, he concluded, since Fiona seemed to have disturbing foreknowledge of everyone's intentions and movements.

He looked suspiciously at his mobile phone, and then at the dozens of ventilation registers, smoke alarms, and other menacing fixtures in his flat that might hide high-definition cameras, listening devices, or even brain wave scanners. As ever, the local reputation of America's intelligence services far exceeded its abilities. On another discarded page, he had detailed an elaborate plot in which Amir would turn the tables on Fiona, threatening to go public with Bank Von Raab's money laundering history and the operation directed at Iran. For a moment, he persuaded himself that *he* held all the cards. Fiona and her friends would have to negotiate on *his* terms if their operation was threatened with exposure. But as he drew the arrows and filled in the circles with probable outcomes, the wet fragment of a cold noodle fell on the page, and the paper absorbed a spreading stain that reminded him of his insignificance in relation to the forces invested in this operation. He and Sara would disappear long before Amir could make good on any threats.

As he did most evenings, careful to choose time zone appropriate hours, he checked in with Sara with the customary exchange of passive aggressive texts. Lately, he had noticed a surprising softening of her descriptions of life as an *au pair* working for Little Satan. Perhaps she was self-censoring for the presumed interception of her communications, but there were unexpected reflections on her new quality of life. She mentioned, for example, that she was spending time with girls her own age who were part of the extended family, from whom she said she was "learning a lot." She described them as "sophisticated," and "not provincial" like her "silly Nablus friends." Amir felt creeping alarm at her reference to "learning," which evoked his own life-changing tutoring from the acrobatic Aaliyah after her *au pair* experience in the settlements. But Sara's shift in tone was not complete. Every text exchange concluded with a biting rebuke about Amir's failure to honor his promises to her. She always had the last word.

Resolved not to end any day in utter defeat, his last refuge was the side of paradise that he and Aisha inhabited in his imagination, a gallery of still images and short clips that Amir could animate into elaborate existence by closing his eyes. Whenever a fresh photograph appeared on her feed, a new episode came to life in his richly imagined screenplay, a streaming series that would be renewed for never-ending seasons. His novice author's struggles to hear her voice or smell her hair had long since been overtaken by a Shakespearean command of invention and stage direction that produced acts and scenes as vivid and realistic as any immersive experience. Amir no longer thought of Aisha in Cairo, or speculated about suspected lovers or that maddening unseen photographer, or puzzled over contradictions in her photographic narrative. They were together now in New York, whispering sweetly during brunch on MacDougal Street, or calmly raising a numbered paddle at Christie's, or napping under creamy cashmere with the Sunday *New York Times* entangled in their bare feet. Her voice now came easily to him, with expressions and inflections drawn from that day of the commencement party in Nablus, when she revealed to him her own determination to escape the shrinking confines of that dying place.

Back in the routines of Bank Von Raab, there was a strange, surreal normalcy in his daily encounters. The fact that he was working with a gun to his head seemed unremembered, as if filed offsite with moldy audit records. He reported faithfully to Katrina and Fiona on his introduction to Golestani, and they reviewed his closing checklist for milestones that might reveal new information and future opportunities to extort cooperation from the chain of prominent Iranian beneficiaries of Bump and Split. With the unusual size of these latest transactions, Fiona—uncharacteristically aroused—speculated that Golestani himself might be the flip candidate who could deal a winning hand from her deck of cards imprinted with the faces of Iran's last remaining nuclear scientists.

It would have been a surprise to Amir, but Fiona's stardom in the clandestine service was new. Her colleagues in Vaduz and London, clawing their way up the grimy meritocracy, resented her aristocratic manner and savage beauty. They worked openly to undermine her. But the Americans on the team, as ever oblivious to Europe's invisible but indelible clues about social status, cared only about results. Only five people in the world knew it was Fiona who designed and ran the operation that produced the explosive deaths in Meyghan, and the extraction of Dr. Mousavi. While her colleagues were busy attacking her, Fiona patiently developed the sources in Dubai that eventually tipped her to the weekend visit of Mousavi, his colleagues, and their chaperones. She orchestrated the touchless contact, the flip, the C4 he would hide in his ugly overcoat, and the extraction to adopt his new identity in an Albuquerque suburb. Fiona personally negotiated Mousavi's eleventh-hour "deal-breaker" demand for a Whirlpool dishwasher.

She was on a roll and determined to convert Amir's lucky invitation from his Lebanese friends into a death blow for Tehran's atomic ambitions.

While the immediate focus was on Golestani, her new flip candidate, Fiona insisted that Katrina and Amir also carry on business as usual, maintaining all appearances that Bank Von Raab in Dubai remained dull and beyond suspicion of anything more exciting than an irrevocable deed of trust in the Channel Islands. They continued their routine of client development dinners, following the same repetitive script. The cast of characters never changed. An aging Emirati patriarch listened warily as an ambitious son—never a daughter—volleyed business school buzzwords in meaningless combinations, while his office manager inserted obsequious suggestions designed to demonstrate his indispensability. Amir played his role faithfully at these tables. But he was increasingly conscious of the sadness and emotional pain that he was witnessing, and indeed, enabling. Aging fathers, some born in Bedouin tents, had built fortunes in the racke-teering Dubai economy but still remembered poverty and portfolios measured in date palms and camels. These meetings forced them to come to grips with the inevitability of family succession plans that would transfer wealth to their reprobate offspring, the classic next generation of new money, unworthy and unanchored by history, val-ues, or faith. The deep lines in the fathers' faces made Amir reflect on his own fast money trajectory, as the enabler for crooked Persian deals exploited by superpower intelligence agencies engaged in transnational blackmail. It was hard to feel good about his career progress. Someday he would have to explain all this to Aisha. The thought made him sick.

But for now, he was Katrina's wing man, dressed in his Emirates' passenger uniform and armed with a PowerPoint deck.

Chapter 26.

IN Nadia's comfortable sunny villa, her decorating business hummed. Clients came and went, always reassured that good taste and self-worth could be purchased. Yasmine had seamlessly joined Nadia's atelier, where she was no longer introduced as new or recently arrived. The two women fell into a relaxed daily rhythm, respectful of their separate spaces and missions, collaborating when needed, and gently competitive in the timeless race among women to be more of everything. During their regular morning swims, separate but equal, they admired each other from a polite distance, each inspiring the other to make small adjustments in the style of their strokes, or the number of laps, or the shrinking slivers of swimwear, if any, that would decorate their toned shapes. In the early evenings, they exchanged frocks and fashion critiques in studied preparation for the gatherings that were chosen for Yasmine's circulation, and lately, for the more targeted encounters with Kirk and Spock.

Despite her intuition that Kirk was not a fish worth the fly, Yasmine gave him a decent interval to prove her wrong. She knew he had been identified in Tehran, and it would take more than her instincts to persuade them to lose interest in him. In their coded messages, Yasmine and Leila bantered about this until an impatient edge appeared in Leila's deciphered prose.

"Stay on Kirk until I tell you to stop," Leila demanded in her latest coded message.

After the first clumsy encounter that provoked a blistering critique from Nadia, Yasmine saw Kirk twice. Nadia insisted on more preparation for these occasions, though she was careful to preserve a lawyerly distance from the substance of Yasmine's mission.

"I don't need to know that," she would say, interrupting Yasmine in midsentence while rehearsing an approach to Kirk. But Yasmine always wondered how much Nadia *did* know. She never spoke about previous sparrows under her care, but it was quite obvious that there had been more than a few. Unlike Leila, Nadia never adopted Yasmine with the intimacy of a mother or sister, worrying about her feelings or nurturing her self-confidence. It was all business. The most that Nadia revealed about herself was that she had her own escape plan, the price of which, for now, was shepherding Yasmine through her undisclosed assignment in Dubai.

At the second encounter with Kirk, a lightly attended gallery opening with large format monochrome images of miserable refugees, Nadia and Yasmine chatted with the photographer, a young Ethiopian woman with flamboyant braided hair, rings on every digit, and earrings the size of Olympia oysters. Kirk approached the women, introducing himself to Yasmine for the second time, and proceeded to make some surprisingly educated observations about the artist's technique. The Ethiopian woman was enchanted and conducted the little group through an impromptu tour of her best work, happily addressing a stream of well-informed questions about ISO, apertures, contrast, shadowing, and telephoto lenses.

He was performing, but he did it well, Yasmine thought.

Kirk didn't purchase any of the work, but he gave every impression that he would and lingered over one particular image after the artist described it dramatically as a "shriek that disturbs her dreams." Kirk asked Yasmine's opinion of the gloomy photograph of an apparently abandoned child in a smoldering hellscape. She whispered to Kirk that it might be staged, noting that the subject appeared well-fed and, beneath her rags, was wearing expensive and clean sneakers. Kirk laughed brightly at the insight They exchanged good-natured cynicism about the gallery world, petulant artists, and the silly patrons that support them. In a segue, Kirk asked Yasmine about her decorating clients. He asked Yasmine whether they actually knew what they liked, or simply paid the decorator to supply that answer. They agreed it was a complicated question, and like photography, it seemed that Kirk knew a great deal about the decorating business.

Yasmine was enjoying his company, but the clock was ticking on Nadia's meticulously planned departure. It was important, she said, to dispel any suspicion in Kirk's mind that their second meeting was anything but a fortuitous accident. Yasmine waited for a break in the clever dialogue, and then made her excuses.

"I'm afraid my friend and I have another commitment," she said to Kirk, looking in Nadia's direction and receiving an almost imperceptible nod.

As she stood, Kirk proposed that they meet again and suggested dinner on the next Friday. As planned, Yasmine demurred, citing her difficult client schedule. Kirk persisted and succeeded in receiving her mobile number, with the suggestion that they "stay in touch."

During the debrief in the back of Nadia's car, they agreed it was a flawless second encounter, and they went to work planning the next. Yasmine felt restored by Nadia's gestures of approval, but her opinion of Kirk was unchanged. He was charming and charismatic, she acknowledged, but probably not an intelligence operative. Closeted back in her secret space in Nadia's villa, Yasmine wrote a detailed report to Leila, which was misleading only in omitting her assessment of Kirk as a waste of time. All signals from Leila indicated that Tehran was not ready to give up on him. She turned her attention to her journal, now as fat and dog-eared as a Baptist's family Bible, stuffed with random notes on cocktail napkins in which she had catalogued the names, institutions, relationships, and likely connections of the individuals she had encountered in Dubai. She kept a running list of possible targets of opportunity, ignoring much of the "intelligence" that Leila was channeling to her from Tehran, which Yasmine recognized as the work product of adolescents on attention deficit drugs. But her own list of potential targets, which she considered better informed by her presence, was shrinking. Names previously annotated hopefully with promising asterisks, and sometimes exclamation points, were gradually stricken after subsequent encounters, unspoken but unmistakable signals from Nadia or Yasmine's own reconsideration. She worried that her patrons might lose patience with her progress, and at some point, even Leila may not be able to protect her from a failure to produce results as her deadline approached.

Yasmine's own sell-by date, which had seemed both secure and far away, now loomed larger in her imagination. The initial attractions of sparrow life in Dubai, if not fully depreciated, had at least diminished with the routinization of cocktail dress evenings, the pressure to deliver, and the colorless, odorless inauthenticity of Dubai. To Yasmine's surprise, she sometimes thought about Nablus. It wasn't nostalgia exactly, but during a lingering bath or in that half-conscious space just before sleep, she closed her eyes and clicked through warm images of home, her family, the piano almost hidden under generations of photographs, Mrs. Al-Qasem's secret boudoir, and the silly boys who were paralyzed with infatuation in Yasmine's presence. The pleasant, faded memories didn't last. She forced herself to remember the checkpoints, the ubiquitous dust that collected in her eyes and hair, the small-minded gossip, and most of all, the certainty that nothing would change. By the time the morning light appeared and the lap pool beckoned, she was back in combat-ready condition, with a singular focus on the imaginary wall calendar with her own exit date.

It might be self-deception fed by urgency, but the pictographs in her journal pointed to Spock as a real possibility. His cover fit the profiles that were familiar from Leila's training—a government job with a plausible anodyne portfolio and flashes of deep knowledge of the uninteresting subject matter, as if to reinforce the existence of such an unlikely position. And she imagined something lurking beneath, like a gun behind the counter of a small neighborhood shop. But first, she had to deal with Kirk.

Several days passed before Kirk placed a call to the number that Yasmine had "reluctantly" shared with him. In the interim, she was embarrassed to experience the textbook sensations of annoyance and anxiety triggered by his failure to demonstrate immediate and urgent interest in her attentions. Eventually, he did call. For his tardiness, she retaliated by ignoring the first two calls and respond-ing to the third with an automated text, "Sorry, I can't talk right now." That ballet continued until dinner finally was arranged.

They met at one of the newish "dining clubs" that were part of Dubai's parallel universe designed to accommodate the behaviors of western expatriates in an emirate that pretended to be conservative. Yasmine was impressed that he did not choose a showy venue, like one of the upper floor restaurants in the Burj Khalifa with names like "Curvature of the Earth." Those places were strictly for the un-imaginative. In contrast, the members-only dining clubs were placed discreetly inside office towers overlooking Dubai Creek, accessed through side entrances with private elevators at which tiny brass plaques marked the establishments with obscure names or dates that recalled the glories of old empires. The interior floorplans fol-lowed a familiar formula and were decorated in a style that might have been chosen by Lord Mountbatten.

On arrival, at a club identified with a plaque that read simply, "1588," Kirk was greeted by name by an imperious doorman, and he and Yasmine were directed to a cozy lounge where small groups of attractive Europeans murmured over cocktails. The art was equestri-an. The leather club chairs were deep and smelled of saddle oil. An unseen ambient sound device blurred all conversations into the dull rush of a desert wind.

Over dinner, they exchanged pleasant conversation, but no topic was probed very deeply. There was no flirting in either direction. Their chemistry brought to mind genial strangers seated together on a long flight. Kirk told stories that he had polished and embellished from his professional encounters with autocrats and oligarchs, the shady characters who invariably lurked behind project finance deals to protect their cut. He expressed polite interest in Yasmine's busi-ness. That provided an opening for the probe that Captain Sadegh and His Boys had formulated for this very moment.

"My clients are much less interesting," she said. "Although . . . I started a new project recently for a nervous Iranian guy who wants to decorate an enormous empty flat not far from here."

She paused, waiting for a reaction, and then finished her script. "His taste is awful. He told me he is some kind of scientist. And he pays for everything in advance with bundles of U.S. currency."

Nothing. No reaction.

"Swag curtains. Can you imagine?" she added.

"Well," Kirk offered, "surely you know by now that cash in Dubai is more plentiful than taste." And then he returned to one of his well-worn stories about negotiating the financing of a pipeline in a former Soviet republic where, as he put it, caviar was abundant but hot water was not.

The evening had been pleasant enough, but Yasmine was bored and relieved when they left in their separate cars. Definitely, Kirk was not what Tehran was looking for. He revealed himself to be merely alone, like so many in Dubai, having made bad life choices that pitted career against family. Kirk may have been mildly more interesting than others, Yasmine thought, with his manufactured charisma and stories from exotic backrooms. But he never even leaned into the challenge of seducing her, as if he had decided it would undermine his reputation to behave so predictably. She was first glad that it wouldn't be necessary to fend him off and then mad that he couldn't be bothered.

The first draft of the report to Leila included some flashes of irritation about wasting Yasmine's time with Kirk, which she later edited out to produce a more cool, analytical assessment. When Leila studied the report, she detected the undercurrents that Yasmine tried to suppress, but still was persuaded that her conclusions about Kirk were correct. Captain Sadegh was unhappy when he read the report, but he would accept Leila's judgment because she was always right. And because he could never say no to her.

Kirk's grainy photograph would be removed from the target board in Captain Sadegh's office, and His Boys would repurpose the code name for another mission. Meanwhile, from Tehran to Cairo, the urgency to produce results was approaching panic. It had been some weeks since the explosion in Meyghan. There were no leads and the trail was going cold. Someone would have to pay. Possibly someone in Prison 59, if no one better turned up.

Leila's coded reply to Yasmine was succinct. "Focus on Spock."

Nadia said nothing when Yasmine asked her to recalibrate the social calendar, dropping Kirk like a canceled magazine subscription and accelerating the insertions into Spock's orbit. It was classic Nadia, protecting herself with plausible deniability by hearing and saying as little as possible about Yasmine's mission, but plainly understanding it as well as anyone. Yasmine was comforted when Nadia agreed that Kirk should be removed from the social register. Surrounded by carefully tied bundles of fabric swatches freshly delivered by her hard-working colleague from Mumbai, Nadia lit up her phone with an artillery barrage of calendar adjustments, invitation replies, and fashionable intelligence to make course corrections in Yasmine's program.

It was hard to tell whether Nadia thought Spock was a more promising lead. The small slices of information from her sources were inconclusive. At the moment, his key qualification was that Yasmine's handlers cast a light on him, and no one else looked more promising. Everything else was intuition or hope. Yasmine worried that she was not given the traditional resources with which to build the case against Spock, like surveillance reports or signals intercepts. Leila said she was assured those files existed but didn't lie to Yasmine when she said, "They were not shared with me. Do your best."

Since their dinner encounter at Ferdowsi, Spock had called Yasmine twice. Each time, she deflected his invitations, citing a punishing work schedule. But she was playful and left the door slightly open. When he called again after Kirk's dismissal, she was ready, and suggested a benign rendezvous at a well-attended gathering to celebrate the launch of a new hotel. She would be there with clients, she said, adding, "It should be fun. I'll send you an invitation."

Nadia joined her this time, both to add her own decorative contribution to the encounter, but also to appraise the situation with Spock. The event was a massive soft opening. The showy new hotel was an empire expansion by a family from Hyderabad who had built a successful chain of middle-market hotels at home and now wanted to upsell with a luxury brand in the Gulf. There were grand entrances by Bollywood celebrities, and a performance by a London hip-hop artist whose stage name was a single angry syllable. A heavy concentration of paid influencers meant that the attendees appeared in their most photogenic ensembles. The crowd rippled with well-practiced camera poses, which Nadia and Yasmine artfully avoided. As always, everyone knew Nadia. A murmuration of admirers maneuvered into her vicinity to deliver kiss-like greetings and threads of whispered dish. She was, it seemed, everyone's encyclopedia of such information, and there was a marvelous spirit of community volunteerism that kept her data refreshed. If it was not always accurate, it was at least up to the minute. Yasmine coasted on the residual pull of Nadia's presence, being noticed and automatically credentialled.

Spock found them easily and presented himself to Yasmine, shouting a greeting over the hard-edged music with vulgar lyrics that had been only lightly sanitized for local standards. Yasmine introduced Nadia, who flashed an impish smile at Spock. As it turned out, the event was perfect for Yasmine's second live encounter with Spock. If he actually was an intelligence operative, and naturally apprehensive of new arrivals in his battle space, there was nothing in this evening to provoke a suspicion that Yasmine had the slightest interest in Spock. She sent him the invitation by forwarding, without comment, an email that had a long list of recipients. The fact that he appeared at all at such a splashy public event seemed to undermine the idea that he was undercover in a sensitive operation. But Yasmine watched him carefully for signals that he might be her target.

As the colony of beautiful guests swarmed about, approximating kinetic harmony with the musical performance, the Hyderabadi host circulated with his entourage of attractive family members, harried handlers with earpieces, and a security detail that was useful only to exaggerate the host's prominence. The host paused to chat with Nadia, and all eyes caught his grateful glow in her presence. The handlers issued frantic instructions into their communications devices, and photographers came forward to capture the moment, just as Nadia turned her back to them. It may have been his party, but Nadia's presence transmuted it from merely commercial to socially significant.

Spock seemed to work hard to achieve relevance in Yasmine's space, though the competition was fierce. His haircut and suit stood out in the sleek and tailored company. Nevertheless, he kept up a competent and versatile colloquy with Yasmine and her circle, appraising the architecture of the new hotel (an "*homage* to Philip Johnson," he called it, in bad French), the bronze sculptures commissioned for the atrium ("nude rocks"), and sarcastically, the "absolute originality of the musical act." Everyone who could hear him above the awful percussion blasts and infantile rhymes agreed on his last point, nodding and crediting Spock with a winning observation. He added that Dubai was nothing but "a collection of masterworks in misappropriated art." Yasmine rewarded Spock with a little laugh and drew closer, with Nadia just over her shoulder.

"Who *are* all of these people?" she asked Spock, as if she had just arrived at the Barbizon from Tulsa.

Yasmine worried that it was a little too easy to keep him talking. Spock pointed out some characters who he recognized in the crowd, usually shady men with suspicious incomes. *Dubai's fish in a barrel*, thought Yasmine, *but still outside his "climate change" portfolio*. She considered trying a teaser remark that might foreshadow a reference to her strange Iranian client with lots of cash, but Nadia had warned her to go slowly.

"Beware of the money shot that comes too early," Nadia had said.

Spock went on cataloguing the familiar personalities. He was reasonably up to date, but not more so than anyone who faithfully accepted all the B-list invitations that arrived like unsolicited mail-order catalogues. Just as Spock seemed to fully relax in Yasmine's presence, Nadia's eyebrow signaled that it was time to go. Yasmine made polite excuses, and the two women abruptly left him in the crowd. He tried to say something as they disappeared.

Chapter 27.

AMIR was in his office early, clicking through the closing checklist, rechecking the SWIFT code entries in the wire transfer instructions, and chatting by telephone with his friend Balz at Switzerland's largest bank. They rehearsed the imminent transaction in the dullest possible terms. Balz could make a mass extinction event seem routine. Rashid texted Amir frantically for updates. Amir's replies were restrained and calculated to leave no relevant record.

"All good," he texted Rashid. "Best to Rula and the kids," Amir added, to distance his message from anything obviously transactional.

They waited until noon in Dubai, when the markets were open in Europe and trading liquidity was deep enough to hide most volume spikes. With a prearranged signal, Golestani's first tranche of Bump and Split proceeds entered the global banking system as an electronic pulse transmitted from a UAE trading company to Bank Von Raab. The money lingered briefly as an accounting entry at Balz's bank in Zürich. It then reappeared in the form of photons fired underwater through the Cross Channel Fibre, finally to be rechristened as a bird of prey in the dusty trust account books and oxidized brass plaques of Guernsey in the Channel Islands. There, Mr. Golestani, together with the various ayatollahs for whom he served as trustee, and "their heirs and assigns in perpetuity," could rely on the absolute discretion of the local bar to shield their good names from prying eyes, and to assure that this new wealth could be accessed in any tradable currency without intrusive questions. It was all over by lunchtime in Saint Peter Port, where the regular town diners at Fat Rascal had an extra glass of wine to congratulate themselves on the generous trustee fees, and fees on fees, they earned that morning.

Amir sent Rashid the customary transaction confirmation, slightly altered for the benefit of Rashid's employer. The sheikh would be comforted to see a very large transfer and a corresponding credit for his usual commission. He would remind himself to send Rashid a nicer gift for the Eid this year. The actual commission, of course, was now in Rashid's own trust account in Cyprus, an old-school bulwark of bank secrecy, impervious to the global fad of ratting out clients to overreaching tax authorities.

"Now, can we celebrate?" Rashid asked in a breathless text message that Amir left unanswered.

At the bank, Amir met with Fiona and Katrina, delivering a dry recitation of the unfolding operation. He chose to forego colorful terms like Bump and Split, referring instead to Mr. Golestani and his very dirty money as "our important new client and his family office portfolio." The first tranche moved without incident, he told them, and the bank had cemented the client's trust. Two larger deposits would follow in a week or two. Fiona methodically probed the details, and Amir was ready with the closing binders, checklists, and the other liturgical records worshipped in the tabernacles of modern finance. Obviously satisfied, Fiona moved on to review plans for the sting that would convert their important new client into an unconventional weapon, obliterating what remained of Iran's nuclear program. Confronted with the option of being exposed and losing both his clients' money and his own, or fingering the remaining scientists, Fiona seemed certain that Golestani would do the right thing. She mentioned the sweetness of victory after decades—indeed, after the millennia since Thermopylae—of being outmaneuvered by cunning Persians. Fiona even took time to acknowledge Amir.

"We owe a lot to you, Amir. I think you are going to be pleased with the way this works out—for *you*, I mean. You shall see."

Amir accepted the recognition silently. He noticed that Fiona often used "shall" in her vocabulary, in place of "will." In contrast to common usage, she applied it in second and third person contexts, but seldom in the first person. It was obvious that Fiona preferred to give, rather than obey, commands.

The three turned their attention to the ongoing schedule of Katrina's client dinners, an essential element of the pretense that Bank Von Raab operated a forgettable, normal business in Dubai.

Chapter 28.

IT was agreed that Nadia would not join Yasmine for her next close encounter with Spock.

"It's better that way," Nadia said with conviction. "Make him focus on you." Nadia had studied the landscape and settled upon arranging for an American friend, a banker, to invite Spock and a "plus one" to a small dinner at a local restaurant. Her friend vaguely recalled meeting Spock at some embassy events, and they had agreed—not very sincerely—to meet again to continue their discussion. Nadia's friend reported that Spock was thrilled to receive the invitation. As expected, Spock asked Yasmine to join him. She accepted, after two intentionally missed calls from him.

In especially ruthless terms, even for them, the two women plotted the assault. Spock's invitation was carefully arranged so that he would arrive thirty minutes later than everyone else. Yasmine would visibly consult her wristwatch when he arrived. Spock would be off balance from the beginning, wondering if he was wrong about the invitation time, muttering apologies to the host, and checking his fly. By the time he finally took his seat next to Yasmine, Spock would be hopelessly backfooted. She would let him stumble through clumsy attempts to position himself as the VIP dinner guest—perhaps even the nominal guest of honor—or worst case, an authority on a subject of profound interest. All of that would fall flat with blank stares at the table. And then, Yasmine would rescue him. She would comment favorably on Spock's reputation as a "trusted advisor in Washington" (so she heard), and "the go-to source on climate policy initiatives." Once Yasmine had the table's attention, and before cueing Spock to deliver his retread carbon disaster speech, she would remind the dinner guests sternly that an "apocalypse" was looming, whether "we denied it or not." With that celebrity endorsement, the other diners would put down their salad forks and turn to Spock, resurrected from his shameful arrival. His gratitude to Yasmine would be boundless, and his clandestine service secrets eventually would melt into her ear, accompanied by intimate entreaties.

After this rehearsal, they affected mock serious nods at each other before Nadia and Yasmine laughed at the unlikely scene they had conjured. Even if Spock really was the high value target they were looking for, it was not going to be so easy to persuade him to reveal an ongoing operation to an Arab interior decorator with a fake name and fictitious backstory. They reworked the program a little, but what remained was more or less the same. Yasmine would test the water with Spock, delivering the lines that Captain Sadegh had developed, and Leila had refined. With or without a promising response, they agreed Spock was worth chasing over a few more fences, if only to put him to ground.

It was Yasmine's first visit to the restaurant, a local legend. Nadia knew it well, and with great authority, she informed Yasmine that a few special preparations would be wise. Expect it to be dark, she said, adding that the restaurant's signature blue accent lighting will render everything cold and harsh, like the winter solstice. Some extra makeup would be in order, they agreed. They made a mess of Yasmine's dressing room before finally settling on a navy dress with ribbed form-fitting fabric and a mid-calf hemline. A teasing stripe of black grosgrain ran down the front, plotting a course from the Spratlys to the Strait of Malacca.

"And let your hair run wild," Nadia suggested, passing her a pair of drop earrings in knotted gold.

Yasmine conferred with Leila in the run-up to the event,

exchanging messages in which the coded versions never quite captured the imaginative energy that she was delivering to the operation. As ever, Leila's tone was dry and methodical, but between the lines of encrypted characters, Yasmine detected an elevated pulse. Gone, for example, were Leila's familiar admonitions about moving too fast, or taking the shot too early. Still missing were updates from the surveillance teams or intercepts that might validate Spock's targeting. Whatever Tehran knew about Spock, they were not sharing it with Yasmine.

Not far away, Katrina and Amir were making their own preparations to launch against a different target. For Amir, tonight's dinner with a local sheikh was only a diversion to keep up appearances for Bank Von Raab while the main event was underway with Rashid and his employer. But Amir had still done his homework for the evening, checking with his sources to build a profile of the family trading business, a pro forma of performance results from the principal portfolio companies, and an artistic genealogy depicting the sheikh's marriages, complete with a pivot table that projected free cash flow from the separate income streams of his four wives. According to Katrina's sources, this Sharjah sheikh had recently reinvented himself as a European sophisticate with a tailor in Naples and a shoe collection that would challenge the closet space of a Mandarin merchant princess. While in the permissive atmosphere of Dubai, he preferred the nightspots frequented by expats, where he would dispense with his thobe, and often turn up in a terracotta-colored silk jacket with navy suede Chelsea boots.

Katrina selected the restaurant, not recalling that it was the site of her first encounter with Amir. When she texted the venue details to Amir, he wondered if she was trying to signal something meaningful to him, like a twisted recognition of his graduation from stateless striver to espionage field commander. He shrugged it off as a European blind spot, like their incessant redrawing of sovereign borders based on trapezoidal symmetry, unaware that they were lighting fuses for future ethnic conflict.

Smiling and backlit in dazzling cobalt, Yasmine took her seat in Hakkasan, with Hodding Easterbrook to her left at the head of the table. He was multitasking, interrupting his wife to ask that she make introductions, while he negotiated with the beleaguered sommelier and tapped on his phone to superintend an exotic arbitrage trade underway in London. Lindsey Easterbrook, who addressed Yasmine as "Dah-Lyn," made a loud show of mispronouncing the other guests' names, pausing at the empty chair to Yasmine's right to observe with disapproval that "someone is *lay-ate*," and then resuming a tedious anecdote about "my time at the White House."

As planned, Spock appeared thirty minutes later, his sunken features and strange hair looking ghoulish in the blue glow. He was mortified when he saw Yasmine glance at her wrist.

"Now that we're all here," Hodding began, smiling at Spock to soften the rebuke. Lindsay looked irritated when her husband took command at the table, repeating all the introductions, and adding his own flourishes and mispronunciations. Since he barely knew Spock, and only just met Yasmine, he relied on marvelous inventions to present their stories to the table. He skirted the edge of manifest lying by prefacing his remarks with exculpatory questions like, "Someone may have told me that Yasmine has a PhD in molecular biology. Do I have that right?" Then he would move on quickly to the next victim before Yasmine could protest or correct the record. But it was all considered good fun, and the exaggerations—delivered in his deep, theatrical dialect—were so extravagant that no one took them seriously, or even felt obliged to issue denials.

There was a momentary alert, however, in Yasmine's antennae when Hodding described Spock as the occupant of a government position that was "so obscure and dull that it could only be deep cover for spying." There was nervous laughter at the table. Spock laughed too, evidently still trying to recover from his entrance. Yasmine tried, unsuccessfully, to read something deeper in his expression. Nothing.

It was *Hodding's* table, and he made that clear. He caromed among obscure topics, and occasionally let others speak, but only to reinforce whatever point he was making. Yasmine wasn't sure, but thought she liked Hodding's company—in the way that one might enjoy dinner with the mastermind of an unsolved museum heist. He had a strange cachet. During the intermissions when Hodding was badgering the waitstaff or indulging Lindsay in some reminder of her presence, Spock leaned toward Yasmine and bowled a few balls.

She deflected the probes about her background but was happy to speak about the decorating business in Dubai. A comfortable conversational cadence unfolded, sometimes looping in the other table guests. Yasmine was disarming in referring to her inexperience in the business, but she was fluent in the language of interior design and seductive in choosing words to describe her artistic vision. She sprinkled into the conversation design-world words like "intimacy," "private spaces," and "sanctuary." Her terms were polite, but visually suggestive of glass-walled rooms on the upper floors of impossibly tall urban needles where the stylish inhabitants could enjoy morning sex in the bright light from the east, undisturbed by anything except a silent, passing airliner.

Hodding became absorbed in remonstrations about the disappointing occupational habits of Dubai natives. He complained that the locals sat on piles of accumulated wealth, much more than they could ever spend, agonizing over keeping it safe. "No imagination!" he complained. "No idea how to spend their money!" He seemed unaware of the irony of sharing these critical views while lavishly spending his employer's money on exotic sushi and precious burgundy, expenses he would never cover himself.

Hodding and Spock exchanged tasting notes on the wine, each making faces of critical appraisal, followed by expressions like, "a little too fruit-forward." But Hodding seemed to quickly lose interest in Spock, who swirled but didn't fully experience his wine, and whose visual presence was a bit too outré for a Dixie Boy. The other table guests appeared better adapted to Hodding's tastes and were happy to be his faithful audience.

"This restaurant attracts quite the crowd," Spock said, inspecting Yasmine's earrings. Nadia was right about the wild hair. The blue light shot through it like flashes from an arc welder. She had Spock's full attention.

Yasmine shared a story that Nadia provided about a famous, possibly true, recent incident at Hakkasan. It seems that a billionaire couple from Australia was present at the restaurant one night. Both were heirs to mining fortunes, and they were favorites of the London tabloids. Each was dining with a secret lover at tables that were only a couple meters apart—close enough to hear their respective entree choices. But the wife and husband completely ignored each other, refusing even to acknowledge the awkward situation to their very uncomfortable dinner dates. Eventually, each of the formerly secret lovers excused themselves with some pretext, leaving the spouses alone at their separate tables, still not looking at each other. When they were still seated alone after twenty minutes, it was evident that their respective lovers had left the restaurant. This speculation was confirmed the following day when tabloid photographs appeared of the pair leaving Hakkasan together and later checking in at the Grosvenor House, both looking disheveled but still hungry after some frolicking in the back of a taxi. Meanwhile, the Australian couple calmly finished their dinner, and each in turn summoned the chef for compliments on the meal. They left separately but were photographed by the same tabloids arriving in different cars at the ground floor entrance to their sumptuous apartment, where they kissed warmly and disappeared together in the elevator. It was, said Yasmine, a perfect metaphor for Dubai, where social conventions and norms of behavior are suspended by mutual agreement for a brief interval, after which the visitors calmly return to the places where gravity and law apply.

Spock clearly liked her story, and his attentions lingered on Yasmine's hair and the tantalizing grosgrain pathway on her torso. He ignored his meal, adjusting his chair and posture to face her as if he was about to perform a dental examination. The table conversations drifted while Spock shared with Yasmine some saucy portraits of his colleagues at the American Embassy, where he said that work and play competed for intensity. He volunteered that the defense attaché, a female air force officer with pilot wings and combat ribbons, was legendary for "onboarding" newly arrived junior foreign service officers in her secure office behind a giant vault door.

The timing was right, thought Yasmine. She mentioned the eccentricities of her decorating clients and then floated a version of the story about her new Iranian client, a scientist with too much cash and too little taste.

At another table on the opposite side of Hakkasan's vast bar, Katrina and Amir were settling into their evening with the unorthodox sheikh, who had arrived in an ivory-colored sport jacket of linen and silk, double breasted, with two humidors conspicuously aimed like miniature missiles behind a pink pocket square. He ordered Glenlivet. The sheikh was a picture of urbanity, though not very bright. In matters of business, it was obvious that he was quite dependent on his son and the office manager, who were more serious and conventionally dressed for the occasion.

The meal unfolded and the dinner conversation flowed comfortably toward a successful closing. Amir and Katrina had developed such a natural rhythm for these client dinners that preparation was hardly necessary, and the coordination of their respective roles was as smooth as the gyroscopic stabilizer on a luxury cruise ship. With rare exceptions, these dinners concluded with a new or expanded client relationship with Bank Von Raab, and crucially, a growing network of relationships that might tap into more Iranian Bump and Split money.

As the sheikh ordered an exotic digestif, Amir's phone hummed, illuminating an incoming call. It was Rashid. Katrina saw the screen, and with a nearly invisible adjustment of her right eyebrow, signaled to Amir that he should take the call. Amir excused himself and walked to a quieter section of the restaurant, standing in near darkness beside an enormous vase with a tropical flower that resembled a Georgia O'Keefe painting washed in blue. Rashid had some technical questions about the wire transfers arranged for Mr. Golestani, all routine and quickly dispatched by Amir in the brief call. He pivoted to return to his table when a familiar voice made him stop.

The voice emerged from the polylingual din of the other patrons, like cream separating from milk. It was a man deploying a full palette of Alabama vernacular, nearing the punchline of a story that was constructed from molasses, rising creeks, and a sister who lost her britches.

"Merde," said Amir to himself. Amir's memory of his previous Hakkasan encounter with Hodding was filed away with other episodes in his life that involved choosing the wrong fork in the road. *But life had moved on*, he thought, *and he should at least say hello.*

His guests were laughing at Hodding's story as Amir approached the table. Lindsay spotted him first, announcing, "Well, I declare! Look honey, it's *Aaay – Mear*, as handsome as ever."

Hodding instantly was on his feet, snapping his fingers at a non-existent waiter to summon a chair for Amir. Amir smiled politely, hastily scanning the assembled dinner guests between Hodding and Lindsay. His eyes and heart stopped on the woman seated to Hodding's right, noticing first the glowing corona that framed her rich, dark hair, exactly as Herodotus had described her forebears twenty centuries ago. Amir approached, and as he started to say the first syllable of her name, she rose from her chair abruptly and pulled Amir to her in a tight embrace, her lips at his ear.

"*Do not* say my name. *Please.*"

She was as startled as he, but Yasmine took command. Stepping back, but still holding Amir like a brother just returned from the war, she introduced him to the table as an old friend from university, a "star student" of literature. Hodding and Lindsay picked up the ball, asking about his banking career and inventing a grandiose narrative that he was a rising star in Dubai's wealth management scene. Some windy banter followed, with Hodding announcing that he had "discovered" Amir but lost him in a bidding war with one of those "nasty European banks." Spock and the other guests shrugged off the episode, an unremarkable restaurant encounter with a casual acquaintance from the past, certain to end with the usual promise to "get together for lunch," and "I will call you."

Amir stammered that he had to return to his client dinner, as Yasmine pressed a cocktail napkin into his hand with an urgent grip, adding a cheerful, "So good to see you, Amir. Let's catch up soon!" On the napkin, she had written her mobile number and, "Call me!"

Amir watched her take her seat, and then she blew him a kiss, the same heartbreaking projectile she had fired in his direction after their last meeting, a lifetime ago, back in Nablus.

He turned and left the little party, moving through the dark space to return to Katrina and the flamboyant sheikh, but found himself circumnavigating the bar in the wrong direction. Young couples with Australian accents were absorbed in their colorful cocktails and various stages of foreplay. He reversed course, maneuvering back through the crowded assembly of faces glowing like glacial ice, and quietly returned to his seat next to Katrina. The sheikh's earnest-looking son was in mid-paragraph, methodically reviewing some of the fine points of the bank's money management proposal.

"Can we assume that the inflation-adjusted returns will at least stay positive for the foreseeable future?" he asked.

Amir took the question, answering calmly and with authority, as if he had never left the conversation. The son was reassured and nodded with satisfaction to his office manager, who tapped twice on a pack of Marlboros to express his concurrence. The sheikh was distracted, deploying a corner of the tablecloth to polish the richly tooled bezel of his weighty wristwatch.

"Khalas," the sheikh said softly. Finished. Everyone stood to commence the ritual dance that marked the end of a successful evening and the beginning of a profitable partnership. The sheikh fumbled with the complex collection of buttons on his creamy jacket. The maître d' appeared, breathlessly soliciting assurances in Arabic and English that everything was satisfactory, and the party moved like a royal wedding through the happy crowd to their waiting cars.

Inside the car, Katrina gave Amir a look. She was a master of clarity in unspoken communication, Amir thought, reading her very precise question about whether Rashid's call indicated a problem. He wondered if she could read him with the same accuracy.

"Everything's fine," he said. "He just wanted to coordinate the wire transfer schedules and double check the time change to Liechtenstein. It's all good. You can tell Fiona that the second and third tranches are on schedule."

Katrina relaxed but said nothing.

"By the way, I ran into Hodding Easterbrook at the restaurant."

"Oh," she responded, only half-interested. "He's always there. They treat him like an Ottoman Pasha. I don't know why. I suppose he's generous with his bank's money. He makes such a ridiculous show out of everything, and he treats the restaurant staff horribly. And his wife . . . *Oh my God.*"

Amir thought he was doing a good job of disguising his unsteady state after the surreal discovery that Aisha was in Dubai. When Katrina's driver dropped him at his flat, she was laconic as always, and spartan in her commentary about the results of the evening.

"I assume you will send the papers to the sheikh's office tomorrow?"

Amir nodded. That was the extent of her farewell address.

The light in his bedroom was harsh. A high intensity fluorescent bulb froze the scene in a paparazzi flash, startling the objects in the room and burning their shadows onto the white walls. Amir opened the cocktail napkin, read the instructions again, and weirdly, held it to his nose as if to verify its authenticity. There was no fragrance, only the careful handwriting of a woman, hastily but emphatically drafted. The telephone number began with the familiar UAE country code, not the 202 of Egypt. But reminded of his own Boca Raton number, that could mean anything. Her decision to underline, "Call me," electrified Amir.

She had posted her most recent image two days ago. It was another example of fine photographic art, with her searching, melancholy eyes rendered dazzling in a black and white image. The grimy windows of the Cairo Stock Exchange lurked in the background, where some of the uniformed traders were taking a cigarette break on the crowded sidewalk. There was a blurred outline of a passing taxi. Amir looked at the date stamp on her photograph and consulted a calendar. It was posted on a Saturday. The Stock Exchange was closed on Saturdays.

While puzzling through the disconnected dots, it occurred to Amir that he would have to explain to Aisha why he was in Dubai, not New York. With her large community of followers in Nablus, that news would travel quickly back home. Possibly, it already was too late. With all the dreamy imagery he had constructed around his eventual exit to Wall Street, as amended by Bank Von Raab's unexpected plans for him, he had given no thought to a contingency plan for being discovered on the wrong continent. For Amir, his mother was only the first problem, with her mysterious but emphatic admonition to him to stay away from Dubai. His New York lie was so monumental that the ripple effects were too awful to imagine, including the ill-timed exposure it might generate in the middle of the delicate Golestani operation. He began to fabricate half-plausible explanations to hold his fragile story together. He was on a business trip, or a training exercise, or a package holiday to escape the harsh Manhattan winter. But Aisha was seated next to Hodding Easterbrook, and by now, Hodding must have shared with her the whole unlikely story of Amir's banking career.

His panic reached a crescendo of dissonant notes when it was challenged and quickly overtaken by Amir's euphoria. "Call me!" she had written. Silence and distance had separated them for months. Their exquisite future together, despite Amir's detailed and artistic renderings, was always blemished by doubt. It was like a nagging imperfection in a marble carving, a small fissure that shadowed the divine perfection. Did she care for him? Was he worthy of her? Was there someone else? Could he extricate himself from Fiona's dark web? Suddenly, impossibly, Aisha was with him. Amir chose to focus on that. He still felt her breasts pressed against him, her warm lips at his ear, and the thrilling whispered command, "Do not say my name." They both had secrets, it seemed.

Chapter 29.

HODDING'S party at Hakkasan lingered for a while after Amir's surprise appearance. Lindsay remarked that Amir was even better looking than before and probably "had his pick" of the attractive expat women in Dubai looking for a break in the monotony. From the desperate look on her face, she was speaking from experience. For his part, Hodding reflected that Amir looked "lean and hungry," the kind of young banker who would work twice as hard as his counterparts from Greenwich with their "fancy" degrees. This was a favorite autobiographical theme from Hodding, both resentful and admiring of graduates from better schools. And with that, the conversation at the table reverted to its previous state in which the prevailing topics were local scandals and oil prices.

Yasmine was rattled. She tried to steer Spock back to her Iranian dangle story that Amir interrupted. But he had moved on, and his attentions now were plainly focused on post-dinner appetites. She needed something for her report to Leila, but apart from keeping the ball in the air with Spock, she had no information to share. He definitely heard her refer to her Iranian scientist decorating client, but with the ill-timed distraction from Amir, she lost focus on Spock's face. If he reacted, she missed it. Now he was asking for decorating advice about his own apartment. With all the finesse of a middle school boy, he invited Yasmine to stop by for a quick assessment of his window treatments, which he described as "in need of attention." For the benefit of Tehran, and the survival of her exit package, she would have to keep Spock in play, though her doubts about him as a worthy target were growing. If it would require giving him a closer look at her and sharing some of her "decorating skills," she would do it.

But not tonight, Yasmine thought. Her Cairo cover was now at risk with Amir, and *that* needed immediate attention.

The dinner party devolved pleasantly into its terminal phase, with Hodding gesturing for the check, and others offering, without conviction, to share in the damage. There were handshakes, half-hearted embraces and air kisses before Yasmine and Spock found themselves alone, standing outside in the thick, sweaty evening. Caffeinated valet drivers hurtled past them.

"Shall we have a look at those window treatments?" he suggested. "They will seem a little more interesting with a nice vintage port, which I just happen to have in my kitchen." He cradled her elbow, as if to steer her to his car. His hand felt damp and clumsy.

Really? thought Yasmine. *This is the best the Americans can come up with in producing spies to prevent nuclear war?*

Yasmine suggested a rain check, which provoked a surprised and wounded expression on Spock's face.

"I'm definitely interested in your . . . window treatments." She pronounced "window treatments" with prolonged syllabication, to be certain that Spock understood they were both referring to the same thing. "But I have an early client meeting tomorrow. With the crazy Iranian scientist, I told you about." At the risk of being too obvious, she was trying once more, this time concentrating on his expression. Again, nothing. Except a petulant look of disappointment, his arousal deferred for an unspecified duration. Maybe forever.

Then she cheered him with an unexpected kiss, full on, pulling him tightly to her lower abdomen. It was fast but infused with possibility. He was still in play. Yasmine had made certain of that.

Nadia was wearing jeans and working late when Yasmine returned to the villa. Yasmine reported on the highlights of the evening, with Nadia paying close attention to her assessment of Spock's performance, which she summarized wearily.

"It's still too soon to know. So far, he's just another creep."

She did not mention the encounter with Amir. A strange and unsettling thing about Nadia was that she seemed already to know the information Yasmine shared with her, and worse, she seemed also to know what Yasmine chose not to reveal. Yasmine wondered if Hodding may have called her already. Those two were close, and after all, Spock's dinner invitation was a favor for Nadia. It would be a mistake—a breach of trust really—if Nadia knew that Yasmine was holding back something important. Or it was all paranoia.

Nadia's overstuffed atelier was quiet while the two women reflected on their parallel paths, and their next moves. Both needed a win, and even at her carefully measured distance from the particulars of Yasmine's sortie, Nadia could feel the urgency from above. There obviously was something different about this project. When Nadia finally spoke, it was a steady voice of experience.

"I know your friend in Cairo really wants this. Or maybe your friend's employer really wants this. But wanting it is not the same as good intelligence. They've given you nothing about Spock. And my sources, which are pretty good, tell me he's just a wannabe. Like a million others in Dubai, he's trying to reimagine his dead-end life as something intriguing and mysterious. At some point, your friend needs to level with you, and tell you what they have on him."

"Or I need to level with them," Yasmine proposed, "and tell them he's nobody."

"Up to you," Nadia said, leaving for bed. "But tick-tock."

It was cold upstairs in Yasmine's room. Faithful to Dubai tradition, the housekeeper obediently kept the thermostat locked on the snowflake icon. Yasmine pulled a down-filled duvet over her shoulders and loaded the encryption application for a coded message to Leila. Just like the uncertainty she felt in Nadia's presence, Yasmine always wondered how much Leila already knew. She assumed that her telephone was monitored, and possibly, there also were surveillance teams in Dubai to track her movements. Not for the first time, she looked suspiciously at all the vents, smoke detectors, and assorted fixtures attached to the walls and ceiling in her room, frowning at the thought of the greasy tech team in Cairo watching her undress, or crudely awarding scores as she tried various alternative costume combinations before an evening out. Depending on her mood, she sometimes gave them an elaborate performance of raunchy poses, punctuated by projecting her tongue in the direction of a dubious wall-mounted device with a tiny glass hemisphere. More often, she couldn't care less, and just ignored whoever was watching.

In fact, Leila and her threadbare Cairo team did not have those Hollywood resources. They had installed a location tracking device on Yasmine's telephone when she first arrived in Cairo, but that served principally to alert Leila if she unexpectedly left town. There were no cameras or microphones in her villa, and no surveillance teams to follow her around Dubai. Of course, Leila found it useful for Yasmine to suppose that she was being watched closely. But Leila knew that, by far, the most effective tool to keep Yasmine focused was the brutal fact that her exit package depended on a successful mission outcome.

Staring at the computer screen, which had been blank for a long time, Yasmine considered a visit to the kitchen for a glass of wine. But the housekeeper slept lightly, or not at all, and doubtless would be offended if Yasmine served herself. Reverting to the comfort of her journal, where Yasmine could idealize without commitment, she sketched arrows and circles around numbered options, for the first time adding "Amir" to the pages. What was *he* doing here? She was furious at him. He had always been just a harmless figure among the many faceless boys in Nablus, differentiated in Yasmine's memory only by his dreamy and oddly boring ambition to go to Wall Street and, of course, by his mother. When Chief Nurse Hala recruited her, it definitely had not occurred to either of them that Amir might turn up in the middle of a mission.

Who knows how his mother would react to this? Yasmine worried. And if he casually mentioned his encounter with Aisha to his loud-mouthed sister in Nablus, the carefully constructed Cairo cover story would explode into a local scandal. For Nabulsis, social media speculation about Aisha in Dubai would spread like videos of celebrity infidelity. The operation, and her exit package, would be finished.

Yasmine considered her options.

She could say nothing about the encounter and try to persuade Amir to keep her secret. After all, he had his own secret to preserve. Yasmine liked this approach. If she revealed the news to Leila, the reaction was unpredictable, but no one in Cairo or Tehran would be thinking about Yasmine's best interests. To protect their cover, she feared Tehran would abruptly cancel the operation and ship her back to Cairo for a version of indefinite house arrest, or worse. *Better to say nothing,* Yasmine thought, *and make sure Amir does the same.* She thought about their brief previous encounters—in Professor Fathy Shambli's class, at that pathetic graduation party, at the coffee shop in Nablus. In her memory, he had the face of a lost puppy. *He would keep quiet,* she thought, *for her.*

And yet. The risk that Leila already knew, or soon would find out, swept away the specious attractions of that option. After their months together in Cairo, it seemed that nothing could be hidden from her. She thought about the catalogue of photographs they had produced together—deep, penetrating, revealing expressions of Yasmine's wants and fears. Whether Yasmine told her about Amir, or failed to tell her, Leila would surely suspect some unreported news. Lying to Leila and being caught in the lie, was not an option.

The thought experiments cleared her head. Yasmine returned to the keyboard and composed a concise, just-the-facts, report on her evening at Hakkasan. The focus remained on Spock, noting his non-reaction to Captain Sadegh's provocative talking point, and lingering uncertainty about his presumed clandestine responsibilities. But Spock *would* reveal more, Yasmine assured Leila, and soon. Then, in closing, she added the briefest possible account of Amir's appearance. It was a simple declarative sentence, stripped of all modifiers, in the style of a military weather forecast. She pressed "send."

The reaction from Cairo was instantaneous. A terse response appeared on her screen as Yasmine wrestled her dinner dress over her head. She momentarily lost her balance when the audible incoming message alert broke the silence. With one arm still in a sleeve, her bare legs now purple from the cold, she opened the message from Leila.

"Will call you on the secure voice line. Ten minutes."

Since Yasmine had arrived in Dubai, she had never used a voice line with Leila. Despite the security features, it was considered vulnerable to electronic surveillance and was presumed to be a last resort.

"For emergencies only," Leila had told her in Cairo, "and there will be *no* emergencies."

Yasmine looked suspiciously at the glass hemisphere on the wall, recovered her balance, and pulled on some jeans. The call came in five minutes.

Voices were flattened on the secure line, suppressing gender clues and the natural pitch variations that accompany familiar human conversation. The effect was even worse in Arabic when all musicality is hammered into the rhythm of an industrial assembly line. Despite those features, Leila's voice was rich with urgency, even anger. She demanded more details of the Amir incident, using language that felt accusatory, as if Yasmine had been intentionally oblique to minimize its significance. They spoke for a long time—far too long according to their security protocols.

"Why didn't you tell me you had a relationship with Hala's son?" Leila demanded to know. "And why didn't Hala tell me?"

"I don't have a relationship with him. Nablus is a small town. I know him, in the same way I know everyone there. It's nothing," Yasmine said, speaking honestly.

"You say it's nothing, but if he speaks to his mother, or to anyone about meeting you in Dubai, this operation is exposed. How do we know he hasn't done that already?"

Yasmine waited for an opening in the interrogation and then made her pitch.

"He won't do that. Amir told his family, and everyone, that he is in New York. Whatever he's doing here, he wants it to be a secret. And if I approach him, and ask him to keep *my* secret, I promise you he will do it. I know these Nabulsi boys. They do what women tell them."

Leila was quiet for the first time, calculating the risks. Yasmine sensed progress and pressed on.

"And if I sense any hesitation from him, I know how to be persuasive." The word she chose in Arabic implied seduction rather than a gun to the head.

"You're getting ahead of yourself," she told Yasmine sternly.

Leila liked to control risks. This one blindsided her. But it was too late for recriminations. For this mission, there was no plan B. If Leila could not produce the foreign devils responsible for the Meyghan blast, the twisted logic in Tehran would demand accountability inside the family. The list of inevitable conspirators surely would include her, and before they were finished, it would enumerate the capital crimes of Yasmine, Nadia, Chief Nurse Hala, the harmless Dr. Reza, Captain Sadegh, his idiot colonel at Prison 59, and whoever happened to be unpopular that week among the Revolutionary Guard commanders. That outcome would be certain and swift.

Or she could take a chance on Yasmine's plan. A shot in the dark, she thought, since Amir was a faceless name, nowhere on her radar. If she approved this plan, and Amir still let it slip that Yasmine, under an assumed name, was a fixture in the Dubai social scene circling Kirk and Spock, it would be a humiliating scramble. She would have to roll up the operation before the Americans leaned on their friends in Abu Dhabi and Cairo to rendition Leila's whole team to a desert black site.

"I'm going to give you twenty-four hours to settle things with this boy," Leila said quietly. Even with the distortions added by the secure line, Yasmine could tell she was not convinced, but felt cornered. "And if I were you, I would start now."

Chapter 30.

YASMINE scrolled through old texts and was surprised to find an overlooked message from Amir to which she never responded. He had written, "Good to see u on Saturday. Hope u will visit me in NYC." She responded now.

"Can we meet?"

The reply was immediate. "Yes. When?"

"Now."

Nadia's driver finally answered her call after three attempts. When he appeared with the car in front of the villa, it was well after midnight. In the darkened rearview mirror, he looked like a vampire. Tomorrow she would need a story for Nadia to explain this outing, but for now, Yasmine rehearsed her performance for Amir. She debated whether to begin with her lie or his lie. She chose the latter. She wanted him on the defensive, and it would give her the chance to tailor her own story, if necessary. Yasmine's recollections of Amir were hazy. Another boy from Nablus. She remembered their last meeting, a convenient invitation she had accepted to reinforce her Cairo cover story among the Nablus natives. When they met over coffee, she had pretended to be deep in her political science studies and hoped Amir would spread that image, especially to his sister, a notorious local gossip and teenage influencer. At that meeting, he was, she recalled, very attentive to her, but his eyes sometimes left their conversation and seemed to linger in indefinite directions, like he was dreaming. Unlike the others, Amir was never forward. He was gentle, respectful, even kind. And otherwise, not memorable at all.

This late-night meeting between two unmarried Muslims violated every possible social convention, even in Dubai. Yasmine chose a tearoom attached to an international chain hotel in the marina, where she often met Nadia. In keeping with the local business imperative of catering to all seventeen time zones between Los Angeles and Tokyo, the place never closed. It was rare to see anyone but Europeans there, and the staff were well trained to notice nothing. For this meeting, Yasmine dressed like an auditor on a business trip from Frankfurt and accessorized with a professional looking leather portfolio, which was empty.

Yasmine arrived first and positioned herself at an isolated table beneath the shadow cast by a rubber tree that looked ridiculous in a desert country. Amir arrived moments later. He looked eager, smiling brightly when he saw her. There was an awkward moment when he joined her at the table. He appeared to maneuver for another embrace, but she remained seated, hoping to minimize attention. They recovered.

"I was so surprised to see you," she said, firing the first shot. She was nervous, noticing a slight tremor in her hand. "I'm sorry if I seemed mysterious, but it was just such a shock to see someone from Nablus. I thought you were in New York."

"I thought you were in Cairo," Amir replied, surprised he was not nervous. The glow around Aisha cradled him. "But anyway, I'm glad to see you."

"You first," she insisted. "What are you doing here?"

With all the richly imagined dialogue in the screenplay of his future life with Aisha, he had never quite written this particular scene. *His detour in Dubai would pass unnoticed,* he thought, *a dull footnote in his resume that would never require a full explanation.* Clearly, he was wrong. Amir lacked the guile that came easily to Aisha, and without considering the consequences, he told her the truth. As he related

his journey from Boca Raton to Hakkasan, and from there to Bank
Von Raab, Amir felt it sounded implausible, like the Vonnegut novel
they had read together in Professor Fathy's class, which Aisha had
dismissed as "too fictional." He paused for breath and stopped before revealing the bank's real business.

Yasmine sensed he had limited powers of imagination, and accepted the story as true, or, at least, probably true. After all, it was
no less strange than her own path, which she definitely would not be
sharing with Amir.

"OK," she said, which instantly felt insufficient to acknowledge
his beautifully detailed narrative. "So now you're a banker. You succeeded in getting out of Nablus. Why maintain the New York fiction?"

Amir appeared to struggle with a reply, obviously embarrassed
by his dishonesty. Finally, he spoke. "You've met my mother, I think?"

This unexpected topic alarmed Yasmine. She looked down at her
coffee, forcing an expressionless look. Amir continued.

"We were never close. She's not a happy person. We disagree on a
lot, but I don't . . . I can't openly disobey her."

A good Nabulsi boy, Yasmine thought.

"There's something in her past. I don't know what it is. But she
was determined to keep me away from the Gulf, and especially
Dubai. It's strange, but she would be much more comfortable with
me in New York than here."

Yasmine held her breath, wondering if he suspected her connection to his mother. But he continued in a different direction.

"I wasn't going to fight with her about Dubai. And once I hatched
the New York story, it was too late to backtrack." Then he added,
"Anyway, I will get to New York soon. Now it's your turn."

Relieved that the reference to his mother was benign and nothing in Amir's narrative required rewriting her own, Yasmine breezily
shared an abridged version of her Dubai cover story, lying with absolute comfort and confidence. Graduate school in Cairo was a dead-
end, she said, and the Egyptians were insufferable. The decorating
job in Dubai came along, and she took it. She adopted "Yasmine
Khoury" as her "trade name." But just like Amir's situation, her parents would never approve, so she kept up the Cairo pretense.

"Eventually," Yasmine said, "I know I will have to unwind this. But hopefully not now. I'm not ready."

And then, some theatrics. Yasmine closed her eyes tightly, first suppressing and then generating tears. She reached across the table and took both of Amir's hands in hers. She looked at him like a lost child. The tremor in her hand added to the effect.

"Amir, you have always been very special to me. I'm not ready to face my family on this. Please promise me you won't tell anyone. At least until I . . ." She corrected herself, "at least until *we* can make a plan."

She read him perfectly. When she said "we," Amir looked renewed. He folded his hands around hers, and promised, with total conviction, that her story was safe with him.

"We are in this together," he assured her.

Success, thought Yasmine, and easier than she expected. She would report to Leila that her cover was secure, and she could get back to the business of pulling the truth from Spock. She wondered whether Amir would require more handholding, which could be complicated. Dubai was not a small town but gossip far surpassed European football as the favorite local sport. It was only a matter of time before someone whispered to Nadia that Yasmine was spotted with Amir. She decided to worry about that later.

Having settled the safety of her cover, Yasmine relaxed in Amir's company. It was late, but for a change, she felt comfortable to be with someone who reminded her of home. She flirted, placing her long fingers on his arm for emphasis. She pressed him for details about his life in Dubai, filling in the blanks in his story about the peculiar journey from the West Bank to a very different bank. Amir obliged, sharing information without apparent restraint. He described his job as money management. "Dubai style," he added, with an expression that hinted at shady practices. He joked about his client development dinners with local sheikhs, painting pictures of the comical interplay among the usual table guests. Strangely, he even recounted select parts of his memorable evening with "a truly evil English woman," which he summarized as an example of European duplicity, and his introduction to "what life would be like at Bank Von Raab."

Yasmine was not entirely paying attention to his banker banter

until Amir, in a casually reckless reference, said that he never expected his career plan to include "money laundering." "Especially
for the Persians," he added.

Startled, and wondering if he was serious, she gave him a look of
worried curiosity. He walked it back only a little.

"I probably shouldn't talk about it. And that's enough about me."

Amir shifted direction and asked about Aisha's elaborate photographic record of her life in Cairo. She was still reflecting on the
reference to Persians when, to her astonishment, he chronicled in
perfect order and from memory the images of Aisha that were posted and were still being posted regularly. His descriptions made it
clear that he had studied every detail, not in a way that might seem
perverse or obsessive, but as an art historian might deconstruct the
work of classic photographers, comparing their techniques, subjects,
and influences. Referring to examples that Yasmine herself did not
fully recall, Amir commented on subtle differences he had perceived
between the early and most recent shots. Comparing one photo to
a museum piece, in which she cradled her head in her hands, hair
lush and amiss, he circled around the subject before coming to a
point that very obviously preoccupied him.

"Who is the photographer?" he asked with hesitation. "I mean,
he's really an artist. And it's like he sees inside you."

Surprised, but realizing that Amir suspected something intimate, Yasmine laughed.

"It's a *she*. A friend from grad school. I'm amazed you remember
these in so much detail."

Amir looked surprised and relieved. "But tell me about the
Mogamma photo," he said.

She didn't remember the image. Amir explained the anomaly,
reminding her of the incident with the divorcing couple in Cairo,
the faceless bureaucrat, the arson, the scorched facade of the infamous building, and the date stamp on her photograph.

"It makes sense now," he said, "since you're here and not in Cairo.
But it was a real mystery to me."

A rare slip-up by Leila, thought Yasmine. *Did anyone else notice this?*

"OK, Amir. You caught me. I've been posting these photos to
keep up my Cairo presence—for my family. I just hope you're the

only one looking at them with a microscope and a calendar."

The patrons in the tearoom had recycled a couple of times since Amir and Yasmine arrived. They both sensed it was time to say good night. Unsure when they might speak again, Yasmine decided to circle back to the "Persian" reference.

Except in the dreamworld in which Amir dwelled happily with Aisha, he had never spent so much time with her or shared such deep and revealing thoughts. But for him, her magical presence, the displays of vulnerability, and the power of their shared chemistry aligned so neatly with his invented story that there really was no distinction. *They were together now*, he thought, just as they had been. He trusted her completely, and in fact, confiding in her felt like investing in their shared future. They would be in this together.

"Since we're keeping each other's secrets, I may as well tell you," Amir began.

He leaned forward, speaking in a conspirator's voice, as if planning a heist. Aisha listened, now rapt, as Amir explained Bank Von Raab's graduation from small-time facilitator of foreign corrupt practices, to an American intelligence front targeting Iran. He described, with some unintended pride, his role in converting Bump and Split proceeds into offshore portfolios that would be used by American spies to extort information and cooperation in the long-running campaign to find and kill nuclear scientists. Amir mentioned Rashid, fondly and by name, as his interlocutor to the Dubai sheikhs whom the Iranians trusted. Perhaps he thought he was being discreet by not exposing Fiona by name, but even her cover was left rather thin when he described her as a "creepy English woman spying for the Americans." He stopped just short of revealing the names and details from the Golestani operation, but anyone could infer from the narrative that the scheme was actively underway. For cinematic effect, Amir couldn't resist telling Aisha that the unnamed Iranian accountant in Dubai had a monstrous facial scar. And finally, Amir rationalized his role by mentioning Fiona's threats to Sara if he did not cooperate, adding with absolute confidence that his participation would be rewarded with a seat on a trading floor in New York, where he could put all this behind him.

Amir started to go further and suggest that there was a place for

Aisha by his side in New York, but her expression implied that she was distracted. He saved that for another time, which would come soon enough. For the second time in his life, Amir made the mistake of saying far too much to a woman whose loyalties were elsewhere.

Chapter 31.

IN his office the next morning, Amir was a man in full. At last. His emotional scars and moral compromises now were internalized, accepted and forgotten like the ubiquitous little pathogens in the atmosphere. He could see the finish line now and was invigorated, even resurrected, by the clarity and beauty of his path. Amir was no longer working under coercion by Fiona or Bank Von Raab. Now he was working for himself and for Aisha.

The second tranche of the Golestani money was about to move. Much larger than the first, it was Golestani's affirmation that the test tranche was successful, that Rashid and Amir were trusted partners, and now they would be the primary channel for the private corruption of Tehran's ruling class. Amir had attended lovingly to the preparations. He was now a club member who was welcomed—at least on the telephone—among the circle of polished European bankers who shared in the superbly generous transaction fees. He had chatted that morning with Balz in Zürich, Ian in London, and Abigail in Saint Peter Port, and each had congratulated him on the "elegance" of his deal structure. Amir had, as they put it, "retired the trophy" for burying the ownership of the funds behind a fortress of inscrutability, which even they couldn't entirely follow. They promised to meet for an obscenely expensive closing dinner soon, and each of the three competed in insisting to pay the tab in honor of Amir.

"To you, Amir. And to the Eagle Trust!" Abigail shouted through the telephone line, referring to the predator appellation suggested by Rashid for this unique set of transactions.

While Amir exhibited his mastery of international finance, Yasmine lingered in her bed. She chose not to swim that morning, with or without a suit. And she skipped breakfast with Nadia, their usual planning session for the day. Nadia would know she had gone out alone the previous night. Both the driver and the housekeeper almost certainly had reported it, probably with some embellishments from the indignant, disapproving Bengali. In good time, Yasmine would share the information with Nadia, or at least what Nadia needed to know.

After a sleepless night, and now wrestling eyeshades poorly designed to shield her from the fearsome Dubai morning sun, Yasmine battled disbelief. After the elaborate ballet of her recruitment and training, the Cairo ruse, Nadia's web of intimates, and the disappearing breadcrumbs on the trails of Kirk and Spock, was it really possible that this half-forgotten boy from Nablus was her target? And that *he* found *her*, not the opposite? *It was incredibly unlikely*, she thought, b*ut so were the other explanations.*

Was it a trap? She had to consider that. Perhaps Yasmine's shark circles around Spock had aroused suspicion, and his handlers decided to send in their own messenger. Maybe, but how would they find their way to Amir, and why would they choose him of all people? If they vetted Amir—as they obviously would have—how would they miss the connection to Chief Nurse Hala, or her connection to Tehran? *Not possible*, thought Yasmine.

Was it a test? It could be one of those outlandish experiments from Prison 59 to prove Yasmine's loyalty to the mission. But Leila would never stand for that kind of paranoid nonsense, nor would Chief Nurse Hala, if they told her. How would Yasmine pass or fail the test, she wondered? With the elevated drama and urgency of this mission, constantly repeated from Tehran, why would they sideline the targets now with a diversion?

Trap, test, or happy accident, Yasmine knew she had to report the full details to Leila. That was a dilemma too. *Amir is working for the Americans,* she reminded herself. The chessboard on which Tehran and Washington faced off had medieval but mostly precise rules about which pieces were expendable without provoking total war. Generally speaking, neither side would intentionally kill an Iranian or American intelligence officer, which would be considered inelegant. And very bad manners. But a hapless Palestinian recruit, coerced with threats to his family and promises of a future in Disneyland? Both sides would consider him acceptable collateral damage, or possibly the fair price of a face-saving de-escalation. She winced at the thought of poor Amir in the custody of either side. Yasmine wondered if she could betray him, and still protect him. Behind her eye shades, she test drove a couple of scenarios in which her report might neglect to mention the "Persian" reference, or downplay Amir's role, reducing him to an office clerk who didn't really understand what he was doing. Leila would be suspicious, she was certain, and in any event, it wasn't Yasmine's job to be an analyst.

"Just collect and report the facts," Leila had told her a thousand times in Cairo. "Someone else decides what it all means."

There was, finally, the issue of Yasmine's own interests. The price of her exit plan was a limited mission: penetrate the American operation in Dubai that was reaching Iran's scientists. *Mission accomplished, and ahead of schedule,* thanks to Amir's careless revelations. *It wasn't her job to do anything about it,* she reminded herself. That was someone else's problem to solve, and by then, she would be in London, and out of the game forever. That was her deal. Amir had his own deal, he told her, and he should take care of himself. Yasmine was confident of her powers of persuasion, but she was at her absolute best when persuading herself. Now in repose under her cool white sheets, with warm daylight filtered through the thread count, there was perfect clarity in her mental calculation of the way forward.

For the second and last time, Yasmine and Leila used the secure voice line. Above the electronic distortion and distracting static, Yasmine spoke clearly. "My cover is safe with him. I'm certain of it."

Faithful to the facts and avoiding any hint of suspicious sentiment, Yasmine recounted Amir's story to Leila. She shared every detail, in the clinical tone of a radiologist's dictations. "The axial sesamoid view confirms acute fibular fracture," she might have said.

Leila said almost nothing during Yasmine's recitation. She interrupted once to probe unsuccessfully for clues that Amir knew something about the Meyghan explosion or the extraction of Dr. Mousavi, but her questions necessarily were obtuse since those events were never disclosed to Yasmine. Yasmine had been told only that the Americans had scored a successful recent penetration, with the help of someone in Dubai, and they were running a bigger operation to target nuclear scientists. But the intelligence that Amir shared was stunning in its detail. He provided the names of the Emirati and Lebanese interlocutors, the timing and routing of the money transfers, and the American connection to Bank Von Raab. Best of all, Amir provided a description of the Iranian officer handling the money, whose vivid scar would be easy to verify. Among case officers, no one was more capable than Leila. She recognized actionable intelligence, and for this, saw no need to waste time imagining false flags or counterespionage traps. This information and its source were too outlandish to be fabricated, she concluded.

"I will speak to our friends," Leila told Yasmine. "Wait for instructions. Tell Nadia only that there has been a development, and we are reviewing our target list. She will understand."

It was early in Cairo. The morning sunlight competed for attention behind a heavy curtain of dirty fog in the air. Leila was alone in the office, except for a security man, who was smoking a cheap local cigarette in the corridor, a Cleopatra Golden King, which produced the aroma of a smoldering mummy. They didn't like or trust each other, so they kept their distance. It had rained briefly overnight, and the city smelled of damp rags. She liked the relative quiet, which helped her plan the next move.

Yasmine's information either would be verified or discredited in Tehran, but Leila knew it would happen quickly. The inner circle paid close attention to their money. Like their prostitutes, they remembered every detail about their bankers in these dirty transactions. If any of the information Amir revealed was familiar, the reaction would be immediate.

Who was the Americans' flip target? she wondered. *This Iranian with the scar on his face?*

It had to be someone prominent, with impeccable revolutionary credentials. No one else was trusted both to handle this money and to keep nuclear secrets. Had he been flipped already? Whoever he was, he needed to be the last to hear about Yasmine's report. If Scarface was tipped off prematurely, he might use his position to make himself disappear or, more likely, make Yasmine and Leila disappear.

It was a peculiar feature of Leila's working relationship with Captain Sadegh that, while she loathed his amateur methods and his unwanted amorous insinuations, she trusted him. In Sadegh's unhappy reflections on his failed personal life, he all but admitted that Leila was the woman he should have married. She was certain he would never betray her confidence.

Leila departed from protocol again and used a voice line to call Captain Sadegh. The signal quality was wretched. *Maybe that was the real security feature,* she thought. Even if intercepted, no one could understand what was being said.

"We've had a lucky break," she said. Leila fed him the highlights, efficiently, in the spoken equivalent of bullet points.

There was silence for a moment, as if he was waiting for a missing bullet to tie it all together. "But what about Spock?" He was still clinging to his hunch.

"Forget Spock. We were getting nowhere with him. If this information checks out, we have found what we are looking for."

Sadegh obviously was suspicious. He said he thought it was too convenient, too fortuitous that Yasmine's "old boyfriend" turned up in Dubai with this story. "Her cover must be blown," Sadegh argued. "I always thought this Nablus girl was too green for this project. Let's get her out of there."

Leila pushed back. "You're wrong about her. But it doesn't matter. What I need right now is verification. From the top. If they tell us they never heard of this bank or these characters, then we will do as you suggest and pull the girl."

They argued, half incomprehensibly on the bad voice line, until Sadegh's reflexive submission to Leila prevailed.

"Fine, let's submit your report," he agreed.

As soon as Leila mentioned the interception risk, Sadegh saw it. "This may not be the time for the usual channels," she said dryly.

Sadegh was just a captain. But Prison 59 had a reputation. It was feared by just about everyone, and for the handful of others, it would at least have their attention. It was a risk to circumvent his colonel, but Sadegh had one safe route to the top. He despised his wife's family, and the feeling was mutual. Except her youngest brother. Years ago, early in his military career, the brother embezzled air force payroll funds to finance a gambling debt. He came to Sadegh, panicked. Saying nothing to his wife, Sadegh used a Prison 59 remote link to clean up the payroll records. Now the brother was chief of staff to the Guardian Council and custodian of their records of the Bump and Split business.

"Send me your report," Sadegh said to Leila. "I will get it to the right desk. If the information is good, we will be fine. If not, then maybe you and I will be spending more time together. In new accommodations."

"I might like that," he added.

Before lunch, Leila's single page report went to the very top. In the first three lines, the report mentioned Bank Von Raab, Bump and Split, Rashid the Beiruti, Amir the Palestinian banker, and, of course, the Persian accountant with the unforgettable scar. It would have been a good opening to a pulpy detective novel.

The reaction was instantaneous. In matters that involve the personal investment portfolio of the Supreme Leader, there are no bureaucratic delays. The reference to the scar left no doubt that Yasmine's information was authentic. Golestani and his wife were escorted with some rough handling from their elegant villa in Tehran's District 6. In a Persian version of the Prisoner's Dilemma, they were questioned in separate rooms and accused of conspiring with American intelligence. In addition to vague promises of God's grace if they cooperated, both were threatened with predictable consequences if they failed to implicate each other. Both were indignant, and Golestani flew into a genuine rage when he realized he had been set up by Rashid and Amir. The scar on his face flared in violent color as if it would burst open like a cherry tomato in a hot skillet. While the interrogators debated whether he was lying or just responsible for an unconscionable misstep—the consequences likely were the same—orders were given to clean up the spill in Dubai quickly, before it spread.

Leila received instructions from Prison 59 to put her sparrow back to work. "Tonight," the order said, without ambiguity. Yasmine would go to Amir's flat, and "proceed as necessary" to obtain the remaining details of the American operation. "A team will follow," the order added.

Captain Sadegh sent worried messages to Leila through the afternoon.

Will she play her role? Is there a chance she will go soft and try to protect the boy? Sadegh asked. *Shouldn't you mention our insurance policy?*

Unbelievable, thought Leila. He knew so little about Yasmine, or for that matter, about any woman. Did he really think it would be effective to threaten the life of her mother?

She will do what I tell her, wrote Leila in a curt reply. Then she added, *Make sure your team stays out of her way.*

In a few deceptively dull encrypted messages, Leila and Yasmine worked out the details of a high-drama rendezvous. Yasmine would arrange to meet Amir at his flat in a few hours.

For dinner, perhaps, suggested Leila, *but use your discretion.*

Yasmine would learn what she could about the bank's plans for the Iranian money transfers and flipping Golestani. She would leave Amir's flat before midnight. She would take precautions to arrive and depart undetected. Leila mentioned midnight a second time.

Yasmine suspected she might not be the last to visit Amir that night. *What happens at midnight?* she typed and then deleted the message.

Leila read her thoughts from the discontinuity in the messaging cadence. Leila sent one more message. *Don't worry about the boy. Nothing will happen to him. He's just a little fish,* Leila added. She lied like the professional that she was.

Yasmine telephoned Amir. The incoming call appeared on his phone as "No Caller ID."

"OK if I make dinner for you tonight? Do you have a kitchen?"

Chapter 32.

NADIA received her own instructions and departed quietly that afternoon for an impromptu ski trip to Sochi. She left the villa and her business in the capable hands of the gentleman from Mumbai, who would reschedule her appointments and make polite but vague excuses until she returned. Nadia was told only that the mission was completed, and that it was—in a manner of speaking—successful. Before leaving for the airport, Nadia joined Yasmine solemnly amidst the fabric and wallpaper bundles. Uncertainty hung over the room like cold drizzle at a summer wedding. Both women were professionals now, and they each observed the essential rules of leaving unsaid anything that might compromise the other.

"One piece of advice," offered Nadia before leaving. "Don't try to write a happy ending for everyone. Just focus on your own story."

Yasmine seldom experienced guilt. She remembered it as a remote childhood experience, encouraged by older family members, excessively religious people, and Anglo-Saxon literature. It mostly left her when she left Nablus. But as she dressed for dinner with Amir, it was hard to suppress the feeling that he got an unfair break, that he deserved some kind of consolation prize at least. After all, they both were recruited by scheming foreigners swept up in their own blood feud. Yasmine and Amir had the same objective, and their exit plans turned out to be remarkably similar. If she was honest, it was only dumb luck that Yasmine would leave Dubai with a winning lottery ticket, and Amir, probably not. And he confided in her, sharing the information that would pay for her plane ticket to London, the house in Cadogan Square, *and* her retirement plan. *Surely, she owed him something,* Yasmine repeated.

Then she reproached herself for thinking so transactionally, like a suburban divorcee trading sex for a restaurant dinner, or more optimistically, a kitchen renovation. Yasmine reminded herself that Amir was working for the Americans. *They will take care of him,* she assured herself. And to be fair, he brought this on himself—talking too much; taking no precautions; ignoring basic tradecraft. *He was never very bright,* she remembered.

During this inconclusive debate with her conscience, there were a few false starts with her choice of evening wear. She started with something from Nadia's closet that was, on reflection, too unsubtle. At the opposite extreme was the dark tunic that looked severe and forbidding.

No need to look as cruel as I feel, she thought. Before finally settling on a simple pairing with white jeans, she cast an exasperated look at the glass hemisphere on the wall. Then she offered a defiant projection of her bare bottom in the direction of the supposed voyeurs. *When this is all over,* Yasmine mused, *they will miss the entertainment.*

The driver, still disapproving of her after-dark solo adventures, drove her to Amir's building. Over his objections expressed with head shaking, she stepped out of the car in front of an adjacent building and walked in darkness to the destination. She told him to wait at a discreet distance. Her head was fully covered, and a capacious abaya billowed in the warm evening wind like a spinnaker on a pirate ship. Obscured beneath was Yasmine's resolute expression and a bag of essential groceries from Carrefour.

She entered without speaking when Amir opened the door to his flat. Still anxious and undecided about her intentions, the head scarf and abaya came off with an impatient sweep and fell in a pile. The grocery bag still hanging from her arm, she kissed him hard. It was unplanned. They both laughed, happy to break the tension.

Yasmine showed herself around his small flat, dramatizing her decorator's appraisal of the design choices, turning to Amir with a lifted eyebrow after studying the framed photographs in the dining room. There was a pair of black and white images of fragments of ancient columns, Greek or Roman, lying on their sides. Masterpieces of meaningless, artless, and inoffensive decoration. Along with the black sharp-angled furniture, severely Scandinavian in design, the artwork was part of the fully furnished accommodations, crowding out all possibility of personalization. Yasmine shook her head in Amir's direction, and he gave her a helpless look, accepting her rebuke for tolerating such unimaginative surroundings.

"You know," she offered, "with some very modest effort, I could help make this place a little more comfortable for you."

"I'm sure you could. But this is Dubai, after all. Everything is just a temporary installation. I'm not sure it really deserves your attention to design detail. Or your talents."

Continuing her inspection, Yasmine peeked into the bedroom. More of the same, except in a break from the color scheme monotony, she spotted his small collection of books on the floor by the bed. Paperbacks, with torn covers and spines that were bowed and rippled by loving attention. Yasmine knelt next to the little pile, fondling the precious treasures, pausing to study ancient pencil annotations and coffee stains from prehistory. She recognized some of the titles from Professor Fathy's course. The cover of *Moby Dick* had separated from its moorings and was stuffed inside Chapter 16, where there was a passage that someone had underlined and circled. In the margin, a cryptic penciled note read, "profit-sharing." At the foot of the bed, a faded and stained anthology of Hemingway stories was held together with rubber bands.

Yasmine released a little squeal of delight when she found the battered copy of *Another Country*. She held it up for Amir to see.

"Can you believe I was such a perfect little arrogant bitch in that class?"

"Perfect, yes," Amir agreed. "I'm sure Professor Fathy will never forget you."

Watching Aisha on her knees next to his bed, leafing through his little collection of beloved literature, Amir felt the persistent antiseptic cold of his flat disappear, as warmth radiated from some energy source within her. After living with her on the opposite side of a fine linen scrim for endless months, pasting together their imagined lives from her photograph postings and his dreamscapes from wealth management advertising, Amir was transported by her physical presence. There was a scent that followed her into a room, and a subtle change in barometric pressure. Her playful gestures and dramatic eyebrows. The feeling that they were old friends, and yet intimates. It was inconceivable, Amir worried, that he had willed all this into existence with nothing but the persistence of his vivid imagination.

Yasmine took command in the kitchen, improvising cheerfully upon learning—with mock horror—that Amir had no shallots, and wielding a dull paring knife like a brain surgeon. She asked Amir if there was wine.

"Merde," he said to himself. Embarrassed that he had not anticipated the request, he located in his closet a forgotten bottle of single malt whiskey, still inside a ridiculously elaborate presentation box that he received from one of his grateful banker friends in Switzerland. Aisha looked at the box suspiciously, reminded Amir that she needed *cooking* wine, and then shrugged. She poured a tumbler for herself, and then splashed a healthy quantity into a glaze mixture that would grace a salmon filet, which lay nearby—naked, wet, and suggestive.

Tentatively at first, but enjoying the idea of their lips touching the same object, Amir shared Aisha's tumbler. She chattered easily during the meal preparation, assigning small tasks to him that placed the two of them on collision paths in Amir's tiny kitchen. Sleeves rolled, wiping olive oil from her hands, she stepped away to launch a playlist on her phone, and then kicked off her heels. Back at work in the kitchen, barefoot, she moved her hips with the music. Coltrane was playing, "You Don't Know What Love Is," though neither the title nor the irony registered with Amir. She patted Amir's bottom gently to move him aside as she took custody of the salmon for its final act.

Amir felt the temperature rise in the compressed workspace with the combined contributions of the gas burners, the whiskey, and

Aisha's animated presence. Her aggressive morning swims had sculpted the contours in her arms and neck, which Amir studied intently
when her back was turned. She turned, smiled, and kissed him again.
A quick, sloppy kiss this time. As she danced while conducting the
music with a long wooden spoon, her rich dark hair flowing madly
like a flooding river, he clearly saw their new life together. Far away
in New York. The dirty secrets, grubby characters and ugly baggage
of Dubai discarded and forgotten. Their careers secure. And their
lives perfect.

They lingered over the meal while seated at Amir's small table,
one candle and the Dubai skyline providing the dim light in the
room. Unguarded for a while, they both shared stories about Nablus,
their families, and their sad memories. When Amir mentioned his
mother, Yasmine tightened. She pictured Chief Nurse Hala, that
tormented woman, and hoped she would never learn that her son
proved to be the target of Yasmine's recruitment.

Yasmine recovered her focus.

"How do you know the bank will let you go?" she asked. "I mean,
aren't you worried that you know too much?"

It was a genuine question, not really formulated to elicit anything. Yasmine wondered about Amir's training, and whether he
was prepared to anticipate countermeasures. Surely, he had at least
some suspicions about her very unlikely appearance in the middle
of *his* intelligence operation; her unconvincing response when he
confronted her with the mistakes in her photographic dossier from
Cairo; her contrived "please keep my secret" entreaty; and the wild
pace that sped in twenty-four hours from a chance encounter between forgotten schoolmates to the kiss she delivered like a starved
animal just inside his door. But he acted as if this was all perfectly
sensible, almost preordained.

"Actually, I don't know that much," Amir responded. "All I know
is that the bank is a front for the Americans, and they want to use
it to extort information from Iranians. But I'm not involved in the
extortion part of it. I just move the money. And anyway," he added,
"everyone knows this spy stuff goes on in Dubai. They've been at it
since before we were born."

"You don't need to worry about me." He smiled, stupidly.

Yasmine suddenly felt sad for him, reaching for his hand, pulling it to her lips, and then placing it on her knee where she held it firmly. She was ambivalent about pressing him for more information. Leila and Prison 59 already had what they needed, and probably as much as he knew. She believed his story about innocently joining the bank, doing his best to build client relationships, and then being threatened to secure his cooperation. Maybe it was strange that they recruited someone like Amir in the first place. On the other hand, he delivered, and led them straight to Tehran's bag man and its dirty money. She doubted the promise that anyone seriously planned to exfiltrate him to a happy new life in New York, especially after his employers are exposed, and they realize that the loose lips were his. Not for the first time, it occurred to her that Amir might be facing trouble from both sides of this shadow war.

Despite the several similarities, nothing about this evening reminded Amir of his dinner with Fiona, or the obvious lessons. Like the aftermath of a concussion, his memory of that painful episode resided mostly in a dark closed cabinet in his mind, the key to which was lost. But it was also true that his understanding of tonight's dinner was impaired by a firmly fixed narrative about Aisha that was horribly wrong. Not only had she lied to him about her presence in Dubai, she was not, as he imagined, possessed with the same sense of divine fate that their futures were now joined as happy lovers. Still, he was wildly content in her company. Ignoring all evidence to the contrary, Amir had no expectation of a seduction, and he was neither plotting nor preparing for a move in that direction.

Yasmine looked at her watch and then led the way, though she was not entirely sure why. It was no longer part of the mission. "This is just for me," she told herself, deciding not to overanalyze. She had low expectations, reinforced by her own experiences with Nablus boys, the catalogue of disappointments and cruel descriptions shared by her female friends, and her impression of Amir as a sweet boy with limited imagination. But Mrs. Al-Qasem had taught her to make the best of these occasions, skipping the awkward preludes, ignoring the fumbled probes, and taking command. "You need to control the pace," Mrs. Al-Qasem repeated, as if training soldiers for an amphibious assault in darkness. "It's up to you to place him where *you* want him."

"Make him work! Make him wait!" she would say, memorably. Then, quoting from a classic book in her little library, she added, "Because when he's finished, it's over."

Yasmine didn't wait for a break in the conversation, or for any other conventional segue from this to that. In fact, Amir was in mid-sentence when she calmly stood up, pivoted from the table, pulled the cotton sweater over her head, and dropped it on the floor as she disappeared into his bedroom.

She expected it would gently shock him, a reliable opening move to establish her control of the board. Amir watched this performance with interest but finished his sentence, and the next three sentences. They had been discussing the relative merits of living in New York or London, places neither of them had visited. Looking at her sweater on the floor, Amir had the feeling that he had already lived this exact moment, possibly several times. It was entirely familiar. He could visualize the rewind and the fast-forward. He couldn't actually see her from the table, but knew she was seated on his bed in a half lotus, straight-backed and shadowed by his small reading lamp. She had selected a book—not at random—and was about to read a circled passage on a dog-eared page. As she paused to take a dramatic breath, a well-timed prelude to her performance, her fine breasts rose, cradled in delicate Italian filigree, not red this time, but midnight blue, the color of a deep, turbulent ocean.

"Let faith oust fact. Let fancy oust memory. I look deep down and do believe."

Amir stood in the bedroom door and watched this performance. He had read that line a dozen times and puzzled over it. This time, its meaning seemed to capture the moment. Aisha dropped the book and beckoned by lifting her chin. But Amir held his position, prolonging the moment and signaling a measured, deliberate pace. In all his richly imagined episodes of making love to Aisha, Amir drew upon the unforgettable instruction from his chemistry lab partner, Aaliyah, who was patient, focused, and a perfectionist. She had nothing but contempt for frenzied, wanton sneezes of sex, which she regarded as crude, amateurish, even insulting. The experience required and deserved patient ritual, she insisted, more intricate and spiritual than any mere religion could concoct.

"Always start with her," Aaliyah would say in her confident voice. "Imagine moving slowly, and then move even more slowly. Imagine what she is expecting, and then give her something else. Surprise her. Let her guess what's next. Your time will come, but you have to earn it."

Amir remembered it as a rich philosophy, more than a technique. But in addition to imparting theory, Aaliyah also tutored Amir carefully in the essential architectural elements and delicate maneuvers that differentiated fine art from finger painting.

Amir had heard about Mrs. Al-Qasem and assumed that Aisha had visited her. All the best young Nablus women did. She was a legend in that little world, provoking awe from men, snickering from teenage girls, and horror from their mothers. But after his exquisite instruction from Aaliyah, Amir assumed that Mrs. Al-Qasem's expertise was in the realm of the merely practical—important but dull categories like elementary positions, lubricants, and contraception. He was about to discover there was more to Mrs. Al-Qasem's pedagogy, and indeed, Aaliyah might learn some things from her.

When Amir finally joined her in bed, Yasmine was surprised that he moved with confidence, even elegance, into a sequence that focused entirely on her. He didn't exactly resist her intention to lead the way, but gently redirected her energies while he applied himself to her centers of attention.

"Make him work. Make him wait!" Yasmine repeated to herself, mystified that Amir was not the timid boy she expected. There was a momentary flash of anger at the realization that she was not his first—that much was obvious—but she forced the thought out of her head, blaming her family for such latent provincial prejudices. While Amir worked patiently and deliberately, like a Geneva watchmaker breathing life into a delicate tourbillon, Yasmine momentarily suspended her determination to control her world, and let Amir do his work. He knew what he was doing, and it didn't require guidance or corrections from Yasmine. *But who is he?* she wondered, realizing that she had no idea, but hoping that he would be gently treated by whichever side got to him first.

Amir followed Aaliyah's prescriptions like the dedicated student that he was. Although he had made love to Aisha countless times inside his invented domains of beauteous wealth management meta experience, this was a new version of her, rich with textures of flesh and flashes of hunger that he had never seen before. He had never imagined her as experienced, but rather as a creature that arrived on earth fully realized, for whom experience was unnecessary, or even corrupting of her ideal self. But even Amir recognized the difference between his dreamy inventions and the glistening, fevered figure now kneeling above him.

They rowed hard together as if in a long-distance sprint, until Yasmine was suddenly conscious that Amir was controlling all the strokes. Abruptly adjusting her position, she demanded to know what he was waiting for. It was a fierce and desperate voice that she might have used to secure a place in the last lifeboat. What followed was a prolonged sequence of determined combinations with the fearsome urgency of breech loading cannon while under fire in a great naval battle. Yasmine and Amir eventually found a harmonious rhythm, though each remained determined to obey their respective tutors, and defy expectations.

"I really underestimated him," Yasmine said to herself.

When the storm finally passed, the two of them slowly recovered their breathing, face down in an agitated tangle of linens, their limbs twisted in unnatural angles. The room was deadly quiet, disturbed only by the permanent rush of conditioned Dubai air, now struggling to lower the elevated temperature in Amir's bedroom. Yasmine was at ease, distracted by exhaustion, when she glanced at her watch. 12:15.

Silently, urgently, Yasmine pulled on her jeans. A covert search beside the bed recovered her lingerie in chaotic, knotted coils, which she hastily bundled into the grocery bag, along with the sweater that still lay on the floor of the dining room. The furtive figure, a topless woman with a paper bag, shielded under the tent of her abaya and head scarf, quietly left Amir's flat and closed the door behind her. Amir slept.

Chapter 33.

THE duty officer in Maryland received a flash alert, one of three that she had handled since arriving for the shift that ran daily from five to midnight. She volunteered for the unpopular hours after a bad breakup convinced her to withdraw from circulation. She either was punishing herself or, she preferred to think, punishing those who would be denied her company. Tonight, she couldn't decide which it was. But the choice felt cleansing, like a detox retreat in California. No, she reconsidered after looking at her windowless space, more like a hunger strike in the Baltimore Correctional Center. Her employer, a vast government enterprise with unlimited funding, was headed by a long-serving admiral who, it seemed, answered to no one. The organization occasionally was accused of misdeeds in the media or by some naïve junior member of Congress, but the claims would be discredited in forty-eight hours, and the accusers invariably apologized, resigned, or both. The job paid well enough, though she resented the admiral's autocratic management style, including his insistence on adherence to a dress code that would have been too extreme even for IBM in 1965. She bristled in her mandatory pantyhose, but then shrugged and embraced it as an important component of her new phase of healing by suffering.

The flash was generated by an algorithm that filtered incomprehensibly large data files consisting of surveillance inputs that followed the digital signatures of everything from radioactive decay at a North Korean missile site, to the tiny power surges in a coffeemaker in a Kyiv pawn shop. The algorithm was designed to detect anomalies, to measure their statistical significance as risk predictors, and to flag those that deserved human attention. It was permitted by law to operate only outside the United States, but with a wink, the admiral made a few exceptions. Some of the monitored data, like the flash she just received, were targeted to support specific operations. It was the duty officer's job to assess the flash, discard obvious machine error results, but refer all others to the operation liaison. She was one of twenty-five duty officers presently tethered to their screens during this evening's shift. Her hair was moist and matted under gigantic headphones that made her look like a homeless Mickey Mouse.

In this particular flash, routine footage from a private security camera on another continent captured video of two men leaving an elevator on the twenty-ninth floor of an upscale apartment building. Facial recognition tools identified one of the men as an Iranian intelligence officer who had never been seen outside of Tehran. The algorithm connected the dots and flagged the data as statistically significant to an ongoing American intelligence operation. The security camera footage came from the corridor outside Amir's flat in Dubai.

The duty officer ran through her checklist for machine error assessments. She was fast, but it took a few minutes. She queried the source data file and found slightly earlier footage in the same corridor of a woman, or at least a person, entering the elevator, fully covered in black, apparently carrying a bundle underneath. The algorithm identified that image as "NA"— "not anomalous." The duty officer knew nothing about the operation, but there was no reason to challenge the statistical calculation, and the facial recognition software was never wrong. She sent the flash and the data file to the operation liaison, without comment. *Goddamn pantyhose*, she thought.

The flash alert from the duty officer in Maryland crossed eight time zones before reaching Dubai. Before Fiona received the flash, the same two men left Amir's flat after only a few minutes inside, triggering yet another flash alert from Maryland. Fiona received both alerts seconds apart and immediately dispatched a contractor to check on Amir.

Chapter 34.

IN the last seconds of his life, Amir had never been happier. The dust and heat that had fogged his eyes and ambitions for as long as he could remember were gone. His head was clear, and he imagined looking out over a glacial fjord, still and silent in the early morning light. He even reconsidered a lifetime of doubts about his faith, which now seemed to provide the only explanation for the conversion of his unlikely dream into the reality he had just experienced with Aisha in his bed. *It's really true*, he thought, reflecting on the classics of American literature strewn about the floor. The possibilities are endless. It was just a matter of time now before he and Aisha took their well-earned places in New York. He pictured the two of them, dressed in chic understatement, preparing dinner in their spacious co-op, the Chrysler Building illuminated behind them. Aisha was resplendent in the earrings he remembered from one of the models on the Merrill Lynch web page.

With his face buried cozily in sheets that were still warm, damp, and fragrant from Aisha's exertions, Amir felt a firm hand at the back of his neck. It was her, he assumed, smiling in anticipation. *She had something more in mind.* There was a sharp pain between his toes, like an insect bite, but it passed so quickly that he dismissed it. By the time he rolled his head to face his lover, it was over.

Coincidentally, it was not Amir's first experience with fentanyl. In his second year at university, he was a striker with the football club. In a failed attempt to score, Amir tore the ACL in his right knee after a freak fall on the pitch. The resultant surgery required general anesthesia, for which fentanyl was the surgeon's preference. Amir recalled how quickly and comfortably he slipped into unconsciousness on the operating table, and how he dreamt with such clarity and beauty. The dosage was different this time. That, and the injection between his toes, would be recognized instantly by the local coroner as an accidental fatal overdose by a recreational user, all too common among Dubai's expat community of young, lonely professionals. It was the custom to keep these stories out of the local media, to avoid embarrassment for the family, but more importantly, to keep ugly shadows from falling on the lovely fiction of Dubai as the perfect tourist destination.

With assistance from the resourceful duty officer in Maryland, Fiona's contractor disabled the security cameras before entering Amir's building. The contractor inspected the body, leaving everything as he found it. He looked back before leaving the flat, spotting a handwritten journal stuffed with receipts and cocktail napkins, which he slid into his pocket.

"In the public interest," concluded the Emirati Minister of Interior when he signed the "No Objection Certificate" later that day, no one needed to know about the death of this unfortunate young man. Very surprisingly, the minister had received an early morning call about this from his counterpart in Tehran, and a short time later, from the American ambassador in Abu Dhabi. Conveniently, they both hoped —and gently requested—that the tragic matter would be handled in confidence.

Chapter 35.

No one could remember ever conducting a fire drill at the bank, but a different variation had been rehearsed many times. Always overseen by a disembodied voice on the telephone, as if behind a curtain somewhere far away, they methodically repeated the evacuation that would follow a revelation that the bank's cover was compromised. Small adjustments were made from drill to drill, including in the selection of the broadcast musical alert. These little changes periodically renewed the appropriate sense of high drama. Still, each time they rehearsed, a few stragglers were left behind.

At 3:40 am, twenty employees of Bank Von Raab's Dubai office were awakened by a phone alert, a piercing single tone followed by ominous silence, and then a ragged 1969 recording of "Over the Rainbow." Judy Garland's signature voice was heavily accented by a lifetime of cigarettes and alcohol. "Birds fly over the rainbow, why then, oh why can't I?" A short time later, just a few minutes before the sun came up, eighteen of the bank's employees departed Dubai for the last time aboard an all-white 737 with no tail number, lifting off and climbing steeply from a lightly staffed private airstrip. By then, a very specialized contractor had already performed a deep clean of the bank's offices, wiping the servers, removing the hard drives, and leaving behind only the reassuring fragrance of bleach. It smelled so clean that it hurt.

Two employees didn't make it to the rendezvous point in time but slipped out later that day aboard a small smuggler's vessel bound for Oman. They shared the cargo hold with seventy thousand Captagon pills hidden under crates of lemons.

Fiona, Katrina, and Mr. Swallow departed by helicopter just before the phone alert was dispatched.

"Right!" Mr. Swallow said, as they left the ground.

Chapter 36.

THE sun was barely up, but already blasting angrily, as Rula waited in the drop-off line at her children's school. A long line of indistinguishable white SUVs stretched ahead and behind her, filled with sleepy, bickering children. Most parents sent their children with a driver and nanny, which relieved them of some of the horrors of Dubai's morning commute. But Rula liked spending the time with her children, even if most days brought either sullen contempt from her back seat or the kind of viciousness seen only among prairie predators and preteens.

The line was moving faster than normal, she thought, perhaps since a recent parent meeting erupted in demands for improvements in the tortured morning ritual. Rula looked in the rear-view mirror, dismayed by the breakfast remnant lodged in her daughter's hair.

The SUV in front of her stopped abruptly. The driver stepped out and calmly approached Rula, tapping on the windscreen. *He looked just like any other driver*, she thought.

When she lowered her window, the man said, "No school today."

"What?" Rula asked.

He handed her a note and returned to his car, which then pulled out of the line and disappeared. The note read: "1135 flight today to

Beirut. You and your children will be on it. Do not return."

Having lived through the wars in Beirut, Rula did not assume that such things were pranks. She pulled aggressively out of the drop-off line, nearly hitting one of the young teachers who had volunteered for duty as a crossing guard, and sped toward home. The children looked frightened but said nothing. Rula frantically phoned Rashid but there was no answer after several attempts. A text message from Rashid eventually appeared, "Do what they say. I will follow."

At the airport, they proceeded quickly to the boarding gate with nothing but Rula's mom-sized handbag and the garish Disney character backpacks that each child wore like a tiny parachute. By then, the children were loud and disconsolate, enraged by the interruption of their familiar schedules, and terrified by Rula's half-weeping assurances that they were taking a "holiday." Rula assumed, or desperately hoped, that Rashid would be with them on the flight. When the aircraft left the ground without him, she remembered Rashid's cryptic comments about a "project" that soon would deliver their little family, once and for all, to a place far removed from the brutality, literal and figurative, of the Middle East. Since that place clearly was not Beirut, she could fairly assume that his project had not gone well.

Back in Dubai, Rashid unfortunately did not survive the morning's questioning from the two gentlemen visiting from Tehran. He chose to take the high road to the very end, and was truthful even to these thuggish Persians, for whom honesty was as threatening and shocking as a bikini at the beach. Rashid gave up everything he knew about his project with Bank Von Raab, but, of course, they already had most of that information from Yasmine's reporting. When he was unable to comment on the Meyghan incident or Dr. Mousavi's whereabouts, the gentlemen from Tehran grew impatient.

As Rashid went to sleep for the last time, his thoughts returned to the architect's renderings of the house he was building in Marbella, which he studied for hours most nights, long after Rula had gone to bed. In the future yard facing the sea, he posed with a pitching wedge, repeating gentle practice swings, his family happily splashing in the pool nearby.

Chapter 37.

As soon as the banks opened in the Channel Islands, conflicting wire instructions arrived moments apart from two different sources, each directing a large transfer from the Eagle Trust. One of the instructions came from Mr. Golestani's successor in Tehran, who carefully entered the account codes, along with the two-factor authentication that appeared on Golestani's phone. Golestani sat nearby, bruised, unshaven, and handcuffed to a metal desk. His signature facial scar was now just one among several. To his relief, and to the surprise of everyone else in the room, the access codes and transfer instructions were accepted. The handsome proceeds of several weapons-related Bump and Split transactions traveled instantly to a friendly bank in the Maldives, less respectable, perhaps, than an English common-law jurisdiction, but nevertheless, a capable laundry where the Supreme Leader's money would be safe for now. Meanwhile, the Eagle Trust, locked in perpetuity behind Dickensian legal instruments, had been emptied of everything except the assets necessary to continue paying the trustees, lawyers and accountants who would steadfastly protect the privacy of its owners, whoever they were.

The other instructions arrived from a more traditional source, superintended by a clerk in Vaduz, for whom the exercise was purely routine, and one of several that she would process before her mid-morning coffee. She entered the Eagle Trust account codes and frowned at a chip in her nail polish while waiting for the authentication. After a second and third unsuccessful attempt, she elevated the matter, and soon Fiona was on the telephone from an aircraft over the Mediterranean. Fiona realized immediately what had happened.

In the next twenty-four hours, there would be polite diplomatic interventions insisting that the Eagle Trust proceeds must be recovered and frozen "for national security reasons." These were followed quickly by less dignified communications from intelligence agencies in Washington to London, which eventually landed on the desk of HM Attorney General for the Baliwick of Guernsey. Predictably, the replies—in the highest of dudgeon—reminded all concerned of the crucial legal principles involved, and concluded with the majestic observation that, "In the circumstances, you will appreciate that what you propose is quite impossible." The rule of law remained unshaken.

In a fit of pique, the Americans ultimately would cancel submarine-related subcontracts that employed a thousand shipyard workers at Barrow-in-Furness, a struggling Lancashire borough where the unemployment rate would then explode, along with opioid addictions. Insult followed injury when the Pentagon announced that the same subcontracts would be awarded to a French consortium as a "reaffirmation of America's oldest European alliance."

Fiona smiled and looked at the ceiling of the small aircraft cabin, as if acknowledging a higher power. She had underestimated Amir. Of course, he would want his own insurance policy to guarantee his exit plan. He must have inserted a discreet transposition in the bank's record of the Eagle Trust authentication code. This assured that his personal approval would be necessary for the Americans to tap the funds. Amir did not anticipate that Golestani, or his Iranian clients, might also wish to move the funds, but after all, it was their money. Amir also did not anticipate that his insurance claim would be filed from the grave. Even Fiona saw the joke in that.

Chapter 38.

THEY were celebrating at Prison 59. With His Boys assembled and rewarded with precious cans of Coca Cola liberated decades earlier from the basement of the U.S. Embassy in Tehran, Captain Sadegh had them applauding as he delivered a version of the happy news from Dubai. A few facts had been tailored for the senior audiences in Tehran, but the essential features of the now official story were these. The Kirk and Spock campaign was a clever charade (invented at Prison 59) that successfully distracted the Americans. Meanwhile, the real operation, led by a heroic, unnamed Prison 59 asset, penetrated the Great Satan's deepest cover and exposed a diabolical plan to attack Iran's peaceful nuclear research program. The Americans' two front line agents confessed their roles and shared valuable intelligence before they were removed, permanently, from the battlefield. Once again, America is humiliated, he proclaimed. A robust cheer rose from the room, and the Islamic Republic was toasted with defiant, raised hands, all clutching The Real Thing.

Sadegh liked telling the story. Like caring for any blood sport animals, he felt he had to reward His Boys with red meat once in a while, or they will tire of the chase. If the meat is a little rotten, or the facts are a little distorted, the win is what's important. It was much the same when he watched his colonel deliver the after-action report to his Revolutionary Guard commanders. Everyone knew there were some pieces missing—like the unsolved crimes at Meyghan and Dr. Mousavi's disappearance—but they needed a big win, and it was easy enough to imagine that the fleeing criminals from Bank Von Raab were responsible for those things as well. As to that, they were more right than they realized.

At the very top in Tehran, the main thing was that the money was recovered. The fortunes of the few were secure. And the fewer questions asked about that, the better. This being Tehran, good news was infinitely more important than true news. Everyone quickly fell in line behind the great victory and humiliation narrative. In the clerics' dining rooms, caviar was served for lunch for the rest of the week.

Always more serious than her other colleagues in the intelligence service, Leila filed a brief report that stuck to the facts, though—in the interest of survival—she omitted inconvenient information. She chose not to mention, for example, that the nearly successful American operation was made possible by the Bump and Split, a practice that, if continued, will only invite further security breaches. Instead, Leila credited the exceptional work of her unnamed sparrow, who would now be safely retired far from the action.

Captain Sadegh called Leila to complain, gently, about her report, which failed to mention him or the contributions of Prison 59.

"Your work speaks for itself," she said, a comment he accepted graciously, clearly not understanding her meaning.

Leila turned back to business with Sadegh. "We need to do something about our asset in Nablus. If Chief Nurse Hala finds out about the boy, we may not be able to contain it."

Sadegh had been waiting for this. "I have a solution," he said, proud once again of the colorful imaginations of His Boys.

Chapter 39.

THE Jungle Bar was packed. With all the beautiful people pressed into the hallucinogenic space, Yasmine doubted that this was the exclusive members-only club that it claimed to be. On the other hand, she was just a guest and supposed that most of the other women in the room were in the same category. Though it was a venerable establishment on the better side of London's Berkeley Square, guarded by doormen in satirical livery, Yasmine thought the club sometimes felt a bit too . . . obvious. Like the aspiring model who chases the paparazzi. A small, printed notice in the ladies' room warned members and guests that Annabel's Club did not welcome "visible nipples." Yasmine looked around and laughed. Plainly that was an ironic challenge designed to encourage guests to test the limits of enforcement.

She reprimanded herself. *Mustn't be so snobbish.* Her frequent invitations to the club came from some good client referrals from Nadia, all London personalities who were perpetually redecorating. They generally came with benefactors, sometimes multiple benefactors competing to support the expensive habits of their spoiled charges. Yasmine had come a long way in the three months since she arrived. Her little one-room office garret in Mayfair started merely as a respectable cover story for a single woman in London, and a place to go each morning as her neighbors in Cadogan Square left for offices, schools, and hairdressing appointments. Now it was a thriving enterprise that *actually* provided decorating services. Yasmine continued to be amazed that people who lived in posh addresses begged her—pleaded with her—to be told what they should like, and then paid her handsomely for the privilege.

Her Dubai exit plan unfolded without incident. Leila did exactly as she promised. There was no last-minute haggling about details and money, a remarkable departure from Persian custom. Yasmine was especially impressed, and grateful, that her final communications with Leila were succinct, even terse, and devoid of any uncomfortable information. The work was completed; funds were wired; the matter was concluded. Yasmine knew they could find her if they wanted, in London or anywhere else, but she hoped Leila would see that they didn't.

On her last day in Dubai, her driver made a detour to the desert on the way to the airport, where Yasmine watched her journal burn until it was nothing but little black wafers floating downwind. When she boarded the Emirates flight to Heathrow, the only souvenir she brought from Dubai was a volume of Proust.

Yasmine was getting plenty of attention at Annabel's, despite her faithful compliance with the nipple admonition. Her date that night for the private party in Annabel's "Jungle Bar" was Freddie Schmiegelow, a jolly, paunchy "private banker" who evidently never worked. Freddie knew everyone, and for now, he was Yasmine's idea of the perfect date. He was charming and had absolutely no romantic interest in Yasmine. It seemed he simply wanted to be seen with her at places like Annabel's, and that was very convenient for both of them.

Yasmine visited Freddie's "office" once, which was very near hers. A lacquered black door above a well-worn stone step was identified with a highly polished brass plaque that read, "Bottomley Fund Limited (Bermuda)." *Surely the name was a practical joke,* thought Yasmine. Inside was a nineteenth century partners desk that Freddie, laughing, said he acquired from Scrooge & Marley, and chairs upholstered in cracked green leather repurposed from a renovation of the House of Commons. There was no evidence that any "private banking" was transacted in these premises, but it was a handsome prop for the public version of Freddie's story.

The Annabel's crowd bubbled. Yasmine watched a very attractive man approach Freddie, who turned, brightened as if discovering a lost friend, and then shouted, "Short the market!" The two of them laughed at their obscure inside joke and clutched each other like university rowing club pals. Freddie's friend was a boyish-looking American with a sunburned nose. Yasmine guessed he was a club member since a waiter addressed him by name and delivered a cocktail described as his "usual."

"I'm Charlie Bridges," he said, extending his hand and introducing himself to Yasmine. Freddie apologized for his neglectful manners, and then made a more elaborate introduction that glamorized Yasmine with a fictional provenance among Venetian royalty, and heaped mock scorn on Mr. Bridges as undeserving of the exceptional luck he had found gambling in the securities markets. There was more laughter and easy conversation that drifted into dinner. After the confit de canard, Freddie made his excuses, gave Yasmine a gentle, big brother's kiss on her forehead, and secured a solemn promise from his friend to see her home safely.

Yasmine was charmed by Charlie. He was polished but genuine. He spoke in lovely, lyrical prose that was unpracticed. He listened when she spoke, nodding gravely at her observations about important lessons of history, including the decline of civilization that surely flows from abandonment of the liberal arts. They were still debating English Tory Party politics and drinking claret when most of the guests had dispersed to other, more uninhibited, parts of the club.

"Are you, by chance, from the West Bank?" Charlie asked.

Yasmine was startled, having worked hard to reveal as little as possible about herself to anyone in London. This, she thought, avoided uncomfortable subjects, and also gave her an appealing air of mystery. The English, who are usually hiding something themselves, were generally happy to let her get away with her untold story. But Charlie clearly was interested in her and wanted to know more.

"Why do you ask?" Yasmine hoped a little polite stalling might lead to a different topic, but he persisted.

She was reminded of her fragile biography. For some time, Yasmine's worries had deepened about her Iranian clients, and whether she reasonably could believe that they would keep their word and leave her alone. She trusted Leila, but Leila was far from Tehran. And practically speaking, Yasmine had information that was very inconvenient for the regime of murderous mobsters. She began to notice unusual things; anomalies in the familiar patterns of her London life. A woman seemed to follow her sometimes on the way to her office, and then at the last block, the woman would disappear and a man would take over. Occasionally, the tabletop accessories in her office would be rearranged overnight. Lately, her phone was inundated with unrecognized calls and apparent phishing attempts. While it was all suspicious, she knew it might also be her imagination.

Yasmine remembered her father saying that Persians never give up; never concede anything; and never can be trusted. It might be paranoia, but Yasmine resolved to find an insurance policy. She needed a new life story for herself with more substance, and more connections to real people, instead of the hazy fiction with which she arrived in London. She should at least make it difficult for Tehran to orchestrate her disappearance. In her present circumstances, with a circle of only ephemeral acquaintances, it would hardly be noticed

Yasmine was not particularly looking for a relationship in London. On the contrary, while that thought occasionally occurred to her, she dismissed it as a burden that would be quickly regretted, like packing too many pairs of shoes for a weekend trip. But as Charlie spoke, she felt a surprising protective warmth in his presence. And it soon became obvious that he was solidly networked in at least two continents, with global banks and other enterprises that were not to be trifled with.

The timing might be fortuitous, Yasmine thought, reflecting on her search for an insurance policy.

At their quiet table in the dining room, there were occasional sounds of laughter and cheering from other parts of Annabel's. Yasmine gave up trying to redirect Charlie's inquisition about her personal history.

"My family is originally from Nablus," she finally admitted, as if to suggest that the connection was something attenuated, like ancestors from another century.

"Really?" Charlie asked, happily surprised. "I took a sabbatical from banking a couple of years ago and taught a course at the university in Nablus. Capital Markets 425."

Yasmine gave him a polite shrug. "I studied literature," she said, hoping to move on.

Charlie continued his reminiscence. "The kids were so eager; really ambitious. But I had a run-in with the faculty. They told me I was too nice to the students. Can you believe it? One of my students had big dreams of going to Wall Street. He was a natural trader; really loved the intensity of a risky stock bet. 'Amir' something." Charlie looked distracted, as if deep in fond remembrance of his time in Nablus and his students.

"I don't think I knew him," Yasmine said to Charlie, suppressing a fake yawn. Determined to change the subject, Yasmine adjusted her posture, providing Charlie a brief but inviting glimpse of an exquisite undergarment. Amir was forgotten.

Chapter 40.

Two nurse trainees were absorbed in a dating app when Chief Nurse Hala emerged from a patient's room. She gave them a withering stare, and they resumed their well-practiced routine of looking busy. It was a quiet night. The few patients were stable. Their monitors chirped with the comforting sounds of nominal vitals.

Dr. Reza paid her a visit earlier that evening with news from Tehran and a fresh letter from her father. The letter mentioned a lingering cough from bronchitis but was upbeat about their imminent reunion. He promised to prepare breakfast for her when he arrived— a happy ritual from her distant childhood, invoking images of her father singing Puccini excerpts and cheerfully wrecking the kitchen. Captain Sadegh's Boys had extracted that little memory from a journal that Prisoner 361 kept until the day he died.

Cloistered in the dusty file room, Reza informed Hala that her latest project had been wildly successful. Her recruit delivered the objective and was safely relocated to what he called, her "new circumstances."

"It was a crushing blow for the enemy," he said. "And, Hala, it fortunately was not necessary to call upon the 'insurance policy' we had discussed."

Hala noted his relief and reflected that *she* would not have hesitated to induce a recurrence of Ms. Dajani's cancer symptoms if that had been the price of Aisha's compliance.

"Our friends are very grateful to you. Orders were given to accelerate your father's return." He handed her a copy of an exquisite forgery of a medical examiner's report signed a few days earlier. There were familiar details about her father in the barely legible handwriting for which physicians are famous everywhere—date of birth, the ancient scar from an appendectomy when he was a teenager, and comments about his bronchitis—followed by a purple stamp, "Cleared for Travel." The document was the result of a fierce competition among Captain Sadegh's Boys, after he hatched the idea, and then promised the winner a subscription to a wildly popular gaming app, forbidden in Iran, called DisMember. The finalists demonstrated impressive artistic aptitude and quite advanced personality disorders, but there was a clear winner. The winning proposal included photos of Prisoner 361's body, which revealed the scar that only his family would remember.

Except for the barking dog chained to the drainpipe outside Mrs. Darwish's house, it was calm when Chief Nurse Hala returned home just before sunrise. For weeks, her husband had been slipping ever deeper into a strange dementia in which his waking attentions were entirely limited to the painstaking copying of his library card catalog, in antique Arabic calligraphy. Her daughter, Sara, had given up her job in the settlements. Hala was relieved to have her back home, despite disturbing new flashes of rebellion from her and slivers of neighborhood gossip about her "slutty" circle of new friends.

For some weeks, Hala had turned her attention to redecorating Amir's old room, preparing it to welcome her beloved father. She relocated the remnants of Amir's book collection to the vicinity of her husband's library, where they remained undisturbed. He showed no interest in adding Steinbeck or Salinger to his precious catalog. Hala chose not to explain the redecoration of Amir's room to anyone, and consistent with the household's pervasive atmosphere of withdrawal, no one mentioned it. Hala repainted the room, and then repainted it again after concluding that her first choice of color bore a strong resemblance to the ICU. She assembled some old family photographs on the fresh walls, including her favorite. Her handsome father, smiling and holding Hala tightly, maneuvered her down her first gentle ski run at a snowy Iranian mountain resort as several stylish women in the background looked on with cigarettes and wine glasses. Above that photograph, a crack in the plaster ceiling resisted several repair attempts. When her dabs of putty dried overnight, the crack reopened like a stubborn wound, and a tiny pyramid of dust lay on the table beneath it.

As the first suggestions of the morning sun appeared, Hala sat at the kitchen table contemplating her glass of Johnnie Walker. There was no ice in the freezer, so she drank it warm, like the English prefer to do. She smiled with happy anticipation. After years of patient effort in the shadows—neglecting her husband, her children and herself—and deferring even the smallest of personal pleasures, Hala saw a glorious new beginning. Her father's unspeakable suffering finally would be over, and she would care for him, lovingly, for the rest of his days. She would quietly retire from the dark duty of recruiting young women to spy, and sometimes to be killed, for a regime that she despised. And based on the surprising new correspondence that began just a few weeks earlier, Hala and her family might soon leave Nablus to start new lives abroad, where the possibilities were endless.

In the months since Amir moved to New York, he and his mother had exchanged no more than a handful of perfunctory texts. She wanted to be sure he felt the depth of her anger after he abandoned his family. He wanted to minimize lying to her, and the possibilities of being caught lying to her, about where he actually was. Until recently, his correspondence with Sara was only slightly more active, though burdened by evasive sentiments from him, and hostile recriminations from her. Amir's tone, and the frequency of his correspondence, suddenly changed.

When Captain Sadegh proposed the idea at Prison 59, his colonel was skeptical. "How long can you realistically keep up this charade?" he was asked. But fresh from celebrating their latest win in outing and dismantling Bank Von Raab, His Boys went to work. It required only rudimentary hacking tools to unlock Amir's various social media accounts, along with his Boca Raton telephone number and a complete history of his calls, text messaging, and even voicemails. As if they were in the writers' room of a daytime soap opera, the Boys met for days and produced a brilliant teleplay of Amir's future life. They carefully assembled and posted photographs of fictitious friends, pets, restaurant meals, and iconic New York events, inadvertently generating a large community of social media followers of Amir. Eventually, Amir would receive unsolicited messages from several New York establishments offering complimentary tickets and meals if he would share the experiences with his followers. In time, he became an influencer of some repute. Captain Sadegh loved His Boys. Amir would live forever.

It was shortly after Dr. Reza's last visit that Chief Nurse Hala received a message from Amir, the first in some time. More messages followed after she replied, warily, and soon a regular correspondence developed that sounded more like a mother and son. The messages were brief at first, but there was a noticeable shift in tone. There was sentiment where there was none before. Amir chose words that signaled regret, even apology, for his past decisions, and the strains that had existed in the family for years. He hoped things could change. He wanted the family to be together again. Hala warmed to this correspondence, and her replies, also for the first time, conveyed genuine interest in Amir's life, even in his career, which she had made a point of ignoring before.

There were similar exchanges with Sara. His first few messages produced missiles of contempt from her, but as he persisted, she softened too. Amir hinted at real progress toward opening doors at NYU for Sara, and this electrified her. "I think things will happen fast," he assured Sara.

Hala hinted to Amir that she might have some good news to share with him soon. "Maybe," she told Amir, "we should think about leaving Nablus." "A fresh start," she called it, "for all of us." Amir's messages seized on this opening. After one late-evening exchange of increasingly warm messages, he wrote:

> Now that I am more established at the bank, I really hope you and Baba and Sara will think seriously about joining me here in New York. We should all be together. It needs a little preparation, but I can do it. Please say yes.

His mother was touched. *I really underestimated Amir.*

Made in the USA
Middletown, DE
10 September 2024

60096506R00201